D0483925

dog company six

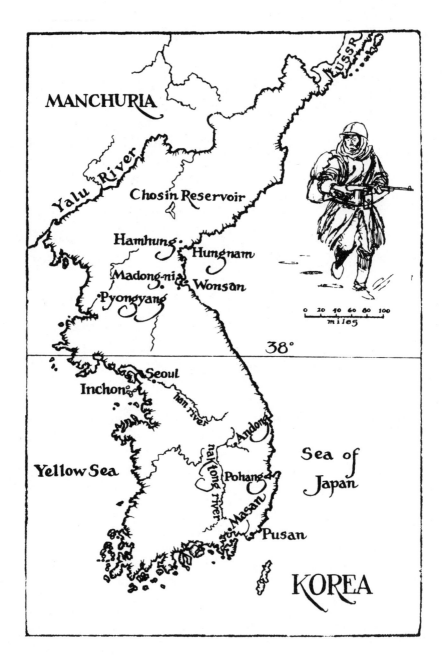

MANCHURIA

Yalu River

Chosin Reservoir

Hamhung .

Hungnam

Madong-ni

Wonsan

Pyongyang

USSR

38°

Seoul

Inchon

han river

Andong

Yellow Sea

naktong river

Pohang

Masan

Pusan

Sea of
Japan

KOREA

0 20 40 60 80 100
miles

DOG COMPANY SIX

Edwin Howard Simmons

Naval Institute Press
Annapolis, Maryland

Naval Institute Press
291 Wood Road
Annapolis, MD 21402

ISBN 1-55750-898-4

Printed in the United States of America on acid free paper ⊚
07 06 05 04 03 02 01 00   9 8 7 6 5 4 3 2

Map drawn by Charles Waterhouse

For all the marines who served
in the Korean War

chapter one...

Bayard regarded his outstretched legs with a great deal of interest. They were floating in front of him like two silver-white fish on the surface of the rusty-red water. All his civilian fat was gone. The legs were thin, and the wet, white skin was stretched tight against the bone and muscle. He must look, he decided, like one of El Greco's gaunt and attenuated figures.

Bayard was in his bathtub.

He had been wounded in April; it was now June. This was the Hotel Otsu on Lake Biwa, a few miles from Kyoto. He had arrived at the Otsu that afternoon. The hotel had been built, he supposed, twenty or thirty years ago for the American and European tourist trade. Now its shabby elegance was made available to dependents, special visitors, transient officers, and convalescents through the good offices of U.S. Army Special Services, Far East Command.

The porcelain of the tub was cracked and stained. The shoddy Oriental imitation of Western plumbing creaked and groaned and worked its secrets spasmodically. Above the chipped and broken shoulder-high tile, the walls and ceiling were painted a strident yellow. The underpowered electric lightbulb hanging bare from its cord glowed a sullen brown.

But the water was hot, and this was the bath he had promised himself—the long, hot soaking that would wash away the ingrained pore-deep smells of Korea and the overlying antiseptic and fecal odors of the hospital.

The soaking went on for a long time. At last Bayard broke free from the lethargy induced by the bath and climbed reluctantly from the tub. He stood in the center of the tiny bathroom and rubbed dry with the thin and slightly stale towel, examining his bare body as he did so with the diligent curiosity of a child.

He dried his legs thoughtfully. They were oddly smooth. Then he remembered that the months of living in woolen underclothing had worn off the body hair.

The scar from his wound crawled like a many-legged red lizard from the angle of his hip to the lower edge of his ribs. The surgeon in the Yokusuka hospital had said, "If that piece of grenade had been one inch this way or that. . . ."

Still naked, Bayard moved over to the washbasin, where he had laid out his shaving things. He studied his face critically in the mirror. The skin lay firm and clear against the bone. The red windburn had changed in the hospital to a deceptively healthy-looking tan. But his eyes were still tired, and his brown hair, cut to regulation length this afternoon by the hotel barber, was beginning to show streaks of gray.

If it had been an American-made fragmentation grenade, it probably would have killed all three of them. As it was, the casing had been poorly cast in some Chinese foundry, and half of it in one large fragment had ripped across Bayard's abdomen while the rest shivered into pinpoint-sized splinters that had peppered Baby-san and Havac.

Bayard shaved carefully using a new blade, combed his hair, and then went into the bedroom. He put on a new set of cotton underwear. The drawers were his regular size, but they were too big and to hold them up he had to tighten the tapes on the sides all the way. In the nine months between Inchon and now he had lost twenty pounds.

The mama-san who looked after his room had brought his uniform from the tailor shop, and it lay on the bed, the green kersey jacket and trousers neatly pressed. The uniform was enlisted issue, and the cloth felt stiff and unfamiliar. The green wool would be hot and uncomfortable on a June night, but his summer service tropical worsteds were lost, along with the rest of his officer's uniforms.

The lieutenant in charge of the warehouse had been more than apologetic for the loss. He had been practically grief-stricken. He insisted on showing Bayard that the division's personal effects were now all neatly sorted and stacked, tagged and palletized. Everything was very systematic.

But, the lieutenant had said, you remember the helter-skelter confusion of seabags and footlockers you left behind on the Kobe docks when you loaded out for Inchon in September. Then there was the typhoon, and later some of the baggage was pilfered by the dock workers before things were gotten under control. And, for a while during the worst part of the Chosin Reservoir in December, the casualty reporting system had broken down and some of the division personnel had been mistakenly reported dead or missing in action and their personal effects sent prematurely to their dependents in the States.

Bayard had listened politely to the lieutenant's explanations. The term "personal effects" bore a nice, clean antiseptic quality. A man's belongings were reduced to a neatly typed inventory and a carefully packed box. Before shipment any items of government property and all such things as condoms and pornographic pictures were removed so that what the dependents received of their son's or husband's belongings was sterile and immaculate and something like a retouched photograph.

Bayard didn't much care that his own things were missing. What was it he had lost? There was nothing, as he remembered it, that really mattered in the trunk, just his uniforms, some insignia, a few books he might have read again, some old letters, and a cheap camera.

And the large photograph of Donna—a Harris and Ewing photograph—younger and perhaps better looking than she really was. But he didn't need a photograph to remember Donna's tall, full-curved figure, her warm chestnut hair, or the faint violet shadows under her eyes.

Gratuitous issues of clothing were supposed to be made only to enlisted marines, but the lieutenant seemed to feel he had to make up for the loss of the trunk. Bayard accepted just what he thought he would need for the trip home. Then he had gone to the army PX in downtown Kobe and bought himself a new set of insignia and ribbons and a few other essentials.

Now, in his hotel room, Bayard pinned onto the green jacket his silver captain's bars, the bronze Marine Corps insignia, and the two rows of World War II ribbons, now topped off with the Silver Star and the gold-starred Purple Heart.

That twice-awarded Purple Heart was his ticket home. Two wounds requiring hospitalization, and back to the States you went. That was Marine Corps policy. He would finish his convalescent leave, present his orders for endorsement, and get air transportation back to the continental United States. His ribbons were his passport. He had done his share. No further explanations were required. No apologies to anyone. None needed. He didn't owe anything to anybody.

"Dearest Donna," he had written from the hospital just before his release,

> Please thank your father for his offer to contact the Secretary of the Navy but it isn't necessary. I am practically home. Everything has been repaired. You have nothing to worry about. All the essential parts are functioning perfectly—a fact which I will demonstrate to you at the earliest opportunity. Also I have a very handsome scar. Unfortunately the damned thing is located where only my very best friends will ever see it.
>
> The powers-that-be tell me that returning officers, especially perforated heroes such as me, get their choice of duty stations, so I am asking for Quantico. I think that will be better for all concerned than Washington itself. Close but not too close. As you know better than I, your father can sometimes be a little over-powering.
>
> It won't be long now, so till then,
> All my love,
> George

It wouldn't be long. He would finish his tour of active duty, secure behind the breastworks of his combat decorations. He wouldn't have to put himself to the test once again, to wonder if his thin reserve of courage had been expended or whether it would be sufficient for the next attack, the next assault against some new hill.

There would be no more nights of lying in a foxhole, waking in the dark to feel the wet earth and to wonder if you were already dead and if this were your grave. At first you were cloaked in the secret illusion of your own immortality. You got over that. When you saw your own blood spilling out of a wound, then you knew that you too could die, that it was just a matter of time and the weirdest sort of chance.

He put on a clean, new shirt, buttoned it, and tied the khaki tie three times before the knot suited him. He grimaced in the mirror and stretched his neck against the unfamiliar constriction of the collar around his throat. His brown socks came next, then the green trousers.

His combat boots stood there waiting, like a pair of shining sentries. Mama-san had labored long on them in exchange for a pack of cigarettes, and now only the deepest scars showed through their gleaming mahogany surface.

When the medics cut off his blood encrusted utilities, they had wanted to take the boots, but he hadn't let them. The boots had ridden the stretcher with him to Japan. They were part of him. He had worn them ashore at Inchon, and he had walked down the hill in them from the Reservoir. They were his lucky boots, nonregulation but lucky, given to him by an army paratrooper on Okinawa just before the end of the war. The war. The real war. World War II. When he got home, he was going to have the boots bronze plated.

He pulled the boots on now, secured them tightly with the new laces he had bought in the post exchange, and let his trouser legs drop down over their shining uppers.

Baby-san had cut down the Chinese grenade thrower with his Browning automatic rifle. First Sergeant Havac had stood there cursing "those goddamn sonsabitches," and Baby-san, his own face flecked with blood from the grenade splinters, had lit Bayard a cigarette and crouched there beside him with worried china blue eyes.

"It's my fault, Captain," he said. "I fouled up. I never thought to look at the rafters."

Then Pilnick had injected Bayard with a syrette of morphine and he had slid off away from things. He would remember the battalion aid station only dimly.

"I've done the best I can for you, George," the battalion surgeon had said, his round face smiling whitely out of the darkness. "I think you're going to be all right. It was something like a Caesarian section. Tell the surgeons in Japan that Goldberg did the job—Goldberg the baby doctor."

Was Goldberg still with the battalion? Bayard went to his bag and pulled out a square brown bottle of Scotch. Ballentine's was only two dollars a bottle at the Yokusuka club. He took a glass from the top of his dresser and poured himself an experimental half inch. He had not drunk any whisky in Korea.

Baby-san's letter was also on the dresser. Bayard picked it up and looked reflectively at the large uneven handwriting on the dirty envelope. He put the letter down again without rereading it. Dog Company was no longer his concern. All of his life Bayard had known when a thing was over, when it was opportune to let go. This time was no different.

But unfortunately this time there was no convenient curtain in his mind that he could close on the parade of unwanted memories. They kept marching past, like a record that kept replaying itself.

He sipped wryly at the Scotch. Havac and Baby-san, the two who had been closest, the two indestructibles. He remembered the first meeting with Havac in the brick company barracks at Camp Lejeune.

Bayard had gone into the company office escorted by Gibson, the company executive officer. There, squarely facing the door, sat Havac. Bayard's first impression of the man was purely visual: short spiky black hair turning gray at the edges; a hard broad Slavic face; massive chest; and an ironed khaki shirt, immaculate despite the North Carolina summer heat.

Gibson had made the introductions.

"Nice to meet the Captain," said Havac in those gravelly tones Bayard had gotten to know so well. "The sergeant major phoned me that the Captain was on his way over."

What was there about that first meeting that had put Bayard on the defensive? Had Havac deliberately been a trifle slow in getting to his feet? Had it been his exaggeratedly formal use of the third person?

Even now, Bayard was not sure. Perhaps it was simply that Havac was so obviously armored in self-assurance. Havac had been with Dog Company since the reorganization of the Fleet Marine Force at the end of the war. He had argued his way off a dozen transfer orders. Other master sergeants could take their well-earned ease at post headquarters or at the rifle range, but in Havac's view, there was no place for a marine to be except in the Fleet Marine Force and there was no billet for a master sergeant except to be the first soldier of a rifle company.

When Bayard joined Dog Company, Havac was in his nineteenth year of service. He had enlisted in 1931, the year, in fact, of Baby-san's birth— although this was no particular coincidence, for there were many in Dog Company who were nineteen.

As Havac told it, 1931 had been a gray year for the bohunks who worked Pennsylvania's anthracite mines, as gray as the endless mountains of slag that surrounded the company town. Havac was seventeen, the youngest of four sons and three daughters. The big mine was shut down. The only money coming in was the little his father and oldest brother made from working in a bootleg shaft.

A poster in front of the post office showed a marine in laced leggings and a flat-brimmed campaign hat standing guard with a Springfield rifle in the shade of a palm tree. In the background was a red-and-gold pagoda.

Havac succumbed to the lure and never regretted the choice. As a private he had chased banditos in the jungles of Nicaragua. As a private first class he had patrolled the Standard Oil docks in Shanghai and had known the exotic pleasures of Nanking Road. As a corporal he had stood watch with the Legation Guard in Peking. Then there had been the war, the big war with Japan.

Senior among Havac's ribbons was the blue-and-white Navy Cross, then came the Silver Star, and then a gold-starred Purple Heart. There were many Purple Hearts among the noncommissioned officers of Dog Company. The Purple Heart, reflected Bayard, was as much the hallmark of the professional marine as the saber scar was a Prussian's badge of honor. There were also a good number of Bronze Stars and two other Silver Stars in the company. But there were no other Navy Crosses. The Navy Cross alone would have marked Havac as an exceptional marine, but that Havac had both the Navy Cross *and* a Silver Star meant that among the master sergeants of the Corps he stood almost alone.

Bayard had not known all this at the time of his first meeting with Havac. He had just come from his initial interview with the battalion commander, and that in itself had been disconcerting.

Bayard had been ordered to extended active duty in July of 1950, almost as soon as the Korean trouble began. He had no dependents, nothing upon which to base a request for deferment. He had reported to Camp Lejeune and there was joined to the 2d Battalion, which had already been alerted to move out. He remembered the mixture of alarm and elation he had felt when he learned that the battalion commander was Lieutenant Colonel Quillan.

Quillan was *the* Red Snapper, one of those sulfurous characters around whom a thousand stories—some irrefutably true, others possibly not so true—are told. He was one of the living legends of the Corps. He ranked with Jim Crowe, Chesty Puller, and Big Foot Brown.

Just to be in the Red Snapper's battalion conferred a special status on a marine. Bayard remembered how it was during World War II. The second lieutenants at Quantico had been much impressed when certain battle-tested lieutenants and captains came to the staff of the Marine Corps Schools from the Pacific and it was known that they had served with the Red Snapper.

Bayard remembered the tale that had been circulated after Guadalcanal, about how the Red Snapper, then a marine gunner, had gone into the cave on Tanambogo and had come out soaked to the elbows in Japanese blood. They said that he had bayoneted all six members of that gun crew.

A happy fantasy had built itself in Bayard's mind. He saw himself at some future time, date unspecified, standing at the Waller Building bar in Quantico, slightly war-worn and suppressing a properly cynical smile as he heard the stage-whispered comment of some member of the current crop of Basic School second lieutenants—"See him? That's Captain Bayard. He was in the Red Snapper's battalion."

As he pursued this highly satisfying line of thought, Bayard's enthusiasm for his prospects had been suddenly dampened by his recollection that it was Quillan's battalion that had been caught in the Gorge at Peleliu. After that, there were some who called him the Red Butcher rather than the Red Snapper.

He had recollected too that Quillan as a lieutenant colonel had commanded a battalion at Peleliu and Okinawa. Now, five years later, he was about to be in a new war, still as a battalion commander. It struck Bayard as strange that Quillan was still no more than a lieutenant colonel. Bayard, counting up the years of seniority, was certain that the Red Snapper's contemporaries were wearing colonel's eagles or even brigadier general's stars. Why was it that the famous Red Snapper had lagged behind? If all had gone well, he would have had a regiment, not a battalion.

With these conflicting thoughts to bemuse him, Bayard had found the red-brick building that housed battalion headquarters and had presented himself and his orders to the battalion adjutant, who received them with a noticeable lack of enthusiasm.

Bayard had been unabashed by the coolness of his reception. This was in character, he thought—an occupational trait of adjutants and sergeants major.

The battalion adjutant, a first lieutenant in his late thirties or early forties, told Bayard to sit down and wait, that the executive officer would see him in a few minutes.

At the desk next to the adjutant sat the sergeant major, so similar to the adjutant in appearance and mien that they might have been twins. The pair formed an island of impassivity in a room filled with frantic activity. The center of the office floor was piled high with field desks and stationery chests painted dull green on which a working party was stenciling red-and-gold battalion markings. A half-dozen clerks were manning their typewriters as though they were machine guns, filling the room with a great mechanical clatter, and in the corner a mimeograph machine, the sine qua non of modern military operations, was rhythmically *ka-chunk-ing* out what was probably the battalion movement order.

A slender, deeply tanned major with a thin dark mustache and a hawk-like face came in from the outside, passed through the adjutant's office without a glance to the right or left and, after rapping peremptorily at the inner office door, entered that sanctorum.

"Is that the executive officer?" asked Bayard, getting halfway to his feet.

The adjutant looked up from his coffee and morning reports. "That was Major Mansell, the operations officer, in from the rifle range. He's got a bug up his ass over something. And when he's got a bug up his ass, it's a good idea to stay out of his way."

Bayard settled back in his chair. More minutes passed. Then the intercom on the adjutant's desk buzzed.

"Major Crenshaw will see you now," said the adjutant. "Let's go on in and meet him."

They passed through the inner door. A fat, balding major with a harassed and anxious smile arose from behind his desk and extended a moist hand to Bayard in greeting.

"I'm Major Crenshaw," he said. "The exec. I've sent your orders and officer's qualification jacket in to Colonel Quillan. He'll make your assignment himself."

The major left his desk and tapped tentatively at the connecting door that opened into the commanding officer's office.

"Come in," rasped a voice from the other side.

Major Crenshaw swung the door open, and Bayard for the first time was in the presence of the Red Snapper. His initial reaction was one of disappointment.

Physically, the man was smaller than his legend suggested. Sitting there behind his desk, he seemed pinched, withered. The famous once-red mustache was now wispy and faded to a rusty gray.

This is the three-time winner of the Navy Cross, Bayard reminded himself. This is the man who as a jawbone *teniente* had gone into the Nicaraguan backcountry and had brought out single-handedly the bandit Garcia. And who as a chief marine gunner had been the first man ashore at Tarawa, who had walked the length of the beach, red mustache flaring, roaring his defiance at the Japanese defenders.

Major Mansell was standing behind the lieutenant colonel's chair. He looked at Bayard coldly, dispassionately. Bayard felt he was being appraised, analyzed, evaluated. The thought made him uncomfortable.

"Captain George Edward Bayard, U.S. Marine Corps Reserve," read the Red Snapper from the address line of Bayard's orders.

"Yes, sir," said Bayard, standing at attention in front of the battalion commander's desk. This flat croaking voice couldn't be all that was left of the stentorian lungs that had reportedly boomed across a hundred drill fields from Quantico to Shanghai.

The Red Snapper waved an impatient hand. "Stand easy, stand easy," he said, getting to his feet. He moved so stiffly that Bayard almost believed he could hear the creaking of the bones.

"I'm Quillan," he said, extending his hand.

As they shook hands, Bayard caught the strong odor of last night's whiskey. The battalion commander's nose and cheekbones were heavily crisscrossed with red and blue lines, like a hard-used situation map.

"This here is Mansell, my operations officer."

Bayard shook the major's hand. Mansell's thin fingers were cool and dry. Bayard was aware that his own palms were unpleasantly wet with perspiration.

The Red Snapper tapped with a stubby forefinger the green file folder that lay on the desk in front of him. "This jacket tells me that you graduated from Ohio State University in 1943, that at Quantico you finished in the lower third of your Candidates Class and the middle third of your Reserve Officers Course. Then you went to Camp Lejeune, and after farting around for a while, you joined a replacement draft and were sent overseas. You were assigned to III Phib Corps headquarters, it says here, as an assistant Special Services officer—what does that mean?"

"I was information and education officer, sir. I was in charge of the USAFI program—you know, the correspondence courses. I majored in education at Ohio State."

The Red Snapper grunted. He can't be more than forty-five, thought Bayard, but he looks sixty.

"I don't doubt but what your qualifications for the job were admirable, but we don't need no full-time Special Services officers in this battalion. What about infantry experience?"

"I commanded a provisional platoon that formed part of the perimeter defense of the Corps CP on Okinawa."

"Did the Japs ever get *that* far back?" Major Mansell addressed the question to the ceiling, not to Bayard.

"No, sir, they didn't," said Bayard. He was conscious now that his hands were trembling. He put them behind his back and locked them in a parade rest position. "I was simply answering the colonel's question."

"Major Mansell was just curious," said the Red Snapper with a tinge of sarcasm. "At the time of Okinawa he was in the Atlantic commanding the marine detachment in an aircraft carrier. But that's beside the point. We're talking about you. What have you done since the war?"

Bayard paused for a moment before answering, trying to marshal his thoughts. How do you summarize five years in a sentence?

"After my release from active duty, I went back to school under the GI Bill," said Bayard speaking slowly, conscious of the half-derisive, half-hostile look on Major Mansell's face. I have no friend here, Bayard said to himself.

"Where was this?" asked the Red Snapper.

"Princeton, sir. I took my master's in European history. I spent one semester in Paris at the Sorbonne doing research for my thesis."

"What was your thesis on?"

"The military reforms of Charlemagne."

"Fascinating," said Mansell to the ceiling.

"You ever been to Paris?" the Red Snapper addressed the question to his operations officer.

"Yes, sir," said Mansell. "I lived there three years as a boy while my father was the naval attaché. I also visited it on my plebe cruise while I was at the Academy."

"I've always wanted to get to Paris," said the Red Snapper with an unmistakable leer.

"I know what you mean, sir," said Major Crenshaw, entering the conversation for the first time.

"I was disappointed," said Bayard recklessly, well aware that he was advancing on very thin ice. "I found it old, worn-out, decadent. I was very disappointed."

Major Mansell's expression had hardened; he had caught Bayard's innuendo.

"Too bad," said the Red Snapper. "Then what did you do?"

"I taught history for two years at St. Swithins—that's a boy's preparatory school in Baltimore. Then this past year I have been a research assistant on the staff of the Senate's Subcommittee on European Affairs."

The Red Snapper raised a quizzical eyebrow. "That's the committee that's headed by that old bastard from the Middle West—what's his name—Senator Wilson?"

"Yes, sir, that's right."

"And all this time you've kept up your connection with the Marine Corps Reserve?"

"Let's say, sir, that I just never got around to severing that connection."

"Well," said the Red Snapper, "that's enough of this horseshit. I'll come straight to the point, young fellow. I'm giving you command of my Dog Company."

He paused. "You needn't look so goddamned pleased. There's nothing in this here qualification jacket of yours or in what you've told me about yourself to recommend you as a rifle company commander. But I got to put you somewhere. Dog Company's got a first lieutenant named Gibson who's a damned capable exec. They also got Hunky Havac, who's as good a first sergeant as is in the Corps. You listen to them, young fellow, and keep your mouth shut until they get you squared away. That's all for now." He nodded his head in dismissal. The interview was over.

Major Crenshaw led Bayard out of the room, back into his own office. He closed the connecting door behind him. "How about a cup of coffee, Captain?"

"Thank you, sir. I could use it."

The executive officer poured two cups of very black coffee from a pot that was simmering on an electric hot plate. "I'm sorry there's no cream or sugar."

"That's all right. I like it black."

"Good," said Major Crenshaw. "You find our Old Man a little rough?"

"Your operations officer bothered me more."

"Mansell? He takes a little understanding."

"It was pretty obvious that he was against me getting a rifle company."

"You'll find that Mansell is a professional perfectionist. Is that how I want to say it? What I mean is that he is professionally very keen, a dedicated marine, and he's apt to be intolerant of others who are less so. Tell me—did you *want* a rifle company?"

The coffee was bitter. Bayard wondered how long it had been in the pot. "I don't remember anyone asking me what *I* wanted. Let's just say that I didn't expect to get a company. I thought something on the battalion staff—S-1 or S-4 maybe."

"You'll make out all right with Dog Company if you bear in mind what the Old Man said about Gibson and Havac."

So Bayard had gone to Dog Company with the knowledge that the Red Snapper had given him the command, not out of confidence in him but because the company had a good executive officer and a proven first sergeant who could be expected to carry an untried company commander.

Now the cycle was complete. Bayard was out of Dog Company. Out of it for good, and on his way home. The people in charge of such things had intended to transfer Bayard straight from Yokusuka to the States, but when he had told them he wanted time enough to see a little of Japan, they cooperated. The fact that his footlocker was supposedly in storage at Kobe was excuse enough for them to give him travel orders. The orders were so written that Bayard could go to Kobe and then report to the marine transient center at Otsu—where by no great coincidence there was this Army Special Services hotel. Later, when he felt like it, he could get his orders endorsed, go back to Kobe, take a train to Tokyo, and get a flight out of Haneda Airport for the States.

Bayard enjoyed the Japanese railroads. There was something especially exciting about them. Part of it was the smell. They were electrified, and the rails gave off a burnt-oil odor that reminded Bayard of the subways in Philadelphia and New York.

But this wasn't Philadelphia or New York. This was Occupied Japan, and everywhere there were symbols of the occupation—separate restaurants, separate waiting rooms, special occupation force trains. The American military police and railroad transportation corps soldiers filled their crisply starched uniforms snugly: the light khaki cloth the Army called "suntan" accentuated by polished brass insignia, shiny brown leather, white plastic chin straps, service ribbons, unit badges, brass whistles and chains, shoulder patches, and side arms secured with white braided lanyards. These rear-area troops had a different look from the combat troops Bayard had known in Korea. He tried to imagine these immaculate creatures going up a long Korean hill against machine-gun fire.

Shoulder-high to these paladins in khaki scurried the myriad Japanese railroad employees, uniformed in black or green cotton: conductors, engineers, brakeman, porters, railroad police, all mixed into the throbbing tempo of the new railway station, sprung up bright and glittering from the bombed-out skeleton of the old.

The undersized train was old-fashioned, musty with green plush seats and slick with yellow varnish, everything a bit too small to be quite comfortable to an Occidental. Bayard, watching the picture-postcard countryside pass by outside his window, theorized that this was perhaps part of the reason for the pomposity of the American occupation: the very reduced scale of things in Japan had a way of making a Westerner feel nine feet tall. It made you feel gauche and out-sized but also powerful and belligerent. An interesting theory, decided Bayard, turning it around in his mind. Weren't there psychological experiments in which the subjects were placed in a room where everything was of a disproportionate size?

But Bayard was not to be left alone with his thoughts. A gray-haired middle-aged American civilian, a hearty, florid man, dropped uninvited into the green plush seat opposite him.

"I see you are a marine," said the man. "Back from the front, I suppose, for—what do you fellows call it? Rest and rehabilitation?"

Barge right in, Bayard thought morosely. Who are you, with your professional cheerfulness? Red Cross field director, YMCA secretary, Sunday school superintendent? Cheer me up if you can. That's what you're set on doing. Here's a lonely marine captain, you said to yourself, I'll extend to him the right hand of good fellowship.

"Why do you people always talk about the front as though it were spelled with capital letters?" Bayard asked abruptly. He supposed that in Far East Command headquarters in the Dai-Ichi building they could show you the front—a neat blue grease-pencil line drawn across the waist of Korea. But in Dog Company they had never talked about the front. In Dog Company they had spoken of going up to the lines, or of being in the attack, or on the MLR, or in reserve.

"I don't know," said the man, somewhat taken aback but pushing valiantly on. "I guess it is something left over from World War I. You know, *All Quiet on the Western Front* and that sort of thing."

"Were *you* in World War I?" asked Bayard, knowing what the answer would be.

"No," said his visitor, "actually I wasn't. I'm one of those fellows who was too young for the First World War and too old for the Second."

There it is, thought Bayard with savage satisfaction. American males of that particular age always felt compelled to confess their failure to get into one war or another, and they always explained their failure with that same pat phrase.

"We are luckier now," said Bayard. "We get a new war every five years. No one need be left out. And they come in sizes. Big ones. Little ones."

The civilian looked confused for a moment; then he plunged on with renewed heartiness. Apparently he was an educator or statistician or something like that with the Occupation. He talked a great deal about the New Japan and the democratization process. He asked Bayard what he thought of the beneficent effects of the Occupation.

"I think," said Bayard slowly, "that the Japanese—if they could—would kick us out on our ass. And I wouldn't blame them."

An uncomfortable embarrassment settled between the two men, and after a minute or two of silence the older man excused himself stiffly and went on to the next car.

Bayard had continued to sit there staring somberly at the Japanese countryside rolling past the window. The farmers and their women were working in the rice paddies, knee-deep in water, cotton trousers up around their hips. The little boys, too young to work in the paddies, were flying their kites in the fresh early June wind. The kites kept the birds away from the rice fields.

chapter two...

The rice paddies of Japan were many thousands of miles away from the sandy pine barrens of North Carolina, and that other train trip now seemed far longer ago than a year.

Bayard was only two days at Camp Lejeune before the battalion departed for California. Those hectic forty-eight hours of processing and packing had left him with little more than a blurred impression of sunburnt grass, red-brick barracks, and the smell of hastily cut yellow-pine crating.

Then the troops boarded a troop train destined for the West Coast. The locomotive was a museum piece, and its cars were antiques. The battalion was five hot days crossing the United States. They went by the southern route, the train dipping down through red-clay Georgia, green Tennessee, across the Mississippi River, and through the long sun-baked and treeless stretches of Texas, New Mexico, and Arizona.

Dog Company occupied two cars and shared a third with Easy Company. The old-fashioned sleeping cars were supposedly air-cooled, but after the second day, no more ice was added to the antiquated refrigeration system.

Bayard shared a compartment with Gibson. The other four officers in the company also had compartments as did the first sergeant, gunnery sergeant, and platoon sergeants. There were berths for the rest of the men. The train would have been comfortable except for the unrelenting heat.

Bayard had Havac leave the company administration field chest in his compartment and put himself to work at reading through the service record books. The company was at half-strength, but still there were more than a hundred books to be examined, more than a hundred personalities to be dealt with.

A service record book is a masterpiece of compressed information, thought Bayard. It gives you a thousand facts about a man. It shows you his picture, gives you his height, weight, and gas mask size. It tells you what kind of a swimmer he is and how well he is qualified in what kinds of weapons. It reveals where he came from, who his next-of-kin is, how well he is educated, and what his special qualifications, if any, are.

If the man had been in combat, there was a concise listing of campaigns and engagements. If he had been decorated, the medals and decorations were enumerated. There were also markings to indicate how well a man performed his assigned duties and how well he behaved himself.

"That's mighty dry reading," said Gibson.

"It's a long trip," answered Bayard. "I've got time."

"Will you be able to remember all that? Will you be able to associate the book with the man?"

"Not in detail, but some of it will stick. I am getting a sort of composite view of Dog Company."

"What does the composite view look like? If you don't mind my asking."

Bayard looked up sharply at Gibson. Was the executive officer being sarcastic? There was no sign of guile on his open, boyish face. Gibson was a first lieutenant and had been acting company commander. He looked about twenty-four, but Bayard knew he was older. He was very blond and, like the other lieutenants, deeply tanned from Caribbean maneuvers. He had an abrupt way of speaking, which Bayard at times found disconcerting.

"There seem to be three kinds of marine in the company," said Bayard, "or perhaps I should say that there seem to be three levels of experience."

"You sound like a college professor," said Gibson.

"That isn't so strange," said Bayard. "I taught school for a couple of years."

"Well, tell me about these three kinds of marine you say we have in Dog Company."

"All right," said Bayard. "First there are the staff noncommissioned officers. They are older. Most of them enlisted before the war. They have ten years service on an average. Havac and Agnelli are the two best examples."

"I am with you," said Gibson. "Next."

"Then there are the buck sergeants and corporals. I notice that most of them are on their second enlistment. They came in during the war. Some of them went out for a while and then came back. The rest, the privates and PFCs, are youngsters, eighteen or nineteen, with just a year or two of service."

"You have a very analytical mind, Captain," said Gibson.

"I try to have."

"Of course, there are exceptions."

"Of course," said Bayard. "I was generalizing."

"Here's one of the exceptions," said Gibson, pulling one of the service records from the file. "Have you looked at this one yet?"

Bayard took the book and turned to the first page. The small square identification picture showed a dark, hard-visaged man. This was no eighteen- or nineteen-year-old boy. The name was Kusnetzov. The rank was private first class.

"Yes," said Bayard, "I remember this book. A second enlistment PFC. There aren't many of those. Good proficiency marks but marked down on behavior. What's the story on him?"

"He's a throwback," said Gibson. "A hash-marked PFC. A professional private. Talks of service in a European army. Before the war we used to have a lot of that type. The Marine Corps was almost a Foreign Legion."

"So I've heard," said Bayard dryly. "I wasn't around then. Were you?"

"I saw a little of the prewar Marine Corps," said Gibson. "I enlisted when I graduated from high school. That was in 1937."

"The officers' qualification jackets are in the battalion adjutant's chests," said Bayard obliquely. "I haven't had a chance to go over them. Do you mind me asking questions?"

"No, sir—not at all."

"You enlisted in 1937. Then what?"

"After Parris Island, I went to Shanghai for duty and then to Tientsin. I was in the old *Concord* when the war began and stayed with her until late in '43. Then I went to Candidates Class. I got overseas again in time to make Guam and Okinawa."

"You didn't revert to your enlisted rank after the war?"

"I passed the college equivalent test and got a permanent commission."

"You've had thirteen years continuous service. I've had less than four years active duty. Yet I am the company commander. How does that set with you?"

Gibson drew a deep breath. "Now the questions are getting tough, Captain. Sure, I minded it when you took over. Who wouldn't? I've been acting company commander, and I had hoped to take the company to Korea. But you're a captain and I'm a first lieutenant. It's as simple as that."

"How about the other officers in the company? How do they feel about it?"

The four second lieutenants were in the next compartment playing bridge. The sounds of the game came through the partition. Bayard had looked in earlier. Seeing him, the boisterous group had fallen respectfully silent.

They were all regulars, and all gave a first impression of being singularly alike: young, lean, close-cropped, deeply tanned. They had stripped off their utility jackets because of the heat and were sitting there in their undershirts. From the neck of each on a slender chain hung two stainless-steel identification disks. Like talismans, thought Bayard. In addition, one lieutenant wore a Catholic medal. This was Miller, a thin, tautly drawn officer who had the 1st Platoon.

Miller and Reynolds, the machine-gun officer, were the oldest of the four. Both had had enlisted service during the war. Both had graduated from the Basic School in 1948. Reynolds, muscled like a middle-weight, had a hard, competent look about him, like the weapons he commanded.

Thompson, who had the 2d Platoon, was a Naval Academy graduate. He had been with the company for a year. He was junior to both Miller and Reynolds, but in many ways he appeared to be the natural leader of the foursome. Rank among second lieutenants, as Bayard had heard so many times at Quantico, was like virtue among whores. Thompson had a sardonic quality. He managed to convey an air of indolent superiority, even in utility trousers and undershirt.

Burdock was the most junior in rank and the youngest of the four. He had just joined the company in June from the Basic School. He was that very blond type that tans deeply. His eyebrows and lashes, by contrast, were bleached almost white by the North Carolina sun. He had the 60mm mortar section—the "pop guns," as they were called. There seemed to be a lack of maturity in Burdock. Perhaps because the gap between Quantico and the Fleet Marine Force was not yet closed in his mind, he was almost painfully deferential, not only with the other lieutenants but also with the staff NCOs. He had to curb a tendency to address First Sergeant Havac as "sir."

All the lieutenants but Burdock had been with Dog Company in the Mediterranean with the Sixth Fleet and at Vieques in the Caribbean for spring maneuvers. In addition, Gibson, Miller, and Reynolds had been to Labrador, the winter before last, on a cold-weather training exercise called NORTHEX.

All of my junior officers with the possible exception of Burdock, thought Bayard, are technically more competent, better qualified for command of the company than I am.

Gibson had not answered his last question.

"They think you got a raw deal, don't they?" persisted Bayard.

"I suppose they do," said Gibson reluctantly.

"The same goes for the staff NCOs?" pursued Bayard. "Particularly the first sergeant?"

Gibson paused before answering. "Sir, is it all right if I speak perfectly frankly?"

"I expect you to."

"Well, then—just before you reported in, the company received a draft of ten recruits from Parris Island. We were glad to get them. They helped to fill up the company. On the same day we received an issue of six new light machine guns from the depot. The guns had been inspected and okayed for issue. That night Havac and Gunny Agnelli and the machine-gun platoon sergeant tore the machine guns down and checked them out. The guns were fine. They were in A1 shape, just like they had been certified by the ordnance people. But Havac wanted to make sure for himself. It's the same with the ten boots from Parris Island. They've finished their recruit training, and technically they're qualified as riflemen. But

Havac is going to watch them and check them out the same as he checked out the machine guns."

"I gather your little parable applies to a new company commander," said Bayard dryly. "Particularly if he's a reserve from civilian life."

Gibson shook his head. "It would be the same if you were a regular straight from the Naval Academy and the Basic School. Havac isn't hostile. He's seen a lot of officers come and go in his time. Some of them made it, in his judgment. Others didn't. You have to remember also that no one—no officer, at least—can ever quite measure up to Havac's idea of what a marine should be. When he first came into the Corps, men like Cates, Shepherd, and Edson were company commanders. That's stiff competition."

"Well, at least I know what I'm up against," said Bayard. "That's something. If I'm going to make the grade, if I'm going to do even a halfway decent job, I'll need all the help I can get. Particularly from you, Gibson."

"You'll have it," said Gibson. "One thing more, sir, I think you should know: there's no plot against you. Nobody wants you to fail. The officers and men, they want you to turn out to be a good company commander."

Gibson's sincerity was obvious. He also appeared a little embarrassed from having talked so freely.

"How about walking through the cars and seeing how the men are making out?" suggested Bayard.

"Aye, aye, sir," said Gibson. He left the compartment.

The long train journey dragged to a close. The battalion finally arrived at its staging area at Camp Pendleton in California. There was a tent camp set up and waiting for them in the brown hills above the dry Santa Margarita River. A platoon was drawn from each company and sent down to San Diego to help with the loading. From here they would mount out for overseas—a "verbally designated destination," the orders read.

They were ten days at Camp Pendleton. In that time Dog Company was filled out with reservists and casuals from posts and stations to its wartime strength of two hundred twenty-one marines and seven officers. Dog Company drew most of its new men from a San Francisco reserve battalion. Among them was a first lieutenant of unprepossessing appearance named Naheghian, squat, swarthy, and of Syrian or Armenian extraction.

In contrast to the other lieutenants, who were lean, Naheghian appeared to be fat. They were brown from the sun; his skin was sallow, almost greenish in cast. Their utility uniforms fitted well and were soft and faded from many washings; Naheghian's utilities were stiff and new.

Bayard had surreptitiously soaked his own utilities in a strong solution of bleach to remove the telltale newness, but Naheghian's uniform was a reminder to him that they were birds of a feather, reserves whose protective coloration wasn't quite the same hue as that of the regular species.

Bayard had been most concerned over Naheghian's date of rank because if he had been senior to Gibson, he would have had to make Naheghian the company executive officer. Bayard was much relieved, therefore, to learn that Gibson ranked him by nearly a year. A problem remained, though, as to where Naheghian should be fitted into the company organization. By seniority he was entitled to the 1st Platoon, which now belonged to Second Lieutenant Miller, but Bayard did not wish to disturb existing arrangements.

In the end he gave Naheghian the 3d Platoon, which was all new, not being a part of the peacetime company. If Naheghian had any objections to this assignment, he did not voice them, and eight days later, when Dog Company went on board ship at San Diego, there was nothing—in outward appearance, at least—to distinguish the 3d Platoon from the rest of the company.

The troop transport was a big Military Sea Transportation Service ship, the twenty-thousand-ton *General Braxton Bragg*. She had a civilian crew and, until the outbreak of hostilities, had been on the diaper run, carrying dependents to the Far East. Her accommodations were remarkably fine; except for her gray paint she could have been a commercial liner. Dog Company, used to the Spartan austerity of the Amphibious Forces, luxuriated in this atmosphere where even senior corporals were treated as cabin-class passengers.

There were incongruities. Officers' school was held in the music room off the main lounge. The battalion office was in what had been the children's nursery. First Sergeant Havac sat with Dog Company's green field desk so situated that a painted clown with orange hair and a red nose peered over his shoulder from the bulkhead.

There were Filipino mess attendants and printed menus in the dining salon and four meals a day to be eaten. The fourth was a late buffet supper laid out for the officers and staff noncommissioned officers after the evening movie. The sight of First Sergeant Havac in his utility uniform sitting in the lounge with a plate of cold cuts and assorted salads balanced uneasily on his knee was enough to excite the risibility of even the most disciplined PFC.

Bayard shared a very adequate stateroom with Gibson. It was an outside room with a porthole opening onto a weather deck. They had their own washbasin and shared with an adjoining stateroom a lavatory with shower stall and toilet. In addition to the double-decked bunks with thick, firm mattresses, there were built-in chests of drawers, and a desk.

Bayard was inclined to feel squeamish on even the most comfortable of ships. He dosed himself with dramamine and stayed close to his stateroom. It wasn't that he was exactly seasick, but he did feel distinctly better lying down.

On the third day at sea, about nine in the morning, after Bayard had returned to his stateroom to recover from an unnecessarily heavy breakfast—he had had no business eating the oatmeal, the hot cakes, *and* the pork sausage—Havac brought him a mimeograph stencil to be signed.

"Here you are, sir," said Havac, putting the stencil down on Bayard's desk and holding out a stylus. "If you'll just sign where I've put the check marks."

Something about Havac's manner—or perhaps it was the pork sausage—rubbed Bayard the wrong way. He decided to be obstinate. "What's this?" he asked.

"Embarkation slips," said the first sergeant. "We put one in each man's SRB to show when he embarked. You'll see that we left the time and place of debarkation blank. We'll fill that in later."

"Has Mr. Gibson seen this?"

"He knows about it, sir. It's strictly routine."

"But I asked you to have Mr. Gibson initial everything you brought me for signature."

Havac looked pained. "Captain, sir, when First Sergeant Havac gives the Captain something to sign, the Captain can be sure it's right."

"I don't doubt that, First Sergeant," said Bayard, determined to be as stubborn as Havac. "The fact remains that I don't see Mr. Gibson's initials."

"Captain, sir, Mr. Gibson was busy with the ship's first officer inspecting the troop spaces."

Havac's tone was faintly accusatory. The company commander should have made the daily inspection, but with his queasy stomach Bayard had no wish to spend an hour or so each morning in the fetid troop compartments, so he had delegated the job to the executive officer.

Bayard looked again at the offending stencil. He read it carefully. There were no typographical errors, but still he did not reach for the stylus that Havac held poised in his hand. "I don't think this is quite right," said Bayard finally.

"What's wrong with it?" The first sergeant was visibly and audibly shocked.

"Isn't there a regulation that all entries in a service record book are to be signed in the witnessing officer's own handwriting?"

"Yes, sir," said Havac. "But this is the same thing. You sign the stencil, and that saves you the trouble of signing each of the books."

"It isn't the same thing," said Bayard. "It's a reproduced signature, not an original."

"This is the way we've always done it, Captain, sir," said Havac heavily. "I've been a first sergeant nine years now, and this is the way I've always done it."

"That doesn't make it right, though, does it?"

"Not if the Captain says it isn't right, sir," said Havac stiffly.

Bayard moved quickly to consolidate his gains: "I think you better make these entries in the SRBs, and then I'll sign them."

"Aye, aye, sir. If that's the way the Captain wants it done, that's the way we'll do it." Havac spoke in the tones of a man just ordered to fling himself bare-handed against a T-34 tank. "Is there anything else, sir?"

"No, First Sergeant. That'll be all."

"May I be excused then, sir?"

"Certainly."

The first sergeant turned on his heel and marched out of the stateroom. Bayard smiled faintly to himself and then climbed into his lower bunk for a nap. It was a small victory, but a sweet one.

Two hours later he was awakened by a tapping at the door. "Come in," he shouted, swinging up into a sitting position.

It was not Havac but Pinky, the company clerk, the corporal who was the first sergeant's good right arm in matters of company administration.

"We have the entries in the SRBs ready for signature, sir," said Pinky. The company clerk had the face of an anemic horse. This morning his countenance was even more lugubrious than usual.

"Good," said Bayard. "That was fast work. I'll be right down to the battalion office to sign them."

"I have them here," said Pinky mournfully.

"Well, then bring them in."

Pinky stepped aside, and a two-man working party staggered through the doorway into the room with the awkward field chest. They deposited it in the center of the room so that it monopolized the small amount of free floor space, and then they dodged back past Pinky and on into the passageway.

"Sir?" said Pinky, hesitating at the door before departing.

"Yes?" answered Bayard, opening the field chest. He pulled out a service record book at random. The proper page was marked with a paper clip. A mimeographed slip had been pasted on the page, ready for the company commander's signature. "What is it?"

"Could I ask the Captain a favor, sir?"

"That depends what it is."

"I was wondering, sir, if I could be transferred to the machine-gun platoon. I was a machine gunner before they found out I could type."

"Were you a good machine gunner?"

"I was a better machine gunner than I am a company clerk," replied Pinky with a tinge of desperation.

"Have you the first sergeant's permission to talk to me about this?"

"No, sir. Not exactly."

"I suggest you take it up with him. If he has no objection to the transfer, I have none."

"Yes, sir. Thank you, sir," said Pinky resignedly. From his tone Bayard knew that Pinky considered his petition denied, his position hopeless.

For the second time that morning, Bayard smiled as his stateroom door closed. In this instance, however, his smile was much warmer. He was still smiling when he sat himself down at his desk to sign his name to two hundred twenty-one service record books.

chapter three...

After twelve days at sea at twenty knots, the regiment arrived at Kobe. The 2d Battalion off-loaded onto the confusion of the docks while a welcoming Negro military band played "St. Louis Blues" in march-time. There was a week's combat conditioning, along with a welter of operations orders, maps, and aerial photographs, a series of intelligence briefings, and a typhoon to stir up the combat loading. Then they were at sea again.

Dog Company crossed over from Kobe to Korea in LST 557. The landing ship was an unlovely thing—rusty and scabbed with yellow chrome and red lead. Only recently had she been recovered from the Japanese shipping firm that had operated her in the interisland trade, and a faint but pervasive odor of fish and the starchy smell of rice persisted in her passenger spaces.

That the 557 was rotten and unseaworthy was of less concern to Dog Company than the disappointment of her being a poor feeder. The expectation of good navy chow failed to materialize. The marine cooks learned that there were no refrigerators for fresh stores, that the LST's previous Japanese crew, with no greater culinary demands than boiling water for rice and tea, had disconnected and carted off most of the galley equipment.

The food, consequently, was poor. Half because of this and half because of boredom, Dog Company began to make inroads into the combat rations that were deck-loaded on the LST. The same C rations that they would curse with polished invective once they were ashore now seemed to exert an irresistible lure. Bayard stationed sentries over the rations and assigned an officer-of-the-day to check the sentries. This cut down the pilfering and left Dog Company with nothing to kill the monotony of the voyage except writing letters, reading paperback novels and comic books, and playing cards. Each member of the company had been permitted to draw twenty-five dollars in military scrip the day before sailing. Two days at sea, and those funds were largely concentrated in the hands of the six or eight most adroit players of poker and black jack. The major portion of Dog Company spent its time sitting stoically on deck under the leaden autumn sky watching the yellow-gray sea and waiting for the next phase of its own private purgatory to unfold.

The lurching vibration of LST 557 was a far different and a far more disturbing motion than the slow majestic pitch and roll of the *General Bragg*. This time Bayard drugged himself even more heavily with dramamine to a point where his seasickness subsided to a dull nausea.

The rest of Dog Company's officers apparently found the odor and the unending, shuddering bounce of the ship less objectionable.

Naheghian, it developed, was an inveterate and expert player of bridge. The other three members of the marathon game changed, but Naheghian seemed content to sit at the mess table in the wardroom, braced against the bumps of the Japanese Sea with a fan of greasy cards in his fist, a cup of stale coffee at his elbow, and a well-chewed stub of a cigar between his teeth.

The wardroom itself was a gray-painted steel box of a room, its walls wet to the touch with condensation and the air foul because the blackout covers on the portholes were welded shut and the ventilating system did not work.

The lieutenants most frequently at the blanket-covered mess table with Naheghian were Miller and Burdock. Surprisingly enough, this oddly assorted trio seemed to be on the most intimate of terms. Naheghian was growing a mustache—he was a hirsute type, with stiff black hair covering most of his body except for the top of his head, which was bald—and lighter smudges had also appeared on the upper lips of Miller and Burdock.

The fourth member at the table could be almost anyone, any of the remaining lieutenants or one of the ship's officers. Reynolds was more apt to be out on deck holding machine-gun school or conducting gun drill in what space he could find between the deck-load of drummed fuel and the Athey trailers filled with rations and ammunition. Thompson had a Naval Academy classmate in the ship's company—the engineer officer—and this had revived his interest in naval machinery. Gibson also tended to remain somewhat detached. He was an omnivorous reader, and somewhere he had found a copy of Frazer's *The Golden Bough*.

Occasionally, out of sheer boredom, Bayard took a hand in the bridge game. For the most part, however, he spent his time wandering restlessly between the open deck, the wardroom, and his "stateroom," which was a euphemism for the cubicle, about seven feet square, he shared with Gibson, Miller, and Thompson. Along with the mingled odors of its past and present occupants, the cubicle also smelled of fish. LST 557 didn't furnish linen to its passengers; Bayard's sleeping bag was unrolled on the bare and much-stained mattress of his bunk.

These accommodations were a sharp contrast to the pleasant stateroom of recent memory on board the *Bragg*. Still, though, they were infinitely superior to the troop spaces below deck. There, only a select few—the NCOs in the upper pay grades—had the luxury of a canvas bunk, slung in tiers of three so that a man's nose nearly brushed the canvas of the bunk above him. The lesser ranks spread their sleeping bags or blankets wherever they could find the room. In good weather many slept topside, which was pleasant enough on a clear night, but after they rounded Pusan, the weather turned wet and all four hundred enlisted souls embarked in LST 557 had to crowd themselves below decks.

There were other inconveniences. Once a day the men had to stand in line during water hours for a canteen of fresh water. This was for drinking. There was no fresh water for washing, only seawater, and there was no saltwater soap on board. The plumbing worked no better than any other part of the ship. The urinals and stools were soon choked to overflowing, and below decks reeked with the smell of excrement and vomit.

The captain of the 557 was not proud of his ship. Lieutenant Huggins, USN, was a former boatswain who had served in landing ships during World War II. This new war was not to his liking, nor was the ship. As he told Bayard, he had been finishing out his thirty years service with just a couple of months to go, stationed at Coronado and looking forward to retirement on a lemon and avocado ranch he was buying near Escondido, when the North Koreans crossed the Parallel.

As they stood together at the rail marking the narrow bit of space that was called officers' country, the volubly morose Huggins complained to Bayard that of all his ship's officers, only the engineer—Thompson's Naval Academy friend—and Huggins himself were regular Navy. The rest were reserves freshly recalled, and none had had any experience in the amphibious forces. The crew was as bad off. Only a handful of the petty officers had been in landing ships, and some of the seamen had never before been to sea.

"Shit," said Huggins disgustedly, looking forward at the rusting deck of his ship, "I get a chief machinist's mate, and it turns out he got his rating during the war being a reefer mechanic at Great Lakes. I got a bosun that can't tell the difference between a hawser and a halyard. Two weeks they give me at Sasebo to get the ship and crew ready for sea."

Bayard looked around at the rest of the convoy spaced out on the lead-colored horizon. "Do you think we'll make it to Inchon?" he asked.

Huggins shrugged his tired, fifty-year-old shoulders. "I'm doing my best, but her hull is strained and a really rough sea'd break the ship in half."

Bayard, looking forward toward the bow, thought that he could see the whole ship bending under the impact of the roughening sea. Huggins assured him that this was no optical illusion. He also glumly pointed out the precarious condition of the deck cargo.

"The decks're rusted so thin I don't dare use a chipping hammer on them, but here I've got them piled high with a full deck-load of trucks and ammo trailers and fuel drums. I expect them to bust through any minute and land on top of your marines. Or else maybe we'll have some of those deck chains break loose, and then we'll have some broken legs from those fuel drums rolling around."

Huggins shook his head in total disgust.

"Rust held together with paint," he muttered dolefully, accepting a thick mug of coffee and a sandwich from the wardroom steward. "You want one of these?"

But Bayard had no appetite.

That night Bayard was suddenly awakened by a change in the motion of the ship. He lay still in his bunk, not certain of what had happened, not even sure of what it was that had awakened him. Then he realized that the plunging vibration of the ship had ceased. The 557 was curiously silent; the throb of the engines was absent. They were lying dead in the water, wallowing in a deep uneasy roll.

"You awake, Captain?" It was Gibson's voice.

"Yes," said Bayard. "What do you suppose it is?"

"I don't know."

"Maybe Thompson knows. You awake, Thompson?"

"He's not in his bunk, sir." This was from Miller.

Bayard slipped out of his sleeping bag and fumbled for the light switch. He flipped it on, but nothing happened.

"Something's wrong with the power," he reported to Gibson and Miller. He pushed aside the heavy curtain that served as a stateroom door. There was no light in the passageway except for a faint glow from a battery-powered emergency lamp.

"Maybe we hit something—or something hit us," said Gibson.

"Do you think we're sinking?" Miller's voice squeaked a little when it got to the sinking.

"No," said Gibson firmly. "If we were, they'd have us at our abandon-ship stations."

"I don't know," said Miller dubiously. "With this crew you can't tell what might happen."

"I'm going up on the bridge to find out what's going on," said Bayard. "Who's got a flashlight handy?"

He had been sleeping in his underwear. He found his utility trousers and boots with the help of the flashlight, held by Gibson. As an afterthought he put on his cap, which bore a Marine Corps emblem and his rank insignia, just in case he was stopped by some member of the crew who failed to recognize him.

He went out into the passageway and found his way to the weather deck. It was raining and the night was very black. There was no sign of the remainder of the convoy. He should have taken time to put on his field jacket; he was getting soaked.

The ship fell into the trough of a particularly heavy sea, and Bayard was thrown up against the rail, his leg scraping painfully against some unseen obstruction. Clutching the rail, he moved toward the ladder that led upward to the bridge. The steps were greasy-wet with the rain and salt spray, and he climbed them with an effort. At the top of the ladder another sudden convulsive motion of the ship catapulted him through the doorway to the bridge.

There was a faint bluish glow coming from the binnacle; that was the only light. It reflected eerily off the faces of the three or four crew members manning the bridge. The men looked startled at Bayard's precipitous entrance.

"Is the captain here?" asked Bayard recovering his balance.

"Of course he's here," growled a voice. Bayard swung around.

Huggins was sitting in a chair bolted to the deck. "What're you doin' on my bridge?"

"It's me—Captain Bayard."

"I know who it is," said Huggins. "I asked: What are you doin' on my bridge?"

Somewhere in the darkness a sailor snickered. Bayard bridled angrily. "As commander of embarked troops I've a right to know what's going on," he said stiffly. The sailor in the darkness snickered again.

I must have sounded like a prize horse's ass, thought Bayard, suddenly and acutely embarrassed. I came pounding up here like I was scared to death.

"Shut up," said Huggins abruptly, presumably addressing the sailor who found Bayard's presence so amusing.

"You want to know what's wrong?" asked Huggins, continuing in a more moderate tone. "That's reasonable, though you have no business coming onto my bridge to find out. That's an ancient law of the sea designed to protect the ship's company. If the passengers keep coming up to the bridge, they're liable to find out how fouled up we are. You want to know what's wrong? I'll tell you what's wrong. Some smart-ass Jap engineer had trouble with the oil filters, so he bypassed them. That's what's wrong. The fuel tanks are loaded with dirt and rust that's shaken loose from the working of the sea and the weight of the deck load. The injection system keeps clogging, and there are no replacement parts on board for the filters themselves. That's what's wrong. We've had to shut down to clean out the fuel injectors. That's what my engineer and your trade-school lieutenant and that refrigerator mechanic are doing."

"What if they can't get them fixed?"

"Then we better find a tow, or you won't be making the landing."

Bayard had one beautiful moment in which to savor this possibility; then the engine room telephone buzzed. Huggins took the telephone, listened, and grunted his satisfaction.

"The engineer says we're ready to get under way again. You can go back to your bunk, Captain Bayard."

Twice again before reaching Inchon, LST 557 had to drop out of convoy while the engineer officer and the machinist mate worked on the worn-out engines, but somehow, despite all of 557's deficiencies and Huggins's own frequently expressed misgivings, they reached the transport area on schedule.

The day was overcast, and the smoke of the prelanding bombardment was mixed with the mist so that the city was wrapped in a yellowish gray blanket. Some of the naval gunfire ships were using time fuzes, and their airbursts were dirty blobs of smoke hung in the dingy sky.

The word was passed for the marines to lay below to their debarkation stations. Bayard went forward, picking his way across the crowded open deck until he found the hatch that led down to the tank deck. His foot slipped on the greasy rung of the ladder. His cloth-covered helmet banged deafeningly against the hatch combing. He caught himself and, moving awkwardly and self-consciously under the unaccustomed weight and bulk of his combat pack and equipment, finally reached the dim cavern of the tank deck.

His amphibian tractor waited in the bow of the LST. The ramp of the landing ship was down, and through the open bow doors Bayard could see a destroyer engaging a hidden shore battery with its five-inch guns. The shells exploding ashore sent up brownish fountains of debris.

Inside the bowels of 557, the drivers of the LVTs were warming the engines of their squat amphibious monsters. The exhaust gases were stifling. The tank deck stank with sweat, oil, and the other effluvia of a troop-carrying landing ship.

Bayard looked at his watch—4:20 P.M.—1620 by the military way of telling time. His wave was scheduled to take to the water at 1630. The timing was very important because of the tides: they rose and fell an incredible thirty feet. White Beach had the further barrier of a seawall. Major Mansell had emphasized in his briefing that the landing must be made within a few minutes of 1730 or the amphibian tractors would belly-up on the soft mud of the tidal flats. Floundering ashore through the mud could prove a worse catastrophe than the reefs at Tarawa.

Bayard had found a place to stand on the grill of his LVT, just to the rear of the driver's cab. For perhaps the hundredth time he went over in his mind the memorized details of the landing plan:

"Company D (Reinforced) in Battalion reserve to move over seawall by way of scaling ladders (left in place by Companies E and F) and to proceed to designated assembly area (see overlay) prepared for employment in zone of action of either assault company." So read the 2d Battalion's operation order.

The terse phrases had worn a groove into Bayard's brain. *By way of scaling ladders. Proceed to designated assembly area.*

What if there weren't any scaling ladders? What if he couldn't find the assembly area?

Havac was watching him. Their eyes caught and locked. What was it that Havac was looking for, what telltale symptom? What was he thinking? That this was *his* company and that he and not some untested stranger should be leading it into combat?

Bayard turned to study the instrument panel of the LVT. The 2d Battalion was to land on White Beach Two in the wake of a platoon of armored amtracs. These thin-skinned amphibian gun-carriers were to try to find a way around the seawall and onto the beach. They would touch down at H-hour to be followed one minute later by the assault platoons of Easy and Fox Companies. The support platoons would land after a five-minute interval, and then would come Dog Company at H-plus-Eleven minutes. So went the plan.

Was the queasiness he was experiencing, Bayard wondered, from the roll of the LST and the fumes that filled the tank deck? Or was it from something more fundamental? His mouth was dry. It was as though there were a pad of steel wool in his stomach. A queer, rubbery feeling was affecting his legs and knees. How could a man tell what he would do when the time came? What if, at that crucial moment when he had to jump from the gunwale of the tractor to the scaling ladder, his muscles refused to respond? What if he stayed clinging to the tractor, paralyzed, frozen, while Dog Company, led by Havac, climbed scornfully past him? He had heard of such a paralysis, when the body refused to obey the frightened mind. Experimentally he moved his legs and flexed his arms. They responded, but they seemed remote, as though a puppet master had pulled the strings on a marionette.

A tall marine with a week's growth of black beard was staring at him from the waist of the tractor. It was a bold stare, insolent and appraising. Was he, mused Bayard, wondering too? Bayard had noticed the man before. He was in the machine-gun platoon. He was older and seemed set apart from the rest of the platoon. He was, Bayard remembered, the professional private with the Russian or Polish-sounding name.

Baby-san, Bayard's runner, was nudging him in the side. "Captain," he shouted over the din of the idling engines, "that navy officer is trying to get your attention."

He pointed toward a ship's officer standing by the port side of the ramp. The officer was looking at him and tapping his wrist. Bayard shot a glance at his own watch. The time was 4:29. Bayard nodded agreement, his helmet wobbling uncomfortably on his head. The ship's officer whirled his arm, giving the windup signal.

Bayard's driver gunned his engine and eased his tractor into gear. The old girl shook herself in protest at being called back into active service so long after Okinawa and started waddling down the rusted ramp. She entered the water with an awkward lurch that threatened to send her bow under. Her tracks dug frantically into the water, she got hold of herself, and her driver brought her around in a wide circle while the rest of the wave came out of the LST with swift clumsiness. Bayard's tractor made the circle twice; by then, all of the LVTs were free of the landing ship.

"Okay," said the tractor commander above the roar of the motors and the churn of the tracks, "where to?"

"Where's the wave guide?" Bayard shouted back.

"The what?"

"The wave guide—the boat that's supposed to lead us to the line of departure."

"Don't ask me," said the tractor sergeant. "Six weeks ago I was driving a bus in San Francisco."

Bayard squinted uncertainly through the thickening haze. A great many fires had been set ashore by the naval bombardment, and the breeze blowing seaward carried with it a dense wall of smoke. He looked aft to where Havac crouched stolidly amid the tightly packed mass of marines and combat gear. But Havac volunteered no solution, and Bayard was determined not to ask him for help. A gray navy shape loomed up nearby, half hidden in the wet smoke.

"Head for that patrol craft," Bayard ordered the driver.

"The what?"

"That ship over there. It looks like it might be a control vessel."

Bayard's tractor veered toward the ship, obediently followed by the rest of the wave of LVTs. Bayard wasn't certain what kind of a ship it was. Around the bow she resembled a destroyer, but two-thirds of the way aft, she was chopped off short, and this gave her a high, stubby look. There was a good deal of activity on her bridge, and a string of signal flags snapped from her signal hoists.

Bayard's column came up on the starboard side of the ship.

"What beach?" came a megaphoned query from the bridge.

Bayard caught the officious glint of an ensign's gold collar bars. "White Beach Two," he shouted. "Which way?"

"That way." The ensign on the bridge pointed to where the smoke was the thickest and no beach at all could be seen.

"Well, let's go," said Bayard with more determination and assurance than he felt.

They headed into the smoke. After ten minutes of running, the outlines of the beach still refused to emerge. Just as Bayard was about to order a change of direction and a fresh course, a Higgins boat came angling toward them. That must be the long-missing wave guide, thought Bayard with relief.

"Idle down," he ordered the tractor sergeant. "And let that landing craft come alongside."

"Are you the wave guide for White Two?" he shouted across the water to the coxswain when they were within hailing distance.

"Hell, no," came the answer. "This is a free boat. I got a load of photographers aboard. Want your picture taken?"

"How about you fellows waving and giving us a big smile?" called a fat, middle-aged civilian holding up a Speed Graphic. Twenty or more cameras were pointed toward Bayard's tractor. His marines obligingly waved and grinned.

"Knock that cheap shit off," came a bull roar from Havac in the stern of the amtrac. "What're you? A buncha fairies going for a Sunday boat ride? Get your goddamn heads down below the gunnels."

Obediently, albeit reluctantly, the heads went down and the press boat curved away in search of more cooperative subject matter.

Bayard was still unenlightened as to the location of White Beach Two. None of Inchon's carefully memorized landmarks showed themselves through the shell-fomented fog. If the line of departure, with its carefully regulated controls, was anywhere in the vicinity, he could see no sign of it.

The men crouched in the cargo space were watching him intently. Bayard was more acutely aware than ever of Havac's disapproving presence in the rear of the tractor. He knew he must find the way into the beach and soon. He banged the tractor sergeant on the back.

"You have a compass?" he shouted.

The sergeant leaned over the shoulder of his driver and dubiously searched the instrument panel.

"I don't know," he said. "These things are supposed to have one, I think. I don't know much about this model. We did all our training in A-4s."

Bayard had his own lensatic compass. He unsnapped its canvas case and took an experimental reading. He supposed that it would be far from accurate because of the influence of the steel hull and the engines, but he could try it. Inside his jacket he had buttoned his map of the beach area. On it he had blue-penciled the landing plan and his company's scheme of maneuver ashore. He pulled out the map and attempted to orient himself. The azimuth of the boat lane was fifty degrees magnetic.

Bayard held the compass to his eye and, with the compass dial wavering between fifty and sixty degrees, sighted in on what he hoped was the direction of the beach. He thought he could distinguish the blacker pillar of an oil fire rising behind the general cloud of smoke.

"Head for that oil fire," he ordered the tractor sergeant. "That should be it."

The fourth wave shook off its indecision and started in the direction Bayard had indicated, not in a proper line, but in a column—each LVT following in the trace of Bayard's tractor.

Standing with his head and shoulders above the plating protecting the driver's cab and intent on keeping the black smoke in sight, Bayard was not immediately aware of the snapping and popping overhead. It took him a moment more to associate the sound with the more familiar noise of bullets passing over the target pits of a rifle range. Now the noise had meaning: a number of rifles and at least one machine gun were firing in his direction. Along with the sound, he could now make out the red-orange fingers of tracer bullets reaching out toward Wave Four.

In the cargo compartment there was a sudden awareness that they were under fire. A fringe of curious heads popped up over the sides of the LVT.

"It's not the red ones you can see that'll hurt you," Havac's voice rumbled from the stern. "It's the black ones you don't see. Get your goddamn heads down before I knock 'em down."

Bayard automatically stepped down from the grill to the relative protection of the cab's thin armor plating. Then, stubbornly, he climbed back to his former position and re-sighted his compass. The unseen bullets cracking overhead communicated to him no feeling of danger—rather, they had an exciting, tonic effect. He looked at his watch. It was 5:34. They had been afloat for over an hour. In seven minutes his wave was to touch down—if he could find the beach.

A string of churning shapes appeared close to Wave Four's left. Bayard had his driver throttle down while he shouted across the water. "What wave? Are you headed for White Two?"

"You're too far to the left," someone shouted back. "This is Wave Five headed for White One."

Bayard squinted dubiously through the smoke and got a new fix on the beach. "Keep well to the right," he told his driver. "Well right of that black column of smoke."

Wave Four veered to the right and continued on. Something close to desperation was beginning to grip Bayard. The minutes were ticking by. There was the rigid landing schedule and the menace of the falling tide. He had to get onto the beach.

Then something plopped in front of his LVT and exploded, sending up a geyser of dirty water.

"Mortars," came Havac's crisp pronouncement from the rear of the amtrac in answer to Bayard's unspoken question. If they were within mortar range, they couldn't be too far from the beach.

Now through occasional rifts in the smoke, Bayard could see the flame-dotted darker gray of the shoreline. He began to pick up the landmarks so carefully memorized from the intelligence photographs. There were the twin brick chimneys of the power plant. To the right were the shed roofs of the rolling mill. And crossing his front was the black streak of the seawall.

He estimated they were still three or four hundred yards out from the beach. A great number of tractors were clustered under the seawall. Another column—they were the armored tractors—was circling a few yards out from the wall, firing their snub-nosed cannon and their machine guns at some unseen target ashore. Bayard could now make out the individual gray-green figures of marines attempting to get over the seawall. Something had gone wrong; the scaling ladders seemed too short. Bayard looked again at his watch. It was now 5:46.

He was already five minutes late with the fourth wave, but what was wrong with the waves to his front? The assault echelon should have been well ashore by now.

"Start circling," he said firmly to the tractor sergeant, fighting down a feeling of near-panic. He had to keep his distance. There was nothing to be gained by joining the tight mass of tractors at the foot of the seawall. Wave Four curved in a tight arc to the right. The ominous plopping of mortar shells increased. One round burst close alongside, drenching the occupants of LVT 4-1 with greasy seawater. Bayard looked back into the cargo compartment in time to see a rifleman raise a startled hand to a bloodstained face.

"I told you to keep your friggin' heads down," snarled the first sergeant. "Corpsman, put a battle dressing on that man. The rest of you keep your goddamn heads down below the waterline!"

A round-shouldered figure in stiffly new and unfaded utilities pushed his way through the mass of marines to the side of the wounded man. Bayard saw that the hospital corpsman was Milton Pilnick—whom Dog Company, with its proclivity for nicknames and with considerable logic, had given the nom de guerre of "Pills."

Pilnick was from Baltimore where he was a salesman for an ethical drug company. He lived with his mother and was also working nights toward a pharmacy degree. His ambition was to own a drugstore in one of the new shopping centers that were springing up out in the county. During the war he had been a pharmacist's mate. He had stayed in the Naval Reserve, and now he was the senior medical corpsman attached to Dog Company. He tore open a battle dressing and applied the compress to the wounded man's face.

"Give him room to lay down," he said. "That's all I can do for him until we get ashore."

Bayard looked back toward the beach and saw five of the armored tractors break away from their circle. He saw them head for a break in the seawall off to the right flank. The amphibians crawled clumsily toward the gap, seeking the dry ground that lay beyond. Bayard saw them start to climb up out of the water, saw their tracks churn for a purchase in the rubble of the broken wall. He saw that to their left Easy and Dog Companies were still struggling with their scaling ladders, saw that only a few of the assault wave had managed to get to the top of the wall.

He knew that if he continued to circle in his present position with Wave Four, he could expect nothing but more casualties. A direct mortar hit in the cargo compartment of one of his LVTs could cost him the better part of a platoon.

"Follow those armored amtracs," he ordered. The tractor sergeant shot a surprised look at Bayard. Bayard gestured impatiently toward the gap in the wall. The sergeant got Bayard's meaning, grinned, and pounded the driver on the back. The driver wagged his leather-helmeted head up and down and headed for the beach.

They reached the break in the wall. The churning treads of LVT 4-1 began to dredge up mud. The driver shifted the gears and the amtrac lurched slowly upward. For an instant it teetered precariously and threatened to throw itself over on its back. Then it slammed down on solid ground.

Bayard kept his tractor moving forward until it had cleared enough room for the rest of the wave. When he saw that his whole company was ashore, he tapped the sergeant on the shoulder. "We'll get out here. Drop your ramp."

The steel cables loosened, and the ramp of the LVT fell open with a clang.

"All right," Bayard ordered. "Everybody out. Get away from the tractor. Spread out and keep down."

There was an instant of frozen indecision.

"You heard the captain!" roared Havac. "Get moving!"

Bayard's marines went tumbling out of the tractor. The other LVTs had come up on both sides of them and were also unloading. For an instant there was no organization, just a mob of marines, then the hoarse shouts of the lieutenants and sergeants whipped Dog Company into the semblance of a skirmish line, three platoons abreast. Some of the more sanguine members of the company began shooting at real or imagined targets. As for Bayard, he had not yet seen a Korean, and if it were not for the ever-present snap and whine of small arms fire and the occasional chunking thud of a mortar shell, it would have seemed to him as though a preposterous joke had been played on them and there was no enemy.

The day's last light was dying. Dog Company's headquarters found a place for itself behind the rubble of a fallen brick wall. Some of the more phlegmatic of Bayard's men were already sampling the contents of their assault food packets. Nearby, the hospital corpsmen had set up shop, and several marines, grinning self-consciously or looking theatrically heroic, were having mortar splinters picked out of their arms and legs. A more seriously wounded marine lay on a stretcher awaiting evacuation, his eyes half-closed and his breath coming noisily and blood-flecked from his mouth.

Bayard reached for the handset of his battalion radio and reported that Dog Company was ashore, that they were still receiving small arms and mortar fire, and that Easy and Fox Companies were still, presumably, trying to get over the seawall. Having sent his message, Bayard lay there waiting for further instructions, the handset pressed close against his ear. Somewhere afloat in the murky harbor was the battalion command group.

Bayard's radio receiver cut out, and he heard the operations officer's voice, crisp and metallic: "Firebrand Dog Six, this is Firebrand Three. Stay where you are. I say again—stay where you are until Easy and Fox have passed through you and reached their objectives. Is that understood? Over."

"Roger. Out," said Bayard. He passed the handset back to the radio operator, a boy by the name of Almquist. He had expected a word of praise. Instead, Mansell had sounded coldly annoyed, as though Dog Company were to blame for the miscarriage of the carefully prepared landing plan.

Bayard mentally shrugged his shoulders. At this moment not even Mansell's coldness could dampen his own feeling of self-satisfaction. Out of the corner of his eye he caught the flash of a scarlet-and-gold silken banner. He turned and saw that it was a Marine Corps company guidon, its pikestaff wedged firmly into the ground.

"Where did that come from?" he asked.

"It was my idea," admitted Baby-san. "I brought it from Camp Lejeune. I had one of the guys in the Ordnance Battalion saw the staff into three pieces and fit it with brass sleeves so it'd come apart like a fishing rod. I thought we could use it to mark our company headquarters."

chapter four...

Once upon a time captains rode horseback and led their companies with shining swords, thought Bayard. Now they used jeeps and very high frequency radios. He sat on his hotel bed and looked out through the balcony windows into the thickening dusk of evening.

What was ahead of him? In another week he would be in Washington. He and Donna would pick up where they left off. He had done well in Korea. He had made a creditable showing, and that was the important thing. There was nothing in the record to reveal his shortcomings, his own inner misgivings. Even her father was impressed; there had been short, ponderously approving notes written on blue embossed United States Senate stationery.

Many nights in a tent or a foxhole, unable to sleep, he had imagined this return to Washington, not precisely a triumphant return but at least one in which he could take pride. Why then did he feel so little elation, so little anticipation, now that the moment was at hand?

"Darling," Donna had written, "hurry home so that you will be here in time for a June wedding. Shall it be at the National Cathedral or in that quaint little chapel in Quantico? Does one have to be a certified virgin to wear white?"

Well, wasn't that what he wanted? To be married to Donna?

Bayard, he told himself, you're just scared. Wait until you get home and you'll be all right. After all, he and Donna were a year and ten thousand miles apart. That was a lot of time and distance. The doubts would disappear once he saw Donna again. In the meantime he had to concentrate on getting himself under better control. He held out his hand. There was a noticeable tremor, one more symptom that his nerves weren't all they should be. There was also his short temper.

Like that incident on the train this afternoon. That man had meant well. He was an average middle-aged, middle-class American citizen. The salt of the earth. Why, Bayard wondered, had I felt shut off from him? Why hadn't I been able to talk to the man calmly and rationally? Why did I fly off the handle? Why wasn't I able to bring together the loose ends of my thoughts and put them all in a neat package and say *Look, here it is. This is the way I feel about it. You talk about democratization and the New Japan as though it were something you could slice and wrap in cellophane. You can't export made-in-America democracy the way you can automobiles or fountain pens. You can't even give it away like you can machine guns and dollars.*

Bayard got up from the bed and poured himself another inch of Scotch. Then he put on his green kersey blouse and looked again in the mirror. His mood improved. He toasted his image in the glass. You make a right fair imitation of a Marine Corps officer, he told himself.

He finished the drink hurriedly. If he didn't get to the dining room soon, he would be too late for dinner. He left his bedroom and went down the red-carpeted—shabby but nonetheless genuine red carpet, he said to himself—corridor and staircase into the lobby.

The dining room was almost empty. A platoon of blue-uniformed Japanese waitresses commanded by a white-coated headwaiter escorted him to his table. A menu was presented, a napkin spread, and water poured with a celerity and ceremony rather overwhelming to a man newly released from a military hospital.

Could he get a drink before ordering?

Yes, he could. The waiter in the white jacket bobbed his head enthusiastically as though nothing in this world would give him greater pleasure. A staccato command was issued, and one of the girls broke ranks and sped off in the direction, presumably, of the bar with Bayard's order for an old-fashioned.

While she was gone, Bayard deliberated over the menu. Actually there was very little choice. The cuisine of the house did not appear to be inspired. There were just three entrées: fried chicken, roast beef, and leg of lamb. Bayard chose the roast beef and specified that it be rare. White Jacket sucked in his breath in audible approval over the wisdom of Bayard's selection. He dispatched a courier to the kitchen with the order, then dismissed the platoon of waitresses, leaving one lone sentinel to guard Bayard's table and to keep his water glass filled.

The Scotch he had imbibed was proving a wonderfully effective anodyne. He felt remarkably relaxed. He observed that the sentry posted by White Jacket was pretty. Her skin was pale ochre, her teeth were straight and even, her black hair was cut short and curled, and her name, according to the badge on her blue waitress's uniform, was Janice.

Bayard was framing a witty remark with which to begin a conversation with "Janice" when he was interrupted by the old-fashioneds being delivered with a pattering rush of canvas-slippered feet. The girl who fetched it wore a badge with "Shirley" lettered on it. Interesting but highly unlikely names for young Japanese girls, thought Bayard. I will have to enquire into this.

The drink was weak and too sweet.

"Next time not so sweet," he said sternly, looking severely at the grinning but uncomprehending faces of Janice and Shirley.

"Not so much sugar," he said. Then with sudden inspiration he tapped the sugar bowl with his spoon and shook his head.

Janice giggled behind her hand. Shirley looked confused. Janice pointed at the sugar bowl and then at Bayard's drink. Bayard wagged his head solemnly.

"Have-a-no," he said firmly.

"Ah, so," said Janice. She gave Shirley a detailed explanation in Japanese.

"Ah, so," said Shirley, and she sped off once more in the direction of the bar.

Janice bent over the table to refill his water glass. She was very expert at refilling glasses. Bayard caught a fragrance that was both female and Japanese. She was standing close to the table now, her left hand on the handle of the water pitcher, her right hand tracing idle designs on the table cloth. Under her breath came the faintest humming of "Good Night, Irene."

It reminded Bayard of something. That afternoon, after checking in at the hotel, he had taken a walk through the town and as he passed one house he had heard "Good Night, Irene" being scratched out on a Japanese phonograph. He had looked past the hedge, and there, framed in the window, was an American soldier in khaki trousers and undershirt drinking beer from a bottle. Behind him, less clearly visible, was a Japanese girl crossing and recrossing Bayard's line of sight as though she were busy with some household task. It had all appeared very established and domestic.

Bayard had mentioned it on his return to the army lieutenant who had charge of the hotel. The lieutenant had said that practically all of the permanent personnel had made similar arrangements.

Bayard decided he would not mind reaching such an arrangement, on a short time basis, with Janice.

Meanwhile, through the joint efforts of Shirley—who had two prominent gold-encased front teeth and was therefore eliminated from Bayard's more intimate thoughts—and Janice, his meal was served. The food was a good deal less impressive than the service. Stripped of its ceremonial trappings and flourishes, it was a standardized, master-menued GI meal. The soup was thin and underseasoned. The salad was made of canned vegetables smeared with mayonnaise—the American Armed Forces had an official horror of indigenously grown green produce because of the Oriental insistence upon the use of night soil as a universal fertilizer. The roast beef had been steamed to a tasteless pulp; the potatoes were watery, the ice cream icy, and the coffee weak.

Bayard finished his meal but lingered awhile over his coffee. He was having difficulty advancing his campaign. During the meal he had ventured several tentative verbal openings, but these had evoked no reply other than a high-pitched titter. However, their eyes kept meeting, his water glass was receiving an inordinate amount of attention, and Bayard was sure that Janice was fully aware of what he had in mind.

But even as he went through this estimate of the situation, Bayard's enthusiasm for pursuing the campaign began to ebb. Presuming that she was willing, where could they go? They couldn't very well march side by side up the red-carpeted staircase to his room. On the other hand, she might know of some Japanese inn or house. The army lieutenant had said that there was a place patronized, by tacit agreement, only by officers. Perhaps they could go there.

But Bayard, who had an ingrained modesty and a great fear of appearing ridiculous, mentally pictured the two of them thrashing about on a floor lined with rice-straw mats. He could hear her responding to his best efforts with that nervous giggle. It was quite likely she had a GI boyfriend. In his mind's eye he saw her doll-like figure straining against a sweating, hairy-legged American body. He wondered if they had a phonograph and whether her soldier sweetheart brought home beer and phonograph records from the Post Exchange.

He folded a hundred-yen *presento* into a square and slid it under his saucer, pushed back from the table, and left for the bar. As he passed by Janice, he thought he saw a shadow of disappointment flicker briefly across her face—a face, he now decided, that was cute but flat as a plate. She had no profile. Besides, she had no breasts, and her legs were typically Japanese—sturdy and slightly bowed, with calves knotted with muscle.

Bayard marched out of the dining room feeling very large and awkward. He passed the low-bowing White Jacket, told him that the meal was excellent, and stood speculatively on the threshold of the hotel lobby.

At the desk the room clerk was gossiping with the bell captain. Bayard did not doubt but that they were discussing his abortive campaign in the dining room. He was sure the bell captain, for a suitable presento, could deliver discreetly a girl into his room. It was something to remember for future reference.

A tiny gift shop was fitted into an alcove adjacent to the desk. He had promised Donna a strand of cultured pearls. In the showcase there as an overpriced selection of souvenirs, mostly damascene, silver, or lacquer—cigarette cases, lighters, compacts, cuff links, earrings in the shape of fans, and always the inevitable Mt. Fuji motif. No pearls. Hadn't he seen some pearls there this afternoon?

He asked the room clerk, who gave him a professionally insincere grin, showing his large capped teeth. With his round, black-rimmed glasses, he reminded Bayard of the World War II caricatures of Hirohito. He said that the gift shop was closed for the night. Come back tomorrow . . . very nice.

In another corner of the lobby was a writing table. An American girl, in her late twenties or early thirties, sat there writing a letter. She wasn't particularly pretty. She had bangs cut straight across her forehead, and there were dark circles under her eyes. She had straight brown hair, a squarish face, and a tense angular body. She was drinking beer, and she kept her left hand around the glass while she wrote with her right. She was wearing a wedding band.

chapter five...

Bayard studied the girl for a moment. He was so recently returned from Korea and so recently released from the hospital that any American girl, particularly if she were alone, was a subject for speculation.

Now this one—no, she wasn't pretty, but she could make more of herself if she tried. She was indifferently dressed in a summer skirt and blouse, and she wore no makeup except lipstick. She was alone here; that was obvious. She appeared utterly absorbed in the letter she was writing. Her hand would drive her pen across the page at a furious pace for a minute or so. Then she would stop altogether to read what she had written. She would take a swallow of beer without looking up, and then the pen would race on again.

To whom was she writing?

Her husband must be in Korea, decided Bayard. She was writing to him. You'd think she would do her letter writing in her room.

Now what would happen, thought Bayard, if I were to walk over to her and introduce myself? If I were to ask her to join me in the bar for a drink?

Nothing, he decided after ten seconds contemplation. She is much too businesslike. She is probably writing to her husband to ask him to increase her allotment. She would probably give me a brief, cold smile and say thank you very much but I am busy.

That was that.

Having exhausted the small possibilities of the hotel lobby, Bayard looked for the bar and found the entrance marked by a slightly slant-eyed cowboy painted on the wall, throwing a lariat that spelled out "Dude Ranch" in rope. Inside, the two Japanese bartenders were wearing cowboy shirts. Above their heads an unlikely pair of Texas longhorns jutted out from the back bar. Underneath the longhorns was posted the officially approved price list. Scotch, bourbon, rye, and blend were all fifteen cents. American beer was a quarter. Bayard laid a dollar in military scrip on the bar and ordered a Scotch and soda from the bartender in the Roy Rogers shirt.

He had the place to himself except for three U.S. Army Quartermaster Corps officers seated at a table. They were big, beefy, middle-aged men, a lieutenant colonel and two majors, with quart bottles of Japanese beer in front of them. Bayard looked at their ribbons and saw that they wore no battle stars. The lieutenant colonel caught his eye.

"Hey, marine," he called over. "You alone? Want to join us?"

"No thank you, sir," said Bayard shortly.

"Come on, I mean it," said the lieutenant colonel. "Come over and tell us about the Marines."

"I said no thank you."

The lieutenant colonel looked confused. "Okay, fellow," he said. "Suit yourself."

Fat rear-echelon slobs, thought Bayard, hiding out from the war behind a stack of requisitions. He turned back to his Scotch and finished it off in a single gulp.

So he looked lonely? Well, he had been lonely before. Those years before World War II, those years of growing up. They were cloudy and remote now, gray in his memory, but they had been lonely years. He'd never forget those rooms, strung out one behind the other, above his father's sheet-metal shop on North High Street in Columbus. It had been a dark, sagging frame building held propped up into place by the two brick buildings on either side of it. The front had once been painted white, but during those Depression years the paint was gray and peeling, everything sooty from the trains that went through Union Station. Inside there had been a dusty confusion of half-finished heating ducts, rain gutters, and chimney flashing.

Bayard's mother had been a large pink woman. Bayard remembered her best in a soiled and feathery pink satin wrapper moving her bulk about the dismal rooms in broken-backed house slippers.

On the mantel above the gas-log fireplace in the living room had been a photograph of a slender dark-haired young man wearing the old-fashioned standing-collared olive drab uniform of World War I. Beside it stood a matching photograph of a round-faced, handsome young woman. But there was little resemblance between the jaunty young soldier in the photograph and his gray-faced middle-aged father or between the robust young woman and his fat, ailing, and untidy mother.

Bayard's mother had met his father at a soldier's dance at Camp Chase in 1917. She had come to Columbus from Marysville, where her father was a doctor. They were both twenty-five. She was the oldest of three sisters. He came from the southern part of the state and never elaborated on the facts about his family. He had left home when he was fourteen.

Now why was it, Bayard had often wondered, looking at the two photographs on the mantel, that these two very different persons had come together, had gotten married, and had him for a son?

That first wave of patriotic response in 1917—unbelievably naive now in retrospect, the reaction of a nation still young and unsophisticated—had been part of it. She had come to Columbus to do something—what, she wasn't quite sure—in this war against the Hun who shelled open lifeboats and bayoneted Belgian babies.

She had found a job in the newly opened Signal Corps plant, winding copper wire on things that in some manner unknown to her became part of field telephones. She made thirty-five dollars a week, lived on twenty-five, and put the remainder toward the purchase of Liberty Bonds. She spent three evenings a week and Sunday afternoons at the canteen at Camp Chase, where she entertained the soldiers within the limitations imposed by her Methodist code of morality.

So she had met his father, and Bayard supposed that his father had seen in this large handsome young woman warmth and unsullied purity and all the virtues that had been lacking in the tarnished women he had known in his drifting past. In any event, his father had had no effective defense against her militant determination. The not-well-kept secret that his regiment was shipping out for overseas provided the final impetus. They were married in the barren, pine-board chapel, there was a forty-eight hour honeymoon, and then he was gone.

In 1919 he had come back from the Army of Occupation in Germany, and these two people, essentially strangers, had begun life together. In this they were no different from possibly a million other war couples, their chances neither better nor worse.

In later years his mother had said, in those almost hysterical seizures of hers, that she had thrown herself away on his father, and there was a time, when Bayard was young, that he had believed this. But when he grew older, he realized that no one was really to blame for this mismatched marriage. Looking at the picture of his father, Bayard saw a thin-featured, whimsically good-looking face. His father had had a reputation for cleverness. Perhaps his mother had mistaken his clever talk and his daydreams for ambition and purpose.

His mother's Liberty Bonds had gone toward setting up the shop on High Street. The location wasn't the best, but the rent was cheap. "It'll just be for a couple of years, and then we'll be out of here," his father had said. "There's going to be a building boom, and all the new houses that go up will be having central heating. In a couple of years we'll be set."

They planned on living above the shop while they were getting a start; then later they would build a house of their own.

"In Bexley," Bayard's mother wrote her father proudly, "and without asking you for one red cent. Someday you will realize that you were wrong about Edward."

But there was never to be a house in Bexley. Edward Bayard was right about the building boom, but little of the new business came his way. The developers of the low-priced subdivisions were putting in patented furnaces supplied by the big heating contractors, and the dingy shop on High Street held nothing to attract the attention of the architects and builders who were erecting the individual custom-built houses in the new suburbs.

The bright, promising 1920s slipped away; the dreary Depression-ridden 1930s began. Edward Bayard's trade was limited to the grubby demands of the district in which they lived, old buildings whose owners wanted the cheapest minimum the building code and the fire insurance inspectors would allow.

Dominating the other side of the street was the Olentangy Hotel, a six-story structure of soot-blackened yellow brick. Before the First World War the Olentangy had enjoyed the name of being a good commercial house. That was when there was still a certain advantage to a hotel's being located near the railroad station. By the 1930s it had established a different sort of reputation.

Rates were two dollars a night or ten dollars a week, and the management maintained a very liberal policy toward the social activities of its guests.

The clientele was made up mostly of salesmen on slim expense accounts, second-rate musicians and entertainers who couldn't afford the downtown prices, and a number of semipermanent gentlemen residents with obscure livelihoods and resident ladies with even more dubious employment.

Next to the Olentangy, and immediately across from Edward Bayard's shop, was the Apollo Theater ("Adults 25 cents, Children 10 cents"), a long and narrow motion-picture house smelling strongly of disinfectant.

On the north side of the Apollo was the Coney Island Restaurant, owned and operated by a Greek whose name was so long and complicated that he was never called anything but "the Greek." The window of the Coney Island was decorated with a roast turkey, a ham, a flounder, a dozen oysters, and a strawberry pie, all so perfectly embalmed that they stayed there for years.

In the front of the restaurant was a counter with a row of porcelain-topped stools. In the back were booths blackened by time and alternate coats of varnish and kitchen grease.

The Greek was his own counterman and chef and, as often as not, his own waiter and dishwasher. He was about sixty and had a twisted neck, a bent back, and skin the color and texture of the cabbage he served with the boiled corned beef.

At the Greek's you could get a three-course luncheon for twenty-five cents or a five-course dinner for fifty cents, but most of his trade was coffee and doughnuts (both for fourteen cents), hot dogs (plain, five cents; with sauerkraut, seven cents), hamburgers (small, a nickel; large, with everything, a dime), and oyster stews (twenty cents and popular on Saturday nights).

Next to the Coney Island was Goldie's Wonder Bar. There had been a succession of "Goldie's"; the name went along with the proprietorship.

When Prohibition was repealed, the then-incumbent Goldie closed the alley entrance and opened the front door.

Across from Goldie's was a dingy red-brick building with an elaborate facade and tall, narrow windows. Set in the brick of the edifice was its name and the date, "Scioto Building, 1878." Once it had housed professional offices; now it was tenanted by a printer and bookbinder. The presses and the composing machines were on the first floor, the bindery was on the second, and paper stock and the ghostly remnants of old print orders filled the third and fourth floors.

The Paris Tailors (custom tailoring, alterations, dry cleaning, and pressing) stood between the printers and the Bayard sheet-metal shop. Rocco Giachetti still had a lot of old-country ways. He smoked a villainous twisted cigar called an Italian stogie, and he smelled of garlic and wine and lilac toilet water. On Sundays he went to Mass in the morning wearing a striped black suit and a white satin tie, and in the afternoon he played bocce at the Sons of Italy.

Rocco had a daughter, Rose, who was two years older than George. Her mother was dead, and Rose kept house for her father—like the Bayards, they lived above their shop—and helped him out with the sewing and the pressing. She had quit school after the eighth grade. Rocco let her have pretty much her own way. She had a lot more freedom than most of the other Italian girls in the neighborhood. By the time she was sixteen, she was going out with a succession of boy friends who drove Ford V8s or Chevy convertibles and who, to George's envy, dressed sharply in hard-pressed gabardine suits that they wore with black or dark brown shirts and white or yellow neckties.

The Paris Tailors was on one side of the Bayard shop. A wholesale candy distributor was on the other. Next to the candy distributor's business was Weinstein's Drug Store. The owner was a narrow-chested little man with decayed teeth who wore a black vest, summer and winter, the pockets of which served as his filing cabinet.

He gave George his first regular job. George opened the store at seven and kept it open until Weinstein arrived at about eight-thirty. George came back again in the evening and stayed on until closing time, eleven o'clock on week nights, twelve on Saturdays and Sundays. Weinstein paid him six dollars a week. George was fourteen.

"Not only am I teaching you the business, but you got wonderful hours," said Weinstein. "You got the whole day to yourself."

Weinstein's merchandising policy was simple: Anything, if you bought it cheap enough and waited long enough, could eventually be sold for a profit. It would have taken an archaeologist to classify the Weinstein inventory, which had accumulated in layers with the passage of years. Underneath the Christmas tree ornaments would be the previous summer's sunglasses, and underneath the sunglasses would be last winter's children's mittens—"Special at fifty-nine cents. You couldn't get them so good at Lazarus's for a dollar. If a friend of mine hadn't gone out of business in Zanesville, I couldn't let you have them at this price, believe me."

George learned to pack ice cream according to the Weinstein principle: "Be generous, George. Pile it high on top of the box, where the customer can see it. But you don't crush the life out of it by pushing down too hard. So somebody squeezes the bottom of the box and complains it's empty? Some people you can't satisfy."

As a further lesson in his business education, Weinstein showed George the contents of the drawer in the counter beneath the cash register. "Rule one is that your net on your propherlactics should pay the rent. Three price ranges we got. The ones in the gold foil are three for a dollar. The ones in the little tin boxes are three for fifty cents. The ones in the paper envelopes are three for a quarter. The difference is psychological. If a man feels safer with the three-for-a-dollar's, who am I to deny him that satisfaction?"

Another fast-moving item with the late-evening customers was Weinstein's Palliative, an invigorating tonic whose sales correlated inversely with the open hours of the state liquor stores. It was compounded of grain alcohol, water, caramel coloring, and enough quinine and ferrous sulfate to placate the Weinstein pharmaceutical conscience.

The drug store wasn't George's only place of employment in the neighborhood. At one time or another he had ushered at the Apollo. He left that position permanently, however, after embarrassing a pair of patrons in the rear seats of the balcony by the maladroit use of his flashlight and suffering a split lip and a black eye in consequence. He had also worked as a counterman at the Greek's, but he left that job when asked to take a turn at the unappetizing chore of dish washing. And he delivered dry cleaning for the Paris Tailors—this was the beginning of his longtime business association with the Giachettis.

He had worked, as a matter of fact, at odd jobs with almost every establishment in the block except the Bayard sheet-metal shop. Once or twice his father had mildly suggested the family business as a possibility. The prospect had not appealed to George, however, and his mother had come to his support. No son of hers was going to work as a tinsmith. She also said that working in galvanized iron was unhealthy.

Bayard now smiled wryly at the memory of this. Small bits of iron blown about the countryside by high explosives were also injurious to one's health.

Those early 1930s had been bad years. Bayard's father blamed them on Herbert Hoover. There was a blue NRA eagle posted in the corner of the shop window, but the elder Bayard was also dubious of Roosevelt. He listened to Father Coughlin on the radio every Sunday afternoon. He held the conviction that it was the Jews who were keeping the country flat on its back, preventing a Christian businessman from making a decent living. One thing about Hitler, said Bayard's father, he knew how to handle the Jews.

The neighborhood had continued to disintegrate, rotting away, filling up with Negroes and foreigners. George was constantly being reminded by his mother that he was better than these people—that, whatever his father was, his grandfather had been Marysville's leading physician.

They—his mother and he, but not his father—drove occasionally to Marysville. Bayard remembered his grandfather as a disagreeable old man living out his remaining years attended and jealously guarded by his mother's two spinster sisters. It was the contention of the sisters, unspoken but nevertheless conveyed with complete clarity, that Bayard's mother had voided any claim to patrimonial inheritance by her unseemly marriage. They, on the other hand, had fortified their claim by a lifetime of unstinting and celibate service to their father. They lived with him in a dreary red pile of brick known as "the old doctor's place," outside of Marysville on Route 36. George found these visits dreadful.

George was an only child. He learned early that the best way to get along with his mother was to feed her self-pity. She, in turn, was overly solicitous of him. She considered him delicate. And in those days he was indeed thin and underdeveloped, the result of too much reading and sulking about the apartment and too little exercise.

He read very rapidly. When he found an author he liked, he attacked the row of books on the public library shelf with the systematic appetite of a silverfish. During his first years of high school, he demolished Rafael Sabatini, Jeffery Farnol, and Harold Lamb in a lightning-like campaign;

advanced with fair success against Rudyard Kipling and Joseph Conrad; struck Herman Melville a glancing blow; and moved off to the flank into the more comfortable company of Somerset Maugham, James Hilton, and A. J. Cronin. Then, through Mr. Cavendish, he was introduced to Ernest Hemingway and William Faulkner.

"Introduced" was the proper word because Mr. Cavendish let it be known to his circle of admirers that he and Hemingway and Faulkner had been the closest of friends during Mr. Cavendish's bohemian years in Paris.

Mr. Cavendish taught English 3 at Central High. He also coached the tennis team and was the faculty advisor to the Salmagundi Club. He was in his middle forties, a bachelor with graying, sandy hair and the thin, sparely built sort of frame that wears clothes well. Most of the male teachers at Central wore hard-finished worsted suits—the kind that came with two pairs of pants. But Mr. Cavendish wore soft tweed jackets and flannel slacks.

George had learned a little about clothes from working for Rocco Giachetti. He had left the Weinstein employ when he learned that he could make more by delivering dry cleaning for tips to the guests of the Olentangy Hotel. He had always liked clothes. Rocco taught him how to use the steam iron and the pressing machine. George had only two jackets and three pairs of slacks—similar in appearance, if not in quality, to Mr. Cavendish's—but they were always immaculately clean and perfectly pressed. Most of Central High's male student body wore corduroys and sweaters and went tieless and sometimes shirtless.

Mr. Cavendish had left Amherst College in 1915, it was said, to join the Royal Flying Corps. He had known and flown with Jimmy McCudden, Billy Bishop, Mickey Mannock, and the other British flying greats. Consequently he had a rather slighting opinion of Eddie Rickenbacker, Columbus's own hometown ace.

"Oh, Eddie was a good enough pilot," Mr. Cavendish would say, if pressed on the subject. "But you have to remember that he didn't get into it until the last months of the war. And you have to give his ship some of the credit. He was flying a Spad, and the Jerries were putting up anything they had left with wings. I often wonder how he would have made out when we were going after the Albatross and the Pfalz in the old Sopwith Pups. I remember a time when we tangled with von Boelcke. . . ."

The story had sounded familiar.

"Gosh," said George, "I think I read about that in *Flying Aces*. I didn't know that the English flier was you though."

"In *Flying Aces*?" Mr. Cavendish's left eyebrow had shot upward. Then he smiled whimsically. "Oh, yes, that's the magazine Arch Whitehouse writes for. I think I told him that story, and he's probably dressed it up a bit. Arch always has been a little on the lurid side. I'm certainly glad he didn't use my name."

Mr. Cavendish had won his blue at Cambridge in tennis, and although he no longer played (because of the effects of an old wound received over Arras in '18), he coached. There wasn't much interest in tennis at Central High, and George, lacking competition, was able to make his letter. In his senior year he had also entered the city junior championships, and even though he didn't get past the second round, it was a wonderful experience just to play on the country club courts.

The Salmagundi Club did things such as discussing books and going to plays. Not too many plays came to Columbus, so about once or twice a winter the club would go to Cincinnati or Cleveland to see a show.

The first play George ever saw was *Tobacco Road* with Taylor Holmes. "I sometimes think," said Mr. Cavendish, "that Caldwell gets closer to the true South than Faulkner. I told Bill that once when I was visiting him in Mississippi, and he hasn't spoken to me since."

The second play they saw together was *Victoria Regina* with Helen Hayes. "Watch this fellow Vincent Price," advised Mr. Cavendish. "I saw him in a student thing at Yale a few years ago and through a friend of mine was able to get him started with the Theater Guild. Well, we could go backstage after the play to meet him. Actually, I had planned on it as a little surprise for you. But when I phoned Vince this afternoon, he said that he was as sorry as he could be but that he was all tied up with a party at the Tafts immediately after the performance."

Rocco Giachetti also liked George. "George is a good boy," he would say to Rose. "Not like those bums you go out with. George is gonna get an education. George is gonna amount to something."

There were some nights when Rose didn't have a date, and at closing time Rocco would punch the cash register and take out a dollar and give it to George. "Here," he would say. "You take Rose to the second show and maybe buy her a Coke or something afterward."

In the movies Rose would let him hold her hand, and if no one was sitting too close to them, she would let him press his leg against hers.

Rocco and Rose, like the Bayards, lived in the rooms over their shop. The door to the narrow and dark stairway opened on the street. After the movie and after coffee and doughnuts at the Greek's, Rose would sometimes let him love her up a little on the stairway, particularly if it had been a love picture with Robert Taylor or Tyrone Power or someone like that.

He would flatten her against the wall and kiss her, and she would push her thighs against him, but when he would move his hands to her breasts, she would always stop him. "Don't get yourself all excited, Georgie," she would say. "I gotta go in now. See you tomorrow."

And then, in spite of his protests and procrastinations, she would dodge through the hall door into the apartment. After Rose had said good night and the door was firmly shut against him, George would sometimes sit for a long time on the dark stairs wishing that he had the money, the clothes, and the car to really take Rose out.

His mother naturally did not approve of the time he spent with the Giachettis. George got around this, just as he got around most things with his mother.

Occasionally the Giachettis would have George in for an Italian dinner. George liked the hotly seasoned food, which was so different from his mother's tasteless cooking. He also liked the flamboyant Giachetti apartment. The walls of the living room and dining room were painted an electric blue. The woodwork was varnished a glistening yellow. In the dining room there was a giant framed chromo of Mount Etna in full eruption. Behind the frame was a yellowed palm frond from the previous Easter season. Stuck in the corner of the picture was a small cabinet photograph of Rocco in his Italian Army uniform.

George was sometimes permitted a glimpse of Rose's bedroom. It was painted a bright burgundy and had white net curtains, the whiteness of which bore testimony to Rose's industry in the face of the soot that drifted up from the railroad yards. A figure of the Virgin, in front of which a candle was kept burning, stood on a side table.

On one of these nights, when George was seventeen and in his last year at Central High and Rose was nineteen, Rocco left them alone in the apartment. His lodge, the Sons of Italy, was meeting that night. He left at eight; they were to clear off the table and do the dishes before going to a movie.

A half-emptied bottle of wine remained on the table—the kind called "Dago red." George had tried a venturesome glass with his dinner. The wine had an acrid, harsh taste. In the Bayard apartment, there was never any liquor of any kind; to George the drinking of wine with a meal was an exotic and daring experience. Flushed with an inward warmth that was not altogether caused by the garlic-laden food and the single glass of wine, George sat back in his chair, watched Rose clear the table—she moved rhythmically, with practiced domestic efficiency—and felt a strange new and exciting anticipation. He half reached toward the bottle of wine.

Rose saw his hand move toward the bottle. "You want another glass?" she asked. "Go ahead. Help yourself."

"How about you?" said George.

"I don't like wine," said Rose. "You kill the bottle. Rocco don't care. I gotta get the dishes done. You going to help?"

George followed her into the kitchen, carrying the wine bottle and his glass. She had put the dishes to soak in the sink.

"You want to dry?" she asked, handing him a red-checked dish towel.

"Sure," said George, "I'll dry."

This is what it would be like, he thought, if a fellow had a mistress in a place like Greenwich Village or maybe Paris. She would be a foreigner of some kind and would cook things like spaghetti and lasagna and use a lot of garlic and cheese and tomato sauce. They would drink wine with their meals and talk about art and literature and things like that. She would be real passionate and always wanting it.

He was vague on the details of this demanding passion, but he had heard that there were women who couldn't get enough of it. He laid the towel down and, standing behind Rose, put his arms around her, nuzzling the general vicinity of her ear and reaching for her breasts.

"Cut it out, Georgie," she said. "You want me to drop the plate?"

"The hell with the dishes," said George hoarsely. "They can wait."

"I want to get them done," said Rose. "I don't want to be late for the beginning of the feature."

"We got plenty of time," said George, pulling at her, trying to get her to turn around. "Let's go on into the other room for a while."

"All right," said Rose. "Just for a little while. I don't want to miss the picture."

Rose's bedroom opened off the dining room. From the flickering light of the candle in front of the Virgin, George could see the white ruffles of her bedspread in sharp contrast against the dark burgundy walls.

"George!" Rose was genuinely shocked. "We can't go in there. That's my bedroom!"

She drew him off in the direction of the living room, which fronted on High Street. The room was dark except for the reflected neon glow from the street.

She let him press her back on the sofa until they were stretched out full length next to each other. He felt for her breasts. She pushed his hand aside but not too forcefully. With elaborate stealth he began to unbutton her blouse. He kissed the soft hollow of her throat while his fingers solved the problem of her brassiere. He cupped her breast in his hand. He had never gotten this far with her before.

"George," she said, "we got to stop."

"Why?" he asked, trying to insinuate his knee between her legs.

"Because we got to." Rose kept her legs closed tightly together.

"Why?"

"Because it isn't right." Rose fended off an exploring hand, which had rounded the curve of her thigh.

"Why isn't it right?" demanded George. "You want to and I want to."

"A fellow loses all his respect for a girl if she lets him. I wouldn't want you to think I was cheap."

"I wouldn't think you were cheap," said George, even more hoarsely. He wouldn't have recognized his own voice. It was as though a third person had entered the conversation. "This is different. I *love* you."

George stopped, momentarily appalled. He had never told a girl before that he *loved* her.

Rose took advantage of the respite to consolidate her defenses. They stayed together that way for a long time. George began a slower, more deliberate campaign, but there was a line beyond which Rose would not let him go.

"Why not?" demanded George, growing angry, urged on by emotions he only half understood.

"Because it wouldn't be right."

"Why wouldn't it be right?" said George doggedly. "I told you I loved you."

"If you really loved me, you wouldn't keep it up when you knew I wanted you to stop."

"That doesn't make sense."

There was a moment of silence.

"George, tell me the truth—have you ever gone all the way with a girl?"

"Yes," lied George, "lots of times."

"Who with?"

"Nobody you'd know."

"It was Shirley Cibik, wasn't it?"

"No."

"Yes it was—you and all the rest of the boys in Central High."

Then they heard her father's step on the stairs leading up to the apartment. They sat bolt upright on the sofa and turned on the lamp. Rose rearranged her dress. George scrubbed at the lipstick on his mouth with his handkerchief.

Her father, after fumbling with the lock, came into the room. He was a little drunk. He looked at the two of them suspiciously. "I thought you two were gonna go to the movies," he said. "You better get home, Georgie. It's getting late."

chapter six...

That first night in Korea after the landing, Bayard had held his original position with Dog Company until the two assault units had come firmly ashore and reorganized and had passed through him. It took time before Fox and Easy Companies reached the high ground rimming the right flank of the beachhead. A drizzly rain was falling, and the night was pitch-black except for the periodic brightness of the star shells being put up by the naval gunfire support ships.

Then came Mansell's radioed orders for Bayard to move his company forward to a blocking position behind the wide gap that separated the frontline companies. Dog Company stumbled through the darkness until, more by luck than design, it found the reverse slope behind the hill now occupied by Easy and Fox. It was well after nine before Bayard was able to report that his company was settled in for the night. He had strung his marines out in a long wavering line, following the contour of the hill—it was amazing how far two hundred and fifty men could stretch—and had gotten them dug in. But before he could unroll his own sleeping bag in the hole his runner had dug, a message came over the company's SCR-300 radio ordering all company commanders to report at once to the battalion CP.

The battalion command group had done well for themselves. For a command post they found a reinforced concrete building—part of the power plant—which was almost shell-proof. The bomb-shattered windows were blacked-out with ponchos and blankets, and in the hard, greenish white glare of a hissing gasoline lantern, the room had the unreal, theatrical look of a stage setting. *What Price Glory?* thought Bayard, remembering the film.

The harsh lighting accentuated the finely modeled head and profile of Major Mansell as he stood by the map board. "There, gentlemen, you have it," he said, recapitulating the order he had just given while his thin, nervous fingers traced a route across the situation map with the black mouthpiece of his cigarette holder. "The regiment makes a general advance along the axis of the Inchon-Seoul highway. The 2d Battalion continues to have the right flank. Easy and Fox will be in the assault. Dog Company remains in reserve with the additional mission of flank protection to the south. Are there any questions on this?"

Bayard had no questions, but Beale and Mason, the two regular captains who commanded Easy and Fox Companies, asked about artillery and naval gunfire support. Major Campbell, the Weapons Company commander and an old-time machine gun and mortar man, supplied the technical details of the supporting fire plan. There were no further questions.

"Did you have anything to add, sir?" said Mansell, turning now to the battalion commander.

"Just this," said the Old Man getting to his feet, his gaunt frame wrapped in an oversize green raincoat. You could almost hear his joints creak. While Mansell had been giving the attack order, the battalion commander had been sitting, hardly noticed, in the corner of the room. Now he stepped into the glare of the lantern and stood in front of the situation map. Bayard wasn't sure whether it was the flicker of the gasoline lantern or whether the man was a little unsteady on his feet.

"Today was the goddamnedest landing I've ever seen in the twenty-five years I've been a marine. You couldn't have fucked it up more if you tried. If the enemy had been the Japanese, you wouldn't have gotten a goddamn man ashore alive. You'd all be out there face down in the mud with the crabs feeding on you."

Except for the hiss of the gasoline lantern, there was complete silence in the room. Bayard looked uneasily at the other company commanders. How were they reacting to this invective? He couldn't tell. They had had more experience with this sort of thing than he. Their faces remained respectfully impassive.

The Marine Corps cherishes its legends, thought Bayard bitterly, and so it clings to the Red Snapper. He is a museum piece, an anachronism, something left over from Haiti and Nicaragua, the gendarmerie and the Guardia Nacional. He's used up.

"The night isn't over," the Old Man went on. "If these goddamn gooks know anything about soldiering, they'll find that dangling right flank of ours before morning. Keep 50 percent of your people on the alert. And you, Dog Company, you be ready to face around to the south to protect that flank."

That was all he had to offer. He could have said something good about Dog Company, thought Bayard. We did our job and more.

"Thank you, Colonel," said the S-3 smoothly, deferentially. "If there are no more questions, gentlemen, that will be all."

Mansell is a different sort from the Red Snapper, thought Bayard. He is the new-type professional, a different generation—cold, bloodless, impersonal, as efficient as a well-engineered piece of machinery. War is a problem to be solved. He welcomes it the same way a brain surgeon might welcome a particularly malignant tumor. And he tackles it with the same deft, detached precision. He's an opportunistic bastard, but he knows his job.

The meeting closed with a muted chorus of "good nights" and a general exodus from the command post. Beale and Mason, who had had nothing to say to Bayard, not even a "well done," wrapped themselves in their ponchos and went out together into the wet night. Bayard hesitated for a minute. The whole evening's performance had angered him. He was going to say something to Mansell, but then thought better of it. What was the use? What was there to say? He ducked through the soggy blankets that covered the doorway and followed Beale and Mason out into the night.

A small knot of marines in ponchos were huddled together, waiting just outside the battalion command post. As the company commanders emerged from the briefing, the orange-red tips of several cigarettes were hastily extinguished.

"A good way to get your goddamn heads blown off by a sniper," said Beale in a dispassionate growl. He had a Silver Star from Iwo. His opinions on such matters were respected. His runner joined him, and together they struck out in the direction of Easy Company.

"Let's get back to the company," said Bayard to Baby-san, who had gotten to his feet at Bayard's approach.

From out in the harbor came the booming and the heat-lightning flashes of the naval gunfire ships firing their harassing and interdiction fires. From over in the direction of the 5th Marines came the distant rattle of machine-gun fire and the cough of mortars. From in front of them came the occasional crack of rifle fire. Bayard remembered the World War II stories of trigger-happy sentries. Some of that had happened on Okinawa, even in the division rear. He was glad to have the company of Baby-san during the walk back to the company area.

While they were still in Camp Pendleton, Havac had brought up the subject of a runner. "Has the captain thought about picking out a runner for hisself?" the first sergeant had asked one morning as they started off on a conditioning march.

"No," said Bayard, preoccupied with something else, "I hadn't given it any thought."

"A company commander needs a good runner," said Havac judiciously. "Somebody with good legs, a strong back, and some common sense. Somebody to take care of the housekeeping details—heating rations and digging holes. And he should be good with a rifle and know radio voice procedure."

"You have somebody in mind?" asked Bayard, knowing full well that Havac had already made his selection.

"I been thinking about a lad in the 2d Platoon," said Havac. "PFC Wade Hampton Caldwell—helluva name. He's a rebel from some place in the South. Don't let his looks fool you. He's short and kind of chunky, but he's husky. Nineteen years old. Has two years in the Corps. Expert rifleman. First on my corporal's list if we ever get authority to make any promotions. I'd like the captain to try him—see how he works out."

Bayard had accepted Havac's recommendation, and Wade Hampton Caldwell of Goldsboro, North Carolina, had become part of Dog Company's headquarters, Bayard's official family. Caldwell's round face made him look younger than nineteen. He had the nickname of "Baby," and during the company's brief stay in Japan, this had become Baby-san.

Now Baby-san walked along, slightly in advance of Bayard, head and shoulders hunched a little forward, rifle at port arms.

Dog Company's CP was in a thick-walled courtyard. As they approached, they were challenged by a hoarse, self-conscious voice out of the darkness. Bayard, just as self-consciously, gave the countersign.

"Over here, Captain." The new voice was Gibson's. Before going down to Battalion with Bayard, Baby-san had scooped out a shallow foxhole close to the wall. While they were gone, Gibson had slanted a shelter-half across it to keep out the rain.

"In here, Captain, where it's dry," said Gibson.

"You better get the other officers," Bayard said to Baby-san. "And First Sergeant Havac."

Baby-san, with his rifle held at high port, trotted off into the wet night. Bayard slid under the shelter-half and joined Gibson. "I got this little old gasoline stove going," said the exec. "How about some chow? I got a can of beans hot here."

The gasoline stove was a collapsible affair about the size and shape of a quart-sized oil can. It gave off a faint blue light. Bayard reached for the beans. The lid of the can had been bent back to form a handle. Bayard hadn't had anything to eat since leaving the LST.

"They're a little burned," apologized Gibson. "I've boiled up some soluble coffee to help wash them down."

"Thanks," said Bayard.

By the time he had dug the last half-burned bean from the bottom of the can and had finished drinking the bitter, scalding mixture in Gibson's canteen cup, his officers were assembled and waiting outside his hole.

They had crouched around his map, a circle of heads under a poncho held suspended, tent-fashion, by Baby-san and Havac. Bayard could barely see the lieutenants' faces in the dim glow of his blue-lensed flashlight: Miller, Thompson, Naheghian, Reynolds, and Burdock. Strange that except for Naheghian they had at first seemed so much alike—young, tanned, slender—using the same words, talking about the same things: maneuvers at Vieques, duty with the Sixth Fleet, liberty in Mediterranean ports of call. Now that he had gotten to know them better, they weren't alike at all. He gave them the company's mission for the next day, lied and said that the Red Snapper had complimented Dog Company for being first ashore, and bid them good night.

Dawn crept in slowly. Bayard had slept intermittently. When there was enough light to see, he slid out of his sleeping bag. Baby-san, already up and around, handed him a cup of soluble coffee and a can of C ration biscuits. With the plastic spoon that came with the rations, Bayard scooped jam out of its own little can onto the thick, dry crackers—crackers not much changed, he guessed, from Civil War hardtack.

Close by, Havac was also up and about. Bayard watched him take a tightly rolled hand towel from his knapsack, spread it out on the ground, and top it with the other contents: a straight razor, a razor strop, a small steel mirror, and a bar of soap. Pinky, the clerk, brought Havac a fire-blackened canteen cup filled with hot water. Havac splashed the hot water onto his face and then rubbed the bar of soap across the day's growth of beard. Wiping his hands dry, he held the opened razor up to the growing light and then gave the razor a few tentative swipes against the leather strop.

Bayard imagined, rather than heard, the scrape of the razor as it swept over the whiskers. Finished, Havac gave a grunt of satisfaction and wiped his face clear of remaining thin lather with the towel. Havac reassembled the shaving gear into the towel and returned the roll to his knapsack.

"Why the straight razor?" Bayard asked Havac.

"Was a time, Captain," said Havac, "when straight razors were issued in boot camp." Havac paused. "Before my time. But they are good in the bush. Don't need fresh blades."

Bayard had finished his crackers and coffee. He summoned Baby-san and Almquist, his radio operator, and together they climbed the reverse slope to the top of the hill to look at the ground. The zone of responsibility assigned to Dog Company was just a few neat square inches on Bayard's map, but from their vantage point they saw it stretching in front of them as a confusing jumble of sparsely wooded red-clay hills with sharply incised valleys terraced into gigantic green steps. His map showed his zone as a peninsula dangling pear-shaped south of Inchon, formed by an arm of the sea jutting inland. A single-tracked railroad ran diagonally across the peninsula and crossed the inlet by means of a causeway. At this point there was a village labeled Pusu-ri.

The rain had long since stopped. The sun was now up. Bayard went back to his command post and met with his lieutenants. He cleared his throat. "All right," he said, "you know the general situation. We'll patrol our zone in line of platoons. The 1st Platoon will move along the high ground left of the railroad."

Miller had the 1st Platoon. His thin, sharp-featured face was almost lost under his helmet. He was so slender as to appear frail. He had left a wife and two very young children in Jacksonville, North Carolina. Bayard found him remote and uncommunicative, but he seemed to be an efficient platoon leader. He accepted his orders with a quiet nod.

"The 3d Platoon will be on the ridge to the right of the tracks," Bayard went on with the order. "Naheghian, you and Miller try to keep sight contact with Thompson and me in the center."

In the few days of field duty the company had spent at Pendleton and in Japan, Bayard had learned that Naheghian's bulk was not all fat but in good part muscle. He had also learned that before the war—the real war, not this affair—Naheghian had been a near All-American guard at the University of California. Everyone had spent the night in the mud, but Naheghian managed to look a little filthier than the rest.

"Each of the two flank platoons will have a section of light machine guns attached. The rest of the company will move along the railroad—company headquarters, the mortars, the machine-gun platoon less two sections, and the 2d Platoon. We'll join up at Pusu-ri. I want to be there by noon. Then we'll turn north and strike back toward the rest of the battalion. Any questions?"

"Where will Mr. Gibson be?"

The question came from Thompson. The leader of the 2d Platoon had a patronizing quality, an air of superiority, that irritated Bayard. Thompson's father was a navy captain retired in the grade of rear admiral—a "tombstone promotion," it was called. Thompson had grown up in the service and had a way of referring too often to past associations with various senior personages.

Bayard gave Thompson what he hoped was a hard look. Are you wondering if I can conduct an approach march without Gibson's help? Is that what you're trying to imply? But he did not say this out loud.

Aloud he said, "I guess I left that part out. The battalion exec ordered all company execs and property sergeants to the beach this morning to help get the battalion gear straightened out. Reynolds and Burdock, you, of course, will move with me."

Reynolds, who had been a platoon sergeant at the end of World War II, was a methodical, earnest, and unimaginative officer wholly dedicated to the premise that his machine guns formed the backbone and framework of Dog Company's tactical structure. Thompson constantly baited him on this point, and the two lieutenants would get into long, involved arguments on machine-gun techniques and tactics, the details of which were beyond Bayard's comprehension.

Burdock, who had the 60mm mortars, was likable. He was eager and anxious to please, but Bayard had doubts as to his maturity. The slight, almost white, fluff of a mustache he was encouraging on his upper lip looked ridiculously out of place, like a bit of pasted-on cotton.

"If there are no other questions," said Bayard, "that's it. We'll meet at Pusu-ri for lunch."

Despite his resentment at Thompson's question, Bayard wished that Gibson might have gone with them, but he could not ask the battalion executive officer to make an exception in the case of Dog Company. So Gibson would move with the battalion train—that is, if the vehicles got ashore today—and they would meet up when the battalion dug in its defenses for the night. In the meantime Bayard was very much aware that his every action would be observed by the watchful and appraising eyes of First Sergeant Havac.

Well, thought Bayard as the lieutenants trotted back to their platoons, I have just delivered my first five-paragraph field order, although in slightly scrambled form. I wonder how they would have graded it at Quantico. Would I have gotten a "satisfactory"?

He remembered the day in 1943 when he had arrived at Quantico for the Officer Candidates Class, getting off the train, being formed up with the other candidates into a company, and standing in ranks on the sidewalk in front of the brick barracks on Barnett Avenue. He remembered the portly, immensely dignified gunnery sergeant—who was wearing the rainbow-colored World War I victory ribbon, so he must be long since retired by now—walking up and down the ranks of Bayard's platoon, looking searchingly into each man's face and then going to the front of the platoon and saying, "I have just ten weeks to make you young gentlemen into second lieutenants and platoon leaders. This will require your utmost in concentration and cooperation. If I say run, you run. If I say jump, you jump. If I say crawl, you crawl. If I say shit, you shit. Platoon, dismissed."

chapter seven...

To patrol the peninsula that first morning after the landing, Dog Company shook itself out into what amounted to a long skirmish line and swept across the countryside like a loose-meshed net. Its immediate catch was a large number of Korean refugees, of both sexes and all ages, drifting back toward Inchon.

When he was a child in Columbus, Bayard had once had a toy, a sort of puzzle. It had come, as a matter of fact, from the Weinstein Drug Store. It was a little glass-covered box, and in it were three tiny metal mice. Each had a ball-bearing in its underbelly, and the object of the puzzle was to get each mouse into its own hole. The slightest tilting of the box sent the mice running every which way.

These refugees reminded Bayard of the mice. Each tilt of the war's fortunes sent them scurrying back and forth. Yesterday the shelling of Inchon had been a pageant of fire and smoke; today it was ten thousand homeless families. Here a lifetime's possessions were reduced to a bundle tied in a square of cloth.

The Korean men for the most part wore baggy white trousers, shirts, and vests. The ancients among them were further distinguished by the black horsehair hats they wore and the long-stemmed tiny-bowled brass pipes and walking sticks they carried. Bayard could see that even though all their other possessions had been swept away, the old men inevitably clung to these three symbols of their patriarchy.

Most of the women wore trousers tied at the ankles, and some had a skirt wrapped over the trousers. The weather was warm, and from below the short jackets of the women, the naked breasts of the more mature hung pendulously. The effect might have been provocative if the nipples had not been encrusted with dirt and if the whole countryside had not smelled like an open sewer.

The children were smaller copies of their elders. Some of them were in Japanese-style school uniforms, the boys crop-headed and the girls Dutch-bobbed. At close hand, all ages stank of garlic, red peppers, and pickled cabbage.

A solid column of this depressing humanity trudged along the railroad and the dirt road that paralleled it. Dog Company had been told that the enemy would try to infiltrate in civilian clothing and that all refugees must be searched. Dog Company before landing had worked out a standing operating procedure for this eventuality, and now Thompson's platoon set up four-man checkpoints to search and screen the civilians. It was a tedious and unrewarding business. It bothered Bayard to see these people's miserably few belongings dumped into the dust of the road at the impatient hands of his marines. He had no stomach for this kind of work.

Due to the sheer numbers of persons to be searched, the center of Dog Company's advance came to a halt. Bayard was on the verge of countermanding his standing order, dissolving his checkpoints, and letting the mass of refugees flow through to be searched by someone else in the rear.

Then a marine searcher gave a yell of surprise. More thorough than most of his companions, he had thrust his hand deep into a sack of rice carried by a husky young peasant. Pulling his hand out of the sack, he held up the drum of a submachine gun.

The peasant twisted free of the marine and started at a run across the paddies.

"Get him!" someone yelled. There was a frozen second of inactivity, then a rifle shot, and another and another until a veritable fusillade pursued the fleeing figure. The peasant dodged and twisted, almost made the temporary safety of a dike, then stumbled, raised himself to his hands and knees, and then fell forward and lay still.

"Let's go get a look at him," said Havac, taking his carbine down from his shoulder.

Bayard pushed through the milling mass of Koreans and, following Havac's lead, bounded over the checkerboard of rice paddies until they reached the prostrate form. While a half-dozen marines watched with fascinated eyes, Havac ran practiced hands over the dead body. He slipped his knife free of the sheath in his boot and slit open the Korean's baggy trousers leg. There, strapped to the dead man's thigh, was the weapon.

"Russian burp gun," growled Havac, cutting it free from the leg. "Now let's see what else we can find." He tore off the dingy white shirt. Bayard saw a mustard-colored uniform underneath. It had red-and-yellow shoulder boards.

"A goddamn gook sergeant major," said Havac. "I wonder how many of these bastards have slipped through us."

It was the first dead enemy that Bayard had seen. The North Korean had been hit at least three times. Already in the warm September sun, flies were beginning to cluster on the caking blood.

Dog Company moved on. The day's heat increased. Bayard watched the widening patches of sweat staining the green utility uniforms. He was carrying his haversack and sleeping bag, and the pack straps chafed his shoulders. Canteens had not been refilled since the men left the LST. Bayard swallowed down the cottony taste in his mouth. He saw some of his people eyeing slyly the wells and ditches they were passing. They had been lectured by the battalion surgeon on all manner of infestations and diseases they could expect to get from contaminated water. But Bayard could see that present thirst would soon be more compelling than the half-believed threat of some strange Oriental sickness.

Behind Bayard plodded Baby-san laden down with a full packboard and Almquist similarly burdened with his SCR-300. Intermittently there was radio traffic from Battalion, and Almquist would hand him the handset. The hills between Dog Company and the main body interfered with the transmission, but from what Almquist could pick up, Bayard concluded that the battalion was moving steadily forward without meeting serious resistance anywhere in its zone. At noon there was still no sign of Pusu-ri. Bayard's back ached, and his feet were beginning to swell inside of his boots.

"When do we stop for chow?" asked Baby-san. It was half a question, half a complaint.

"We'll eat when we get to Pusu-ri. Not before," Havac answered, making Bayard's decision for him. Bayard wet his lips with his tongue and shook his two canteens experimentally. One was empty. The other was almost full. He pulled the filled canteen out of its canvas carrier.

"Have some," he invited Baby-san.

Baby-san took a pull at the canteen and would have returned it.

"Pass it around," said Bayard. Havac scornfully waved aside the offered canteen. Others were less proud. When the canteen was returned to Bayard, there was only enough left for him to rinse his mouth.

That was a mistake, he said to himself, putting the empty canteen back in its case. Havac is thinking I did it as a grandstand play. Maybe I did.

It was two o'clock before they rounded a bend in the railroad track and could see the village, the causeway, and the inlet laid out in front of them, just as it was drawn on the map. Pusu-ri was a handful of brown mud-walled thatch-roofed houses lining two dirt roads, which crossed at right angles. The most pretentious building in the village was a Japanese-style school, its unpainted board siding weathered to a dark grayish brown. Except for a pair of yellow dogs romping in the dust of the street, there was no immediate sign of life.

A squad from the 2d Platoon was detached and sent on ahead to scout out the village while the rest of Bayard's party waited and watched. The street remained quiet. The dogs sniffed curiously at the leggings of the riflemen in the lead squad. The sergeant squad leader sent a fire team— a corporal with three men—forward to search the schoolhouse; he then disposed the remainder of his squad in watchful attitudes on both sides of the village street. The fire team disappeared into the building.

Bayard trained his binoculars on the schoolhouse and braced himself for the glassy explosion of a grenade or the noisy stutter of an automatic weapon. Instead he heard the wheeze of an old-fashioned reed parlor organ. One of the marines inside the schoolhouse was pumping out the first several bars of "The Marines' Hymn." *From the Halls of Montezuma . . .*

"All right," said Bayard, "it sounds like the village is secured. Let's go on in and wait for the rest of the company."

As company headquarters moved into the village, a marine came toward them from the schoolhouse holding high a yellow-stocked rifle.

"Bring it here," called Havac.

The first sergeant took the Russian rifle from the marine and expertly snapped open the bolt. A brass cartridge, bright in the afternoon sun, flew out of the chamber. Havac ran a stubby finger inside the receiver.

"Freshly oiled," he said. "I wonder where the guy is who goes with it."

Bayard beckoned Thompson. "Have your people go through all these houses carefully."

The marines of the 2d Platoon, delighted at having the opportunity to do some systematic souvenir hunting, broke up into fire team–sized fragments and descended with a will on the houses.

Bayard himself searched the high ground on both sides of the railroad with his field glasses for some signs of his 1st and 3d Platoons. They were not yet in sight, and he had had no contact with them for the last hour or more.

"See if you can raise them on the 536," he ordered Baby-san.

His runner looked at his handy-talkie radio in disgust. "Hell, Captain, I can shout further than this thing can carry."

"Look," said Havac, calling his attention back to the village street, "I knew there had to be somebody to go with that rifle."

A forlorn North Korean soldier was being urged toward Bayard's group by the triumphant bayonets of a 2d Platoon fire team. He was only the first. There were others. Some were found hiding in the irrigation ditches, some under the thatched roofs, some in the pig sties and outhouses. They had no fight left in them. They gave Bayard to understand that they had been waiting to surrender since the village had been strafed that morning by the dark blue airplanes with the bent wings. Bayard recognized this as a description of the Marine Corsair fighter-bombers.

Dog Company took away their prisoners' weapons and then argued among themselves for the possession of these souvenirs. Later in the war they would scorn such booty as so much additional weight to be carried. Half as a precaution, half for the sport of it, they stripped their prisoners bare. Soon twenty-four North Koreans were huddled in the street, as naked and yellow skinned as two dozen freshly plucked chickens.

Meanwhile Naheghian and Miller had come down from the high ground with their platoons and closed into the village. A mutual exchange of compliments and congratulations was interrupted by a snappish radio inquiry from Battalion as to just what the status and positions of Dog Company were.

Bayard, as modestly as possible, reported that he was at the company objective, that he had no casualties, that he had twenty-four prisoners, and that he would march north to rejoin the main body as soon as Dog Company had had a chow break.

Thirsty marines found an iron water pump in the village. Pilnick, the company's senior corpsman, came forward to give a professional appraisal. He filled a canteen cup, looked at it, smelled it, and said that the water would be safe enough if it were boiled or if water purification tablets were added. Bayard stationed him by the pump to insure that each man added a half-dozen halazone pills to his canteens. The resulting product had the smell and taste of household bleach.

Baby-san fired up his little gasoline stove—one man in every four was supposed to have one—and served ration cans of coffee to Bayard and Havac. It was a poor excuse for coffee, but the bitterness did disguise the chlorine taste of the treated water.

Time was getting away from them. It was almost four o'clock before Dog Company was on its feet again, formed into column, and moving north along a road that was nothing more than a rutted trail. The road wavered around the foot of the hills that pressed down like knuckles against the shoreline of the inlet. Each curve around each hill could have been the site of an ambush.

The men had been marching for about an hour when the sudden rattle of small arms fire up ahead brought the tired column to sharp attention.

"Sounds like the point got hit," said Thompson. His implied question: What are you going to do about it?

Bayard eyed the ground to his front. He could see nothing. "They must be up in that clump of trees," he reasoned aloud, hoping that his voice carried more conviction than he felt. "Thompson, you take your platoon up the draw and see if you can flank them. We'll put some machine-gun and mortar fire up there and see if we can flush them out. I'll keep pushing forward with the rest of the company."

"Just like Quantico, eh, Captain," said Thompson, white teeth gleaming in a sardonic grin. "All right, 2d Platoon, let's go."

Thompson's platoon peeled off of the road and disappeared into the brush that filled the ravine.

Just like Quantico, thought Bayard. Enemy on the high ground, establish a base of fire, flank with a maneuver element moving up through a convenient corridor. The old Candidates Class limerick came to mind:

Here lie the bones
  Of Lieutenant Jones,
A graduate of this institution.
  In the midst of the din
He died with a grin.
  He used the school solution.

Burdock's 60mm mortars got themselves set up in a ditch at the edge of the road and began lobbing their little shells into the suspected center of enemy resistance. The short-barreled mortars looked like toys. It was hard to take them seriously.

Reynold's machine guns were raking the hillside with ball and tracer. There was no return fire.

"God knows what we're shooting at," grumbled a machine gunner as he worked his bolt hand to start a new belt of ammunition through his gun, darting a questioning look at his platoon leader.

"I'll worry about that," said Reynolds. "You just keep firing."

Reynolds himself appeared undismayed at the lack of a visible target. He seemed content to demonstrate the volume of fire that he could deliver.

Bayard, not quite sure of the effect of all this, cloaked his uncertainty by staring stonily through his binoculars at the offending hillside until the last camouflaged helmet cover belonging to the 2d Platoon was lost to sight in the vegetation. Then he ordered the two remaining rifle platoons to continue the march down the road until they reached the lead squad.

They found the members of the point strung out in the ditch alongside the road, unharmed but laboring under the impression—caused, no doubt, by the heavy volume of fire engaging the hillside—that they were cut off from the rest of the column.

Time passed. Radio contact with the 2d Platoon failed due to the inconstancies of the SCR-536s. The first eager excitement faded and turned, as the evening grew chilly, into restless impatience. Burdock had reported himself out of mortar ammunition, and Reynold's machine guns had long since ceased to fire at their illusory target. Battalion, at first alarmed lest Dog Company be inextricably trapped, was now testily urging Bayard to get on with it.

It was almost dark before Thompson's platoon came sliding down the clay slope.

"What did you find up there?" asked Bayard going over to meet Thompson.

"Not a goddamn thing," reported the platoon leader. He grinned sourly through the sweat-caked dust that masked his face. "Nothing up there but some empty foxholes."

"What took you so long, then?" demanded Bayard.

"Nothing," said Thompson sweetly. "Nothing except a rough climb and the fact that you had us pinned down with our own mortar and machine-gun fire."

In mortified silence Dog Company got to its feet, a little more slowly this time; tired muscles had begun to stiffen during the long halt. The march was resumed. The company reached the position designated by Battalion well after dark. The defenses for the night straddled the main highway at a point where it cut through a ridge of hills. A roadblock manned by Weapons Company's antitank-assault platoon barricaded the center of the cut, and Easy and Fox Companies had the high ground on each side. A string of jeeps and trucks lined the road to the rear of the roadblock. These belonged to Headquarters and Service Company and its attachments.

"You guys get lost?" jeered battalion headquarters as Dog Company slogged past.

"Go fuck yourselves, you lousy office poges," answered Dog Company wearily.

Lieutenant Gibson was standing in the road waiting for Bayard. "I got a batch of prisoners here," Bayard told him. "What do I do with them?"

"There's a sergeant from Battalion S-2 here waiting to take them off your hands," said Gibson.

A short, squat figure stepped forward out of the shadows. "I'll take 'em from here, Captain."

"We got twenty-four of them," said Bayard.

The intelligence sergeant was unimpressed. "We been sending 'em to the rear all day by the truckload," he said. "I hope you didn't take their clothes away from 'em. Regiment has been on our ass for sending back naked prisoners. Seems we shocked some female war correspondent."

"I'll show you the company position before it gets any darker," said Gibson.

"Good," said Bayard. "Let's go." He was not overly eager to be around when the intelligence sergeant discovered that Dog Company's twenty-four POWs were sans clothing.

"I walked the line with Major Mansell," said Gibson. "We've got the high ground to the right rear of the battalion. The battalion MLR—main line of resistance—sort of curves around like a fishhook. The Old Man is still worried about that exposed right flank."

"We went all over that ground today," said Bayard. "There was no sign of resistance except for that little ambush we ran into. There's nothing down there that could give us any trouble."

"Try telling that to the Red Snapper," said Gibson.

"No, thanks," said Bayard, "I'll leave that up to Mansell. By the way, what about our baggage?"

"It's all up, sir, including the bottom halves of the men's packs."

"Never expected to see those again," said Bayard. "The men can't carry them anyway. They've got too damn much to carry now."

"I know," said Gibson, "but I've fixed it with Battalion Supply to take them back after the men have had a chance to go through them and get what they want."

Bayard left his headquarters group on the reverse slope while he walked the line with Gibson and his platoon leaders.

The highest ground in the company sector was in the center and assigned to Thompson's platoon. An argument arose over the siting of machine guns. Reynolds wanted to put his guns well down on the forward slope so that he could get something like grazing fire. Thompson was against doing this because his riflemen would have to conform to the positioning of the machine guns.

"If you had your way," said Thompson coldly, "you'd have my people down in the rice paddy. What's the use of having the high ground if we don't make use of it?"

"I'm not asking you to move 'em down to the paddy," argued Reynolds doggedly. "All I'm saying is that I need a decent field of fire for my guns. Didn't you ever hear of the *military* crest? That isn't the top of the god-damn hill!"

"There's no such thing as a military crest in this cut-up kind of country," snapped Thompson. "Can't you see that this ground calls for individual guns and sectors of fire—not final protective lines?"

Bayard listened and compromised. He traced out a line for Thompson's platoon, a main line of resistance that was not as far forward as Reynolds would have liked nor as close to the topographical crest as Thompson would have had it.

Then he moved on to the 3d Platoon area. Naheghian, chewing the stub of a cigar, walked the length of the line with him. The members of the 3d Platoon were industriously digging in, and Bayard could find no fault with the positions selected by their platoon leader.

Bayard reached the right flank of his company; there was nothing beyond, only darkness. Naheghian grunted and pointed with his cigar stub. "If the bastards come tonight, that's where they'll come from. Down that ridge."

"Well, we'll be ready for them," said Bayard.

"I expect so," said Naheghian dryly.

Having completed the inspection of his company front, Bayard returned to his own hole on the reverse slope of the hill. It was marked by the scarlet-and-gold guidon, faintly visible in the darkness. He found Baby-san, whom he had left behind to dig their holes while he toured the company position, working in his hole in the carefully shaded light of a candle stub, completing the reassembly of a Browning automatic rifle.

"What have you got there?" demanded Bayard.

"I got me a BAR," said Baby-san. "If we keep running around these here hills, we're going to be needing some firepower before long."

Bayard looked at his wristwatch. It was almost midnight. He kicked off his boots and slid into his sleeping bag. He was just dozing off when the field telephone rang. As he groped for the leather-covered case, a small avalanche of loose dirt cascaded down into his upturned face. He finally got the handset free of its slot.

"Dog Six? This is Three-Able. The major wants all the company commanders down to the CP in fifteen minutes to get tomorrow's attack order. Okay?"

Resignedly Bayard worked his way out of his sleeping bag and reached for his boots.

chapter eight...

The war had an excitement during those early days. War is exciting when you are winning and the danger isn't too great. Bayard supposed that no expeditionary force in history was ever more self-confident or more imbued with its own success than was the 1st Marine Division during that headlong rush from Inchon to Seoul.

The division crossed the intervening hills in giant steps. Field manual formulas for frontages and distances were forgotten, and Dog Company found itself advancing on a mile-wide front, three, four, five thousand yards a day, against an almost unseen enemy who managed sometimes to do quite well, considering its obvious state of disorganization.

Dog Company's losses were not heavy—three men one day, six the next. A sniper's bullet might take one; a cluster of mortar shells falling on a column walking unwarily along a ridgeline might cause the rest.

Each day there was a new set of objectives—goose eggs to be drawn on Bayard's map between the parallel lines that marked the battalion's zone of action. "Seize the high ground" was the dictum. Each morning's work would begin with the artillery pounding the day's first objective. Then, after the high explosive had fallen, the hill would blossom beautifully with white phosphorus, and this would be the signal for Dog Company to go forward.

"Firebrand Dog Six, this is Firebrand Three," Major Mansell's radioed voice would lash at their heels. "Why haven't you moved out? Get your people moving."

Dog Company would reach the top of the first objective and find the enemy foxholes or trenches empty except for a spilled bowl of rice or a bloody bandage.

"That was a lung-buster," Havac would say, his great chest heaving. "What comes next?"

Then the artillery and mortars would go to work on Objective Two.

"Jump off as soon as you see the Willie Peter," would come the order. The white smoke would rise above the pine trees scantily covering the next ridge, and Dog Company would get to its feet and start forward again.

"Christ," Baby-san would say, laboring under the combined weight of his BAR and packboard, "I'm so goddamn tired I couldn't assault a piss-ant, less alone a gook."

Then, late in the afternoon when they were going against the last objectives for the day, when they had lost all contact with the units on their right and left, and when they had outstripped the range of their supporting weapons, the men of Dog Company would stumble onto a nest of stubborn North Koreans, and a violent sort of hide-and-seek would be played.

"We're setting up on Objective Four," Bayard would radio when the game was finished. "I've got four men badly wounded."

"Get them down to the road, and we'll pick them up with the jeep ambulance."

"They're too far gone. They'd never make it."

A pause. Then "Okay. Put out your panels. We'll try to get them out with a helicopter."

By the fifth day they were outside of Yongdung-po, an unlovely town just across the Han from Seoul. It had been an easy day. Casualties had been light, and the battalion had advanced four thousand yards across the red-clay hills against insignificant resistance. As the day ended, Dog Company began the nightly ritual of digging in. Bayard had walked the line earlier, assigning positions to his platoons, and now he walked the line again, rechecking the siting of his automatic weapons with Reynolds.

"Skipper," said Reynolds as they threaded their way along the ridge connecting the 1st and 2d Platoon positions, "I got a problem."

"What sort of problem?"

"It's this guy Kusnetzov. You know who I mean?"

Bayard thought for a moment. Kusnetzov was the rugged black-haired machine gunner who had been in the original company at Camp Lejeune and who had ridden in to the beach in Bayard's LVT. "Yes, I know him," said Bayard. "What about him?"

"He's too much for me. I think he's a psycho."

"What's he done?" You got something specific?"

"Well, like today. He was missing all day from his section. Went off by himself on some screwy deal."

"You want me to talk to him?" asked Bayard. "Is it something you can't take care of yourself?"

Reynolds closed his right hand into a fist and looked contemplatively at his knuckles. "You know, Captain, sometimes I wish I was still an enlisted man. Sometimes I get so mad at this guy Kusnetzov that I could belt him one. Maybe that's what he needs. You know he's in my first section. That's Griffith's section. Griffith is a good machine-gun sergeant— he knows his guns, but he isn't the physical type. He can't handle a rough character like Kusnetzov. I can't either—not by just talking to him. Maybe you can."

Bayard turned to Havac. "What do you know about this, First Sergeant?"

Havac rubbed the blunt features of his face with the palm of his hand. "Let's see. He's a Polack or a Russian. I don't know which. In some ways he's a good soldier. He knows his weapons. But he's a troublemaker. Gets into fights. Just before you took over the company, we had to get him out of the pokey in Myrtle Beach. He had cold-cocked a couple of Fort Bragg paratroopers in a gin mill. Which would have been all right, except he did it with a chair."

The three men, accompanied by Baby-san and Reynolds's runner, moved along the ridgeline to the 1st Platoon's area. They found Kusnetzov lounging behind his machine-gun position. At their approach he leaped to his feet and stood at an exaggerated attention. His squad leader and his section sergeant moved in expectantly.

Kusnetzov was a big man. He stood taller than the first sergeant, and Havac was better than six feet. Bayard judged Kusnetzov to be about thirty. His heavy black beard had sprouted an inch or more, and he was wearing a knitted blue watch cap instead of his helmet. He had an M1 rifle, two extra bandoliers of ammunition crisscrossed his chest, and four hand grenades hung from his pack straps.

"What is your job, Kusnetzov?" asked Bayard.

Kusnetzov took a deep breath that swelled his deep chest. "I am assistant gunner, second squad, first section, light machine-gun platoon."

"What are the duties of that position?"

"I carry the machine gun and help the gunner when the gun is in action."

"Where were you today?"

Kusnetzov looked uneasily at his platoon leader, then at First Sergeant Havac, and then at Bayard. His big hands fingered at his cartridge belt.

"You're at attention," growled Havac.

"We had no targets, so I took my rifle and went to look for communists."

"Was that your job?" asked Bayard.

Kusnetzov's eyes narrowed stubbornly. "To kill communists? Yes. That is why we are in Korea. To kill communists."

"Your job is assistant machine gunner. You're not a rifleman. You're not a scout-sniper. Do you understand?"

Kusnetzov seemed perplexed. He held up three thick fingers. "I killed three Nort' Koreans."

"That's beside the point. Who do you think you are that you can take off from your platoon whenever you feel like it? Your job is with that machine gun. Do you understand?"

"Yes, sir," said Kusnetzov reluctantly.

"I could court-martial you for what you did today. I'm not going to, but I never want to hear of you leaving your machine gun again. Never. Is that understood?"

"Yes, sir," said Kusnetzov.

"Very well. That's all," said Bayard, turning away abruptly. Perhaps Reynolds had expected him to do more—the machine-gun platoon commander had half hesitated as though he were about to say something.

That night, although he was tired to the point of exhaustion from the day's exertions, Bayard lay awake for a long time. To the north the thunder of artillery and the sight of tracers ripping across the black sky told him that the battalion on their left was receiving a sharp attack. But within Dog Company's position all was quiet except for the mournful sighing of the wind passing over the crest of the ridge, the *snick* of an M1 bolt being opened by a cautious sentry ensuring that there was a round in his chamber, and the comfortable sound of snoring from Havac's nearby hole.

Old memories, uninvited, had crowded in on Bayard. It was strange about the past—how it got stretched and distorted and twisted out of shape so that what came back to you was series of brightly lit scenes, where even the tones of the voices were faithfully reproduced. Bright, vivid scenes set against the dimmer, less clearly perceived, less clearly heard, background of graying memory.

Why, for example, should he be thinking tonight about Rose Giachetti? Rose—he had no idea where she might be, or if she were married, or how many children she might have. He did not even know what had happened to Rocco.

Conscience was the balance wheel of personality. Where had he heard that? Or was it something that he had put together himself and tucked away in the back of his mind? Was it his conscience that made him think of the Giachettis? Had he used them so badly?

Rocco had been tremendously enthused when he learned that George had enrolled at Ohio State. "What you gonna be, Georgie?"

"I don't know. I think I'll take education, be a teacher."

Mr. Cavendish, his beau ideal, was a teacher. But Rocco was disappointed. "A teacher? That's all right for a woman maybe. But I think you want to be something big, something important like a doctor. I think you make a good doctor, Georgie."

"I don't want to be a doctor," said George. "Besides, it takes a lot of money to be a doctor."

What he remembered most of his freshman year was the start-and-stop streetcar ride back and forth each day along High Street.

It wasn't by choice that he had gone to Ohio State. He would liked to have gone to Amherst, which was Mr. Cavendish's undergraduate school, or one of the other New England colleges. He had never visited any of them, but he had sent for the Amherst, Williams, and Dartmouth catalogs and had constructed a mental picture of white-painted, green-shuttered buildings and tall, arching elm trees, an intimate academic world.

The costs of these schools put them beyond all possible reach. It was Ohio State or nothing. When you left the streetcar at Long's Bookstore corner and went onto the Ohio State Oval, you also entered another world, but it was a blunt, massive, impersonal world where your class-mates numbered in the thousands. If you lived in town, you *went* to Ohio State. You couldn't say that you *belonged*. You could only belong to some smaller segment of the university, a fraternity, for example, but it wasn't easy for a town boy, of undistinguished attainments and no money, to belong to a fraternity.

So each day he had the streetcar ride to school, the large classes—where by the end of the academic quarter the instructor might know his name—and then each evening the ride home again.

Rocco was shrewd enough to perceive George's disappointment. "How you making out at school?" Rocco asked him one night.

"Oh, good enough," said George.

"You like it?"

"Pretty well. It's all right."

"How you making out with the money? Not so good, huh?"

"I get along."

"I wish I could pay you something regular for helping out in the shop, but you know how business is."

"Sure."

"But I gotta idea," said Rocco. "If you could build up a dry-cleaning route at the university, I could pay you a commission."

George was unenthusiastic. "There are already a lot of dry cleaners doing business with the dorms and fraternities."

"Yeah, I know," said Rocco, "but maybe we could do it a little quicker and a little cheaper than the rest. You want to try?"

George said that he would. Rocco had an old panel truck, which George used in making his evening rounds to the living groups. Then he delivered the garments to a central dry-cleaning plant. At six in the morn-ing he drove out to the plant again and brought the cleaned articles back to Rocco's for pressing. In the evening he retraced his route, making his deliveries. That way they were able to give one-day service.

George's commission was 25 percent of his collections. The money at first was small, but gradually his weekly take increased as he added more and more fraternities, sororities, and dormitory sections to his route. It went from five dollars a week to ten dollars and then got up close to twenty-five dollars. By then Rocco was doing more business with the university than off the street.

"You getting much fun out of school?" asked Rocco one night during the winter quarter of George's second year at State.

"I haven't got time for fun," said George. "Between studying and working the route, I don't have time for anything else."

"What about Rose? You don't take her out anymore."

"What do you mean? We see a show together every once in a while or have an oyster stew at the Greek's."

"I mean, really take her out—to one of them big school dances or something like that."

"She seems to get along."

"I don't like the bums she goes out with," said Rocco. "I'd rather she go out with somebody nice like you, Georgie. So how about it? When's the next big school dance?"

"Do you have any idea how much those things cost?"

"Who you kidding, Georgie? I know how much I'm paying you each week. There're men in this town who're raising families on less."

"I haven't got the clothes," said George. "I'd need a tux."

Rocco said nothing, but a week or so later he told George that he had something for him. He took a dinner jacket off the rack.

"What's this?" asked George.

"What's it look like? Try it on. A customer left it. He skipped out on his bill at the hotel. I think he was a musician."

Bayard put on the jacket.

"That's what I thought," said Rocco. "A little alteration, and it'll fit you good."

There didn't seem to be any way out of it. The big midwinter dance was at the Neal House. George bought the tickets. Artie Shaw's band was playing.

After Rocco made the alterations, George's tuxedo fit passably well. He bought a dress shirt and a wing collar, and a maroon tie and cummerbund to go with it. The haberdasher added an imitation carnation made out of maroon feathers.

The florist said he could let him have an orchid for five dollars or a corsage of gardenias for three. George took the orchid. The florist threw in a red carnation—a real one.

Rose wore a lavender taffeta dress she had bought especially for the dance. She had wound her black hair up into sort of a coronet, and she had a kind of tiara of artificial lavender flowers.

"Thirty-fi' dollars that dress cost me," said Rocco with pride. "How she look to you, Georgie?"

"Just fine," said George with some misgivings. "Just great."

"Sure," said Rocco. "She going to be the best-looking girl at the dance."

"I guess we better be going," said George uncertainly.

"You going to take the truck?" asked Rocco.

"I guess so. I cleaned it up this afternoon."

"You rather take a cab?" asked Rocco, shoving his hand into his pocket. "I could letcha have an extra five."

"No," said George hastily. "No, thanks. We'll make out with the truck. We can park it around the corner from the hotel. That all right with you, Rose?"

Rose shrugged her shoulders. "For once I'd like to do something first class, all the way. But if you want to take the truck, let's take the truck. Just so we get going."

The truck had gotten them to the dance. They left it in a parking lot on the street two blocks down from the hotel. Artie Shaw was doing a clarinet ride on "Frenesi" as they went up the marble steps to the ball-room.

"That's my favorite they're playing," said Rose. "I been here before to lodge dances and things like that, but they never had a band like Artie Shaw's. Let's get out on the floor."

Ordinarily they danced well together, but tonight George felt stiff and awkward.

"Loosen up, Georgie," said Rose. "Have fun. That's what we're here for, isn't it?"

"Give me a little time," muttered George. He didn't see anyone else wearing things in her hair like Rose had.

"Don't you know any of these people?" asked Rose. "When you going to introduce me to some of these other fellows and girls?"

"I don't know too many of them," said George defensively. "Ohio State is a big school, remember."

It was true that he didn't know many, but he did know some. Between the sets, the other couples gathered in little knots and circles. Rose and George stood alone. There were short nods of recognition, brief exchanges of greetings, but no invitations to join any of the groups. "They're mostly the fraternity crowd," explained George. "They stick pretty much together."

"Why don't you belong to a frat?"

"Why don't fish fly?" snapped George.

You could tell the ones who belonged. They were the ones whose evening attire fit them and didn't look as though it was rented or was altered hand-me-downs. He should have known that he and Rose wouldn't fit into a crowd like this. Not that Rose was going unnoticed. You couldn't overlook a girl like Rose. George intercepted more than one wolfish look and knowing grin. He grew sullen, half-belligerent. His mood communicated itself to Rose.

"What's wrong with you?" she asked.

"Nothing's wrong with me. I just don't think much of this dance, that's all."

"How long does it last?"

"Until two."

"What time is it now?"

"Almost one."

"Why don't we leave now and beat the rush?"

"All right, if you want to."

"I want to."

George went to the cloakroom and got their wraps. In silence they walked to the parking lot. It was a cold night, and George had a hard time starting the truck, but finally he got it going and they left the lot and began the drive up High Street.

Still, Rose said nothing.

"I'm sorry you didn't have a better time," said George. He realized that he hadn't behaved very well.

"I've had worse," said Rose. "Sometimes things just don't work out the way you think they will."

"You hungry?" asked George. "We could stop at the Greek's. He ought to be still open."

"No, thanks. Let's just go home."

George turned off at Weinberg's corner and threaded the truck through the alley that ran parallel to High Street. He parked behind the Paris Tailors. "Well," he said, "we're home."

"Yeah," said Rose. "I wonder if Rocco's waiting up for us."

"I bet he is. Maybe we shouldn't let him know things didn't go so well."

"We wouldn't want to disappoint Rocco, would we?" Rose's voice was suddenly harsh and strained.

"Well," said George. "He put out a lot of money for tonight—so we could have a good time."

"It was his idea in the first place, wasn't it?"

"I wouldn't say that exactly."

"I would," said Rose. "How come you never asked me to anything else the school gives, until this time?"

"You know," said George uncomfortably. "Money, mostly. And time. Going to school and working the route doesn't leave me much time for anything else."

"There's lots of things the school gives that don't cost money. And don't take much time either."

George remained silent.

"You let Rocco push you into it, didn't you?" pursued Rose. "Rocco's always pushing us at each other."

"Rocco likes us to go out together. What's so wrong about that?"

"Rocco thinks you're so much," said Rose. "He'd like to have you for a son—or maybe a son-in-law. He don't know you're ashamed to take me out where your college friends can see us."

"That isn't so," said George, reaching for her hands. "You know I like you, Rose. I've liked you for as long as I can remember."

He drew her across the seat toward him, turning her so that she was facing him, her back against the steering wheel. It was a practiced movement; they had done it often before. He kissed her, but her lips were taut and unyielding.

"I'm a cheap date," said Rose. "So cheap that your mother don't even speak to me on the street."

"My mother, your father—what've they got to do with it?" said George through clenched teeth. "Why can't it be just you and me?"

Rose ran her finger from the lobe of his ear down to the point of his jaw. "Because, Georgie, there's no future in it for you and me."

And George knew that she was right. This is the end of it, he said to himself. I've got to break off with the Giachettis. Rocco and Rose. Both of them.

This time her kiss was open-mouthed.

"Let's get in the back of the truck," said George roughly.

She didn't argue. "I saw the blanket you've got spread out back there," she said. "You must have felt pretty sure of yourself."

They groped their way over the seats into the back of the truck. They stretched out together on the blanket. The smell of woolens and dry-cleaning fluid flooded up around them. Rose shivered a little.

"You cold?" whispered George.

"No," said Rose. "I was just thinking that if you hadn't been such a kid, I would've let you do it to me a long time ago."

chapter nine...

"When we get across the river and into Seoul," the first sergeant had pre-
dicted, "then the war is really going to get rugged. This has been Boy
Scout stuff so far."

Dog Company watched the city from Hill 108, the hill that overlooked
the bridges leading into the capital city. The bridges would be of no use
to them. Bombs and demolitions had dropped the center spans into the
Han. Beyond the naked abutments Dog Company could see the barricades of sand-filled rice bags blocking the streets. They glimpsed the
brown specks that were the enemy, fleetingly seen through the gray
shroud of smoke that wrapped itself about the city. They sat on their hill
and waited the word to move, one day, two days. . . .

On the second morning on the hill, Major Mansell came up to inspect
Dog Company's position. He looked more Florentine than ever. He was
allowing his mustache to fill in to *condottieri* proportions. Otherwise he

was freshly shaved and faintly aromatic, indications that he was able to find both time and sufficient water for shaving and bathing—two things that Bayard had not been able to do. Mansell was wearing laced boots; they too were clean and freshly greased. His field jacket fit him trimly, and the hood fell away handsomely, like an abbreviated cloak, from his shoulders. Only a rapier belted to his waist needed to be added to complete the effect. In lieu of the sword, however, Mansell carried a light walking stick. "What percent alert do you have here, Bayard?" he asked.

"Twenty-five percent, sir."

The question was ritualistic, a formality, and so was the answer. Both officers knew full well that the prescribed alert for daylight hours was 25 percent.

"Would you mind walking your line with me?"

"Not at all, sir."

Bayard was determined to remain unruffled, unannoyed.

"Please have your platoon commanders meet us at the flank of their platoon positions."

"Aye, aye, sir. First Sergeant, pass that word over the sound-powered phones."

They started down the line—a string of foxholes that wavered just below the crest along the forward slope of the hill. It was a fine autumn day, and Dog Company was enjoying the warmth. The men had hung their sleeping bags from the trees to air; the bags swung in the light breeze like giant khaki cocoons. Rations simmered over an occasional gasoline burner and over dozens of little wood fires. The smell of the fires was like that of the autumn bonfires back home. Dog Company, barefooted and bare-headed, was relaxing, its members writing letters, playing cards on a poncho, napping, eating, reading, watching the opposite bank of the river with their field glasses.

"Where are their helmets?" asked Major Mansell.

"There hasn't been a shot fired all morning," said Bayard.

"My question was: Where are their helmets? Regulations are that they will be worn at all times, Captain."

"Yes, sir." The helmets were heavy and a nuisance. Dog Company, having seen what happened when they were hit by a rifle bullet, had no great faith in them. But there was nothing to be gained by arguing the point. They were in Miller's platoon area. Miller was wearing a cloth utility cap.

"Where is your helmet, Mr. Miller?" asked Major Mansell.

"In my foxhole, sir."

"And what about your individual weapon?"

Miller pulled back the skirts of his field jacket. He had a .45-caliber pistol tucked into the waistband of his trousers.

"Here, sir."

"I was under the impression that the M2 carbine was the prescribed weapon for platoon commanders."

"Yes, sir," said Miller. His thin face was perfectly guileless. "But I don't think much of the carbine as a weapon. I carry a rifle."

"Which I presume is in your foxhole with your helmet."

"That's right, sir."

They left Miller at the flank of his platoon position.

Things went better in the 2d Platoon area. It was not in Thompson's nature to be caught unawares. He had gotten the word on the operations officer's inspection over the company's sound-powered phones, and he was prepared. When he joined Mansell and Bayard at the limiting point that separated his area of responsibility from Miller's, he had his carbine correctly slung over his shoulder, he was wearing his helmet, and his field jacket, while not clean, was neatly buttoned and the bellows pockets were flat, not bulging with the usual load of ration components, maps, and other miscellaneous impedimenta.

A good 25 percent of the 2d Platoon were in their foxholes behind their weapons, staring intently at the opposite bank of the Han. All were wearing their helmets.

The remainder of the platoon were deployed on the reverse slope of the hill virtuously pursuing various constructive enterprises. The platoon sergeant was holding demolition school for the benefit of a rapt audience. At another site, socks and underwear were being washed in water brought up from the river by a carrying party. Elsewhere, individuals had field-stripped their weapons and were scrubbing the metal parts industriously with toothbrushes dipped in gun oil.

Mansell, followed by Bayard and Thompson, marched without saying a word along the ridgeline trail that bisected the 2d Platoon's position.

"This is as far as I go, sir," said Thompson when they reached the flank of his platoon position.

"Thank you, Lieutenant," said Mansell dryly. "I am very impressed by the show you have put on for my benefit. But I suggest that you relocate your main line of resistance. You have violated two of the battalion's basic rules for the organization of a hillside position. You've allowed your people to dig in too close to the crest of the hill, and you've allowed them to bunch their foxholes together. We organize the military crest of a hill—not the topographical crest—and I want to see five yards between single foxholes and ten yards between double foxholes. Understood?"

"Aye, aye, sir," said Thompson. Only someone who knew Thompson very well could have detected, from the slight change in expression and tone, the dent that had been made in his self-esteem.

Naheghian was waiting for them at the flank of the 3d Platoon position. He had stopped shaving altogether. With his matted beard he looked like something out of the Dark Ages. His platoon called him Ali Baba, and they were the self-styled Forty Thieves. Naheghian was wearing a cloth cap and carrying a rifle in the crook of his greasy sleeve.

"G'morning, Major. G'morning, Skipper." He spoke without removing the soggy stump of a cigar from his mouth. Bayard never saw him without a cigar. Even on night patrols he would have the cold, dead end of a cigar clamped between his teeth and as soon as he was safely under cover he would light up. The Forty Thieves had developed a proclivity for patrolling—even for night patrolling, an activity of which marines were not notably fond. The platoon was building a reputation for craft and guile, and their casualties tended to be fewer than those suffered by either of the other two rifle platoons.

"Where's your helmet, Lieutenant?" asked Mansell.

"I don't know, sir," said Naheghian ingenuously. "I must've lost it."

"May I see your weapon, please?"

Naheghian held out his rifle. It was an M1903 Springfield fitted with a telescopic sight.

"Where did you get this?"

"It belonged to the scout-sniper assigned to my platoon. He didn't seem to know how to use it, so I took it away from him."

Mansell cocked a dubious eyebrow but said nothing. He resumed his walk along the ridge trail. The fighting holes on the forward slope appeared to be manned by the requisite percentage of men although it was difficult to determine who was on watch and who was not. Rations were being cooked and eaten, letters being written and read, and some members of the 3d Platoon had crawled out of their holes and were lying flat on their backs, staring up comfortably at the sky.

"A form of antiaircraft precaution, I presume," said Major Mansell caustically.

"No, sir," said Naheghian blandly. "They're not on watch. They're just crapping out."

By this time they had reached the end of the 3d Platoon position, and Mansell's thin lips had tightened to a very narrow line. "Mr. Naheghian, if I hadn't seen it myself, I wouldn't believe it. Your platoon position is one gigantic rat's nest. You've allowed your people to mix up their house-keeping arrangements with their fighting holes. Your camouflage is miserable. Your field sanitation is nonexistent. You blithely ignore standing regulations concerning weapons and protective equipment. The appearance and manner of your men is deplorable. All I can say is get yourself and your platoon straightened out."

Mansell paused to look significantly at Bayard. "Captain, I'd like to speak with you alone for a moment."

The two men walked a few yards further along the crest of the hill in the direction of Easy Company's zone of action.

"Captain, it's very obvious to me from that short walk we've just taken that there is very little overall supervision being given your platoons. You have allowed your officers entirely too much freedom of action. You're supposed to be the company commander. I suggest that you start acting like one."

"I'm doing my best," said Bayard doggedly. "And I don't think Dog Company has done so badly."

Major Mansell cocked his head back slightly and smiled thinly, humorlessly. "We know about your connections, Captain. We know about your friend, the senator. But while you're in this battalion, you will do your job and do it to the same standards as any other company officer. If you can't get hold of your company and start running it the way it should be run—well, then, we'll find someone who can. Is that understood?"

Bayard forced himself to salute. "Yes, sir," he said. Mansell returned the salute, nodded curtly, and walked off in the direction of Easy Company, where the squat figure of Captain Beale stood waiting.

In bitter, silent anger, Bayard turned back toward his own company position. He had never discussed Donna or her father with any member of the battalion. Nor had he ever hinted at any political influence. He had asked for no special favors or extra consideration. He was in a savage mood as he retraced his steps to his company command post.

Miller intercepted him as he passed through the 1st Platoon's position. "The men were wondering," he asked, "if they could go back for showers. The engineers have set up a water point and a bath and shower unit a couple of miles back."

Bayard looked at him scathingly. "Do you have any more brilliant suggestions?" he snapped.

Miller's eyes dropped. "I'm sorry, Captain, if I embarrassed you when the major was here. I know the platoon area doesn't look so good. But I thought it was all right to let the men crap out a little. Christ knows, they haven't had much rest since we landed."

Bayard muttered something unintelligible even to himself, jammed his hands into his field jacket pockets, and walked glumly back to his command post.

Gibson and Havac were waiting for him with apprehensive expectation.

"Pass the word," said Bayard to Havac, "to get the company position squared away. Anybody too close to the crest will have to dig a new hole. I don't want to see any single foxhole closer than five yards to the next hole. The double holes for the BARs can be ten yards apart. Move all the housekeeping gear to the reverse slope. Everybody's to wear his helmet at all times. I want all the garbage and trash cleaned up and slit trenches dug behind each squad."

Bayard looked at his watch. "It's almost ten o'clock now. I'll inspect again at 1500."

Havac reached for his helmet and carbine. "Aye, aye, sir. I'll go round up the gunny and the platoon sergeants."

Bayard was left alone with Gibson.

"Did the major chew you out?" asked Gibson. You could always depend upon the executive officer to say exactly what he was thinking.

"The good major doesn't think Dog Company comes up to Marine Corps Schools standards," said Bayard. "Where does he think we are— Quantico?"

"Don't let him get you all upset," said Gibson. "He doesn't mean it personally. He's the most impersonal guy that ever lived. I've told you that in 1943, when I was a buck sergeant, I was in his detachment on board ship. He must remember me, but he's never brought it up. He's that impersonal."

"All right," said Bayard, "I'll take your word for it. Maybe it isn't personal with Mansell. But it's sure as hell personal with me."

That afternoon Bayard walked the line again and found his company, including Naheghian's platoon, a model of neatness. Nearly every man in the company had on his helmet. Those who didn't had lost them earlier. Bayard told his property sergeant to check with Battalion Supply for additional helmets.

The next morning Major Mansell inspected Dog Company again, almost without comment—there was no tête-à-tête with Bayard at the end of the company line.

chapter ten...

It wasn't until the middle of the night of September 24 that Dog Company was roused from its holes on Hill 108 and sent marching north along the Han to the bridgehead thrown across the river by Division. They crossed the river in LVTs and DUKWs, unloaded onto the opposite bank, and stumbled off in the black night into bivouac in a pear orchard. There was scattered firing somewhere in front of them. Someone said that it was the 5th Marines. Someone else said that the 187th Airborne had jumped into the city. Another voice argued that there wasn't any U.S. Army unit closer than Suwon.

They broke bivouac before first light. Baby-san complained of stomach cramps and squatted over a cat hole dug with his entrenching tool.

"I told you those goddamn green pears would give you the shits," said Havac without compassion. "Now wipe your goddamn ass and get under way."

By dawn they were on the road, marching southward toward the city. Another regiment had crossed the river the day before. Except for the occasional crack of a sniper's bullet and the answering fire of the flank patrols, there were no sounds of war coming down from the hills. The villagers along the line of march stood warily in their doorways and peered cautiously through shuttered windows. Hastily colored Republic of Korea flags sprouted here and there—hopefully placed, as if to announce: "We under this roof are loyal South Koreans. We welcome your return and plead for your protection."

But only the very young were completely unafraid of the marine column. The children laughed and chattered and edged close to the marchers. The little girls waved shyly, their slanted eyes shiny with excitement. The little crop-headed boys, wooden sticks on their shoulders, marched along parallel to the column, mimicking the slouching stride of the Americans. The marines of Dog Company searched their pockets for candy and chewing gum. "*Presento*" they said, tossing whatever they could find to the children.

The little boys were now firing in furious make-believe in the direction of the hills, reenacting with elaborate pantomime the firefight that must have been fought here the day before.

A man's work becomes a boy's play, reflected Bayard, thinking of the imaginary battles he had fought in the backyards and alleys off High Street. He remembered the fascination that soldiers and war hold for the young. Maybe this fascination, this inborn instinct for destruction, is the real and fundamental cause of war. Perhaps all the other supposed causes—ideologies, religions, territorial ambitions, population and economic pressures—all the reasons historians give—perhaps these are nothing. Perhaps man's urge to destroy his fellow men is as much a part of the life cycle as conception, birth, death, and decay. Perhaps it is the fatal flaw that will finally cause man's obliteration.

It was too bright and pleasant a morning to contemplate for long such a morbid philosophy. Bayard shook off the thought and looked up and down the length of his marching company. His eyes sought and found Kusnetzov. Ever since the evening on the hill he had made a point of watching the machine gunner. Sometimes in the midst of an attack against a hill he would get a glimpse of him when his gun was firing, on the left of the gunner as the assistant gunner should be, feeding the canvas belts of bright cartridges into the hungry maw of the gun. Then in quiet times Bayard would sometimes see him with the gun torn down and spread out on a poncho, going painstakingly over the steel internals with an oily rag. This morning he cut a piratical figure, marching along with the perforated jacket of the Browning light machine gun riding easily on his shoulder.

The road gradually widened and became a broad street lined with houses and shops, some of them empty and gutted by fire. Dog Company was in Seoul. They marched along in a loose double column—a row of men in each of the gutters that edged the street. The city dwellers along the sidewalks were less apprehensive and more articulate than the villagers had been. There were cheers and more of the hurriedly painted signs and many more of the South Korean flags.

"Man," said a marine, "I'm gonna open up a flag factory in this here part of the world and make me a fortune. No Korean home should be without a completely stocked flag locker. These poor folk don't know who's going to come marchin' through their town next."

Bayard remembered the end of the other war, when the marines had gone into Tientsin and Peiping. The Chinese had also cheered, and there had been much displaying of the Nationalist flag.

"*Mansei, mansei*," the people shouted, waving their Republic of Korea flags furiously, and the older ones, perhaps confused, kowtowing in the old Imperial fashion. In North China, Bayard recalled, the people had shouted "*Ding hao.*"

"Monnzy bonnzy," Dog Company yelled back happily. "Lookit that old bag. Here you are, you lovely, lovely creature. Chocolate. *Chocoletto*— for we are the chocolate soldiers marching as to war."

"Bunch of candy-ass marines," muttered Havac balefully, looking mean-ingfully at Bayard. But Bayard had no intention of interfering with his men's enjoyment of their small triumph. These city people look more like the Japanese than the peasants do, he remarked to himself. There were fewer wearing the traditional white costume, more wearing Western-style clothing.

"Happyness Comes," read the signs and banners. "Welcome U.S. Marine. Greeting to UN Police Force."

"Man," said the marine who was going to start the flag factory, "these poor folk can't spell worth shit. I don't reckon though that they mean any offense calling us a police force."

"Yep," gloated Baby-san, loose bowels forgotten, "that's us—Horrible

Harry's police force. I guess the gook army bugged out for sure when they heard we were coming."

Then Dog Company marched around a corner, making a ninety-degree turn, and the street was suddenly empty and silent.

But before Dog Company had a chance to translate the sight of an empty city street into a threat, the enemy's counterattack materialized from nowhere. One instant the street was empty; the next it was filled with North Korean soldiers rushing toward Dog Company, submachine guns and rifles banging wildly. Dog Company's 1st Platoon, caught in the broad, open street, began to fall like a row of tin soldiers knocked over by a giant hand.

For a moment Bayard had no thought except a primeval instinct that urged his own self-preservation. He scrambled for the protection of a thick rice-bag barricade and found most of his headquarters huddled behind it. Bullets plucked at the straw matting, sang off the paving blocks, cracked overhead. The enemy attack came through the 1st Platoon. You could see the individual faces. Brown faces. Slit-eyed. Hard faces, wide through the cheekbones. Yellow-and-red shoulder boards on those mustard yellow uniforms.

Bayard clung to the shelter of the rice bags. He didn't know what to do. His leading platoon was shattered. He did not know what his 2d and 3d Platoons, somewhere to his rear, were doing.

You're the company commander, Mansell had said. Act like it. But how? Did it mean stepping out in the street and dying? What good would that do? A string of submachine-gun bullets ripped across the top of the barricade, showering Bayard with bits of straw and dirt. Numbly he looked for his SCR-536, the midget radio that theoretically gave him communications with his platoon leaders. The thing must have gotten lost in the melee.

Then from behind him came the slower, harsher coughing of a light machine gun. A line of tracers reached out its probing yellow fingers and caught the leading edge of North Koreans. The attacking column wavered, its forward elements sliced down as though by a knife.

"Where's that coming from?" demanded Bayard. "Where's the machine gun?"

"There," said Baby-san, pointing. The LMG was set up in the shadowy recesses of an alley. Two marines were serving the gun. As Bayard watched, something struck the gunner, flung him half around. The assistant gunner lunged to his feet, straddled the prostrate gunner, seized him by the collar and cartridge belt and literally hurled him into the shelter of the alley. Then he dropped down behind the gun, jerked the bolt handle back, and resumed firing. Bayard saw that the marine behind the machine gun was Kusnetzov.

"Give him some help. Get the fuckers," roared Havac. The first sergeant stepped out into the street, his .45 thrust forward in his big square-cut hand. The pistol began to bang out a measured cadence as though Havac were firing at the bobbing targets on the pistol range.

Baby-san slid his BAR onto the top of the rice-bag barricade, scrambled up into firing position, and let go half a magazine.

Thompson's 2d Platoon came up strong. Their rifles and BARs added to the yammering din. The Red assault dissolved back into the doorways and alleyways.

Once again the street in front of Bayard was empty of movement, but now there were huddled bodies, some grayish green and some yellowish brown. Pilnick unslung his field medical kit and scuttled crab-wise out into the street to see what he could do with battle dressings and morphine syrettes.

The battalion radio began crackling. "Firebrand Dog Six, Firebrand Dog Six, this is Firebrand Three. What's holding you up? What's going on up there? Why aren't you moving? Over."

Come on up and find out for yourself, thought Bayard savagely. He closed his eyes and swallowed hard to steady his voice. "Firebrand Three," he answered, "this is Firebrand Dog Six. We have been hit by an enemy counterattack, strength about two-zero-zero. See if you can expedite artillery and mortar fire. Also tanks. We could use tanks. Have taken approximately fifteen casualties. I say again one-five casualties. Send up jeep ambulances as far as rice-bag barricade just east of railroad overpass. Do you read me? Over."

"Roger your last. Is there anything else you need? Over."

"Negative your last. If you have nothing more for me at this time, out."

Bayard passed the handset back to Brown. He looked appraisingly at the street. There was not a single living North Korean to be seen, but from the alleyways, the buildings, and the barricades there came the continuing rattle of small arms and automatic fire. The 1st Platoon had been badly mauled, but the rest of his company was still intact. He sent Havac over to help reorganize the 1st Platoon and told Thompson that the 2d Platoon would be in the assault with Naheghian immediately behind him.

The 60mm mortar section had found a firing position and was busy popping out its little shells, but so far as Bayard could see, they were not having any great effect. Most of the shells were exploding on the roof tops. Something a good deal heavier was needed to blast the enemy troops out of their hiding places.

Within the next few minutes, several things happened. The artillery came through with a crashing preparation, the interstices filled with the lighter shells of the medium mortars. Two tanks came rumbling up in support, probing inquiringly with their long-snouted 90mm guns. Dog Company leaned forward expectantly.

Bayard checked the magazine of his carbine. "Okay, Dog Company," he said. "Let's go."

He stepped out from behind the shelter of the barricade and into the open street. Dog Company got to its feet and followed. Bullets thudded into the rice bags, screamed in ricochet from the paving stones. Dog Company put its head down and went forward.

Bayard's marines cleared the houses and shops on both sides of the street with rifle fire and grenades ("Throw one anyway and make sure."). Every few yards there were yellow rice bags filled with sand stacked thick and high. There were machine guns behind some and antitank guns behind others. Always there was small-arms fire coming in unseen from the flanks and the front.

From one house a Red lieutenant popped his head out of a street-level window and shot a sergeant with his pistol. The sergeant lunged at him and dragged him through the window onto the street, covering him with his own blood. A rifleman bayoneted the Red lieutenant and cursed him as a lousy son of a bitch when the point of his bayonet broke off on a paving stone.

By eleven o'clock Bayard was able to report to Battalion that the street was cleared for four hundred yards. Nothing remained to be done except the old savage game of hide-and-seek, hunting down the few bypassed survivors.

Battalion was pleased and elected to push Easy Company through to continue the attack and so give Dog Company a breather in which to reorganize. The hot edge of the fight moved forward and was soon a safe half-mile ahead of Bayard's position. Except for the occasional ping and crack of a chance rifle bullet passing overhead and the clatter of a loosened tile falling from a roof to the street now and then, the war had moved on. Dog Company lay quiet in the midday sun waiting for what might come next. Havac had gone off to question the platoons and learn their casualties. Baby-san and the company clerk were searching the ruins of a nearby shop in their ever-optimistic hope for treasure. Bayard tried to coax enough heat from a burning ration box to warm a can of hash.

Then gradually the empty street filled with civilians. They seemed to emerge from every nook, alley, and cranny.

"Red Rover, Red Rover, it's safe to come over," said Bayard to himself, remembering a childhood game played in Columbus's streets. He detailed a squad from the 2d Platoon to set up a roadblock and search these people as they passed through to the rear.

Havac came back with his notebook in his thick fist.

"How bad is it?" asked Bayard.

"Pretty bad," said Havac. "We got eight killed and seventeen wounded. The 1st Platoon caught it worst—eleven casualties countin' the lieutenant."

"The lieutenant?" questioned Bayard sharply. "What's wrong with Miller?"

Havac looked surprised. "I thought you knew. He's dead."

"Dead?" echoed Bayard. The word had a leaden sound.

"He was shot through the head," said Havac. "His helmet didn't do him a damn bit of good."

"That's rough on the 1st Platoon. Eleven out of—what was their strength this morning? Thirty-seven?"

"Martinez got 'em squared away. They'll do all right."

"Sergeant Martinez is a good man," said Bayard.

Miller, who didn't like to wear his helmet and who didn't think much of the carbine as a weapon, was dead. Bayard recalled little threads of conversations he had had with him. Miller had been a corporal when the last war ended. After being mustered out he had gone to college under the GI Bill. He had told Bayard that he felt strangely adrift while out of the Marine Corps, and after graduating, he had come back in as a second lieutenant. He had a young wife and two babies waiting in Jacksonville, North Carolina. Now he was dead.

"Skipper," said Havac in a hoarse undertone, "you better get your hash outta the fire. It's burnin'."

Bayard ate his hash. It was burned around the outer edges and cold and greasy in the center. He forced it down.

Pinky and Baby-san came swaggering out of a side alley into the street. Stumbling in front of Baby-san's BAR was a North Korean prisoner. His helmet was gone, and his short black hair was wet with perspiration. Baby-san brought him up short in front of Havac and Bayard.

"We found this sonuvabitch in a cellar. Look at what he was carrying." Baby-san brandished a Russian machine pistol. "You didn't have the guts to use it, did you, you slant-eyed bastard?"

A ring of curious marines collected around Baby-san's prize.

"Let's see what else he's got," said a big rifleman from the 2d Platoon. He stepped up, knife in hand, seized the front of the trembling North Korean's coat, and with his knife sliced off all the coat buttons. Rough hands jerked off the coat. The knife then cut the waist string that held up the cotton trousers. They fell in baggy folds to the prisoner's ankles. Bayard, standing to one side, looked at Havac. The first sergeant was watching the proceedings with complete indifference. Taking his cue from Havac, Bayard made no move to interfere.

"He's a skinny sonuvabitch," said one of the marines.

"Take off his skivvies," said someone else.

The prisoner was stripped of his underclothes. He stood there naked, shivering violently although the afternoon sun was warm. He looked fearfully around the menacing circle of bearded marine faces. Then he burst into tears.

"Now look what you've done," said Baby-san to the tormentors. "You done scared my prisoner. Knock it off, you guys. Leave him alone."

"Hell," said the big rifleman with the knife, "he hasn't even got any hair around his balls. He's just a kid. I bet he's no more'n fourteen or fifteen."

"Pull up your britches," said Baby-san to the prisoner. "Nobody's going to hurt you."

The prisoner caught the meaning of Baby-san's tone and gesture. He drew up his trousers and held them clutched around his waist.

The big rifleman returned his knife to its sheath and fumbled in his jacket pocket. "Here, kid," he said, "have a cigarette."

The prisoner took the cigarette mutely, bobbing his head and venturing a frightened baring of the teeth that was apparently meant for a smile.

The rifleman struck a match and held it cupped in a big, steady, dirt-stained hand until the prisoner got his cigarette lit.

"All right, if you're through horsing around," said Havac, speaking up for the first time, "turn that shitbird over to one of the walking wounded and let him take him to the rear."

Slowly the ring of marines around the prisoner disassembled. Bayard went back to his can of hash. It was the middle of the afternoon, and the street was now dotted with civilians, some of them scurrying toward the rear, others curiously watching the lounging marines. It was a ridiculous situation, thought Bayard, like a football game with both the players and the spectators occupying the playing field.

Now Platoon Sergeant Martinez was coming toward Bayard, prodding before him a bareheaded young Korean in a torn white shirt and black trousers. "Captain, thees fellow says he can show us where some gook officer ees holed up," said Martinez.

The 1st Platoon's acting platoon leader was a stocky brown-faced Mexican with a reputation in the company for rock-hard courage.

"Yes?" said Bayard irritably, "how do we know who *he* is?"

"Is so," said the Korean boy anxiously. "Absolutely true. I show you. Come quick." He ran a nervous hand through his long black hair. He must be about seventeen, thought Bayard. He was slender and not very tall, short even for a Korean. Bayard noted that the boy's features were finer than most, his teeth were white and even, and his nose had an aquiline curve to it.

"Where did you learn to speak English?" questioned Bayard.

"Presbyterian School here in Seoul," said the boy. "Come quick, please sir, before the communists leave this place."

"How many are there?" asked Bayard.

"Thirteen," said the boy. "I count them. Four officers. Nine soldiers."

"What do you think?" said Bayard to Havac.

The first sergeant shrugged his heavy shoulders. "It can't hurt to look."

"All right," said Bayard. "Martinez, get your platoon on its feet. We'll take a look."

It was Martinez's patrol, but Bayard and Havac went along, and so did Baby-san with his BAR, his china blue eyes round and eager. They kept their Korean guide well in front of them, and a rifleman was told to drop him first if it developed that they were being led into a trap. The patrol moved through a shadowed side street cautiously, feeling its way and watching its flanks.

Bayard looked sidewise at Havac. The Hunky's face was as stolid as ever, but a slight grin turned up the corners of his mouth, and his lips were pressed wolfishly against his teeth. He likes this, thought Bayard; battle is his natural element.

The side street, which wasn't much more than an alley, intersected with a broader street. In front of them was a house, a fairly substantial house by Korean standards, Japanese in style with a heavy, curving roof of tile. Around it was a shoulder-high wall enclosing a fair-sized court. Perhaps because it was protected somewhat by its wall and courtyard, the house did not appear to be greatly damaged.

"There," breathed the Korean boy, "is the place. They're in there."

"Martinez," ordered Bayard, "take your first squad and look it over. We'll cover you from here."

The platoon eased its way forward. The machine-gun sergeant found firing positions for his two guns in the rubble edging the street. The two support squads deployed to the right and left. Bayard and Havac squatted down to watch and wait.

Martinez led his squad out from the shadows into the sunlit street. They went forward with watchful eyes and tight, predatory smiles. A shot banged out from the house, and the squad raced for the corner of the wall. Bayard caught his lower lip between his teeth. Martinez's marines made it safely and began to work their way along the wall, pressing close to the bricks.

The machine-gun sergeant was looking at him inquiringly. "Now, sir?" he asked.

Bayard nodded.

"Now," said the sergeant to his gunners. "Give 'em some support. Make it good."

The strings of armor-piercing bullets smashed chunks of plaster away from the sides of the house, leaving bare the straw and bamboo lathing. It is like the rest of Korea, reflected Bayard. Strip off the Western facade, and underneath the veneer it is Oriental.

His riflemen started pecking away, aiming below the window ledges to get at any lurking Red sniper who might be waiting for a target. A few rounds of return fire came from the house, not many. Then they heard the glassy explosion of a grenade and a burst from a BAR, and they knew that Martinez had found his way into the house. The rest of the platoon held off firing now, waiting.

Another grenade was heard, then a frantic chatter of a Russian sub-machine gun, the throatier chuckle of a BAR, the deliberate banging of an M1. Then silence.

The remaining members of the platoon looked at each other uneasily. Bayard began calculating his chances of getting across the street and over the wall.

Abruptly the gate to the compound was thrown open from the inside, and Martinez was standing there. "Hello," he called triumphantly, "come into the house. Mi casa es su casa."

Bayard, Havac, and Baby-san, followed by the others, crossed the street. They stepped over the crumpled body of a North Korean soldier lying across the doorway.

"In here, Captain," said Martinez. He led them to a small room, push-ing aside the flimsy sliding-wall partitions. On the thick floor mats were two female bodies. One was an old woman who looked to Bayard very much like any old woman anywhere in the world. Her hair was white, and time had blanched her skin to the color of pale ivory. The other figure was that of a girl, not more than fourteen or fifteen. She had a round, plump body, just swelling to womanhood.

"Oh, Lord," said Bayard, "I didn't expect this . . . we could have held off firing. I mean, if we had known. . . ."

"It wasn't us, Captain," said Martinez. He pointed to the women's throats. Around each, embedded in the soft flesh, was a tightly twisted wire.

"The North Koreans—how many were there?" asked Bayard.

"Like the boy said, Captain—thirteen."

"Where are they? Did any of them get away?"

Martinez's Indian face remained impassive. "None of them got away, Captain. They are all dead."

The Korean boy had slipped into the room and stood now beside Bayard.

"You know these women?" asked Bayard.

"Yes, I know them."

"Who are they?"

"My grandmother and my sister," said the boy quietly.

"I'm terribly sorry," said Bayard, "but I want you to know that it wasn't our bullets. They were—well, you can see the wires."

"I know," said the boy. "They hid me under the roof so the soldiers cannot find me when they search the house. They grow angry and kill them. I wait my chance and slip out of the house to get the Americans."

"What will you do now?" asked Bayard.

"I will go with you," said the boy. "I can be interpreter. Together we kill more communists."

So it was that Kim Kai Kyung—whose name was quickly corrupted to Jim Kim—became a member of Dog Company's headquarters.

chapter eleven...

Bayard's group rejoined the rest of Dog Company, still waiting quietly in the main street. The afternoon was coming to a close. The shadows were lengthening and losing definition. A platoon of tanks came rumbling back from the hot forward edge of the street fighting. A tank gunner leaned out of an open hatch and vomited. Dog Company hooted its derision.

"Goddamn powder fumes," explained the tanker. Dog Company unsympathetically suggested that he get out and walk.

A jeep came roaring up the street from the rear and screeched to a halt next to the rice-bag barricade behind which Bayard and his headquarters were resting. The driver bounded out of the jeep and stood stiff-legged, like a fighting cock, with his Thompson submachine gun cradled in his arms. Bayard saw that the passenger was the battalion commander.

The Red Snapper got out of the jeep more slowly. He steadied himself with a hand against the windshield post. He ignored Bayard's salute.

"Whose goddamn idea is that?" he asked, pointing. Bayard followed the direction of his outstretched arm. The Red Snapper was pointing at the Dog Company guidon. Baby-san had wedged its staff firmly between the rice bags on top of the barricade.

"I'll have it taken down, sir," said Bayard.

"Leave it where it is," said the Red Snapper. "It reminds me—well, it doesn't make a goddamn bit of difference what it reminds me of. That was a different war. How you making out, young fellow? What sort of shape is your company in?"

"We've taken quite a few casualties today, sir. I've lost a platoon leader."

The Red Snapper waved an impatient hand. "Of course you've taken casualties. You've been in a fight, haven't you? A company isn't fighting unless it takes casualties. Tell me how many casualties you've got and I'll tell you how hard you've been fighting. That's a rule of thumb. Real casualties, that is. You send a man to the rear in this battalion and he better be able to show blood. Where's your first sergeant, young fellow?"

"Here, sir," said Havac. The Red Snapper peered around nearsightedly. "There you are, you Hunky sonuvabitch. What'd you think of this war we're having, Hunky?"

"I told the captain it'd be getting rougher when we got across the river, and it has."

"You call this rough?" rasped the Red Snapper. "The real fight's still to come. Wait till the Russians and Chinese get into it."

The battalion commander grunted a good-bye and climbed back into his jeep. His driver left off glaring at Bayard's headquarters group and got behind the wheel. The Red Snapper grunted again, and the jeep spun around in the street and roared off to the rear.

"You two are great buddies, aren't you?" said Bayard to Havac.

"He's been a great marine," said Havac evasively.

The battalion radio crackled. Almquist handed Bayard the handset. Dog Company was told to get to its collective feet and get forward to relieve a platoon of Easy Company. Dog Company shrugged itself into its shoulder straps, picked up its weapons, and shook itself out automatically into the familiar double column.

The sounds of the fighting up ahead had ceased. The evening was almost quiet. Far off to the left was the pumping sound of someone else's artillery supporting someone else's fight.

Dog Company went forward, past the gaping empty windows that stared vacantly onto the street, stepping over the scattered debris, judging from this flotsam with now professional acumen the degree of violence in the fight of Easy and Fox Companies.

They found Firebrand Easy One huddled beneath a rice-bag barricade—the duplicate, triplicate, quintuplicate of the rice-bag barricades that intersected the street every hundred yards or so. Firebrand Easy One was a lieutenant. Bayard didn't know his name. The lieutenant's eyes were glassy, and he was smiling a loose and idiotic grin.

"It's all yours, Captain," he said. "This is as far as we got. There's a bridge just in front of us, and the street makes an angle just past the bridge. We couldn't get around that bend. We tried, but we couldn't get around the bend. I used up half my platoon, but we couldn't get past the bridge."

Tears welled out of the lieutenant's eyes and coursed a muddy streak down his dirt-caked cheeks. "Christ knows, we tried, Captain. I used up half my platoon. I only got twenty-four men left."

Bayard waited in uncomfortable silence.

Firebrand Easy One dragged a filthy dungaree sleeve across his eyes and nose. "Christ, Captain, you don't want to hear my troubles. I guess this is as far as we go tonight. You're to organize in the center of the battalion position to take care of this roadblock. Protect the bridge. The Reds are supposed to have tanks. Fox Company is up there on the right. The rest of Easy Company is on your left. If you're ready to take over, I'll be getting back to Easy Company."

Bayard looked around, tentatively planning his dispositions. The street was a wide one—perhaps fifty yards from gutter to gutter. It was surfaced with stone paving blocks and had a double set of streetcar tracks running down the center of it. The buildings on each side of the street were solidly built. The short concrete bridge to his front was a railroad overpass. The street took a sharp turn to the right just beyond the bridge and sloped upward out of sight, defiladed by the buildings.

While Bayard was talking to the Easy Company lieutenant, Thompson had come up with the 2d Platoon and had taken over the positions behind the rice bags. Bayard climbed experimentally to the top of the barricade. Two bullets in quick succession thwacked into the rice bags. Bayard slid back down.

"Okay, Lieutenant. We've got it. You stand relieved."

Firebrand Easy One grinned wearily and slipped his carbine strap over his shoulder. "Wish you luck, Captain. Come on, Easy One, let's go."

The twenty-four remaining members of the 1st Platoon, Company E, 2d Battalion, formed up and trudged rearward after their lieutenant.

"Where in the fuck are you goin'?" demanded a member of the 2d Platoon, Dog Company.

"Piss on you," answered a big, raw-boned BAR man.

Bayard summoned his platoon leaders to the barricade. "It'll be dark before long," he told them. "We'll have to organize in a hurry. The 2d Platoon will stay in position here in the center covering the road. Reynolds, I want you to put most of your LMGs in support of Thompson. If you can't find enough firing positions in the street, try the first floor of some of these buildings. Maybe behind some of those broken-out shop windows. Naheghian, you and the 3d Platoon, I want you to slide over and make contact with Easy Company on our left. Martinez, you tie in with Fox on our right."

Bayard looked around for his mortar section leader. "Burdock, you got a firing position?"

"Yes, sir, right over there behind that building."

"Good. How much ammunition do you have?"

"I got a jeep-trailer full. Pretty near a unit of fire."

"Well, send the jeep to the rear and get some more. I expect we'll need it."

Bayard switched his attention to Agnelli, the company gunnery sergeant. "Gunny, they say the NKs have tanks somewheres in the city. You take charge of the rocket launchers tonight. I wish we had something heavier, but we'll have to make do with what we've got."

They had all heard the disquieting rumor, which had come up from the south, that the antitank rockets wouldn't penetrate the armor of the Soviet T-34 medium tank. Dog Company had not yet been called upon to test the truth of the rumor.

The platoon and section leaders disappeared into the gathering gloom, setting the component parts of the human machine that was Dog Company into motion, accomplishing the simple and complex tasks of a rifle company preparing for a night defense. In the ten days since Inchon, they had become experts in these matters.

Bayard radioed Major Mansell, told him that he was in position, and asked for some heavier weapons for the roadblock. Mansell told him that a platoon from Weapons Company was on its way.

It was already dark when the lieutenant from Firebrand William arrived with a section of heavy machine guns, a section of rocket launchers, and a pair of 75mm recoilless rifles from the regimental antitank company.

"I hear you're a little nervous about the tanks," said the Weapons Company lieutenant. Bayard thought his tone condescending.

"You think you can stop a T-34, Lieutenant?"

"There's a trick to it," said the lieutenant. "The trick is to hit them. You got to wait until they get close. If you hit them they stay hit. That's what they tell me."

"All right, son"—the choice of the word *son* was deliberate on Bayard's part—"put your people into position and we'll see what they can do."

Gibson came up. "I got a truckload of rations and ammunition parked about a quarter-mile back. The property sergeant's with it."

"Good," said Bayard, "tell the platoons to send back their carrying parties."

Gibson passed the word over the sound-powered phones that the wiremen had already run to the platoon positions. Bayard looked contemplatively at his executive officer.

"Do you feel it?"

"What do you mean?"

"I don't know. It's like electricity in the air. Everything is all charged up. Know what I mean?"

"I think I do," said Gibson. "It's like in the last war before you got hit with a *banzai* charge. You'd feel the little bastards coming before you could see or hear them."

"You ever get hit by tanks?"

"Only once. On Guam. They gave us a hard time outside of Agat before we stopped them. But they were Jap tanks. Nothing as good as these Russian jobs."

Baby-san came over and handed Bayard and Gibson each a ration can filled with hot coffee. "Want something to eat, Captain?" he asked.

"I don't think so. This will do fine."

It was eleven o'clock before Bayard was satisfied that he had done everything he could do to get his company ready for the night. He had ordered a 50 percent alert. Half of his company was on watch; the other half was supposed to be sleeping. He had no intention of sleeping himself. He did not bother to unroll his sleeping bag but lay down to rest with his head pillowed on his pack. His command post group was huddled behind the shelter of the rice-bag barricade. Close to hand was the EE-8 phone leading back to the battalion switchboard. The artillery forward observer had said it was not possible to direct fire from the level of the street and had gone up to the roof of one of the buildings to Bayard's rear. A pair of sound-powered phones tied his position to Bayard's CP.

Despite his intentions to stay awake, Bayard realized he must have dozed off, for suddenly Baby-san was shaking him. Major Mansell was on the EE-8 calling from the battalion command post a half-mile to the rear.

"You're to send a patrol to make contact with the 5th Marines," Bayard was told.

"We know where the 5th is," said Bayard. "They're a mile to our left front. They're in a firefight. We can see their tracers."

"Regiment has ordered us to make contact with them," said Mansell evenly.

"That's what I'm trying to tell you, Major," snapped Bayard. "A patrol couldn't possibly reach the 5th Marines. Half the NKs in the city are between us and them."

"That remains to be seen. You have your orders, Captain."

Mansell broke down the connection. Bayard was on the point of ringing him back but decided against it. He had his orders. He told Baby-san to follow him over to Thompson's position. He found the leader of the 2d Platoon in his sleeping bag but still awake.

"I want you to detail a fire team to make contact with the 5th Marines."

"A what?" Thompson's tone was incredulous.

"A fire team to patrol to the flank of the 5th Marines," repeated Bayard. "Contact is from right to left."

"Good Christ, Captain, a patrol couldn't get two hundred yards in that direction." Thompson gestured toward the north, where red and yellow ribbons of tracer laced the sky.

"You heard the orders, Thompson."

"But why us? Easy Company is on our left. Why shouldn't they do it?"

"Because Battalion told us to do it, that's why," said Bayard coldly. "Have the fire team report to me in fifteen minutes."

It was impossible to see Thompson's face in the dark. "Aye, aye, sir," he said, very formally.

Twelve minutes later, a corporal fire-team leader, a BAR man, and two riflemen presented themselves to Bayard at his position behind the barricade.

"What's your name, Corporal?" asked Bayard.

"Jones, sir." He was a slightly built marine. Bayard supposed him to be about nineteen.

Bayard inspected the patrol very carefully, almost ceremoniously. He wanted to communicate to the men in some way his concern for them. They were equipped very lightly; cloth caps—helmets were not suitable for night patrolling—individual weapons, and cartridge belts. All was correct.

"Very good, Corporal."

"Thank you, sir."

"Do you hear that firing off to our left front, Corporal?"

"Yes, sir."

"You're to patrol to that vicinity and make contact with the flank of the 5th Marines. You'll go straight out to the front for a thousand yards—better have one of your men count the paces—and then make a ninety-degree turn to the left and proceed until you make contact. You'll return by the same route."

"Aye, aye, sir."

"Any questions?"

"No, sir."

No questions, thought Bayard. Just do what you're told, even if it makes no sense.

"Well, then—take care of yourselves."

The patrol members picked up their weapons and moved out through the gap in the barricade. In seconds they had blended into the darkness of the night.

Bayard waited. No one was asleep in Dog Company's command group now. All were straining their ears for some telltale sound to mark the patrol's progress. Minutes passed. Then they heard an angry outbreak of rifle fire just on the other side of the bridge.

"They've been hit," said someone.

"I knew they wouldn't get beyond the bridge," said Havac.

Thompson appeared out of the darkness. "Let me take a squad out there, Captain, and help them out."

"No," said Bayard shortly.

"What chance do four of them have out there?" said Thompson.

"That's enough," said Bayard. "I think you better get back to your platoon."

The firing stopped as suddenly as it had started. It was as though a door had been opened and then slammed shut. The night in front of Dog Company was ominously silent.

"Well, I guess that finished them," said a quiet voice out of the darkness.

The telephone rang. Baby-san touched Bayard's arm and then handed him the receiver. "Telephone, sir. Conference call with Battalion."

Bayard held the receiver to his ear.

"Everybody on the line, sir," he heard the battalion operator say.

"This is an attack order." It was Major Mansell's voice. "The battalion jumps off at zero-one-three-zero hours. There will be a fifteen-minute artillery preparation at 0115. As soon as it lifts, we move out."

There was a heavy silence.

"Any questions?" asked Mansell sharply.

"What are the company objectives?" growled Beale, Easy Company's commander.

"Each company will attack straight ahead and keep going," said Mansell.

Bayard could not believe his ears. Mansell went by the book, and the book said that night attacks were made with a well-rehearsed plan and against limited and well-defined objectives.

"We'll be stopped in our tracks," prophesied Mason of Fox Company gloomily.

"An aerial observer has reported to Corps that the enemy's fleeing the city," said Mansell curtly. "Chances are there's nothing in front of you."

"I have a patrol out there," Bayard reminded Mansell. "They were in a firefight to my immediate front not three minutes ago."

"That could have been an isolated pocket," said Mansell.

"And what happens to my patrol—if they're still alive—during the artillery preparation?" pursued Bayard. "It will come right down on top of them."

"Fortunes of war," said Mansell. "They'll have to take their chances. We're wasting time, gentlemen."

"Give us a time check," asked Mason.

"When I say 'mark' the time will be exactly zero-one-zero-two."

There was a pause. Bayard cautiously turned on his blue-lensed flashlight and held its hooded light over his wristwatch.

"Mark," said Mansell.

Bayard's watch was a minute slow. He made the correction. The conference call was concluded and the wire connections broken down. Bayard reached for his sound-powered phones and told his platoon leaders of the impending attack. They listened in stunned silence. Bayard checked his watch again. It was now 1:08.

"I'm going up with the artillery FO to check his preparation fires," Bayard told Havac. "Almquist, you come with me."

Bayard, followed by his radioman, made his way back the fifty or so yards to the building where the artillery forward observer's party was set up. On the rooftop the artillery lieutenant told him that he planned to walk the fires right up the street beginning at the far end of the bridge.

"We still got a patrol out there," said Bayard.

"I know it," said the artillery observer grimly. "It's your choice, Captain. Either we shoot or we don't shoot."

Bayard watched the remaining minutes tick slowly across the face of his watch. At 0114 he called the roadblock.

"Any sign of the patrol?"

"Not a sign," reported Havac.

"Almost time," said the artillery observer.

Then from out in front of them there came a new sound, an unmistakable, clanking rumble and the accompanying roar of engines.

"Hear that?" yelled Bayard.

"Tanks," confirmed the artillery lieutenant.

"Tanks coming straight down the road toward you," yelled Bayard into the phone to Havac.

"We hear them," said Havac.

There was a muzzle flash from out in front of the roadblock, and a high-velocity shell slammed past Bayard. He threw himself down on his face. There was no explosion. Bayard stirred, looked around. The rooftop was clustered with huddled bodies. Bayard could not tell immediately if they were alive or dead. He got to his feet and cast wildly about him for the battalion radio. He stumbled over a body. It was Almquist's. The shell that had passed Bayard had cut Almquist nearly in half. The boy was crumpled over his SCR-300. Bayard rolled him aside and checked the radio. It was still working. He flashed a mechanized attack warning. His hands were sticky with Almquist's blood. He wiped them on his trousers.

"I've told the 105s to start shooting," said the artillery lieutenant, coming to life at Bayard's elbow. "All they have to do is pull the string. They're laid on the street."

From far to the rear came a rippling thunder like the banging together of a string of freight cars on a siding. The sky was filled with the sound of projectiles passing overhead, like the tearing of cloth greatly magnified. The shells began crashing down out in front.

"We were lucky they were all ready with the preparation," muttered the artillery lieutenant.

The tank gun that had opened the attack was still firing, the shells screaming overhead.

"He's got a range error and don't know it," said the artillery lieutenant. "We're safe up here as long as we stay low. He must have spotted us up here before it got dark. If that first round had been high-explosive instead of armor-piercing, we'd all be dead."

"We got to get some illumination," said Bayard. "We got to see what's going on out there. Can you get some illumination shells?"

"Mortars would be quicker," said the artillery lieutenant.

Bayard reached for the phone to the roadblock. "How are you making out?"

"We're still in business," said Havac.

"Call Burdock and tell him to put up some illumination."

"Aye, aye, sir."

Soon there was the *chungging* pop of the 60s putting up their flares. Swinging down from their parachutes, the flares sent long black shadows dancing eerily across the front. In stark silhouette Bayard could see the lumbering shapes of the enemy armor coming down the street toward them.

"I got some white phosphorus on the way," said the artillery lieutenant. "Maybe we can set those buildings on fire and get some more light that way."

Major Mansell was on the phone. "What's hitting you? What's your estimate?"

"I think there's a battalion of infantry out there and maybe twelve or fourteen tanks. We need something heavier than 105s to stop them."

"You got three battalions of 105s shooting for you now," said Major Mansell. "And you're going to get a battalion of 155s."

Mansell rang off. Bayard tried to call the roadblock once again. He could not raise an answer. The line must have been cut by shellfire.

"I'm going down to the street," Bayard told the artillery observer. "Have your wireman trace that wire or lay a new line. And keep the artillery shooting. Don't let them stop."

He left the rooftop, scrambled down the stairs and across the street to the barricade.

The leading enemy tank had reached the bridge approaches. The heavy machine guns from the roadblock were engaging it, their tracers pinging off the armor plate in a cascade of orange sparks. Bayard caught a glimpse of the Weapons Company lieutenant pacing back and forth behind his weapons, shouting fire commands. One of the 75mm recoilless rifles fired; the back blast nearly stunned the Dog Company members closest to it. The North Korean tank crept through the converging fires and onto the bridge. A second tank came around the bend and moved into the position vacated by the first tank at the far end of the bridge.

Behind the tanks the white phosphorus shells and illuminating flares did their work. The whole city seemed to be in flames, a bright red-yellow backdrop for the dark encroaching shapes of the enemy armor. In the lurid light Bayard saw the Weapons Company lieutenant step out into the street, forward of the barricade, with a rocket launcher on his shoulder. The first tank was almost to the rice-bag barricade. Its 85mm gun was firing at pointblank range. Somewhere in the black shadows a wounded man was screaming.

With a roaring *shusshh*, the lieutenant's rocket launcher stabbed its flaming finger at the turret of the lead tank. There was a half-muffled explosion; the 85mm gun canted crazily skyward. A second rocket burst against the treads of the tank. The T-34 spun half around and then clanked to a halt. The turret hatch opened. A flame spouted up from inside the vehicle. The gunner got half way out of the turret when a gust of small arms fire caught him and tumbled him back into the burning hull.

There was a new sound in the night—the sharp stutter of submachine guns as the assault waves of enemy infantry attempted to close. They came up in front of Dog Company, black shapes hardly distinguishable from the dancing black shadows cast by the inferno on the other side of the bridge. Dog Company switched its attention to the new threat. Burdock's mortars shortened range until their shells were bursting just on the other side of the rice bags. The 105s kept up their drum fire on the bridge and street. The heavier 155s were seeking the tanks with their more deliberate, more accurate fire. A shell caught the second tank where it had paused at the far end of the bridge, turning it into a funeral pyre for its entrapped crew. A BAR man close to Bayard cursed and hammered at the magazine of his weapon, attempting to clear a jam. The piece continued to fail to fire. Bayard gave the BAR man his pistol.

Baby-san was pulling at his arm, holding out the sound-powered phone that linked them to the artillery observer.

"The FDC asks if they can stop firing," said the artillery lieutenant. "They say the tubes are so hot they're ready to melt."

"Okay," said Bayard, "I think we've broken the back of this one. But tell them not to change the lay of the guns."

The barrage fire of the 105s slackened and then stopped. The night was quieting down.

"I think it's all over," said Bayard. "Where's that Weapons Company lieutenant?"

"He was hit," said Baby-san. "The corpsman's working on him."

Pilnick was holding up a plasma bottle at arm's length. The rubber tube led down to the supine body of the lieutenant. Bayard knelt down to hear the lieutenant's husking whisper: "I told you, Captain. All you got to do is hit them."

Bayard looked questioningly at the corpsman. "He'll be all right," said Pilnick. "But he's lost a lot of blood, and we got to get him out of here."

"What kind of casualties did we take?" asked Bayard.

"I don't know how many. The first sergeant is trying to get a head count now. It don't look too bad."

"That's good," said Bayard. "We'll have enough left if they want to try it again."

But the big fight of the night was over. Still, sporadic outbursts of firing broke out as the night wore to a close, by edgy machine gunners and riflemen who thought they heard sounds of a renewed assault building up in front of them. And from somewhere out there, a 76mm self-propelled gun kept up a persistent fire that sent its high velocity shells screaming over Dog Company's heads. The artillery FO registered on it for counterbattery fire, and the 76mm was abruptly silenced.

The night was coming to an end. The flames of the burning buildings to the front were dying down and giving way to the gray light of predawn.

"There's somebody out there," called a rifleman. "Out there by the burned-out tank."

"Don't fire," yelled someone else. "They're our guys."

They came across the bridge, ghostly in the thin light, Corporal Jones and his fire team. Bayard went out in front of the roadblock to meet them. "I never expected—where in the hell have you been?"

Corporal Jones's dirty face split into a grin. "Well, we didn't get to the 5th Marines, Captain. We was under a bridge. When I heard the NKs coming, I thought we better get out of the way. The whole frigging attack rolled right over us."

Jones looked about him approvingly. "Looks like old Dog Company had themselves a real fight."

chapter twelve...

The night attack had been Dog Company's last violent action in the city. The next morning when their patrols were sent out, they found no enemy in front of them.

Three days later, General MacArthur had reinstalled President Syngman Rhee in his capital, and Dog Company was on the road leading north from Seoul to Pyongyang. The company was in high spirits. It was good to be marching again, free of the city with its filth. When they reached Pyongyang, the war would be over because that city was the North Korean capital. "No contact" was the word—no contact with the enemy anywhere in the division zone. The broken remnant of the North Korean army had disappeared into the hills. Some said they were racing for the sanctuary of the Manchurian border, where there was a river called the Yalu.

Dog Company swung along at an easy three miles an hour. A hill ahead of them, marked with a circle on Bayard's map, was the company's immediate objective—Hill 131. One hundred thirty-one meters high—that would be just about four hundred feet. Dog Company was to occupy it. On the right and left of Hill 131 were other hills uncircled on Bayard's map, objectives for other letter companies. Linked together with patrols and supporting fire plans, these company strong points would form a line defending the northern approaches to Seoul.

The road was strewn with the destroyed dark green armor and transport of the North Koreans. Air and artillery had done that, along with the Reds' own frantic haste to escape. Already American bulldozers were nudging the wreckage aside.

The battalion radio crackled an order to halt the column. Bayard raised his arm and shouted, and Dog Company shuffled to a stop. The more curious, or cautious, faced outward from the double column, peering suspiciously at the houses and dooryards fenced in with bundled brush—likely places for a sniper left behind or a lingering light machine gun. A larger number of marines flopped down in their tracks, willing to accept unquestioningly any rest.

Bayard did not entirely trust the countryside. He told his platoon leaders to set out security and to detail fire teams to search each of the houses bordering the road. This order given, he sat down in the ditch that edged the highway. He was tired. When you were thirty, a pack rode more heavily on your back than when you were twenty. He wondered if the break would be long enough to make it worthwhile to take the damned thing off. The pack straps were cutting into his shoulders. His arms were numb from lack of circulation.

A trickle of muddy water ran along the bottom of the ditch. Some of Dog Company, thirsty from the long march in the heat of the afternoon, filled their canteens. The careful ones added halazone tablets from their C ration accessory packets. Others, eluding the watchful eyes of the platoon sergeants, drank the water raw. Later some of them would pass long parasitic worms, to the disgust and consternation of Dr. Goldberg, the battalion surgeon.

Bayard tried leaning back so that the grassy bank of the ditch took the weight of the pack off his shoulders. It was an uncomfortable position, so after a few experimental shifts of his seating arrangement, he slipped his arms free of the pack straps.

He undid the flap of his haversack and fished around inside to see what he had in the way of rations. He found a can of sausage patties and remembered that he had traded the first sergeant, who did not think highly of sausage patties, a can of pork and beans for two cans of sausage. Bayard's one-burner camp stove dangled from a pack strap. He unfastened the strap, set the stove up, and was pumping the plunger to build up pressure when Baby-san came toward him, leading a small girl by the hand.

"I found her near one of them houses yonder," said his runner. "I guess her folks hid her there. She was in one of them root cellars."

"You better take her back," said Bayard. "Her people will be looking for her after we pass."

"I don't think so," said Baby-san. "There's nobody in none of them houses. Jim Kim says they were all run off by the Reds."

Bayard put down the gasoline stove and his unopened can of sausage patties. He took the child by the arms and stood her in front of him so that he could study her face. She looked like an Oriental doll, with her bangs cut straight across her forehead and her eyes like chips of black glass. She was dressed in baggy black breeches and a short red jacket. Red, Bayard remembered, was the "happiness" color.

The inevitable circle of curious marines ringed itself around the child.

"Talk to her, Jim," said Bayard, singling out his interpreter. "See what you can find out about her and her family."

"She a Chinese girl," said Jim Kim. "Not Korean. My Chinese not so good, but I try to talk to her."

Gradually Jim Kim drew some answers from the child. "Her name Mei-ling. She five years old. Soldiers come last night. They take her mama and papa away. She say she very hungry."

Bayard had nothing to give the child to eat except the cold sausage patties. They seemed too greasy for a five-year-old's stomach. "Who's got something she can eat?" he asked.

"I got some peaches," said Baby-san. He took a half-size ration can of peaches from his jacket pocket and from another pocket pulled out a plastic spoon. He opened the peaches. "Here, kid," he said, "try these."

The little girl fixed her eyes solemnly on the peaches and obediently opened her mouth. Baby-san very carefully fed her the canned fruit. "I got a kid sister at home," he said. "That's how I know how this is done."

When the peaches were gone, Mei-ling continued to stare at the plastic spoon.

"I think she's still hungry," said Baby-san. "Any you guys got anything else she could eat?"

"Maybe she just wants the spoon," suggested Pilnick. "Try giving it to her."

Baby-san held out the spoon, and Mei-ling's grimy little hand closed quickly around it.

"I guess she never saw nothing like it before," said Baby-san.

"Captain," interrupted Havac, "we better get going. The rest of the battalion is moving out."

Bayard nodded reluctantly and Havac let out with a stentorian blast: "Aw right, Dog Comp'ny! Saddle up!"

The company stirred itself and reformed into double column.

"What about the little girl?" asked Baby-san. "We can't just leave her."

"Do you think we could find some Korean family hereabouts to take her?" Bayard asked Kim dubiously.

"A Chinese baby? A girl?" Jim Kim's tone was incredulous. "Nobody want her."

"Let's take her with us," said Baby-san.

"A rifle company is no goddamn place for a kid," said First Sergeant Havac.

"We can't just leave her here by the road," argued Baby-san.

Bayard looked at Havac questioningly. Havac massaged the blunt features of his face with the palm of his hand.

"Aw, hell," he said to Baby-san, "gimme your BAR. You carry the kid."

The column moved out again toward Hill 131. When they got to the place where they were to turn off the road, Three-Able from the battalion operations section was waiting for them.

"There's your position," pointed the lieutenant. "The Old Man wants you to be sure to get dug in good."

"Dug in?" questioned Bayard, half sarcastically, half derisively. "What for? Isn't the war supposed to be over? Isn't that what they're saying in Tokyo?"

"The Red Snapper doesn't give a fuck what they're saying in Tokyo," said the lieutenant with an understanding grin. "He says to get dug in good."

"All right," said Bayard. "I wouldn't know how to sleep on top of the ground anyway. Let's go, Dog Company!"

It was a green hill, made that way by the Japanese with their reforestation program. The pine trees were evenly spaced, and the terraced hill was almost parklike. Close to the crest it was girdled by a North Korean trench. The clay parapet made a raw orange line against the dull green. Aside from this, there was no sign of war. The trench appeared deserted. The afternoon seemed perfectly peaceful. But somehow Bayard felt there was something wrong with the hill. He sent a squad-sized patrol forward to sound it out while the rest of Dog Company waited.

"I don't know what it is," said Bayard to Havac. "But there's something not right about the crest of that hill."

It was almost dusk. Bayard followed the progress of his patrol as best he could with his field glasses. The squad disappeared and reappeared as it made its way upward along the trail through the young growth of pines. Bayard saw them reach the trench. No sounds of firing came down to the waiting main body of Dog Company, but the patrol stood on the parapet of the trench for only an instant before falling back.

"Something *is* wrong up there," growled Havac. Bayard fixed his field glasses on the sergeant squad leader. The man was making a circling motion over his head with his hand and arm.

"He wants us to join him," said Bayard.

Dog Company's little headquarters entourage—the first sergeant, the gunnery sergeant, the corpsman, the radioman, the interpreter, the runner, and the captain—began the climb.

The sickening stench reached them while they were still a good way from the top of the hill. Bayard looked at Havac. "Do you know what I think it is?"

Havac nodded grimly. "I haven't smelled that smell since Okinawa. There must be a lot of them up there."

The squad leader met them fifty yards below the trench. His face, under its sunburn and dirt, was strained and pale. "Captain," he said, speaking with difficulty, "that trench is full of dead people. Not soldiers but civilians—mostly women and children."

Bayard and his headquarters went on up to the parapet. It was as the sergeant had said. The trench was packed with tumbled bodies. They had been machine-gunned, doused with gasoline, and burned. A buzzing, green cloud of flies boiled up and then settled back down on the decayed and roasted flesh. Bayard fumbled for his handkerchief. There were men, women, and children, all ages, all indiscriminately and horribly jumbled together. How many were there? Bayard's reeling mind could make no estimate. Hundreds? Thousands?

The taste of vomit rose in Bayard's throat. He swallowed hard to keep from being sick and stepped back from the trench. "Don't bring the little girl any closer," he called back to Baby-san.

Her mother and father might be somewhere in that anonymous pile of blackened flesh, he told himself. Jim Kim was standing silently at his elbow.

"Why do you suppose they did this?" Bayard asked him.

"When the enemy leave Seoul, he take with him all Christians he can find," said Jim Kim. "All friends of Americans. These must be some of those people."

"They could do this to these people just for being Christians? Or friends of the Americans? I can't believe it."

"It easier for me to believe," said Jim Kim.

I suppose it is, thought Bayard soberly. By degrees he had learned Jim Kim's history. His father had been a member of the National Assembly. Young Kim had been a cadet in the Republic of Korea's military academy, but his education had been cut short by the events of the summer. In the general mobilization he was detailed to one of the new regiments as a sergeant. His unit lasted only three days in action against the North Koreans. Kim Kai Kyung made the mistake of slipping back into Seoul. He learned that his father had been taken away by the insurgent communists. One of his neighbors informed the Red authorities that the son was in the city. Now, as a consequence, his grandmother and sister were dead.

There were other Koreans with Dog Company and more would join—with and without official sanction—as interpreters, ammunition carriers, line crossers, clothes washers, and latrine diggers. Kim Chang Shaw, Chong Kyung Wan, Lim In Hup, Pak Su Yong, Lee Nai Chun—names that to Bayard had the sound of corks popping from a bottle or perhaps the distant rattle of a machine gun. But of all these and the others to come, Jim Kim was the undisputed chief and unofficial lieutenant of Dog Company's Korean irregulars.

"All right," said Bayard heavily to his headquarters, "you've seen it. Now get back."

To Havac he said: "We can't do anything about it tonight. It's too late. Tomorrow we'll get the graves registration people or somebody up here. You take the company headquarters back to that leveled-off place with the grave mounds. We'll make that our CP and mortar position. I'm going to put the 1st and 2d Platoons on the forward slope and the 3d Platoon to cover our left flank and rear. We don't need to organize the crest."

With practiced efficiency and in avoidance of the grisly trench, Dog Company readied itself for the night. With a molelike instinct they buried themselves into the hill. They dug their fighting holes, their sleeping holes, and their straddle trenches.

On the next day the people from the city started coming to the hill. Led by an old man and two old women, they made their slow and painful way to the crest. The old man was dressed in shabby Western-style clothing. There was a defeated sag in his shoulders. He was carrying a rudely fashioned wooden cross.

"I know that old man," said Jim Kim. "He was a teacher in the Presbyterian School."

The persons who came out from the city were mostly old. The war had taken away the young. These were the families and the friends of the dead in the trench, and now that Dog Company was securely in position, they had come forward to identify, if they could, the scorched and rotting bodies.

A sanitary detail had also arrived and spread lime and DDT on the remains. Those corpses that weren't carried away by their friends were buried where they lay by volunteers from Dog Company.

Only the most callous or the most compassionate would undertake that job, thought Bayard as he watched the twenty-man working party march with its shovels and pickaxes toward the crest. He saw among them the tall figure of Kusnetzov, distinctive with its blue watch cap and black beard.

Three days passed. Dog Company added small luxuries to its position on Hill 131. Sleeping holes were roofed over with shelter-halves and ponchos. Lean-tos were built of cardboard or corrugated iron hauled up from the valley. There was no tactical activity now except for contact patrols sent out to the friendly units to their front and flanks. The word being passed from mouth to mouth was that the Army was going to push an armored task force through the Marine main line of resistance. The road north led to Pyongyang. Occupation of Red Korea's capital would be the act of American victory.

"Just like when Grant took Richmond," Pilnick needled the rebel Baby-san. You took Richmond, and the war was over. You took Berlin, and the war was over. That's the way it was.

G-2 estimated that only broken remnants of the North Korean People's Army, defeated in the south and trying to filter back to the north, guerrilla-fashion, were in the division's zone of responsibility.

The nights were growing colder, but the days were pleasant and Dog Company was content to lie on the parapets of its foxholes and soak up the warmth of the sun. The company command post was on a grassy shelf cut into the hillside, and Bayard, with Baby-san's help, had developed a very fine hole, insulated with pine twigs and covered with a piece of army tarpaulin. At night, Bayard slept warm and if he wanted to read or write, he had the light of a candle stuck into a reflector made of a shiny ration can.

Mei-ling, the Chinese child, was still with them. Bayard and Dog Company believed with increasing certainty that her mother and father were among those horribly anonymous and unidentified remains that had been dusted with quicklime and buried where they lay in the trench. At first Mei-ling had grieved for her lost mother and father, but already her sorrow seemed to be fading. She responded to the affection and attention of the marines, adapting quickly to the routine of the company headquarters. Pilnick and Baby-san—the one having two young daughters in Baltimore, the other having a young sister in North Carolina—shared the details of her care.

She was a bright, unendingly inquisitive child. Of greatest attraction to her was the brown C ration box that was each man's daily allowance of food. She remained fascinated by the shiny tin-plated cans and the unbelievably good things that came out of them—the canned fruits, the sweet cookies, the cocoa, and the chocolate candy.

And she had never gotten over her first love for the clear plastic spoons. She accumulated a sizable collection of them. It became almost a ritual for each marine in company headquarters, as he finished his meal, to solemnly lick his spoon clean and pass it to Mei-ling. She would put each one carefully to bed with the others in an empty ration box. She treated them like little people, and the Spoon Family was a fast-multiplying breed.

Dog Company could see great activity taking place down in the valley below Hill 131. The engineers moved in with their heavy equipment. The old road was widened, straightened, and resurfaced to handle the traffic of a main supply route. The regimental command post was down there, a busy little village of dull brown tents. The quartermasters had staked out their claims for their supply points. Daily the pyramids of ammunition and tarpaulin-covered stacks of rations grew taller. More and more artillery filled each available battery position. First, the light battalions, the 105s, their snub, well-greased barrels glinting in the sun. Then the heavier 155s, the same in silhouette, more emphatic in authority. Finally, the eight-inch howitzers, army weapons brought up for long-range counter-battery.

The men of Dog Company watched all this from their aerie. The high ground remained their unchallenged domain. The supporting artillery, the rear echelons, and the service elements might usurp and encroach upon every square inch of the valley floor, but the hard-won hills remained the province of the infantry.

chapter thirteen...

Pinky, the company clerk, proudly announced a mail call, and for the first time since the landing at Inchon, there were packages for Dog Company. Bayard received a carefully wrapped fifth of Scotch and three letters from Donna. They were crisp and knowing letters filled with Washington gossip, and like Donna, they were clever, well-turned, and brightly polished.

"Judd Benson has gone back to his old firm in New York," she wrote. "He and Mary have closed up the Connecticut Avenue apartment. They didn't call before leaving. Apparently he still hasn't forgiven you. . . ."

Well, Bayard was sorry about that, because, after all, he still owed Judd a great deal. If it hadn't been for Judd, he would never have met Donna. But, for that matter, if it hadn't been for the Marine Corps and the alphabetical proximity of the names Bayard and Benson, he wouldn't have gotten to know Judd.

In 1943 they had gone through Candidates Class and then Reserve Officers Course together. They had been in the same squad and had shared a wall locker and a double-decked bunk. Bayard had had the top rack and Judd the bottom. In their twenty weeks of living so close together at Quantico, they had come to know each other very well.

Judd was older than Bayard. He was twenty-six when he came to Quantico, already a graduate of Yale Law School and a member of the bar. He admitted he could have gotten a direct commission in the Navy or the Army as a legal specialist, but he had chosen to go after a line commission in the Marines. Bayard had asked him why.

"Because I wanted to," said Judd, smiling his crooked, open yet enigmatic smile. He had the lean patrician features and the easy manners that reflected generations of money and breeding. The Bensons were of Nyack, Bar Harbor, and Palm Beach.

When they graduated from Reserve Officers Course, Judd had gone off to join the 1st Marine Division at Cape Gloucester, where in good time he was the recipient of a Silver Star, a Purple Heart, and a worse-than-usual case of malaria.

They had not seen each other after Quantico. For a while they had written, but gradually they lost touch. It was five years later and George was teaching in Baltimore, when one day he received the telephone call: "This is your old Quantico bunkie, Judd Benson. I saw your name on a list of reserve officers in the Washington area. What in the hell are you doing with yourself?"

"I'm with a boy's school—St. Swithins," said George. "Ever hear of it?" he added somewhat diffidently.

"I think I have," said Judd. From his tone, Bayard knew that he hadn't.

"It's a rather bad copy of an English public school, I'm afraid. We have forms instead of classes, masters instead of teachers, that sort of thing."

Bayard heard Benson's well-remembered chuckle. "I just don't see you in the role of Mr. Chips, old man. How did you get sucked into that?"

"Well, I had to do something," said Bayard defensively. "I couldn't live on the GI Bill forever. As it was, I stretched it out as long as I could. After I was released to inactive duty, I went to Princeton for graduate work. Remember we talked about that? I even managed a summer at the Sorbonne. But what about you? I thought you were with that law firm in New York."

"I still am—in a way. But they have a new policy under which they lend out their bright young men to the government for a year or two. Sort of an internship. I'm with the FSIA."

"Oh," said Bayard.

"You don't know what that is?"

"I'm afraid not. Should I?"

"The FSIA, my friend, is the State Department's Foreign Services Information Agency. It does international public relations. It's an outgrowth of the old OWI. You remember the Office of War Information. Amongst other things, we sit on top of the Voice of Democracy. You've heard of that?"

"Of course," said George. He was vaguely aware that the Voice of Democracy was a Radio Free Europe sort of thing.

"Well, now that we know where each other is, we'll have to get together," said Judd.

"Sure thing," said Bayard, and he took down Judd's Washington address.

Judd told him that he would be expecting to hear from him.

After the conversation was finished, Bayard put down the receiver and looked around at his furnished apartment with mixed feelings. His first year at St. Swithins he had been required to live in as a dormitory warden, but the second year he had found this room-and-bath on Charles Street near Mt. Vernon Place. He had added to the furnishings a few knickknacks he had brought back from China and had hung on the walls the lithographs and the reproductions of the French moderns he had gotten in Paris. He had thought that the apartment had a certain charm, but all of a sudden it looked affected and shoddy.

Judd Benson always had had a way of making him feel uncomfortable and counterfeit.

The next Sunday he drove to Washington in his secondhand Ford convertible and looked up the address Judd had given him. It turned out that the Bensons lived in a very glossy apartment house on Connecticut Avenue. Judd answered the door and seemed a little taken aback to see him. George went into the apartment with the feeling that he should have telephoned first.

The first fifteen minutes were spent in an awkward three-cornered conversation with Judd hurling verbal cues at his wife: "Darling, George is the one at Quantico who . . ."

But it was obvious that Mary had never heard of him, and she did not particularly trouble herself to conceal the fact. Bayard disliked her instantly. Begrudgingly he admitted to himself that she was pretty in a robust, horsy sort of way and was probably an excellent and enlightened mother to the young Bensons—of whom there were two, a boy and a girl, aged four and two.

Bayard doggedly spent an hour with the Bensons. They did not insist that he stay longer. He then went off to have dinner alone at a seafood place on Maine Avenue. It was a restaurant he had gone to frequently as a second lieutenant at Quantico. Eating alone in these nostalgic surroundings only increased the disturbed, dissatisfied feeling he had carried away from the Bensons. He told himself angrily that there was no reason for his dissatisfaction. He was not being fair to himself to compare his prospects with those of a well-connected Yale law graduate. Bayard wished he had stayed in Baltimore and spent the day with Sandra.

Except that Sandra was getting to be a little too much of a good thing.

She was the headmaster's secretary. During the war she had suddenly married a bomber pilot, and after the war she had become, just as suddenly, unmarried. With a little chemical assistance she was very blonde, and she had a figure that was a little overdone. She was really much too glittering an ornament for a headmaster's office.

George had lured her into the Mt. Vernon Place apartment with practically no difficulty at all. On their third date she spent the night with him. After that, it became regular. At first it was one night a week, then two, and then up to three.

The whole arrangement was becoming disturbingly domestic, with Sandra making cocoa and playing records while he graded papers and got together his lesson outlines. She even insisted on getting up first in the morning to make coffee and cook his bacon and eggs. He would not have had this Sunday afternoon free except that she had gone off to visit with her mother, who lived in Frederick.

After the Sunday in question, Bayard did not call the Bensons again, and he did not really expect to hear from them. He was therefore quite surprised two months later to receive a small square envelope with a card inviting him to cocktails at the Connecticut Avenue apartment, from five to seven on Saturday next.

When Sandra learned he was going, she asked very pointedly why he wasn't taking her. He had no good reason to give her. He wasn't quite sure himself. Sandra was a little conspicuous, particularly when she had a couple of drinks. Probably, he didn't want Mary Benson eyeing her in that coldly superior way, guessing at their relationship.

The Benson apartment had looked large and commodious at the time of Bayard's first visit. It looked less so with fifty or so persons crowding the living room and overflowing into the foyer, the dining ell, and even the bedrooms.

George was greeted warmly at the door by Judd, a martini on-the-rocks in a water tumbler was pressed into his hand; he was introduced to a tall, red-headed man who was either in the Navy or a civilian in the Navy Department; and then Judd was off to meet some other arriving guest.

After some moments of an ambiguous exchange of pleasantries with the tall, red-headed man—who somehow seemed to think that *Bayard* was in the Navy or in the Navy Department—George espied Mary Benson at the opposite end of the room and disengaged himself from the red-headed man under the pretext that he must pay his respects to the hostess.

A barrier of elbows and backs filled the twenty-foot interval separating him from Mary. He sought to avoid a collision course by going around the outer edges of the room. This tactic might have worked except that a foursome reemerging from the dining-ell pressed him back into a cul-de-sac formed by an end table and a club chair. It was while he was looking around wildly for an escape route that he first saw Donna. She was sitting on the arm of the club chair.

His first fleeting impression was that her crossed legs looked mighty fine, with a nice contrast between the very full calf and the slender ankles.

"Hello," she said, "I don't think we've met. I'm Donna Wilson."

"I'm George Bayard."

"Who are you with?"

"Oh, no one," he said. "I'm alone."

She laughed. "I meant here in town. Are you in government?"

"No, I teach at a boy's school in Baltimore." He looked at her left hand. There was no wedding band. "What do you do?"

"I work on the Hill."

"That must be interesting," said George. By this time he understood enough of the Washington patois to know that she meant that she worked for Congress. Nearly everyone at the party was in government, and if you were in government, you were either with the administration or on the Hill. Most of the guests were in State because Judd Benson was in State.

Sometime between eight and nine the party began to thin out, and George asked Donna to have dinner with him. They went to Napoleon's, which was close by. He found her attractive and very easy to talk to.

About midnight he drove her home and found that she lived alone in a doll-sized house in Georgetown. She invited him in for coffee, and it was while she was making the coffee and he was prowling about the miniature living room that he saw the picture on the mantel and recognized the iron gray forelock and the steel-rimmed glasses that the political cartoonists loved to accentuate.

Donna had come in with the coffee.

"This is Senator Wilson," said George, holding the picture.

"Yes," said Donna.

"You're related to him?" asked George.

"He's my father," affirmed Donna.

"You must think me awfully stupid for not knowing that," said George.

"No," she said, "I don't think that at all. Do you take cream and sugar?"

Senator Wilson, Bayard knew, had come to Washington in the early days of the Roosevelt administration. He had a reputation for being an opinionated, forceful man who was not always amenable to party discipline. He had a large and vociferous following not only in his own state but throughout the Midwest. There were rumors, no doubt carefully planted and cultivated, that he could be his party's nominee in the 1952 presidential elections.

On the next Sunday, Bayard had seen Donna again, and on the Sunday following that, and then it became a matter of every weekend. She was a good-looking, intelligent girl—that was part of it. But Bayard had to admit to himself that even more of the attraction lay in the fact of her being the senator's daughter. He learned that she lived alone in Georgetown because she preferred being by herself rather than with her mother and the senator in the big place out in Chevy Chase. It gave her an independence and a sense of detachment. Nevertheless she was devoted to her father and very much a part of his public career. She had been his secretary since her graduation from George Washington, where she had majored in political science and minored in journalism.

Meanwhile matters came to a head between Bayard and Sandra. He no longer bothered to give her any reason or excuse for his frequent trips to Washington. From someone, she had found out about Donna. She did not take it well. She threatened to see the St. Swithins headmaster.

"And what would you tell him?" asked Bayard. "That you have been sleeping with me on an average of twice a week for the last year? That might fix me, but it wouldn't do you any good, would it?"

Sandra, after much talk, of course did nothing. But it would be an awkward and embarrassing situation, seeing her every day at the school. It would have been much easier on both of them if she were a good sport about the whole thing.

The Sunday following the blowup with Sandra, he and Donna went to the zoo in Rock Creek Park. It was a crisp cold day, and they stopped in at the zoo's restaurant for a cup of coffee.

"Something's the matter with you," said Donna. "You've been preoccupied all afternoon. What is it?"

"Nothing," said Bayard. "Nothing really, except that I'm fed up with the school."

"You don't like it there at all, do you?"

"I thought I did at first but not anymore."

"Then why don't you make a change?"

"A change to what?"

"Oh, I don't know. Have you ever thought of going into government?"

Donna was eyeing him shrewdly. Bayard was careful, very careful, in the way he answered her question. Actually he had been thinking about going into government for some time, almost from the moment that he had found out that Donna was the senator's daughter. Specifically, the State Department. Her father's influence in that direction was well known.

He managed a self-deprecatory laugh.

"I used to think that I would like to go into the Foreign Service."

"Well, why not?" asked Donna. "Why don't you?"

"I really don't know how to go about it."

"There should be a way," said Donna. "We'll have to get to work on it."

As yet he had not met the senator. Donna, of course, made the arrangements. Ten days later, at her suggestion, Bayard presented himself at the senator's suite in the Senate Office Building for the interview. In introducing him to her father, Donna was crisply impersonal. From her tone he could have been any visiting constituent or job supplicant. Then, having played her role, she left them alone. The senator, in turn, wasted no time in getting to the point of the interview.

"My daughter tells me you are interested in getting a job with the government. You're interested in the diplomatic service?"

"Yes, sir."

Had they passed on the street, Bayard was not sure he would have recognized the senator. The thick gray hair and the steel-rimmed glasses were much less obtrusive than they appeared to be in the caricatures or even in the news photographs. What was more noticeable were the senator's eyes, shrewd and calculating, and the firm, determined mouth. There was no doubt that this was a powerful and purposeful man.

"What sort of a background do you have to offer?"

"Not much, I'm afraid, sir."

"Do you have a law degree?"

"No, sir. But I have a master's in history and government."

"What do you know about current European affairs?"

"As much as the average person. Maybe a little more. I try to keep abreast of what's going on."

"How old are you?"

"Twenty-nine, sir."

"You're a little late getting started. What is it you want from me? A job? A note to the State Department? What do you have in mind?"

"I'm not quite sure, sir. I wanted your advice, primarily."

Senator Wilson grunted. You could almost have called it a snort.

"Are you familiar with my subcommittee?"

"Yes, sir."

"Would you be interested in a temporary position on its staff?"

"Yes, sir. I would be very interested, sir."

"It won't pay much, and it will be temporary," warned the senator.

"I understand that, sir."

"When would you be able to begin?"

"As soon as the spring semester closes."

The senator reached for a blue memorandum pad. He took an old-fashioned thick-barreled black fountain pen from his vest pocket and unscrewed the cap.

"We have some special hearings beginning about then—the first week in June. Towards the end of the session we sometimes take on summer help. We also have sort of an intern program for law majors and political science graduates. I think we can work you in under that."

"I would appreciate it, sir."

The senator wrote a few lines on the memorandum blank. The point of the pen was broad and the ink was black.

"Give this to Colonel Ritchey—he's the chief counsel of my subcommittee. As I said, this is strictly temporary, so don't quit your teaching job. You may have to go back to it in September."

The senator pushed the completed memorandum across the desk, got to his feet, and held out his hand, signifying that the interview was over.

Bayard shook his hand. "Thank you, sir. I appreciate this."

"It's nothing," said the senator. "I expect you'll be worth your hire. If not, you won't be the first one."

Bayard found Colonel Ritchey in the office assigned to the permanent staff of the subcommittee. Ritchey had been the chief counsel of the subcommittee since 1923. He was now seventy-two, and he still wore the starched high collars with the rounded points in the style usually associated with Herbert Hoover.

Colonel Ritchey took the senator's memorandum and looked over the top of it at Bayard. He did not seem particularly impressed by what he saw. He asked for a résumé of Bayard's past experience.

Bayard supplied the colonel with the document forthwith, in a form that bore down heavily on the year he had spent in France. Colonel Ritchey seemingly remained unimpressed.

In 1918 Ritchey had commanded a National Guard regiment. He had arrived in the Meuse-Argonne as the last shots of the war were fired. He had last seen Europe in 1919, when he departed the Army of Occupation in Germany. In those earlier years he had formed all the necessary opinions he needed of Europe, and nothing that had transpired since had ever given him cause to revise them. Colonel Ritchey distrusted the British, disliked the French, despised the Italians, and detested the Russians. The lesser nations were beneath his notice.

"Well, very well," said Colonel Ritchey, dropping the memorandum onto his desk as though it had soiled his fingers. "I think the best thing you can do between now and the beginning of the hearings is to go over these old committee reports."

He gave Bayard a foot-high stack of committee reports. They were printed by the Government Printing Office on thin paper. When he got back to his Mt. Vernon Place apartment, Bayard exercised some elementary arithmetic and came up with an estimate that Colonel Ritchey had given him twelve-million words to read.

Bayard had not yet established tenure at St. Swithins Academy. His teaching contract was renewable annually, and in May he received the contract for the next year from the Board of Visitors. He did not have to return it immediately; actually he had until 15 July, which would have given him a month's trial period on the subcommittee staff. But he looked at the contract and saw that his salary was unimproved, and that fact persuaded him.

He took great satisfaction in writing across the face of the contract: "No thanks, other plans."

With the closing of the spring semester, Bayard vacated the Mt. Vernon Place apartment and moved into a furnished room on Maryland Avenue in the District of Columbia, within walking distance of the Senate Office Building. He hadn't read all of the twelve million words laid out for him by Colonel Ritchey, but at least he had perused enough of the committee transcripts to have a feel for the proceedings.

He learned from Colonel Ritchey that the special hearings were to investigate the Foreign Services Information Agency. Bayard thought it a coincidence that of all the myriad activities in the government, it should be Judd's agency that the senator's subcommittee was going to investigate. The coincidence became even more marked a few days later when Judd phoned, told Bayard that he had learned he had gone to work for the subcommittee, and invited him to lunch at the Occidental.

"What do you think of your new job?" asked Judd over the onion soup.

"I'm not sure," answered Bayard carefully. "I have a desk wedged between two filing cabinets. Every time I ask the colonel a question about what I'm supposed to be doing, he pushes another transcript at me to read."

"Don't underestimate the colonel," said Judd. "He may look and act like something out of President McKinley's cabinet, but he's been in this rat race a long, long time. As for what you're supposed to be doing—what you're doing isn't as important as what people think you're doing. In this town, people accept you at just about the value you place on yourself."

"I'm not quite sure I know what you mean."

Judd smiled indulgently. "I mean that this government of ours is so big and so complex that no one person can ever really know very much of what is going on. Even so energetic a person as your friend the senator must depend a great deal on his subordinates. Just now the emphasis is on bright young men. Except for some die-hards like the colonel, the old-timers have had their day. So have the New Deal intellectuals in the tweed jackets and baggy flannel slacks. Carry a rolled-up *New York Times* under your arm for effect, but be sure to read the *Washington Post*, particularly Drew Pearson and George Dixon. You'll catch on. It isn't too hard."

Bayard went back to reading transcripts. Two days before the hearings were scheduled to begin, Judd called again—this time inviting Bayard to meet him at the Mayflower bar for a drink.

"I suppose you are about ready for us," said Judd after they had their drinks in front of them. "What have you been working on? Lists of questions for the members to ask the witnesses?"

"Something like that," said Bayard cautiously.

Judd laughed. "You don't have to be so damned secretive. These procedures are routine. Hearings are to help the committee get at the essential information and to get it read into the record. Your staff dreams up the questions. We try to provide the answers. Here's something that might help you."

He handed Bayard a legal-size white-bond envelope. The flap was not sealed. Bayard flipped it back and saw that there were several typewritten sheets inside.

"What's this?" he asked suspiciously.

"Questions," said Judd. "Some which might not have occurred to you. You might find them useful in working up your lists."

Bayard eyed the envelope skeptically.

"For Christ sake," said Judd, "put it in your pocket. I'm doing you a favor. My agency wants to get the answers to those questions into the record. If you don't want them, I'll give them to the personal staff of one of the other senators. I'm giving you a chance to look good, boy. Take it."

With some misgivings, Bayard put the envelope into his inner coat pocket.

The hearings began on schedule two days later. The subcommittee's hearing room had an Edwardian elegance. There were crystal chandeliers, heavy velvet drapes in dark blue, and a marble mantelpiece. The walls of the room were lined with Herculean-proportioned portraits of the former chairmen, starting with Henry Clay himself.

The senators sat at a long mahogany table with the chairman in the middle of one side, Democrats to his left, Republicans to his right. There were two smaller tables—one for the staff and one for the press. At the far end of the room were temporary rows of chairs for spectators.

Colonel Ritchey was very particular about the arrangements at the committee table. There were thirteen members counting the chairman.

In front of each chair was a folder of staff-prepared background material, a new blue-lined pad of paper, two new yellow-painted pencils, and a large, immaculate ash tray. Down the center of the table was a row of four carafes of water, each with four water tumblers.

At ten minutes to ten, Marcellus Browne, the head of FSIA—accompanied by three members of his staff, one of whom was Judd—entered the room. Bayard would have recognized Browne anywhere—the deep ruddy tan, the platinum white hair precisely combed in perfect regular waves, and the heavy, very black eyebrows. It was the handsome face of a highly talented actor.

Judd caught Bayard's eye and nodded, smiling slightly.

One by one the members of the subcommittee arrived, the staff assistants scurrying over to the door to escort them to their respective chairs at the table.

The press section was half filled with lounging, unimpressed reporters and photographers. The flicker of interest when Marcellus Browne entered the room subsided quickly.

At 9:57 Senator Wilson came through the doorway. He crossed the room briskly to where Marcellus Browne was sitting, seized Browne's hand in both of his own in a politician's handshake. Browne looked momentarily startled. The photographers caught this fleeting event, and the afternoon papers published the picture of a paternalistic, comforting Senator Wilson and an ill-at-ease, disconcerted Marcellus Browne.

After a moment's brief conversation with Browne, Wilson went to the center of the committee table. There were seven senators already seated at the table. Wilson had a quick, warm word for each of them. Then he brought the gavel down. The time was 10:01.

"Let the subcommittee come to order," intoned the chairman. "Members of the subcommittee, with your permission, I would like to make a brief statement as to the purpose of these hearings.

"We have asked Mr. Marcellus Browne to come up here this morning to tell us something about the workings of his agency—the Foreign Services Information Agency.

"First, I would like to say that we here on the subcommittee are all very much aware of the great public services rendered by Mr. Browne. We are deeply appreciative of the fact that it was at great financial loss that he gave up his position as the vice president and executive director of the Federal Broadcasting Company. More than that, we all remember those words of courage that came to us from him from the battlefields around the globe during the darkest days of World War II. Here is an American, a very fine American, who, having achieved a position of immense affluence and public esteem, has at great personal sacrifice contributed his services and talents to his government. So I want it understood, and I request that the gentlemen of the press note this, that this investigation in no way impugns the motives or character of Mr. Browne.

"We are investigating not the man but the agency. Most of the members of this subcommittee sat at this same table five years ago when this agency was formed. We were told that it was going to be a small office that would perform a highly specialized public information function for our Foreign Service.

"Each year since then we have seen this agency grow. We have seen its budget doubled and tripled and quadrupled. We find that it is operating overseas radio stations and publishing foreign-language newspapers and magazines.

"We don't say that these activities are wrong. We do say that the Congress and the people of the United States deserve an explanation and an accounting. That is why we have called these hearings.

"Mr. Browne, do you have a prepared statement which you wish to read at this time?"

"Mr. Chairman, I do."

Browne's rich, remembered voice made those four words sound like an invocation. The members of the subcommittee and the press had already received mimeographed copies of Browne's opening statement. The reading of it was a formality, but he read it slowly, with measured emphasis. Bayard did not listen but remembered instead the words broadcast in 1940. "This . . . is . . . London. Marcellus Browne . . . speaking. The Luftwaffe . . . is overhead. . . . If you listen . . . you can hear . . . the wail . . . of the air-raid sirens."

"I would like to compliment Mr. Browne on a very fine, very clear, very concise statement," Senator Wilson began his response. "Mr. Browne, our procedure here, as you I think you know, is to allow each of the senators in turn to ask you whatever questions he might think relevant to the matter under discussion. But before my colleagues begin their questioning, I would like to clear up one point that I don't think was completely covered by your statement.

"As I understand it, your agency is about to embark upon a new and greatly expanded foreign-language broadcast program, an expansion of your present Voice of Democracy. Is that true?"

"Yes, sir," replied Browne, "I would like to—"

The senator frowned at the interruption and continued, "And much of the money requested for your agency would go into technical improvements, the electronics equipment which would make that expanded program possible?"

"Yes, sir. We have come up with an entirely new conception of transmission and reception. With a number of very high-powered transmitters strategically placed and by distributing a large number of inexpensive receivers of a radically new design—"

"Just a minute, Mr. Browne. You'll forgive my interrupting, but who is that young man at your elbow, who seems to be so insistent upon whispering into your ear?"

"This is my administrative assistant, Mr. Benson."

"He seems so insistent on expressing himself," Wilson said, "that perhaps we should interrupt your testimony long enough to hear what he has to say. What is your full name, young man?"

"Judson David Benson, sir."

"And what is your position?"

"I am a special assistant to Mr. Browne," Benson replied.

Senator Wilson took a moment to consult a file of papers. "It says here that you are a member of the firm of Bryce, Mellon, and Frobisher. Is that so?"

"I was a member of that firm before coming to Washington."

"Aren't they still paying you a salary?"

"Well, yes, sir. They are."

"Then I think we are safe in saying that you still are a member of the firm. Now isn't it true that one of the largest accounts handled by Bryce, Mellon, and Frobisher is the account of the American and International Radio Corporation?"

"I believe it is, sir."

"You know it is, Mr. Benson. And isn't it true that the Federal Broadcasting System is a wholly owned subsidiary of the American and International Radio Corporation?"

There was a sudden flurry of activity at the press table. Flashbulbs began to pop and a handheld motion-picture camera began to whir softly.

"I think that is the case, sir," Judd replied.

"Yes, Mr. Benson," said the chairman, "I think it is. And isn't it true that these expensive high-powered transmitters we have been told about and these millions of cheap receivers we've been asked to buy, isn't it true that the patents for these are controlled by American and International Radio Corporation?"

"I don't think Mr. Benson can be expected to answer that question," Browne interposed.

"Perhaps not," responded Senator Wilson, "but Mr. Benson, I think we will all agree, has been a most helpful witness."

The subcommittee recessed at noon. In the press of people at the doorway, Judd was pushed up against Bayard. His face was white and strained, but he managed a tight little smile.

"You bastard," he breathed into Bayard's ear. "You complete son of a bitch."

chapter fourteen...

A few days after the hearing, an intern from Senator Wilson's office delivered an envelope to Bayard's desk, addressed to him in broad-nibbed black ink in the senator's unmistakable handwriting. The note inside invited Bayard to have lunch with him the following day at the Metropolitan Club. Bayard hurriedly telephoned his acceptance.

Next day, Bayard hesitated at the steps of the Metropolitan Club, a square, solid, yellow brick building, at the corner of 17th and H Streets, Northwest, and then plunged in. A doorman intercepted him at the double doors with a challenging, inquiring, "Yes?"

"Lunch with Senator Wilson," said Bayard, conscious that he was mumbling.

"Yes," said the doorman, this time affirmatively. "Of course. The senator is not here as yet. Perhaps you would wait in the lobby."

Bayard went through the double rank of double doors and saw that the lobby was a kind of reading room. Doors opened off of it into various other more mysterious regions of the club. Huge portraits of bearded men, most in uniforms of immediate post–Civil War, hung on oak-paneled walls. A vast staircase opened on the opposite side of the room, portraits ascending its walls as well. In the center of the lobby was a large octagonal table almost totally covered with rows of neatly arranged newspapers, ranging, north to south, from the *Boston Globe* to the *Atlanta Constitution*. Bayard found the morning edition of the friendly, familiar *Baltimore Sun* and then sat down in one of the vast leather chairs that were facing the door. The room smelled faintly of leather and cologne and more pronouncedly of cigar smoke mixed with the stagnant smell from the huge fireplace at one side of the room. The day was much too warm for a fire.

Men were arriving for lunch in ones and twos and occasionally in threes. They bustled in, thought Bayard, as though this were an important, welcoming destination. Bayard had dressed carefully for the luncheon, wearing his best suit, a double-breasted blue flannel. The suit had been made to measure the year before at the Canterbury Shop on Charles Street in Baltimore. It cost sixty-five dollars, the most Bayard had ever paid for a suit. He had considered, briefly, wearing his blue suede shoes to match, but he thought better of it and wore his Florsheim wing-tipped shell cordovans. Plain-tipped Florsheim shell cordovan officer's shoes had been the top of the line with Marine Corps officers, along with cordovan Sam Browne belts made by Peter Bain.

Over the top edge of his *Baltimore Sun* Bayard studied the men entering the double doors. Every few minutes he would catch a publicly familiar face: a senator but not Senator Wilson, a Supreme Court justice, several congressmen, a columnist with the *Washington Post*.

He became painfully conscious that his blue flannel suit was a bit too blue. The men coming in off the street were mostly in gray—worsted gray suits, some with faint stripes. Bayard began counting on his fingers the chalk stripes, pencil stripes, and pin stripes. There were some blues, but they were dark navy blue, almost black. As he sat there, the blue of his flannel suit grew brighter and brighter.

A half an hour passed. Bayard had arrived ten minutes before the appointed time. Senator Wilson was twenty minutes late. Bayard wondered if Wilson had forgotten or if he himself had been mixed up on the day. Or maybe the senator had expected him to stop at his office and the two of them were to come over together.

To Bayard's considerable relief, the senator then came through the door. Smiling, he crossed the room toward Bayard, pausing infinitesimally a time or two to nod familiarly toward a friend or acquaintance. Bayard sensed strongly that the senator was on safe home territory.

Bayard got to his feet, clumsily trying to refold the copy of the *Sun* and at the same time extend his right hand to the senator, who was wearing a very dark gray, vested, suit with an almost imperceptible stripe. A small gold Masonic emblem was in the buttonhole of his left lapel. His shirt was white with a stiffly starched collar. The senator's tie was a dark, rich—and, Bayard supposed, Italian—silk.

They went up the grand staircase with the giant portraits on the wall, Bayard trailing one step behind the senator, and then on into the dining room, which was almost filled with men in gray suits. By now, Bayard's suit was almost an incandescent blue. The senator exchanged a cordial word with the maître d'hôtel, who led them to a reserved table by a window overlooking 17th Street.

Now, three years later, Bayard could not remember what he had had for lunch. He did remember that the senator had asked some exploring questions and, as they finished with coffee, had invited him out to his farm, west of Warrenton, for a weekend.

"You and my daughter seem to hit it off," rumbled the senator. "I run a few cattle—Black Angus—on the farm. She has a couple of horses. Four of them. Do you ride?"

"A little," said Bayard, hoping that the senator would take that as an understatement.

"Well," said the senator a bit dubiously, "there are tennis courts. I suppose you play tennis?"

"Yes," said Bayard, "a little."

A car was waiting for the senator at the door of the club. The senator paused as he entered the back seat. "Can I drop you some place?" he asked offhandedly.

"No, thank you, sir," answered Bayard, fearing the senator would drop him too fast and too hard. "I have a few errands to run before I get back to the office."

The senator's black sedan pulled away from the curb, and Bayard was left standing there. He let the sedan reach the next stoplight and then started off at a fast walk for the Saltz F Street Store, between 13th and 14th Streets. He entered the long narrow first floor, the room dim at first from the bright sun he had left on the street. A salesman came forward to meet him.

"Can I help you, sir?" The accent was decidedly British. The salesperson, pale and slightly built, was of an age indeterminately between fifty and seventy. It struck Bayard that the store had almost the same smell as the Metropolitan Club: cigar smoke, cologne, and leather—with the addition of the scent of wool.

"A suit," said Bayard. "A very conservative suit."

"Mmmmm," said the salesperson judiciously. "Good shoulders. Slim through the waist and hips. I think a forty-one long."

He led Bayard to the wall where a row of forty-one longs, mostly gray, stood in a rank. A number of them were briskly pulled loose and thrown across an adjacent lower rack. The salesman removed Bayard's electric blue coat without unfavorable comment and held up a pin-striped gray for him to try on. The judgment of forty-one long was confirmed.

A gray sharkskin suit was added to the gray pinstripe. A subdued brown and green houndstooth jacket cut with side vents was found. Three pairs of trousers—one pair of tan Bedford cord cavalry twill and two pairs of flannels, an oxford gray and a cambridge navy—joined the pile.

"We must match this up with some shirts and things," said the salesperson. Six shirts were placed by the pile—four white broadcloths and two blue oxford button-downs. Six proper ties and two pairs of braces were matched off with the suits and jacket.

"Now you should be ready for any occasion except the most formal," said the salesperson. "Let me show you our dinner jackets."

A half an hour later, after Bayard had been fitted, the salesperson escorted him to the cash register.

"Can all of this be ready by Friday?" asked Bayard.

"Of course," said the salesperson, busying himself with the sales slip. "Altogether that will be four hundred eighty-five dollars and forty-five cents."

"Can I pay that on time?" asked Bayard.

The salesperson's eyebrows lifted an eighth of an inch. "Of course," he said again. "We have a simple form for you to fill out."

As the salesperson took him to the door, he patted Bayard gently on the shoulder. "Remember, sir, for any clothing needs at all, I will be here to serve you. And a little word of advice, if I may, sir. Use a clothing brush, and send your suits and jackets to the cleaner as infrequently as possible. It kills the wool."

Donna did not appear surprised when Bayard told her that the senator had invited him to a weekend at their farm.

Bayard put in a full day at the office before leaving on Friday afternoon for the country. It was a two-hour drive. He had packed the new jacket, the gray flannel trousers and the Bedford cord, and three of the shirts and ties. He also packed his riding breeches and boots, which went back to Quantico. Boots and breeches were not required for wartime officers. Some field-grade officers—majors to colonels—sometimes still occasionally wore them. Bayard had added riding breeches to his uniform order and cheated a little by buying inexpensive riding boots at Sears and Roebuck and dyeing them cordovan brown.

There had been time between assignments at Quantico for Bayard to take the equitation course that justified the continued existence of the riding stable. Instruction was by a master gunnery sergeant who had been a mule skinner in Nicaragua. Later, after the war, when Bayard was in North China, the Marines had taken over a stable near the racetrack in Tientsin, where the Japanese had kept some of their horses—big fellows, reputedly from Australia. Bayard had ridden regularly, sometimes dangerously alone beyond the edge of the city.

The senator had held dinner until Bayard's arrival. Afterward, Bayard and Donna took a lengthy walk along dark country roads that were marked on each side by white-painted wooden fences. Bayard took her elbow as they dodged past a muddy patch. He held her hand for the remainder of the walk.

In the morning Bayard came down for breakfast dressed for riding in his Quantico boots and breeches and new houndstooth jacket. Donna, in jodhpurs and hacking jacket, looked to Bayard much like Gene Tierney, or maybe it was Patricia Neal, in a motion picture he had seen recently.

The red-brick house was on a hill, and the stable was a hundred yards or so below it. The barn smelled strongly of hay and horses. Donna led him to a box stall. In it was a mild-looking mare, who came to the door to meet Donna.

"This is Sweetheart," said Donna. "I've had her since I was a teenager. She will give you a gentle ride."

And Sweetheart did. After the ride came the tennis. Donna played to his game, which was not very strong, but allowed herself to win. In the evening they drove to the Warrenton Country Club for dinner and dancing. On the way home they parked in the lane leading up to the house. Donna set the limits.

chapter fifteen...

On the third evening on Hill 131—it was the day of the mail call—Bayard
was having a last smoke as the sun went down, when Havac came over to
him and asked if they could speak together alone. Havac's breath smelled
faintly of whiskey. They walked to the edge of the command post area.

Havac rubbed his face with the palm of his hand. "I been thinking
about the Chinese girl," he said.

"So have I," said Bayard. The problem of the child had to be solved;
she couldn't stay with the company indefinitely.

"A patrol from Easy Company ran into some guerrillas a couple of
miles north of here today," said Havac.

"So I heard."

"We'll be shoving off from here in a couple a days, and then what're
we going to do with the girl?"

"I wish I knew," said Bayard.

"Some of the men been talking about sending her home to their families," said Havac tentatively.

"I know," said Bayard. "It's a warmhearted, generous thing for them to offer to do. But things like that are complicated—too many technicalities."

"That's what I told them," said Havac. He massaged his face again. "The Captain's heard about those orphanages they got in Japan?"

"Yes," said Bayard.

"Well," said Havac, "the company passed a helmet around, and there's nearly six hundred dollars in military scrip altogether. That ought to be enough to take care of getting her into one of those orphanages."

"It should be," said Bayard. Here was an obvious solution to the problem. Why hadn't he thought of it? "I'll add something to the pot. I'll talk to the other officers. I'm sure they'll want to be in on it."

"We shouldn't put it off too long," warned Havac.

"No," said Bayard. "Tomorrow we'll get a jeep and go into Seoul. The Red Cross or somebody back at Division ought to be able to help us set it up."

"Who can tell—maybe after this thing is over, somebody might be able to get her out of the orphanage and back to the States," said Havac. "If I was married, I wouldn't mind having her myself."

"It's something to think about," said Bayard. He wondered what Donna would say or do if he were to come home with a five-year-old Chinese girl.

"Well, thanks, Skipper," said Havac. "I'll go back now and tell the men."

Bayard slept very soundly that night. He was awakened only once, and that was by the first sergeant reporting that all patrols had returned safely and without incident. Bayard phoned this in to the battalion watch officer and went back to sleep. He did not waken again until it was broad daylight, a bright sunny morning.

"How about a cup of real coffee, Skipper?" asked Havac.

"Thanks," said Bayard, sliding out of his sleeping bag and taking the canteen cup from Havac.

"This is the real article," Bayard said gratefully, sipping the scalding black brew. "Where did you get it?"

"I got a twenty-five-pound can from the battalion mess sergeant," said Havac. "I got some oatmeal too, if you like it."

"Where's Baby-san this morning?" asked Bayard, for breakfast was Baby-san's business.

"Down to the company supply point after the rations," answered Havac. "Sir, you going to do something about the kid today?" He jerked his head in the direction of Mei-ling. The child was having her face and hands washed by Pilnick.

"As soon as we're through here with breakfast," promised Bayard, "we'll go down to Battalion."

"That's good," said Havac. "The longer she's around here, the more the men'll miss her when she's gone."

"I think you're right," said Bayard.

"Hi!" somebody yelled, and up the green slope from the company supply point came the grinning Baby-san with a carton of C rations on his shoulder.

"Hi," Mei-ling tinkled an answer. Pilnick gave her face a last pat with a khaki towel. She gathered up her box of spoons and trotted down the trail to meet Baby-san, just as she had done the last several mornings.

Suddenly, out of the sky came the whispered warning of a mortar shell.

As a reflex, the headquarters crew dived for their holes or flattened themselves close to the earth, as did Bayard himself. During the night the enemy must have gotten past the outposts with a heavy mortar. The shell cleared the company command post and exploded on the slope stretching down to the valley.

Bayard looked up from the ground. A tiny figure stood there on the grassy slope half way between the command post and Baby-san.

"Get down, Mei-ling!" yelled Bayard, forgetting that the little girl knew no English. The confused and frightened child just stood there on the path leading down to Baby-san. Bayard got to his feet and started toward her. A second shell came *cruummpingg* out of the air and hit between them. Then a third shell tossed the little body into the air like a bright bundle of rags.

Bayard and the others got to her as soon as they could, but her small and unimportant life had flickered out. The shell burst had scattered the Spoon Family over the green grass. In the bright morning sunlight they lay there glistening like tears.

chapter sixteen...

"Saddle up! We're movin' out!" Havac roared out the word, and the platoon sergeants took it up and sent it echoing across the hill. Dog Company had struck its shelters and rolled its packs. The squads formed up, and their leaders reported to the platoon sergeants that they were ready to go. The platoon commanders, standing in a group with Bayard and the company headquarters, ground out their cigarettes with their heels and moved to the front of their respective platoons. The company started to thread its way in column down the trail to the road. Behind them they left Hill 131 pocked with the raw, red scars of their abandoned foxholes. Down along the road, ready to head back toward Seoul and Inchon, waited the battered trucks of the 1st Motor Transport Battalion.

Battalion radioed the word to embark. Dog Company boarded its allotted trucks, the lieutenants climbing into the cabs next to the drivers. Bayard got into his jeep with Baby-san and his new radio operator, Ernest

Brown, a reservist from Wisconsin. Then they waited for the column to move.

The marines, wedged into the back of the trucks with their equipment and weapons, began to grow restless. Radios crackled up and down the column in exasperation. A distraught motor transport lieutenant came up to Bayard's jeep, demanding to know what the delay was. Bayard refused to be ruffled. "I am sure I couldn't tell you, Sonny," he said mildly.

Baby-san snickered, and the lieutenant whirled off in a rage. Finally the sharp incisive voice of Major Mansell came over the radio telling the battalion to move out. The truck column lurched into motion along the dust-thick highway. For the last two days U.S. Army troops had been moving north. The convoys of the 1st Cavalry Division were now passing the 2d Battalion, their trucks filled with troopers with yellow scarves and fatigue uniforms a darker shade of green than the faded utilities of the marines.

"What's the matter, Gyrenes?" yelled the troopers. "You're going the wrong way!"

They were cavalry without horses, rumbling north, oiled and glistening, in olive drab armor. Dog Company, self-conscious about its shabby accoutrements, tilted back its collective head and set up a yapping and barking that drowned out the clank of the armored treads. "Sic 'em, doggies! Go get 'em! It's safe. They ain't no Ko-reans left up there. What color are them scarves you're wearin'?"

Shouldering raffishly past the army column, Dog Company's trucks reached the broader streets of Seoul. Just in the week since they had passed through, the city had changed. It now teemed with a hectic, unnatural life. Fungus-like growths had sprung up from the ruins. The shop fronts still gaped empty and blackened, but the sidewalks were dense with tiny markets. An old man pushed a cart filled with cabbages. A boy sat with half a dozen packs of American cigarettes spread out on the curb. The air reeked with the smell of fish, kimchi, and sewage.

Dog Company rolled by without a nod of notice or a cheer. Already the sight of American troops was commonplace, and last week's frantic welcome forgotten. Except by the children: "Hey, GI, you got chocolate? You got cigarette? You got chew' gum?"

They passed the remains of a T-34 tank, the one that had gotten closest to the road block. Souvenir hunters or scrap collectors had stripped it down to its bare hull. Now the trucks of Dog Company were at the intersection just beyond the railroad underpass. The rice-bag barricades were gone, cleared out of the way of the truck traffic going north. Bayard thought of his dead radioman and looked around at Brown, his new operator, sitting next to Baby-san in the back of the jeep.

The boy was oblivious to the scene. He was telling Baby-san about a night club in San Diego. "A body exchange, that's what it is," he was saying. "Any kind of woman you'd want to meet. I picked up one from Coronado who had her own convertible. A real doll."

"You better get some radio checks with the rest of the column," Bayard interrupted abruptly. The boy looked at him with the offended superiority of a communicator with a high GCT score.

They crossed the Han by the way of the pontoon bridge that had been hastily completed in time for the triumphal reentry of Syngman Rhee and General MacArthur into the city. They moved through Yongdung-po along the road to Inchon that had been the axis of their advance. What had been eleven days of fighting now rolled beneath their wheels in less than an hour.

Inchon was a tumult of high-pitched activity. Huge and flamboyant signs announced the presence of such impressive units as the "1784th Medium Ordnance Maintenance Battalion," the "907th Signal Construction Company (Heavy)," the "Young Koreans UN Peace Fighters."

It pays to advertise, thought Bayard.

The streets were crowded with merchant seamen, South Korean soldiers, U.S. Army quartermasters in ODs, sailors in white caps and dungarees, here and there a dusty, bearded infantryman—all mixed in with the swarming civilian populace.

"Well, how does it look to you?" asked Bayard.

"I'll settle for a shower and a clean place to flake out," said Baby-san, "and some decent chow."

Baby-san's modest expectations were doomed to disappointment. The 2d Battalion's convoy turned in between the shell-blasted gates of an iron foundry, and Dog Company was assigned billeting space in the gaunt skeleton of a building filled with rusting and shattered machinery. The corrugated metal roofing had been blown off, leaving only the bare ribs of the structure intact; the floor was an inches-thick accumulation of grease, coal dust, and filth left by a population insensitive to sanitation.

"And we left a nice green hill for this," complained Baby-san.

"Never mind the bitching," said Bayard, pointing to a room framed with rough boards in one corner of the building. "We'll set up the company office there."

Company headquarters fell to, and by nightfall the room was not only livable but, by Dog Company standards, almost luxurious. Baby-san and Brown had nailed sheets of the corrugated roofing over the gaping holes to keep out the weather and had draped blankets and ponchos on the inside of the walls to black-out the room. Pilnick had unloaded a half-dozen stretchers to serve as beds. The property sergeant had found a pot-bellied cast-iron stove. Jim Kim went to the marketplace and traded off cigarettes for a couple of oil lamps made from beer cans. Havac had procured from his friend, the mess sergeant, several pounds of bacon, some potatoes, and some fresh bread. As a welcome change in menu, Dog Company headquarters messed that night on bacon sandwiches and potatoes fried in bacon grease.

The LSTs, rusty and unlovely, were waiting for them, beached across the causeway on Wolmi-do. Dog Company was half-eager to go on board, half-anxious to stay ashore. The next two days were crammed with administrative detail: loading forms, recommendations for awards, letters of condolence, and a partially successful attempt at a consolidated battalion mess. Losses in equipment were made up. Bayard had to explain in writing to the battalion commander why and how Dog Company had lost most of its mess gear.

A company from the 1st Engineer Battalion had rigged up a shower-and-bath unit down the street, and Dog Company had its turn to shed its worn utilities and scrub itself clean. The water was hot, but the new uniforms that had been issued were U.S. Army fatigues. Dog Company complained about this until a sufficient amount of india ink was found with which to stencil the Marine Corps globe-and-anchor on the breast pockets.

Bayard let Gibson struggle with the loading forms, but the recommendations for awards and the letters of condolence he felt he must prepare himself. The letters of condolence were the most difficult. The company commander must write to the next of kin of each marine who is killed in action or who dies of wounds. That is prescribed in regulations.

Bayard would sit staring at each sheet of paper, pen in hand, inching his way, word by word, through each letter. Twenty-two members of Dog Company had been killed; twenty-two letters to be written. Bayard did not feel so bad about the wounded. At least they were out of it—no longer his responsibility. They would recover, most of them. And in most cases, there would be no lasting disability from the wound. But the dead . . . There was a finality about death with which Bayard could not cope.

"Dear Mrs. Almquist," he wrote. "Your son was my radioman. He was killed quite close to me during the street fighting in Seoul on the night of 25 September 1950. He was hit by a high-velocity enemy shell and died instantly. He could not have felt any pain.

"There is nothing that I can write that will lessen your grief, but I do want you to know that your son died fighting for what he knew to be right. Your son was a good marine and a fine young man. . . ."

So it went—twenty-two times Bayard had to search his soul for the right words of sympathy for a mother or a wife. Some of the dead Bayard could remember vividly; others were just a name. "Collins? Let's see, Top Sergeant, was he the stocky boy killed in Seoul by the grenade?"

"No, Skipper, you're thinking of Costello," answered Havac. "Collins was the skinny guy in the 2d Platoon who got hit outside Yongdung-po by the mortars."

One by one the letters were written. Meanwhile, Gibson finished the loading forms, and Bayard signed them. The property sergeant made endless inventories, and Bayard argued out his list of shortages with the battalion supply officer.

An accumulation of incoming letters and packages had to be distributed. Dog Company gorged itself on goodies from home: cookies, cakes, salami, cheeses, potted meats—a well-meaning mother even sent a jar of soluble coffee. There were several letters from Donna—one only four days old. Four days, and it had come halfway around the world.

"Father had luncheon with one of your generals from Headquarters Marine Corps yesterday," she wrote. "The general mentioned that they planned on bringing back some of the combat-experienced officers to instruct at Quantico this Fall. You know that they have greatly expanded the basic officer's courses there.

"I would think that you should have a very good chance of being one of those chosen. Father didn't say anything specifically about you in his conversation with the general as he knew you wouldn't want him to. However, it seems to both father and me that you would be a very logical choice. After all, darling, you are a trained teacher.

"It would be lovely to have you at Quantico—only an hour away from

Washington. I don't know how you want to go about this but it seems to me that the right word to your regimental commander—or should it be to your division commander?—ought to assure you of getting the assignment."

It was an intriguing possibility. Bayard thought of the months he had spent first as an officer candidate and then as a student officer at Quantico. He remembered also the combat veterans, faces yellowed with atabrine, who had been brought back from the South Pacific to instruct.

"Gentlemen, the title of this period of instruction is *Lessons Learned at Guadalcanal.*"

Bayard had stood in awe of these men who had been initiated into the Great Mystery. He wondered if any of the current crop of officer candidates would be as ingenuous as he had been. He wondered if they would listen as attentively and as believingly as he had listened seven or eight years before to the voices of combat-tested authority.

Did they still use those wooden, bare-raftered classrooms? Did the instructors still wear the public-address system microphone around their necks? Did they still trail behind them the wire from the microphone like an umbilical cord tying them to the Academic Board? Did each instructor bear the imprint of the Instructor's Orientation Course? Bayard could see himself on the platform and hear himself saying:

"Gentlemen, the title of this period of instruction is *Over the Seawall at Inchon.*

"Gentlemen, this morning we will have a presentation on how to stop a T-34 tank.

"Gentlemen, I will now tell you what it feels like to write twenty-two letters to the next of kin. . . ."

It was about this time that Reynolds reported renewed trouble with Kusnetzov.

"I thought we had him straightened out," said Bayard. "I'm recommending him for a Bronze Star for that day in the street in Seoul."

"He was doing pretty well," said Reynolds slowly. "There was something that happened north of Seoul I should have told you about. It was when we were pulling those gooks out of the houses. Two came out, and Kusnetzov shot them. He said they had grenades, but Griffith says their hands were up in the air and their hands were empty."

"Why didn't you tell me at the time?"

"I don't know. I wasn't sure exactly how it happened—you know, he could have thought they had grenades. But last night something else happened. He got into a fight with Sergeant Griffith. Kusnetzov threatened him with his bayonet. Captain, something has to be done about that guy. I think he's off his rocker."

"Have you talked to the battalion surgeon about him?"

"No, sir. I wanted to talk to you first."

"What do you want me to do, hold office hours?"

"I think it'd be a good idea."

"All right. We'll hold them tonight. And I'll ask the surgeon to sit in."

That night they met in Dog Company's office—the office that had been the shop foreman's corner. With its empty window frames covered with blankets in the dim yellow light of Kim's oil lamps, supplemented by two or three candles stuck in sand-filled ration cans, the place had a raffish, dramatic quality of which Bayard was quite aware.

Baby-san was posted at the blanketed doorway to keep visitors out until office hours were over. Bayard sat behind his appropriated South Korean desk with Dr. Goldberg next to him. Lieutenant Reynolds and Sergeant Griffith stood to one side of the desk. At Bayard's order, the first sergeant marched in Kusnetzov and stood him at attention in front of the desk.

"Well, Kusnetzov," said Bayard, "do you know why you are here?"

"Because I told Sergeant Griffith I would stick him wit' my bayonet."

"What made you threaten Sergeant Griffith?"

"It was just an argument. I didn't mean nothing by it."

"Where was the bayonet?"

"In my scabbard."

"Did you take it out of its scabbard?"

"Yes, sir."

"Did you threaten Sergeant Griffith with it?"

"Maybe I pushed it toward his belly a little."

"Then what happened?"

"Nothing. Sergeant Griffith went and told the lieutenant."

"Sergeant Griffith, do you have anything to add?"

"No, sir," said the section leader. Griffith was a very youthful sergeant, probably eight or ten years younger than Kusnetzov. "It was just about the way the Polack—I mean, Private Kusnetzov—has told it."

Bayard turned back to Kusnetzov. "You know that threatening another man—particularly a superior noncommissioned officer—with a deadly weapon is a very serious offense?"

"Yes, sir."

"Then why did you do it?"

A puzzled expression spread itself slowly over Kusnetzov's bearded face. "I don't know, Captain."

"What do you mean, you don't know? What kind of an answer is that?"

"I got mad. It just happened."

"Kusnetzov," said Bayard suddenly, "are you an American citizen?"

Kusnetzov's massive frame flinched slightly. His dark brooding eyes narrowed. "I am an American citizen."

"Kusnetzov—that's a Russian name, isn't it?"

"The name is Russian. I am Polish."

"Did you ever serve in a foreign army?"

"What has that got to do wit' it?" a tinge of anxiety crept into Kusnetzov's voice.

"Answer my question."

"I was in the Polish Free Corps."

Was this the truth? Bayard searched his mind for some detail, some technical trap that he might set. "Who commanded your Corps?"

"General Anders."

"Anders? That sounds like an English name."

"He was a Pole like me."

"Did you see action?"

"Yes, sir."

"Where?"

"In Nort' Africa and then in Italy."

"How did you get to the United States?"

"Do I have to answer these questions? I am a good marine. I know my job. Since 1939 I have been a soldier."

Until this point Dr. Goldberg had said nothing but had sat there next to Bayard thoughtfully kneading his plump cheeks with his stubby fingers. Now he laid a hand on Bayard's wrist and softly interjected a question: "Private Kusnetzov, tell me in your own words, why do you think we are in Korea?"

"To kill communists."

"You mean to fight communism, don't you?" asked the doctor.

"I am here to kill communists." Kusnetzov's voice rang out harshly in the blanket-muffled room.

"Why?" asked Dr. Goldberg. "Why do you say that, Private Kusnetzov?"

"That is a private matter."

"I see. In any event, you now have this compulsion to kill communists, and sometimes Sergeant Griffith stands in your way—is that it?"

Kusnetzov made no reply. Dr. Goldberg gave Bayard a slight nod to indicate that he was finished with his questioning and settled back in his chair.

"That will be all," said Bayard to Kusnetzov. The first sergeant faced the machine gunner about and marched him out of the room.

"Well," said Bayard to the battalion surgeon, "what do we do now? Do we court-martial him, or do we put a casualty tag on him and send him to the rear?"

The doctor put his pudgy finger tips together and sighted over them at Bayard. "Why do either? You say he already has been court-martialed three times. Has that solved his problem? If I evacuate him as a combat fatigue case, they won't find very much wrong with him. He will sit around the division hospital quietly for a few days or a week, and then they will send him back to us. The experience would most likely do further damage to his ego, and the problem would be aggravated rather than helped."

"What do we do then?"

"Why do anything? You tell me he is a good machine gunner. You need good machine gunners, don't you?"

"What if he hurts one of our people? What if he kills somebody?"

"I don't think he will. There's a tremendous compulsive drive there. Part of what he does is a dramatization of his situation. It may win him the Navy Cross—or it may get him killed. But I don't think he's a threat to your marines."

"Anyway," said Bayard, "I'm tearing up his recommendation for the Bronze Star. We'll say the two things cancel out."

"Do you think that is wise?"

"What do you mean?"

"Don't think I'm telling you how to run your company, Captain, but I'm wondering if that would be a wise thing to do. More than anything else, Kusnetzov craves recognition. He feels that he has to exact a revenge. A medal would be official recognition that he had retaliated against his enemies."

"Perhaps," said Bayard, "but under the circumstances, I can't forward the recommendation."

Dr. Goldberg shrugged his shoulders. "Do as you wish, Captain. It will be interesting to see what happens."

The next morning Bayard was summoned to battalion headquarters. It was the Red Snapper's custom to hold a meeting with the company commanders and the battalion staff at 1600 each afternoon— "Officers Call" he called it—but this was a special meeting assembled at 1000 in the morning.

When Bayard arrived at battalion headquarters, which was set up in the ramshackle office building that was part of the iron foundry, he found Beale and Mason from Easy and Fox Companies already there. They were waiting in the outer office, which was shared by the adjutant and the sergeant major. Neither of these worthies saw fit to inform the rifle company commanders as to the purpose of the meeting if, in fact, they knew.

Promptly at 1000, the door to the battalion commander's office opened, and Major Mansell, standing on the threshold, peremptorily invited the company commanders to come in.

Bayard, Beale, and Mason followed Mansell into the small room that for the last several days had served the Red Snapper as a combination office and sleeping quarters, which he shared with Major Crenshaw and Major Mansell.

At the opposite end of the room from the doorway was the Red Snapper's canvas cot and unrolled sleeping bag. The cots belonging to the two majors were against the side walls of the room. Also in the room were a field desk, a table covered with a green marine blanket, and three or four canvas camp chairs. "Make yourself comfortable, gentlemen," invited the Red Snapper in a blurred voice.

He was sitting on the edge of his cot. His boots were off, and he was in his stocking feet—heavy woolen socks pulled up over his trousers legs. His hair was rumpled, and it was obvious that he had neither washed nor shaved that morning. "I apologize for making a goddamn mystery out of this meetin', but it's a matter that only concerns you rifle company commanders. Major Crenshaw will tell you what it's all about."

Bayard did not know Major Crenshaw well. The battalion executive officer was a rotund, rather fussy little man who concerned himself primarily with the battalion's administration and logistics. Bayard had neither a liking nor the technical background for these affairs, so he ordinarily delegated them to the meticulous Lieutenant Gibson for execution. Hence it was Gibson who usually dealt with Crenshaw.

Crenshaw, for all Bayard knew, was an efficient and capable officer, but his pallid personality was overshadowed both by the flamboyant reputation—based, in Bayard's opinion, on past rather than present performance—of the Red Snapper and by the dominating influence of Major Mansell.

"Yes," said Major Crenshaw. "Thank you, Colonel. I think we can finish this up in a very few minutes, gentlemen. The facts of the matter are simply this: Regiment has asked us to nominate one rifle company commander—he has to be a captain and a rifle company commander—to return to Marine Corps Schools, Quantico, Virginia, as an instructor. It is our understanding that each of the infantry battalions in the division has been asked to make a similar nomination so as to make up the quota. The colonel would like to make his selection on as equitable a basis as possible."

"If any of you has got a good reason for going home, now is the time to speak up," said the Red Snapper.

Donna's information was correct, thought Bayard. He looked up and saw that Mansell was watching him with half a smile on his face. Here, Bayard, Mansell's expression seemed to say, here's your chance to get out of this business.

"Come now," said Major Crenshaw, "aren't we going to have any volunteers?"

Beale, the senior company commander, spoke first. "I'd rather stay with my company," he said stolidly.

"So would I," said Mason. The two of them, Beale and Mason, had commanded their respective companies in peacetime. They were both former enlisted men. They had made the Mediterranean cruise and the Vieques maneuvers together. Beale stood out as the more forceful and aggressive of the two, but both were first-class company commanders.

It was Bayard's turn to speak. "I'm not ready to go home yet," he said.

"Well, now," said Major Mansell softly, his eyebrows going up a fraction of an inch.

The Red Snapper got to his stockinged feet. "I'm sorry, gentlemen, but I haven't time for any goddamn heroics. If you won't choose for yourselves, I'll choose for you."

Which means I will be the one sent home, thought Bayard.

The battalion commander went over to his field desk, fumbled in a drawer, and pulled out a deck of cards. "You'll draw for a high card. That'll decide it."

He shuffled the cards and fanned them out on the blanket-covered table. "You'll draw alphabetically. Dog Company, you're first."

Bayard pulled a card from the fan and turned over a jack of hearts.

"Next," said the Red Snapper brusquely. Beale reached across the table and turned up a seven of clubs.

"Knave of hearts is high," said the battalion commander. "Next."

Mason looked at Bayard and then at Beale, grinned a little, and reached for a card. "Anybody want to make any side bets?" he asked, holding the card facedown.

The Red Snapper waved an impatient hand. Mason snapped the card face up on the blanket. It was the king of hearts.

Red Snapper grunted. "Let's see," he asked. "Who's the exec of your company?"

"Lieutenant White, sir."

"He a good man?"

"One of the best, sir."

"Good. As of now he's commanding Fox Company. Major Crenshaw, you tell Regiment we're sending them Captain Mason. Mason, you get your gear packed and make your good-byes."

Mansell was still smiling his thin humorless smile as the company commanders left the office.

On the day following the meeting in the battalion commander's office, Dog Company marched across the causeway to Wolmi-do and embarked in a rusty-bellied LST. There was a new operation plan and a new set of maps and aerial photographs. This time Dog Company would be one of the assault companies with Fox on the left. Easy would be in reserve. The target was Wonsan.

chapter seventeen...

The LST on which they embarked at Inchon was no lovelier than the 557 that had brought them across from Japan. They sailed south, a gray ship in a gray convoy on a gray sea. The weather had turned raw and cool, portentous of the approaching winter. They rounded the southern tip of the Korean peninsula and started north, up the eastern coast to the harbor of enemy-held Wonsan. The landing was then delayed. Dog Company asked why and was told that the minesweepers were having their troubles with a harbor full of made-in-Russia mines. The group of landing ships grooved a path in the Japanese Sea, repeatedly sailing north toward Wonsan during the hours of darkness—would they be landing in the morning?—and then withdrawing to the south during the daylight hours.

Dog Company in their boredom and isolation listened to the fragmentary news reports provided by the ship's radio, enlarged on these in their imagination, conjectured as to their future. They heard that while the amphibious task force plodded back and forth outside the harbor, the South Korean army, magically revitalized by victory, had taken Wonsan from the land side.

When the 1st Marine Division finally went ashore, it was an anticlimactic administrative landing. Dog Company crossed the undefended beaches, ruminating on what kind of defense the North Koreans might have put up if they had chosen to stand and fight. The radio news reported that MacArthur had said that the war was over, the North Koreans crushed. Perhaps it was so. A first hint of a cold wind came out of the north. Someone asked what if the Chinese Communists choose to come in. But the radio news was reassuring. MacArthur had said that it was now too late for the Chinese to intervene effectively; they could not now change the course of the war. Meanwhile the U.S. Army and the ROK Army were hard on the heels of the fleeing North Koreans. Pursuit! On to the Yalu! On to the Rhine!

All these fucking army generals think they're a bunch of Georgie Pattons, grumbled the marines of Dog Company, sitting on their packs on the sand of the Wonsan beach. Hearing that the Red capital of Pyongyang had fallen to the 1st Cavalry Division, they remembered the shining new armor and the yellow-scarved troopers who had passed them, heading northward outside of Seoul. And here Dog Company sat in the rear with the gear.

A runner from Battalion brought Bayard a march order penciled on a bit of overlay paper. Bayard laid the overlay on his map and saw that the bivouac for his company was on the far side of the city, that they had a twelve-mile hike ahead of them. He briefed his platoon leaders quickly, telling them to get their people ready to move out. The battalion radio crackled an order for Dog Company to fall in on the road.

"Let's go," said Bayard getting to his feet. The separate segments of Dog Company arranged themselves in proper order. By now they did these things automatically. They moved out. Bayard looked back with a lifting feeling of pride at the twin columns of dingy gray-green marines. This was not a heads-up chest-out parade. Dog Company marched at route step, leaning forward under the weight of their packs.

They carried their weapons slung across their shoulders, or in the crook of their arms, or as convenient. They had lost the look of uniformity of stateside marines and had gained the lethal individuality of the combat veteran. They marched with a slouching stride that had nothing of the drill field in it. They could march that way all day or all night, Bayard knew, and still have enough in them left to fight at the end of the march.

Their route led them across the airfield from which a marine squadron of fighter-bombers was already operating. The dark blue gull-winged Corsairs were painted with a checkerboard insignia. Dog Company looked, half-hostilely, half-admiringly, at the ground crews solicitously arming and grooming the familiar F4U birds.

"Look at those lucky fuckers," said a rifleman. "Tents and hot chow. I hear they already had a USO show."

"Who needs a USO show?" grunted a machine gunner, shifting the weight of his weapon from one shoulder to the other.

Dog Company marched through an industrial area, past a chemical plant reduced to scrap iron by naval gunfire, past an oil terminal, its storage tanks puffed and blasted into curious and grotesque shapes. They were now in a built-up area. A few furtive figures watched the marines march by. They looked different from the South Koreans of Inchon and Seoul. More of the men wore black, a sort of mechanic's uniform; fewer wore the peasant's traditional white. There were some red-white-and-blue South Korean flags being waved desultorily, an occasional patter of hand clapping, but no cheers.

"They don't seem happy to see us," said a rifleman.

"They frightened," said Jim Kim. "Communist leaders tell them that of all Americans, those that wear yellow leggings and spotted cloths on their helmets are the most savage."

"Oh, hell," said the rifleman. "We ain't that bad. Sometimes I go for weeks without raping nobody."

"Quit bragging," said his fire-team leader. "The only piece of ass you ever had in your life was in Tijuana, and you paid for that."

"Look at all these goddamn houses," said the rifleman. "You'd think they'd billet us in a house, just once. No, we got to march a hundred fuckin' miles to find an open field so we can pitch shelter-halves."

"Don't you remember your field sanitation?" said the fire-team leader. "Don't you know these gook houses are lousy with germs and parasites and stuff?"

"So we got to find a rice paddy some farmer has just covered with shit," said the rifleman. "I think maybe I'll write a letter to my congressman."

Dog Company found its designated field and pitched its shelter-halves.

During the night, Bayard was called to the schoolhouse where Battalion had set up its headquarters. He learned that in the morning the battalion would move inland to a village called Madong-ni, that the village was twenty-seven miles from Wonsan, that here the road from Wonsan forked in two directions: one route led across the peninsula to Pyongyang, the other to Seoul. Madong-ni had been taken from the guerrillas by a battalion of the ROK Capital Division. Now the 2d Battalion was to relieve the ROKs. Attached to the 2d Battalion would be a battery of 105mm howitzers.

At first light the trucks of Able Company, 1st Motor Transport Battalion, were ready and waiting along the road bordering the battalion's bivouac area. The order of march was Dog Company, Easy Company, Weapons Company minus, Headquarters and Service Company, Item Battery, and Fox Company.

Bayard organized his company into a routine advance guard. He used a squad in three jeeps as a point; then came the rest of the 3d Platoon under Naheghian in two trucks as an advance party; then Bayard's jeep, overcrowded with himself, his driver, his runner, his interpreter, and his radio operator; then the remainder of his company, wedged tightly into six more trucks.

The macadam highway quickly narrowed to a badly rutted gravel road climbing abruptly into the mountains that rose behind Wonsan. The road edged its way along a narrow shelf hacked into the side of the hills. Far below them purled a blue-green mountain stream; above them the hills were yellow and dark red with autumn colors. Bayard thought of Colorado, wondered if there were trout in the stream below, thought too of a hundred cowboy-and-Indian pictures he had seen, and how this mountain road was a classic invitation to an ambush. He half expected to see a row of war-bonneted Sioux appear along the crest of the canyon, accompanied by a thundering chord of music.

The convoy moved slowly. The artillery trucks hauling their howitzers were having difficulty with the steep gradient and the hairpin turns. Frequent radioed orders to halt the column caused a rubber-band effect. At each halt, Bayard's apprehension increased. He insisted that as each truck ground to a stop, its passengers disembark and his automatic weapons be set up to cover the menacing slopes from which, he felt, a thousand pairs of hostile eyes were watching.

But the convoy continued to inch its way along the mountain road without incident. After five hours had passed, the trucks rounded the last curve, and down below them, brightly etched in the cold white light of the late autumn sun, was Madong-ni. The village was a cluster of mud- . walled thatched houses and a schoolhouse differing from the usual pattern in that it had a Russian-style onion-shaped dome. A bridge crossed a mountain river that bisected the village, and on the far side of the bridge, two roads led off through valleys opening up through the mountains. The north road went to the northern capital of Pyongyang; the south road to the southern capital, Seoul.

Bayard's jeep passed a black-clothed corpse lying by the side of the road. "It looks like maybe the ROKs did some fighting here," said Baby-san.

From the village they heard the sound of a ragged fusillade. "It sounds like maybe they still are doing some fighting," said Brown.

Bayard halted the column, radioed back to Battalion that he had heard shots, and was told to take a platoon into the village to investigate. Bayard and his little entourage—Baby-san, Brown, and Jim Kim—dismounted from the jeep and dogtrotted up to where Naheghian was waiting with two squads of the 3d Platoon. The leading squad had left its jeeps and was moving into the village on foot. Bayard and his group, and Naheghian with the remainder of the 3d Platoon, followed along at a respectable distance.

At the outskirts of the village, they passed through a roadblock manned by a grinning and gesticulating squad of South Korean soldiers. The ROKs welcomed the marines enthusiastically, greeting them with garlic-laden breath and pointing proudly at a captured Russian Maxim heavy machine gun.

"Find out where their command post is," Bayard ordered Jim Kim.

With many words and many gestures the ROKs responded to Jim Kim's question. "They say," said Jim Kim, "their major is in the schoolhouse. That they had big fight here yesterday and killed many communists."

Bayard looked toward the onion-domed schoolhouse, a quarter of a mile or so from where he stood. A fresh crackling of rifle and carbine fire came from that direction.

"What the hell they doing over there, holding target practice?" asked a familiar voice at Bayard's elbow. He turned and saw that Havac had come up and joined him.

"I don't know," said Bayard, "but something is funny about this lash-up."

Cannily, with a sophistication won in the street fighting in Seoul, Naheghian's platoon moved through the village toward the schoolhouse. Confronting them as they entered the school yard were four bareheaded Koreans in peasant costume, standing with their backs to the mud-brick wall. A volley of shots stuttered raggedly and the figures slumped down. An untidy pile of twenty or thirty bodies already lay crumpled by the wall.

A squad of South Korean soldiers stood in a firing line about fifty feet from the wall. A group of Korean officers lounged around a U.S. jeep. Fifty or more male Korean civilians were packed into the back of a Japanese-made truck. As Bayard and his headquarters came into the school yard, four more Koreans were yanked over the tailgate of the truck and dragged into position in front of the bullet-pitted wall.

"What goes on here?" said Bayard loudly.

A tall South Korean officer detached himself from the group by the jeep and came toward Bayard. He wore a lightweight army ski parka belted with a polished leather belt from which hung a Japanese-style leather map case and a U.S. pistol holster.

With a feathered war bonnet, thought Bayard, he could be my Sioux Indian chief. Instead of feathers, the Korean officer wore a winter cap with dog-fur earflaps. The cap framed a face the color of weathered copper with slit black eyes and a hard slash of a mouth.

The Korean officer saluted, held out his hand, and said something in Korean. Bayard shook the proffered hand somewhat dubiously while Jim Kim translated.

"He say he is Major Pak," said Jim Kim. "This his battalion."

"Ask him what's going on here," said Bayard, gesturing with his left hand toward the tumbled bodies by the wall. There was a staccato interchange of Korean between Jim Kim and Major Pak. Bayard's marines had edged closer, watching with appalled eyes the grim work of their Korean opposite numbers.

"He say," translated Jim Kim, "that these the guerrillas who attack him in this town yesterday. He execute them."

"Look at your men, Skipper," said Havac in a low voice. "They don't go for this kinda shit."

"Tell him that he will have to stop," said Bayard. "There will be no more killing prisoners now that we're here."

Jim Kim hesitated. "I do not think it good for me to say this," said Jim Kim. "For him to take such order from you would be to lose much face."

"We're not going to stand around here and watch him kill these people," growled Havac, "face or no face."

The first trucks of the convoy were nosing their way into the village.

"Tell him," said Bayard with sudden inspiration, "that if the trucks are to get him and his battalion back to Wonsan before dark, he will have to be ready to load in twenty minutes. Tell him that he stands relieved of the responsibility for the town, that I will accept the custody of the prisoners."

Jim Kim translated. While he did so, Major Pak stared stonily at Bayard. Bayard did not give way; he met him eye to eye. When Jim Kim had finished, the major gave a short, harsh laugh and, without further palaver or another glance in Bayard's direction, spun on the heels of his polished boots and shouted an order. The members of the firing squad looked at each other incredulously and shouldered their weapons. The major climbed into his jeep, followed by his half-dozen captains and lieutenants. The driver gunned the motor, the gears clashed, and the jeep, with its passengers bulging precariously over the sides, roared out of the school yard.

chapter eighteen...

Dog Company was assigned the western sector of the defensive perimeter that the battalion drew around Madong-ni. Bayard's line stretched from the southern road that led to Seoul up across a razor-backed ridge and down to the northern road leading to Pyongyang.

His observation post was at the apex of his position, where his line crossed the backbone of the ridge. Behind him the ridgeline dropped precipitously down to the valley floor. In front of him—and this was his major concern—it reared almost equally sharply to an intermediate peak about four hundred yards forward of his main line of resistance. Dog Company named this knob "the Nose." Beyond the Nose the ridgeline dropped down into a saddle and then ascended upward to a higher but more remote height.

In reconnoitering his position, Bayard went forward to the Nose. He found there, half covered by the underbrush, the ruins of an old stone tower. Bayard theorized that the tower had been built by some feudal robber baron in Korea's ancient past who, in holding this particular position, thus controlled the old trade routes across the waist of the peninsula. The Nose offered an almost unobstructed view of the three roads leading into Madong-ni and of the village itself.

Looking back down into the valley, Bayard could see the battalion's Headquarters and Service elements busying themselves around the schoolhouse. He could see the battery of 105mm howitzers going into position in the school yard behind a palisade of red-and-white striped aiming stakes, the barrels of the howitzers not parallel as in normal gunnery practice but pointing outward toward all four quadrants of the perimeter. Close to the howitzers were the battalion's organic 81mm mortars, their gunners industriously digging circular gun pits. Along a level strip of ground close to the road on the east side of the bridge, the attached engineer platoon optimistically scraped away with its bulldozer at the beginnings of a landing strip. Upstream from the village, the engineers had established a water point. From his high perch Bayard could see the water being pumped into the water trailers. The engineer lieutenant, after testing the water, had reported to the battalion surgeon that it was pure enough to drink but that he was adding chlorine to give it flavor.

All this activity lay bare and naked to the observer on the Nose. This is what Quantico would call a critical terrain feature, thought Bayard. But Quantico didn't teach me how to do a battalion-sized job with an understrength company. A battalion could have bent its line forward to include the Nose. But I don't have a battalion. I have 178 effectives including attachments.

The best Bayard could do was to establish a forward observation post on the troublesome Nose during the day and outpost it at night with a fire team of four marines.

Battalion issued stern orders concerning any meddling or mingling by the marines with the civilians in the village. The population of the village was possibly five hundred persons—mostly old men, women of all ages, and young children, only a very few young men. In normal times the villagers exacted a frugal living from patches of soil terraced into the sides of the hills. Potatoes seemed to be their chief crop, but most of them were still in the ground. Bayard's marines dug some up and roasted them in their cook fires until the skins were thoroughly charred. The baked potatoes were pronounced delicious.

The barbed wire the battalion had brought for its final protective lines was used to build a POW cage, enclosing a group of thatch-and-mud huts somewhat away from the parent village. Into the cage went the prisoners Bayard had inherited from the ROK battalion.

There was a steady eastward drift of refugees from the interior through the village toward Wonsan. Battalion established checkpoints using its interpreters to screen this traffic. Jim Kim and the Dog Company irregulars were detached for this duty on the north and south roadblocks. They looked for the signs by which they could single out the former members of the North Korean army: short-cropped hair, a sunburned vee at the throat from wearing a uniform shirt, calluses on the ball of the foot from the unaccustomed wearing of Western-style leather army shoes.

These suspect persons were added to the POW compound. Here they were interrogated by the battalion S-2. Some were very glib, others sullenly silent. The interpreters alternately cajoled and bullied. The S-2 fit the bits and pieces of information together, added up his totals, and published an estimate of ten thousand guerrillas, the broken remains of a North Korean division, in the hills around Madong-ni. No one took these figures seriously. They set them down as the product of the Oriental proclivity for exaggeration and the intelligence officer's own dramatic flair.

On its hillside, Dog Company organized its position in accordance with what was by now ingrained habit. The forward edge of the position was marked by a line of fighting holes: double foxholes for BAR men and their assistants, single foxholes for riflemen and fire-team leaders, more elaborate emplacements for machine gunners, rocket launchers, flamethrowers, mortarmen, squad leaders, section leaders, and platoon commanders.

To the rear, wherever defilade afforded protection, the men dug their sleeping holes. Because there was time, because there was no enemy pressure as yet, and because the weather was growing increasingly cold—a thickening skim of ice formed on the mountain stream each night—these housekeeping arrangements were more elaborate than anything previously attempted by Dog Company.

Bayard shared a hut with Gibson. With the help of Baby-san, they had dug into the side of the hill until they had a room about eight feet square. A three-inch poplar gave them a ridge pole, which they secured into the hillside at one end and to a stout post at the other. Additional poles cut from the poplar and pine trees served as rafters. These were covered with old canvas and corrugated pasteboard from ration boxes to keep the dirt from sifting down. Then on top, they added a roof of dirt and sod. "If we're still here in the spring," said Gibson proudly, "we'll plant a garden on our roof."

The unburied end of the hut had a door frame and a window stolen from the schoolhouse. These were a *presento* from Pinky and Baby-san, a gesture that gave these two a double measure of satisfaction: not only had they stolen them out from under the eyes of their mortal enemies, the effete clerks of battalion headquarters, but they added considerably to the dignity of the Dog Company command post. From a peeled pine pole in front of the hut flew the red-and-gold company guidon.

Inside the hut was a double-decked bunk with springs woven from rope and pine-bough mattressing, a minuscule desk (also stolen from the schoolhouse), and a wood-burning stove improvised from an oil drum and a flue made from 81mm mortar-shell packing tubes.

The consummate luxury, however, was the electric light. This was contrived by Bayard's jeep driver, who argued with considerable logic that there was no point leaving the headlamps mounted in the jeep, where they could not be used because all nighttime driving was done under blackout conditions. With the addition of a little wire and a modest expenditure of gasoline to keep the battery charged, the driver reasoned, they could be used to light the men's living quarters.

Next to Gibson and Bayard's hut—and, incidentally, lit by the second headlight—was a larger, if somewhat less elegant, set of quarters known as the "Rabbit Warren." Occupying it were Pinky, Baby-san, Pilnick, Jim Kim, the property sergeant, the jeep driver, the radio operator, the field music, and gunny Agnelli. Only Havac was unbeguiled by these creature comforts. He preferred sleeping in Spartan simplicity in his own individual hole, roofed by nothing more than a shelter half.

During the first several days at Madong-ni, while Dog Company busied itself in these constructive pursuits, not a shot was fired in anger—although an unfortunate mortar gunner did put a .45-caliber slug through the palm of his hand while field-stripping his pistol. This was the official version; rumor had it that the accident occurred while the mortar gunner was demonstrating to a rifleman from the 2d Platoon that the trigger could not be pulled if a firm pressure was maintained against the muzzle of the pistol.

Part of the battalion's mission was to keep open the routes that joined at Madong-ni. Each of the rifle companies was given the responsibility of patrolling one of the three roads. Dog Company was assigned the road that led northwest to Pyongyang. Each morning at 0800, Bayard dispatched a reinforced platoon through the road block. This platoon, under battalion control, would march five miles up the valley to a hamlet marked on Bayard's map as Chipyong-ri and there would establish a patrol base. From this point the platoon commander would send out squad-size patrols to scour the hills for evidence of guerrilla activity until midafternoon, at which time the platoon leader, at battalion order, would gather his platoon together once again and hike them back into the perimeter.

Occasionally these patrols brought back prisoners. The majority of these were disheartened stragglers who had given themselves up under the pressures of an empty stomach and the increasing cold of the approaching winter. For the most part, these patrols reaffirmed Bayard's personal conviction as to the futility of regular forces reconnoitering in hostile terrain against a guerrilla enemy. The marines caught only those who wished to be caught, learned only what the enemy was willing for them to learn.

October ended and November began. Dog Company patrolled, stood watch in their foxholes, shivered in their field jackets as the weather grew colder, elaborated on their huts, and waited for the elusive enemy to make an overt move.

The situation began to coalesce on the third day of November. It was the 1st Platoon's turn to patrol to Chipyong-ri. Bayard had gone forward to the Nose in order to keep sight contact with the patrol as far as possible. At 0800, through his field glasses, he saw Martinez lead his platoon out through the roadblock. Thirty minutes later, not much more than a mile out from Madong-ni, the patrol ran into heavy small-arms fire coming down from the surrounding hills. With his field glasses Bayard saw the distant figures of the marines scurry from the road and take cover. Monitoring the battalion tactical net, he heard Martinez report that he was taking casualties and requested instructions. He heard Major Mansell order Martinez to extricate his platoon and return to the perimeter. From his perch on the Nose, Bayard could see the marines fall back. Every now and again he glimpsed a bent-over, running figure breaking into the open. The thin sound of rifle shots grew more infrequent and then halted altogether.

"Come on," said Bayard to Baby-san. "Let's go down to the roadblock."

They went back along the ridgeline trail to Dog Company's position at close to a dead run and then turned at right angles and plunged down the slope to the roadblock. Winded, Bayard arrived to find Dr. Goldberg already there with a jeep ambulance. Also present and waiting was Three-Able, the lieutenant who was Mansell's operations assistant. Bayard nodded curtly to the lieutenant and walked over to the jeep ambulance, where the battalion surgeon was laying out the tools of his trade.

Martinez brought his platoon through the roadblock in good order, carrying three wounded on litters. Two of them would be all right, but the third—Dr. Goldberg shook his head. The marine was shot through the lungs. Goldberg pulled away the blood-soaked battle dressing from the boy's chest. Bayard saw a bubbling red-ringed wound.

"How many were there?" Bayard asked Martinez.

Martinez's broad Indian features were impassive. He lifted his shoulders in a slight shrug. "Who knows, Captain? They were well hidden. A company maybe. Just rifles and I theenk one light machine gun."

Three-Able interrupted impatiently to say that Major Mansell wished the patrol leader to make his patrol report immediately. He gestured toward a waiting jeep.

"I'll go along too," said Bayard.

"Very well, sir," said the lieutenant. Bayard thought there was a shade of condescension in his tone. Martinez climbed into the back of the jeep. Bayard pointedly waited until the lieutenant, deferring to his seniority, scrambled into the rear seat of the jeep along side of Martinez. Bayard then got into the front right seat next to the driver.

At the schoolhouse they went into the room that had been set up as the operations center. The inside walls had been lined shoulder-high with sandbags to give a measure of protection against possible enemy fire. A cast-iron potbellied stove glowed cherry red with a wood fire. The room was overly warm to a person coming in from the outside. Bayard unbuttoned his field jacket and pulled off the strip of blanket he was wearing for a muffler.

Mansell turned around from his field desk and without saying a word, just by flicking his eyes up and down from Bayard's grease-stained cap to his mud-caked boots, managed to convey the impression of ineffable disgust.

After the most perfunctory of greetings, Mansell turned his full attention to Martinez. Propped up against the wall was an acetate-covered situation map. Standing next to it, red grease pencil in hand, was the young second lieutenant who was the battalion S-2.

"All right, Sergeant," said Mansell, "suppose you show us exactly where your patrol came under fire."

Martinez crossed to the map. "I am not so good with the map reading," he said pointing at the map with a black-rimmed fingernail. "I theenk it was right here."

"Hardly," said Mansell icily. "You're pointing at the wrong valley."

"I saw the whole thing from my OP on the Nose," interrupted Bayard going over to the map. He tapped the acetate with his index finger. "The patrol was right here when it was hit."

"Thank you, Captain," said Major Mansell. The battalion intelligence officer made a short red mark at the point on the map indicated by Bayard.

"Now, Sergeant," Mansell went on, "what can you tell us about the size of the enemy force?"

"About a company, I theenk," said Martinez.

"You *think* there was about a company," said Mansell. "Can't you be a little more precise, Sergeant?"

"They were in the hills, sir. We were down on the road. We could not see so good."

The lieutenant marked the map with the symbol for an enemy rifle company and put a question mark above it.

"Were they dug in?" asked Mansell.

"I theenk so, sir," said Martinez. "They were hid good. We couldn't see much."

"You *think* they were dug in," said Mansell. Martinez's broad face remained impassive, seemingly unperturbed. The battalion S-2 drew a rickrack symbol on the map to indicate a line of trenches.

"How were they armed?" asked Mansell.

"We come under rifle fire and a light machine gun—just one, I theenk."

"Thank you, Sergeant," said Major Mansell. "That will be all."

Martinez picked up his rifle and started for the door. Bayard wrapped his strip of blanket across his chest and began buttoning up his field jacket.

"Just a minute, Captain," said Mansell.

"Sir?"

"Let me recommend that in the future you send an officer along with your patrols."

Bayard hesitated. Mansell had not disguised his dissatisfaction with Martinez's patrol report. Martinez had a stolid impassivity that made him appear slow-witted, and there was that unfortunate error in map reading. But it was not fair to judge Martinez by his performance in front of a situation map—you had to see him handle a platoon in combat. Bayard wanted to remind Mansell that Martinez had been recommended for a Silver Star for the street fighting in Seoul, but, looking at Mansell, he decided that such a defense would be impolitic.

"Aye, aye, sir," he said resignedly.

"Do you want my driver to run you back to your company area?" asked Mansell.

"No, thank you, Major," said Bayard. "We'll walk back."

Later that morning the patrols from Easy and Fox Companies were also beaten back in, and in the afternoon Battalion learned that a supply convoy scheduled for Madong-ni was unable to force its way through and had to turn back.

That night the battalion went on a 50 percent alert in anticipation of an attack. Nothing happened during the hours of darkness except that something—possibly an enemy patrol, probably an animal—tripped a flare in front of Easy Company. Beale called down a mortar barrage and swept the area with his machine guns. There was no return fire.

When morning came, Battalion ordered the companies to send out their patrols once again, but this time they were to travel the ridgelines rather than the roads. Naheghian took the 3d Platoon out in front of Dog Company. He made no contact with the enemy but reported freshly dug holes and brought back in a blood-stained padded-cotton jacket, a basket of rice balls, and some freshly fired cartridge cases.

At 1600 that afternoon the company commanders met with the battalion staff at the command post and listened to the S-2's considered opinion that, without artillery or armor, the enemy was not strong enough to attack the Madong-ni perimeter but would continue its present tactics of harassing the battalion's patrols and cutting the MSR leading back to Wonsan to prevent their resupply.

"Meanwhile," drawled Beale of Easy Company, "back at the fort—"

This broke up the meeting. Even Mansell smiled a thin icy smile.

"Just to remind you that it is six more days until the Marine Corps birthday," said the S-4 as the company commanders bundled up to return to their company areas, "if the convoy gets through from Wonsan, we plan to serve the troops a holiday menu."

It was dusk by the time Bayard got back to his own company and dark by the time his platoon commanders had gathered in his hut. In the warmth of the wood fire and the golden glow of the candlelight, he felt very close to these men, who such a short time ago had seemed such strangers. He flipped open his notebook, talked from the notes he had taken, and watched the serious young faces of Thompson, Burdock, Reynolds, and even Martinez and Naheghian as they listened and in turn made entries in their own notebooks. He watched Martinez's thick brown fingers cramped around a pencil stub and saw the frown of concentration on the broad Indian face. From Martinez he switched his attention to the blond boy-face of Burdock.

"Burdock," Bayard asked, "do you think that Staff Sergeant Laski could handle the mortar section by himself?"

Burdock looked surprised. "I'm sure of it, sir. Sergeant Laski is a very good NCO, and he knows his mortars."

"I think for the time being," said Bayard, "that we'll switch you to the 1st Platoon."

"Aye, aye, sir," said Burdock eagerly, and then he looked questioningly from Bayard to Martinez.

Martinez said nothing but snapped his notebook shut and slid it into his field-jacket pocket.

"That will be all for tonight, gentlemen," said Bayard. "Remember—33⅓ percent alert. One out of every three on the line and awake. Sergeant Martinez—and Mr. Burdock—I'd like to see you after the others leave."

"Do you want me to leave too, Captain?" asked Gibson.

"No, you stay if you will, Mr. Gibson." Bayard waited until the others had filed out of the hut. "Martinez, I wanted to make sure that you understood why I have assigned Lieutenant Burdock to the 1st Platoon. It has nothing to do with the way you've handled the platoon. I think you have done an outstanding job. But we're one officer understrength, and I believe that the mortar section can better do without an officer than a rifle platoon."

"Captain," said Martinez slowly, "I have been with the 1st Platoon four years—at Lejeune, on maneuvers, on the Med cruise, here in Korea. If I theenk that you believe that I cannot handle the men, I would feel very bad. But I know that there is a job in the platoon for a lieutenant and also a job for a platoon sergeant."

"That's it exactly," said Bayard with relief.

"Well, sir," said Burdock, "if it's all right with you, I'll move in with the 1st Platoon tonight."

"I will help you carry your things up to the position, Lieutenant," said Martinez.

The two men stood up to leave.

"One more thing," said Bayard. "This transfer doesn't have anything to do with Major Mansell."

"Doesn't it?" said Martinez.

The blanket hanging from the door frame closed softly behind the two men as they left the hut.

"It's time to set the watch," said Bayard to Gibson after a minute's silence.

During the day, the company command group operated from the company observation post either out on the Nose or in the center of the middle platoon, where the company straddled the ridgeline. At night they operated from Bayard's hut, with Havac, Gibson, Agnelli, and Bayard standing two-hour watches in rotation. The other enlisted men in company headquarters rotated sentry duty and telephone watch on the same schedule.

This particular night, Bayard had the first watch, from eight until ten. Baby-san was standing the duty with him, just as Pinky usually paired off with the first sergeant.

"Sentry's posted, sir," said Baby-san, coming through the blanket flap. "I told him if I caught him ducking into the property tent to get warm, I'd have his ass. It's Turner from the mess section."

The cooks and the messmen from Battalion were divided among the line companies as stretcher bearers during these times when it was impossible to have a battalion mess.

"What're you reading, Captain?" asked Baby-san, squatting on the dirt floor in front of the SCR-300.

"I found a paperback copy of *The Pickwick Papers*," answered Bayard. "It's sort of a collection of short stories by Charles Dickens."

"Sure, I know," said Baby-san. "The guy that wrote *Tale of Two Cities*. We read it in school." Baby-san tilted back his head and said in a fair imitation of Ronald Colman: "It is a far, far better thing that I do—" Baby-san shook his head and declared, "What an asshole!"

"Do you have the schedule for tonight's radio checks?" asked Bayard, cutting short Baby-san's histrionics.

"Yes, sir. Twenty after and ten to the hour. Captain, you keep reading in this lousy light and you're going to ruin your eyes."

"Suppose you let me worry about that," said Bayard.

"Yes, sir, but I don't favor having a half-blind company commander leading me around these here hills."

And so the two hours passed, much in the same way they had passed during every other night watch that had been stood in the command post since Dog Company's arrival at Madong-ni. Bayard read his book, wrote a short letter to Donna, cleaned and oiled his pistol, scraped the mud from his boots with his knife, and worked some dubbing into the leather. Baby-san came up on the battalion tactical net at the prescribed times to get his radio checks and called each phone on the company's wire net every fifteen minutes or so to make sure that the lines were still in and that the talkers on the other end were there and awake. He boiled some water on top of the stove and opened a bread unit from a C ration and Bayard and he snacked on crackers, jam, and coffee. Turner, the messman on sentry duty, reported each time he completed the circuit of the command post area, a soft disembodied voice calling through the blanketed doorway, "All's well." Then it was 9:50, and Bayard told Baby-san to go over to the Rabbit Warren and break out Pilnick, who had the next radio and telephone watch.

Bayard woke up Gibson.

"Anything happening?" asked the executive officer, getting out of his sleeping bag.

"Not a thing," said Bayard, "but tomorrow we better have somebody walk out the wire to the outpost. We've been having a little trouble with our telephone checks."

Gibson took Bayard's place at the school desk and rummaged about for a piece of writing paper. Bayard took off his field jacket and started unlacing his boots. "Another letter home?" Bayard asked Gibson.

Gibson nodded.

"You don't miss a night, do you?" said Bayard.

"Not if I can help it," said Gibson.

Night after night, on board ship and ashore, Bayard had watched Gibson writing to his wife—long letters, page after page of neat small script.

"What do you find to write about?" Bayard asked. "I write Donna about once a week, and then I have a hard time filling a page."

Gibson smiled. "Oh, I don't know. Maybe when you're married and you have a couple of kids, it makes a difference. I sit down with a piece of paper in front of me, and I sort of lose myself—sort of like if Carol were here and I was talking to her. I write about the things I hope we have someday—the house we'd like to build, where the boy and girl should go to school—things like that. Does that make any sense to you, Captain?"

"Sure," said Bayard, "it makes a lot of sense. I wonder though—you're such a family man. How does that fit in with the Marine Corps?"

Gibson was silent for a minute. "I'm not quite certain. I miss not being with them. Sometimes I'm downright homesick. Being separated from them sometimes, though—that's part of being a marine. I have to accept that. Oh, I guess that like everybody else, I wonder sometimes if I couldn't do better on the outside. But whenever I sit down to figure out what I could do on the outside, or what I would want to do, I come up with a blank. The Marine Corps has been pretty good to me. I've had eleven years of it. I enlisted in 1939, right after I got out of high school. I'm twenty-nine now. I make enough to live comfortably and to provide for my family. I've had the good and the bad with the Marine Corps. I've had some pretty rough tours, and I've worked for some pretty horseshit characters. But I think the good has outweighed the bad. I wouldn't even have met Carol if it hadn't been for the Corps. She was working in Washington when I was in Candidates Class in Quantico. I met her at one of those USO dances."

Someone knocked on the doorpost, and a voice from outside said, "It's Pilnick, sir."

"Come in, Pills," said Bayard. The company's senior corpsman ducked in through the blanket, spoke to Bayard and Gibson, and then went over to the radio and telephone. Bayard watched him as he set about checking the frequency of the radio's channel setting.

Pilnick had changed radically since he first joined the company. Bayard remembered the drug salesman who had looked so out of place in his stiff new marine utilities. Now, there was little to distinguish him from any other NCO in the company—only the faded petty officer's rating stenciled on the arm of his utility jacket. Pilnick didn't have to stand the radio and telephone watch; as a corpsman he was exempt from such duties, but he himself had asked to be put on the watch list.

Bayard slid into his sleeping bag and turned his face toward the wall, away from the light of the jeep headlamp hanging over the desk where Gibson sat absorbed in his letter writing, his mind and thoughts ten thousand miles away. Bayard listened to the night noises for a minute or so and then drifted off to sleep. He dreamed that he and Donna were married. Only it wasn't Donna at all. His wife in his dream had Carol Gibson's face, pleasant and plumpish. She was standing in front of a house—a small white house with green shutters. A little boy and a little girl were standing next to her. They seemed to be waiting for him. A sidewalk stretched out longer and longer. The figures of his wife and children receded in the distance. The sidewalk broke off at his feet, and there was a yawning chasm separating him from his house and family. The house seemed to be floating away. . . .

The muted *thu-u-dds* of distantly exploding hand grenades intruded into his consciousness. He was wide awake before Gibson could shake him. "What's happening?" he asked, getting out of his sleeping bag and reaching for his boots.

"We don't know yet," said Gibson. "I think they've overrun the outpost. We can't reach them on the sound-powered phone."

"What do you hear from the 2d Platoon? What does Thompson say?" Bayard buckled the flaps of his combat boots.

"Thompson says he can't see a thing from the OP."

"Have you called Battalion?"

"Yes, sir."

Bayard had on his field jacket by now. He reached for his helmet and pistol belt. "Let's get on up to the OP. Where's Baby-san?"

"Here, sir." Baby-san was standing in the doorway with his BAR cradled in his arms.

"Where's the first sergeant?"

"They're all outside—waiting," said Baby-san.

"Good," said Bayard. "Let's go. Gibson—you and Pinky stay here. Brown—where's your radio? Let's get going!"

Outside the air was knife-cold. A powdering of snow had fallen, and in the moonlight the world was black and white. Bayard and his headquarters group started up the trail that led to the 2d Platoon's position astride the ridge. Ahead of them a burst of orange tracers arced across the sky. Behind them from the school yard in the valley, red fingers of flame stabbed upward as the 81mm mortars began their barrage fire.

"Christ, they've gotten into the MLR," said Bayard.

"Maybe not," said Havac.

They reached the 2d Platoon's position and dropped down into the short zigzag trench they had dug across the apex of the ridgeline to serve as an observation post. Bayard pushed past marines crouching in the trench, indistinguishably alike in helmets and field jackets.

"Where's Mr. Thompson?" he asked.

"Here, sir," answered one of the dark shapes.

Dog Company's machine guns were slicing the blackness in front of the position with glowing, interlacing strings of tracer bullets. A quarter-mile out beyond the 2d Platoon *crummpped* the mortar barrage.

"All right," said Bayard to Thompson, "what's the story? Where do we stand?"

Before Thompson could answer, a marine pushed a telephone receiver into Bayard's hand. "It's for you, Captain. It's the Three, sir."

"What's happening up there?" Mansell's voice came through the wire with metallic crispness. "Are they into your main battle position?"

"I don't know, sir. I don't think so." Bayard covered the transmitter with his hand and called to Havac. "See if you can raise the 1st and 3d Platoons on the sound-powereds. Find out how they're making out."

"I suggest you find out," said Mansell.

"We're checking now," said Bayard. He covered the mouthpiece again. "Where's the mortar sergeant? Have him tell the 81s to shorten range."

Off from Bayard's left came an anguished cry. "Corpsman! Corpsman!"

"Where's your platoon corpsman?" Bayard asked Thompson.

"I don't know where the son of a bitch is," Thompson responded. "He probably sneaked back to Battalion to spend the night with the medical platoon."

A cry came from out in the darkness. "He's bleeding to death! Where'n the Christ is a corpsman?"

"I'm coming," called a voice that Bayard recognized as Pilnick's, and a dark shape pushed by him and scrambled over the parapet of the trench.

The threads of the situation began to weave themselves together. Bayard could see that the 2d Platoon stood firm in its foxholes, that the 1st and 3d Platoons had not been budged, that the integrity of his line remained inviolate.

The telephone receiver, forgotten these last several minutes, was still in his gloved hand. He raised it to his face. "Major?"

"Mansell here."

"We're lifting our final protective fires. They didn't reach our main position. We've beaten off the assault."

"What about the Nose?"

"They've still got that."

"You'll have to get it back."

"Aye, aye, sir."

"Will you need any help?"

"We can manage."

Bayard handed the telephone back to Baby-san and turned to Thompson. "We've got to get the Nose back as soon as it's light. You got any ideas?"

"Not much room for maneuver along the ridgeline, Captain."

"I know it. We'll have to push straight ahead from here with your platoon. That will give us room for Burdock and Naheghian to come up on both sides of the hill from the flanks. It's almost two o'clock now. That gives us better than four hours until first light. That gives us plenty of time to get ready for the jump-off."

Dawn came slowly. In the warming air a heavy fog swathed the ridge in white cotton. In this gray light of the morning, Bayard could not see fifty yards in front of the observation post.

"Can't see a goddamn thing," said Thompson.

"So much the better," said Bayard. "It would take a hell of a lot of WP to give us this good a smokescreen." He looked at his watch. "Just about time for the 105s. Battalion's promised us a hundred rounds of HE. Your people all set?"

"All set, Captain. I'm going to have to attack in a column of squads. I don't like it, but the ridge is too goddamn narrow to deploy any wider."

"On the way," interrupted the artillery forward observer.

Ka-chunngg came the noise of the howitzers firing from down in the schoolyard below them. The range was short. The guns were firing at high angle and with minimum charge. Instead of the familiar tearing sound of shells passing overhead, Dog Company—after what seemed an interminable wait—heard the shells plunging downward, almost like aerial bombs, to strike the still-hidden higher ground in front of them.

"Are they on target?" asked Bayard dubiously. "Are they hitting on the Nose?"

"I can't see," said the artillery lieutenant. "They sound right, Captain. I think they're on."

"How long will it take your battery to get out a hundred shells?" asked Bayard.

"About five minutes or less," responded the artillery observer.

Bayard turned to Thompson. "Let's go," he said.

Thompson climbed out of the trench and stood up on the parapet. "All right, 2d Platoon," he said in a high, strained voice. "Let's run the bastards off the hill."

The center squad converged on the ridge trail and started forward toward the Nose. Thompson, his runner, and his radio operator fell in behind them. The column disappeared into the white blanket of fog, man by man, as though they were stepping off into eternity.

"Get a check with your SCR-536," Bayard said to Baby-san. "Make sure we can receive them."

Baby-san held up the small company radio, called Thompson's operator, and nodded to Bayard. "I can read them, sir."

The 105s still burst unseen somewhere out in front of them.

"How much longer before you're through?" Bayard asked the artillery officer.

"That's the last of them," said the lieutenant.

The drumfire of the artillery ceased abruptly and the ridgeline in front of the company position was suddenly silent. Then Bayard heard the *pop-pop-popping* of a solitary machine gun. He could not make out from the sound whether it was American or Russian. Baby-san handed him the SCR-536.

"Firebrand Dog Six," Thompson's voice came thinly through the receiver, "this is Firebrand Dog Two. We're almost to the Nose. No resistance yet. Out."

The machine gun stopped firing. More silence. The fog still hung heavily along the ridgeline. Bayard looked up at the sky. It was brightening overhead. Someone pressed a sound-powered telephone into his hand. Burdock was phoning from the 1st Platoon area.

"When do we move out, Captain?" Bayard could feel the tension in Burdock's voice. He wants to show me, thought Bayard, that he can handle the platoon.

"I'll tell you when," he said shortly.

Another phone was pressed into his hand. It was the Battalion Three again. "What's happening up there?" Mansell's voice was sharp and incisive. "Keep us informed. I want fifteen-minute reports."

"Everything according to plan so far," soothed Bayard.

The angry sound of a firefight broke out to the front. Bayard dropped the phone and grabbed for the SCR-536. "What's happening?" he asked

Thompson. "Where are you?"

"We're just short of the Nose," reported the leader of the 2d Platoon. "The fog's thinning out up here. We can see them, and they can see us. I got a couple of men hit. You better send some more stretcher bearers forward. I'm getting ready to assault the position."

"Stay where you are," ordered Bayard. "I'm coming up. Dog One and Three, did you monitor Dog Two's transmission? Over."

"Roger," from Naheghian.

"Roger," from Burdock.

"Okay, then," said Bayard, "move out!"

He reached for the battalion phone. The switchboard operator had kept his line jacked through to the Three. "This is Bayard," he said. "My 2d Platoon has developed the position. My 1st and 3d Platoons are moving out. I'm displacing my command post forward. I don't expect to be able to keep wire in so I'll come up on the battalion tactical net."

"Very well," said Mansell, "good luck."

"All right, you people," said Bayard to his headquarters group, "let's go!"

They scrambled out of the trench and moved forward in column along the ridge trail. The powdering of snow that had fallen during the night had been trampled into thin slush by the 2d Platoon. The fog was lifting. Ahead, dimly, they could see the Nose rearing upward. To the left and to the right, at a lower elevation, they could hear the sounds of the 1st and 3d Platoons crashing their way through the frozen, ice-encrusted underbrush. These flank platoons had the more difficult approach. They would have to move down the slope, and then when they were abreast of the Nose, they would turn in at right angles and climb the precipitous sides of that rocky citadel.

Bayard and his group came up cautiously behind the 2d Platoon. From among the sprawled out forms he found Thompson. "Keep down, Captain," cautioned the platoon leader. "I already lost four men here. They got a machine gun enfilading the trail."

Bayard could now see the Nose clearly. The enemy had been busy with its shovels. The gray rocky eminence was pocked with the yellow clay of newly dug holes. The 2d Platoon was engaging the hidden enemy with rifles and machine guns. A desultory return fire came back from the Nose.

"Think they got any mortars?" asked Bayard, worming up on his stomach alongside of Thompson.

"I don't think so," said Thompson. "They haven't used them, at any rate. They've got a bunch of stick grenades, though. We found that out when we tried to close with the bastards."

"Any sign of Naheghian or Burdock?" asked Bayard.

"Not yet," said Thompson.

The morning sun was burning off the remnant of the fog. The rocky summit of the Nose was perhaps a hundred and fifty yards in front of where Bayard lay. He had not seen an enemy since arriving at Thompson's position. The return fire from the Nose had died down to the occasional crack and whine of an opportunistic rifle shot.

"It's taking Naheghian and Burdock a hell of a long time to get in position," he said. Lying there on his belly, he could feel the wetness of the melted snow soaking through his jacket and trousers.

"Do you want me to move out?" asked Thompson. "I think I can take it without their help."

"We'll do it the way we planned it," said Bayard shortly. Thompson was the most dependable of his platoon commanders, very competent professionally and extremely steady under fire, but he had an air of superiority, an acidity of expression, that sometimes grated on Bayard's nerves. This was one of those times. Bayard reached for his company radio. Baby-san thrust the SCR-536 into his outstretched hand.

"Firebrand Dog One, Firebrand Dog Three, this is Firebrand Dog Six, Over."

"Firebrand Dog Six, this is Firebrand Dog One. I read you. Over," said Burdock.

"Firebrand Dog Six, this is Firebrand Dog Three, " said Naheghian. "Send your message. Over."

"Why aren't you in position?" asked Bayard. "When will you be ready to assault? Over."

"This hill is slick as grease," said Naheghian. "I need ten more minutes. Over."

"I'll be ready as soon as Dog Three," said Burdock. "Over."

"All right then," said Bayard, "I'll give you ten more minutes and no more. Then I'm going to have the 60s dump all the Willie Peters they got on the Nose. That'll be your signal to move out. I want that hill back. Out." He handed the set back to Baby-san and looked at Thompson.

"Did you get that?" he asked.

"Yes, sir," said Thompson.

"As soon as the 1st and 3d Platoons jump off, I want you to move forward with your platoon."

Thompson gave him that faintly sour I-know-my-business look. "Aye, aye, sir," he said.

"Where's the mortar sergeant?" asked Bayard.

"Here, sir," said Sergeant Laski. He had put his 60mm mortar section into firing position close behind the 2d Platoon and had come up and joined the headquarters group.

"You think you can hit the Nose from here?" asked Bayard.

"Easy," said Laski. "I could throw 'em that far, sir. Just tell me when you're ready for 'em, sir, and we'll lay 'em in there."

The mortar chief had a sound-powered phone in his hand and a thin, glistening, black strand of wire ran off behind him, disappearing behind the hummock that hid the mortar section from Bayard's view.

The ten minutes were painfully slow in passing. "All right," said Bayard, watching the last minute crawl across the face of his watch, "start shooting!"

Laski passed the word to fire over his phone. From behind him Bayard heard the *pum-m-m pum-m-m* of the almost toylike 60s spitting out their finned projectiles. Somewhere overhead arced the unseen shells.

"There they come," said Baby-san. Bayard followed the line of his runner's outstretched arm but could see nothing. His eyes were not as sharp as Baby-san's. The shells exploded in a cluster on the Nose. Three—six—nine—twelve explosions, spewing up cottony little fountains of white phosphorus. Then silence.

"That's it," said Sergeant Laski, almost apologetically. "That's all the WP I got."

"That's it," said Bayard over the SCR-536. "Move out."

For a minute or so, nothing happened. All he could see were just those little piles of white phosphorus burning away on the hill. Then there was a yell, a sort of cheer from the right flank, and then two, then three, and then four marines broke out of the underbrush and started scrambling up the last few yards to the top of the Nose. A hidden North Korean began pitching stick grenades. Bayard could see the black shapes, like short sections of pipe, turning end over end in the air. Two or three of them exploded, and the four marines went down. Three of the marines got up again and continued forward. The fourth stayed down in a crumpled heap.

More marines from the 1st Platoon were emerging from the under-brush. Bayard saw one marine stand straddling a foxhole, emptying his rifle down into the hole at pointblank range. He saw another marine point with his carbine toward the top of the Nose. That marine had lost his hel-met, and his hair was like bright gold in the morning sun. It was Burdock. Bayard watched him pick his way upward over the rocks.

"Goddamn," said Bayard. "Where's Naheghian? Why isn't he coming up on the other side? Come on, Thompson! Get your people moving. Give Burdock a little help up there."

Thompson was already on his feet. He and his platoon started up the trail. Bayard followed Thompson, his attention riveted on Burdock's slen-der figure. The boy was almost to the summit. There was a pile of gray stone there, what was left of the old war lord's watchtower. Burdock reached the pile, climbed up on it, held out his arms exultantly.

For I am King of the Hill, thought Bayard almost ecstatic with the excitement of the assault. He started to dogtrot forward, elbowing ahead of Thompson. Then Burdock's triumphant figure buckled. He fell first to his knees and then rolled off the pile of stones and on down the slope.

"Get to him!" screamed Bayard. "Somebody get to him!"

And then from three sides Dog Company converged on the hill. They swept on up and over the Nose. The enemy withdrew back along the ridgeline. Dodging through the underbrush, the North Koreans gave Dog Company only elusive and fleeting targets before they disappeared alto-gether from sight. But not all of them escaped—a rewarding number of bodies remained on the position.

Burdock was dead when they reached him. So were two riflemen from the 1st Platoon and one man from the 2d. There were also six critically wounded to be sent down to the village on stretchers to join the four from Thompson's platoon who had already been carried to the rear. The casu-alty count continued to grow. The bodies of the four marines who had manned the outpost were found laid out neatly side by side in a depres-sion behind the ruins of the watchtower. The enemy had taken their weapons and equipment and had stripped them of their field jackets and boots but had otherwise left them unmolested. Bayard's feeling of exul-tation had long since faded, leaving him with a sick, empty feeling and a pounding headache. He called Battalion, reported the Nose as being retaken, and asked for some additional stretcher bearers to carry the bod-ies down the hill.

chapter nineteen...

Bayard looked into the bottom of his empty glass and thought of that morning on the ridge above Madong-ni, seeing once again Burdock's still white face as the body was carried past him on its stretcher.

He remembered Martinez saying, "He was too eager, Captain. I try to hol' heem back, but he start for the top of the hill an' I could not hol' heem."

He remembered Naheghian's dejection, the crushed look on the face of the leader of the Forty Thieves: "If I could've gotten there sooner. That goddamn hill was like glass. If Burdock only hadn't rushed the hill until my platoon was in position."

Life, Bayard reflected morosely, was studded with *ifs*—a million suppositions. *If* he had handled things differently at Madong-ni. *If* he hadn't pushed Burdock into making the assault—

Women's voices cut into his consciousness. "Are you sure it was the same boy? The cute one with the curly hair?" asked one of the voices.

"Certainly I am sure. He's been in that ward for over a week now," answered a second voice. Bayard swung around on his stool. Three American women had come into the cocktail lounge and were seated at the bar to his right.

"Why I gave him some writing paper just yesterday. He seemed perfectly all right to me," said the woman who had spoken first.

"Three whiskey sodas, boy-san," ordered the center member of the trio. "*Toksan* whiskey. *Sukoshi* soda."

The bartender, imperturbable in his alien cowboy shirt, mixed three strong whiskeys and soda and set them in front of the trio. Bayard watched the process attentively, as though it were of great significance, and then looked at each of the women in turn.

The one in the center was tall and handsome in a strong-featured sort of way. The other two were softer and prettier. Bayard guessed they were army wives. The husband of the one in the center was probably the commanding officer of the husbands of the other two. From their conversation he gathered that they had spent the day at the army hospital in Kyoto doing well-intentioned things for the patients' comfort—such as passing out writing paper, playing cards, and magazines.

"Tell me," said the plump, pretty girl on the far right, "what you two are talking about."

"You mean," said the woman on the extreme left, the one closest to Bayard, "that you didn't hear what happened in the ward today?"

"Didn't you notice all the fuss?" asked the tall woman in the center. "The colonel's coming into the ward and their putting a screen around the boy's bed?"

"I was in the diet kitchen all day today."

"You must have been," said the tall woman. "Well, Marian was pushing the book cart through the ward and this boy asked her to straighten his bedclothes. That should've tipped her off, but, anyway, she started to smooth out the sheets and then he grabbed her hand and—"

The woman on the far right leaned forward with a look of horrified fascination on her face, a slight anticipatory smile turning up the ends of her mouth. "What did he do?" she breathed. "You mean he—?"

The woman in the center dropped her voice to a whisper, but it still carried to Bayard.

"He put her hand right on his thing."

"Oh, no," said the woman on the right, "he didn't. Not right there in the ward!"

"Oh, yes, he did!" said the other two women in triumphant unison.

"Poor Marian," said the woman on the right. "I wondered where she was tonight."

"She went home early. Dr. Billings gave her a sedative and sent her home in a staff car."

"I should think so. What an awful experience."

"I thought," said the plump, pretty one on the far right, "that they gave them something in their food to keep them from getting like that."

"They do," said the woman in the center. "They put it in their milk. Haven't you noticed how the milk sort of curdles on the sides of the glass?"

"I've heard the medics talking about it, but I thought they were joking."

"Joking?" said the woman in the center. "Ask Marian if they were joking!"

"Well, if they put this stuff in their milk, how is it they still get that way?"

"Oh, Jane, don't be so naive. The patients know that they put it in their milk, and when the milk is curdled against the sides of the glass, they won't drink it."

"I guess the boy in the ward didn't like milk," giggled Jane.

More fun than scribbling dirty words in a public toilet, thought Bayard bitterly. Maybe it was the Scotch whisky, maybe it was just his mood, but Bayard felt an impulse to say something shockingly vile to the three women. In his mind, he strung together the crudest words he could think of. He put together a lovely sentence, but he didn't say it aloud. When he spoke it was to order another fifteen-cent drink.

Twenty-five cents in scrip remained on the bar. Twenty-five from a dollar leaves seventy-five. Seventy-five divided by fifteen is five. This was his fifth drink—the first real drinking he had done in almost a year.

He did not particularly feel the whisky except that it seemed to have sharpened his perception. Whatever he concentrated his attention on became enlarged and bright—like the illuminated field of a microscope. Or to be more exact, it was as though he had a built-in radar scanner. He could tune in on the three women, and there they were tittering over their dirty little bits of gossip. Or he could tune them out, make them recede again into a blurred and shadowy background, and there in front of him was the fresh Scotch and soda, little bubbles of carbon dioxide working their way up through the bright amber liquid, around the angled planes of the ice cubes, and exploding on the surface in a tiny shower of droplets.

As he reached across the bar toward his pack of cigarettes, his sleeve caught the edge of his glass and knocked it over. It was empty except for the ice cubes, which slid across the bar onto the lap of the woman to his immediate right.

"I'm awf'ly sorry," he said, getting to his feet, steadying himself with one hand against the bar.

The ladies ignored his apology. "He's drunk," said the acidulous one in the center.

Bayard sat down again on his stool and refocused his eyes on the empty glass and the little pile of military scrip in front of him. Then he swung around on his stool and looked pityingly at the three women on his right.

You poor, frustrated, sex-hungry old bags, he thought. He decided to tell them so. He started to speak but couldn't get the words out. Somehow his tongue was too thick. It filled his mouth. The women were staring at him.

To hell with you, thought Bayard. The bar had become oppressive, stifling. The liquor he had drunk magnified the faces of the women. They were leering at him like a trio of harpies.

Too goddamn bored with your goddamn rear-echelon quartermaster husbands to go home, thought Bayard savagely. To hell with you—I'm going to get some fresh air.

He got off the stool. The room rocked a little. Standing up, he found himself towering to an immense height. He looked down at his feet—they were a great distance away. He steadied himself and headed for the door. With great deliberation he walked across the lobby and through the French doors that led into the garden.

The night air was cool. The breeze coming off the lake chilled the sweat that had soaked through his shirt, and he felt better. The night had a cedar smell. The garden, hedged in with evergreens, was laid off with wandering gravel paths and formalized with stylized stone lanterns. Bayard liked the soft rustle of the gravel under his feet. *Shush, shush, shush.* Peaceful. And safe. A man's footsteps on a gravel walk. A path a man could travel without fear.

He walked for a while thinking that it would be nice to be out here in the garden with a girl. Then he found a bench, sat down, and closed his eyes. The world betrayed him by spinning around him sickeningly. He opened his eyes and the spinning slowed to a stop.

He sucked in a deep breath. Underlying the green fragrance of the garden, was another, altogether Oriental, stink—that of night soil, coming from the vegetable plots beyond the garden's borders. You never got very far away from that smell. It was always there. In Korea during the winter, when you went into bivouac, you pitched your tent on a frozen field, and then, when the heat from the tent stove thawed out the top inch or so of the dirt floor, that same ubiquitous odor came up out of the ground.

Bayard put a cigarette in his mouth and struck a match. The match flared briefly, and a new, sharply acrid odor from the burning match head momentarily filled his nostrils. That smell, the smell of white phosphorus, released another flood of memories. He closed his eyes, and he was walking once again along a shell-pitted ridgeline, putting one foot in front of the other, slowly and deliberately because the ridgeline was mined and he expected at each step to trip a mine that would blow up under him, shredding the flesh away from the shattered bones of his legs, tearing away his testicles.

chapter twenty...

The cost of retaking the Nose had been too high. The officers of Dog Company had held a somber council of war on the site of the old watchtower that morning. They could not risk losing control of that rocky eminence a second time. The question was how could they hold the ground without further compromising Dog Company's already overextended resources.

"It'd take a reinforced platoon to defend this position properly," said Thompson.

Was Thompson implying that Bayard had thrown away the lives of the four men he had placed on outpost? "I can't leave a platoon up here," said Bayard. "That's out of the question."

"You could," said Thompson, "if Battalion filled out our main line of resistance with Headquarters and Service Company people. They got the equivalent of two platoons not doing a goddamn thing but providing command post security. Nothing but a goddamn palace guard. If you could get forty men from H&S to fill in between the 1st and 3d Platoons on the MLR, I could hold this position with my platoon."

"You think that the North Koreans are going to come back—going to try to take this place a second time?"

"I *know* they'll be coming back," said Thompson. "Look at the ground, Captain. The nature of the terrain dictates it."

"They're like the Japs," said Reynolds. "They don't change their minds easy. They'll be back tonight. You can bet on it."

"I got to go down to the battalion CP anyway," said Bayard. "I want to see how the wounded are making out. While I'm there, I'll ask Major Mansell about giving us a provisional platoon. In the meantime, Thompson, you stay here with your people. Naheghian, you and Martinez take your platoons back to your original positions on the MLR. Only, Naheghian, you'll have to extend to the right for the time being and put one of your squads in Thompson's old area."

Bayard signaled Baby-san, and the two of them started back along the ridge trail toward the battalion command post. By the time they had descended to the valley floor, four bubble-nosed helicopters had come in from Wonsan. Two had settled down in the school yard. Two still remained warily in the air.

"Those ugly birds sure look good, don't they, Captain?" said Baby-san.

"They sure do," said Bayard. He saw Dr. Goldberg in conversation with one of the helicopter pilots and went over to join them. Goldberg laid a friendly hand on Bayard's shoulder.

"Major," he said to the helicopter pilot, "this is Captain Bayard, the commander of Company D. Most of these wounded are from his company. I'm sorry, Major, but I didn't catch the name."

"Jim Harper," said the helicopter pilot, holding out his hand. "Nice to meet you, Captain. I was telling the doctor that it will take two trips to get all your people out of here. These choppers I got can't lift too much of a load over these hills."

Major Harper was tall and thin and wore a shoulder holster over his dark brown leather flight jacket. He had a straggling black moustache that hung down at the ends, giving his windburned face an Oriental cast.

"We'll get the more critical patients out on the first lift," explained Dr. Goldberg. "The rest we'll get out on the second trip."

"What about my dead?" asked Bayard.

Dr. Goldberg looked uncomfortable. "I asked the major to take their bodies out," he said, "but he says he can't do it."

"Why not?" asked Bayard sharply.

"Captain," said the helicopter major, speaking slowly, placatingly, "as long as you've got wounded and there's a chance of my helping them, I'll fly in and get them. But I can't risk my choppers or pilots just to fly out your dead."

"What do we do with them?" Bayard asked. "The road's closed, so we can't get them out by truck. Do you want us to bury them here?"

"Maybe the road'll be open in a day or so," said Dr. Goldberg. "The weather's cool. We can keep them for a day or so. If the road gets opened up, then we can send them out with the convoy. If it doesn't—well, then, we'll have to bury them here—just temporarily."

"I'm sorry as hell," said Major Harper. "But that's the way it's got to be, Captain. They're dead, and my flying them out wouldn't help them a god-damn bit."

"No, I don't suppose it would," said Bayard resignedly. "You're right, Major. The big thing is to get the ones who aren't dead back to the beach."

"That's the size of it," said Harper. "I see we're loaded up. If I'm to get that second trip in and out of here before dark, I better get going. Nice to have met you, Captain. Good luck up there on the hill. I'll see you in about an hour, Doc, for that second batch of wounded."

The major walked over to the cluster of helicopters. He signaled the other pilots. One by one, their rotor blades started turning, flailing the air, and the helicopters took off like grotesquely magnified insects, the downdraft from their blades creating a miniature maelstrom of dust and debris. Dr. Goldberg and Bayard stood watching through squinted eyes until the last of the helicopters was airborne and headed east toward the first range of intervening hills.

"I'm sorry about Burdock," said the doctor. "He was a nice young boy."

"That's the trouble," said Bayard. "They're all nice young boys. I got to see Mansell now and see if he can let me have about forty more nice young boys to put up there on the hill. I'll see you later, Doctor."

Goldberg was looking at him intently. "Stop off at sick bay for a cup of coffee before you go back up the hill," he invited. "For you, I got a shot of brandy to go with it."

"Thanks, Doctor," said Bayard. "I'll try to make it." He went into the schoolhouse and learned from Three-Able that Major Mansell was out making a reconnaissance of the perimeter. Bayard decided to wait.

"We're getting an air drop of supplies this afternoon," volunteered Three-Able. "I guess that means that they've given up trying to push that truck convoy through."

Bayard did not pick up the conversation, and Three-Able went back to his field desk and situation map. Bayard was there for close to an hour before Major Mansell returned.

"Oh, you're here," said Mansell. "I expected to see you up on your position. You handled that little action up there this morning very nicely. But I'm sure that you've realized by now that it wouldn't have been necessary if you had assessed the situation properly in the first place."

"I felt that a fire team was all that I could spare," said Bayard, holding his voice level. "They were an outpost. I didn't expect them to be able to hold the Nose against an attack in strength. Their orders were to withdraw if the enemy came in on them. They must have been surprised."

"They must have been," agreed Mansell.

"It would have taken a platoon to hold that piece of ground all night."

Major Mansell raised his eyebrows. "A platoon, Captain? Are you sure of that?"

Bayard went on doggedly. "I want to leave a platoon out there now. But if I do that, I'll need some more people to fill out my main position. That's why I'm here. I'm asking for a provisional platoon from H&S Company. They won't have to maneuver. I just want them to hold the center of my line."

"I'm sure that you could use them," said Mansell, "but I'm not going to give them to you. Those two provisional platoons in H&S Company are all we got in the way of a battalion reserve."

"Up on the hill," said Bayard recklessly, "they call them the palace guard."

"They do?" said Mansell. "That's interesting, but hardly relevant. You don't get the platoon. Of course, if you don't agree with me, we can always go see the colonel. You're a company commander. That's your prerogative. I haven't seen the colonel since this morning, but I think he's in his tent reading Rudyard Kipling. He found a copy of *Plain Tales from the Hills* somewheres. Do you like Kipling, Captain? Our battalion commander is very fond of him."

"There's no point in my seeing the colonel," said Bayard. "He'd only back you up."

"Yes," said Mansell, "I believe he would. Now that we've settled that, I've looked over that piece of ground of yours, Bayard, and I can tell you how to hold it—not with a platoon but a squad. And I'm sure that you can spare a squad."

"How?" said Bayard.

Mansell reached for his field phone. "I'm going to tell the Four to give you all the barbed wire and AP mines we've got left in the battalion dump. With a machine gun to enfilade the trail itself and a barrage of 105s and 81s to box in the position, you can make that Nose so strong that a squad could hold it against a battalion." Mansell paused. "What's the matter?"

"I didn't say anything," said Bayard.

"I know you didn't say anything," said Mansell. "It's the look on your face. What is it—the mines? You don't like to use them, do you?"

"No, I don't," said Bayard. "They've never been anything but trouble for us. You put out a minefield, and then there's a change in the plan and you have to go through it. There's always that one mine that doesn't get picked up or the one man who steps out of the safe lane."

"A mine is a weapon," said Mansell, "just the same as a machine gun or a rifle or a flamethrower."

"I don't like flamethrowers either," said Bayard stubbornly.

"Now you're being childish," said Mansell. "You're an educated person, Bayard. I'm asking you to be objective about this thing. The defense of the Nose poses a tactical problem. One of the complications is the reduced strength of your company. Another is the distance of the Nose from your main line. The use of mines is part of the solution to your problem. It's as simple as that."

"All right, sir," said Bayard reluctantly. "I'll do as you say."

"Good," said Mansell. "You can call Gibson on my phone and tell him to start your carrying parties on their way down to the battalion dump to pick up the mines and the wire."

Bayard made the call and then left Mansell. Baby-san was waiting just outside the doorway, and together they started the climb back up to Dog Company. Bayard had forgotten Dr. Goldberg's invitation to stop at the sickbay. He found Gibson and Reynolds at the company observation post where it straddled the high point in the center of the MLR.

"I got the carrying parties off to get the mines and wire," said Gibson.

"Good," said Bayard.

"Captain?" asked Gibson hesitantly.

"Yes?" said Bayard.

"You didn't get any reinforcements from H&S Company, did you? Mansell didn't give you one of the provisional platoons?"

"Who says we need them?" said Bayard abruptly. "Don't you think we can hold the Nose without asking Battalion for help?"

Gibson looked at Reynolds. "Well—it's not that, Captain. But I thought we were agreed that if we could get a platoon from H&S to fill in the center of the line, we could leave Thompson's platoon out on the Nose."

"We can do the same job with a squad," said Bayard.

"With the help of the mines, you mean."

"With the help of the mines and the wire."

"You've never liked to use mines out in front of Dog Company."

"They're a weapon like anything else. If the situation dictates their use, we use them."

"We're going to put a squad on the Nose and then put a ring of barbed wire and Bouncing Bettys around them?"

"Now you're catching on."

"What if the gooks overrun the squad and take the position anyway? Then when we counterattack like we did this morning, we've got to go through the wire and the mines."

"I don't expect the squad to be overrun."

"But if it is?"

"Then we go through the minefield and take it back again. That's the risk we have to run. I want to reinforce that one squad with a light machine gun—just a gunner and an assistant gunner. Who'd you recommend for the job, Reynolds?"

"Kusnetzov, Captain," said Reynolds.

"Kusnetzov? The gunner we leave out there is going to be on his own. He has to be absolutely dependable."

"For this sort of thing," said Reynolds, "Kusnetzov is the best man I got. Don't forget the day in the street in Seoul."

"Yes," said Bayard slowly, "I think you are right. Have him move with his gun up to the Nose."

"He's already up there. His section is attached to the 2d Platoon, sir."

"That's right," said Bayard. "So it is. Have that section leave all its ammunition with Kusnetzov before they pull back. I want him to have at least three units of fire on position—say twenty or twenty-five boxes."

"Aye, aye, sir."

"Reynolds, you and I'll go forward. Gibson, I want you to stay here and push that wire and those mines up to us. We're getting some sort of air drop today. Find out what's being dropped and if we can use any part of it. Now let's get going—the day's half over."

Reynolds and his runner and Bayard and Baby-san moved up the trail once more to the Nose, where they were met by Thompson.

"I'll answer your question before you ask it," said Bayard. "Battalion didn't give us the provisional platoon. I want you to name one squad to stay up here. The rest of the platoon will have to move back to its old position."

"Just one squad up here?" said Thompson. "That's not enough, Captain."

"It will be," said Bayard grimly, "when we get through fortifying this place. Battalion is giving us all the barbed wire and AP mines they've got left in the dump. The 105s are going to put a box barrage around the position. When we get through with it, this place is going to be as safe as a church."

"Just a squad, Captain," said Thompson stubbornly. "It isn't enough."

"Thompson," said Bayard evenly, "one of your biggest troubles is that you never seem to know when the time for discussion is over. We're not debating the matter. I'm telling you what to do. You got that straight?"

"Aye, aye, sir."

"All right, then. I'm leaving a light machine gun with a two-man crew with the squad," said Bayard. "Their job will be to enfilade the trail. So altogether there'll be about a dozen men here on position tonight. In the meantime, we want the gooks to think we're holding here in strength. I'm not going to have you pull your platoon back until after dark. That way, we can also get three or four more hours work out of all your people. I want a low barbed-wire entanglement as deep as you can make it around this whole position. We won't bother with the iron pickets except where we absolutely need them. I want you to use the trunks of the trees. And keep the wire low—not more than about eighteen inches high. Detail one of your squads as a wire party and start them on the outside of the perimeter so that they are working their way back toward the center. And I want the wire mined every foot of the way. We'll use all the Bouncing Bettys and flares we can get from Battalion. If that isn't enough we'll improvise with hand grenades and composition C."

"What about safe lanes?" asked Thompson. "Do you want them taped or not?"

"What point would there be in mining the position and then taping the safe lanes?" snapped Bayard. "No, we're going to have to orient our people as thoroughly as we can, and then they're going to have to depend upon their memories."

"Pretty risky," said Thompson.

"We can use the tops of C ration cans then," said Bayard relenting a little. "Nail them to the base of the trees to mark the lanes. But not too many of them, and keep them close to the ground—not more than about six inches off the deck."

"We got a lot to do," said Thompson. "We better get humping."

"I'll stay with you until the job is done," said Bayard. Thompson was a truculent bastard, but he knew how to handle a platoon.

After they got into it, preparing the defenses of the Nose was a fascination to the men. About fifty marines busied themselves in the tasks of digging, wiring, and mining. The inherent and impending dangers were forgotten as each man joined in the conspiracy of readying what they now regarded as a gigantic trap being prepared for the night-marauding enemy. An adroitly located trip wire or a hand grenade, its pin loosened, carefully placed so that the least disturbance would set it off—the whole idea held great satisfaction and became the cause of warm and admiring congratulations.

Remembering the helplessness he had felt when the sound-powered telephone line had gone out in the first few minutes of the previous night's engagement, Bayard had his wiremen string two new lines from the Nose back to the company OP. One of these lines he had overheaded in the trees. He also planned on leaving both an SCR-536 and an SCR-300 with the squad that would hold the position. Leaving the SCR-300 would probably bring a lecture from the battalion communications officer, but Bayard was willing to risk the wrath of that earnest young first lieutenant.

It was three o'clock in the afternoon or later before the aircraft from the transport squadron came overhead to make their promised drop of supplies. The members of Dog Company at work on the Nose paused, straightened their backs, and looked up to see four R4Ds, one by one, make their circle and swing low over the drop zone in the valley. The two-engined transports, the Marine Corps version of the Douglas DC-3, were actually at an altitude lower than that of the marines on the Nose. Dog

Company could read the bold black letters "U.S. Marines" on the fuse-lages of the passing aircraft. They could see the marine cargo masters in dungarees and brown flight jackets standing spread-eagled in the opened cargo hatch, ready to kick out each packaged load. It was a free drop—no parachutes to slow the descent—and the dark bundled shapes show-ered down on the village of Madong-ni like so many meteors.

A telephone talker from the company OP reported to the Nose with satisfaction that a reel of barbed wire had crashed through the roof of the schoolhouse. "Those goddamn H&S poges came running out of the build-ing like ants out of an anthill."

A little later Gibson telephoned Bayard that the drop had included small-arms and mortar ammunition, an initial issue of cold weather parkas, and several hundred pounds of white cake mix.

"White cake mix?" questioned Bayard incredulously.

"Yes, sir," affirmed Gibson blandly. "For the birthday cake."

"Whose birthday?"

"The Marine Corps's—remember?"

"Forgive me," said Bayard. "I'd forgotten. I hope H&S has a very nice party. In the meantime, if it doesn't interfere with their getting ready for the celebration, I wonder if you could break them loose from enough of those parkas to take care of Dog Company."

"They'll be up before dark," promised Gibson. "Also, you can have some more barbed wire if you want it."

"I think we've got enough," said Bayard. "At least all we can get strung this afternoon. We've done about all we can do up here. I'm getting ready to knock off. As soon as it's dark, I'm sending Thompson with his platoon, less one squad, back to the main position. I'll be staying with him at the company OP tonight. You go to the 1630 conference for me. Tell them I was too busy to make it. I'll check with you later." He rang off and turned to see Thompson standing just behind him.

"Well, do you think you've done everything that can be done to get things ready?" asked Bayard.

"Yes, sir," said Thompson with a sour hint of a smile. "I'd like to see those slant-eyed bastards get through that wire now."

"Maybe you'll get your chance before the night's over, Lieutenant," said First Sergeant Havac dryly.

"All right," said Bayard. "There are just a couple of loose ends to get squared away. Which squad are you going to leave on position?"

"My second squad. Corporal Jones's."

"Jones?" asked Bayard. "He's the corporal who had the patrol out in front of the roadblock in Seoul. Maybe this time we ought to stick somebody else's neck out."

"I don't think so," said Thompson. "He's had the squad since Sergeant Murphy got wounded. It's the strongest squad I've got. They have ten men left. I don't have a better NCO than Jones."

"All right," said Bayard. "It's your decision. But I'd like to speak to Jones, if you don't mind."

Thompson sent his runner looking for Jones, and in a couple of minutes, the squad leader was standing in front of Bayard.

"Mr. Thompson tells me that he's picked your squad to occupy the Nose tonight."

"Yes, sir," said Corporal Jones modestly, almost demurely.

"You have ten men in your squad?"

"Counting myself."

"The two machine gunners make twelve. That should be enough."

"Yes, sir," said Jones. "Twelve is plenty."

"Mr. Thompson," said Bayard, "unless you have something else for Jones, I think it is dark enough for you to start the rest of your people to the rear. I'll be along as soon as I've given the position a last check."

"Aye, aye, sir," said Thompson.

After Thompson had cleared the position, Bayard, accompanied by Jones, walked the circumference of the minute fortress. The foxholes at the base of the stone watchtower had been deepened and extended to form a circular trench about twenty yards in diameter. At regular intervals firing steps had been dug for the riflemen and BAR men. Extra bandoliers of ammunition were pegged to the dirt walls. Hand grenades, stripped of their cardboard packing tubes, were placed conveniently at hand.

Kusnetzov and his assistant gunner had dug a horseshoe-shaped emplacement for their machine gun. It rested on its dirt platform, its perforated snout pointing outward along the trail leading to the higher ground in front of the Nose.

"This is a mighty fine emplacement you've got here," said Bayard to Kusnetzov. "Just like a page from the field manual."

"Thank you, sir," said Kusnetzov.

"I don't think I know your name," said Bayard peering at the assistant gunner.

"Private First Class Howard, sir. I joined the company at Pendleton, sir."

"Of course," said Bayard. "I know you now. It was just too dark for me to see your face. Now tell me—what's your principal direction of fire?"

"We're laid on it now, sir," said PFC Howard.

Bayard leaned over the gun and sighted along the barrel. The gun was laid to enfilade the trail; the point of impact was about seventy-five yards in front of their position. He took the grip of the gun and tried to move it. The gun was securely locked to the traversing bar.

"All right, now," said Bayard, "show me your sector of fire."

Kusnetzov stood with his two arms outstretched. "On my left, that pine tree. On my right, that bare rock."

"Can you cover your sector without shifting your trail legs?"

"Yes, sir."

"What are you going to do at night when you can't see your reference points?"

"We got aiming stakes." Kusnetzov pointed at a little palisade of wooden sticks out in front of the gun.

"How many boxes of ammunition do you have?"

Kusnetzov waved a hand toward the dark shapes of the ammunition cans lining his hole. "We got t'irty boxes, Captain."

"Very good," said Bayard. "It looks like you're ready for them."

"Sure we ready," said Kusnetzov loudly. Then in a softer, more confidential tone he added, "Don't you worry, Captain. I do a good job for you."

Bayard continued his circuit of the position. A carrying party had brought up rations, water, and enough of the new parkas for the men remaining on the Nose. The parkas had been packed in naphthalene flakes, and the air was heavy with the disinfectant smell. The men looked heavy and clumsy in the shapeless winter garments.

"Hey, does this hood go over or under the helmet?" somebody wanted to know.

One rifleman had a half-dozen rifle grenades, each wrapped with several turns of barbed wire, lying on a shelf cut into the parapet of his fighting hole. Bayard pointed at these. "You aren't expecting a tank attack up here, are you?"

"No, sir," answered the boy seriously. "But I figured that by wrapping them with barbed wire I ought to get a fragmentation effect."

"Sounds like a good idea," said Bayard. "Let me know how they work out."

Having completed his inspection, Bayard left Jones and, with Havac and Baby-san, picked his way along the safe lane through the wire. Breathing more easily once they had their feet solidly on the ridgeline trail, they dogtrotted back through the fast-enshrouding gloom to the company OP. Here Thompson had their sleeping bags and three of the new parkas waiting for them.

Bayard and Baby-san were to share a large double foxhole for the night. Bayard checked his communications. A leather-cased EE-8 telephone linked him to the battalion switchboard. Three CE-11 sound-powered telephones hung from pegs driven into the sides of the hole. One was on the circuit that joined all of the platoon leaders. Another was to the 60mm mortar position. The third was a hot line running forward to the Nose. A shelf had been dug for the SCR-300 radio, its fishing-rod antenna jutting up into the air. The SCR-300 tied him into the battalion tactical radio net. Also pegged to the wall was the capricious SCR-536 that netted him with his platoon commanders in the event the sound-powered telephones failed. Everything checked out in good order. Even the undependable SCR-536 came through loud and clear.

Baby-san started boiling some water over the miniature gasoline stove. "I'll have some hot joe in just a minute, Captain."

"Well, what do you think?" asked Bayard.

"About what, sir?"

"About tonight?"

"Well, sir, if the gooks don't elect to attack after all that there hard work, I'm going to be downright disappointed."

He poured the hot water into two empty C ration cans and tore open the packets of powdered coffee. "Here's your joe, sir. Do you want me to heat up a heavy for you—say, a can of beans?"

"I don't think so," said Bayard. "Do we have any fruit left?"

"Just a can of cherries I've been saving. I'll split them with you."

The EE-8 rang. Bayard pulled the phone out of its case. "Dog Six," he said.

"This is Gibson. How are things?"

"Just fine so far."

"Do you need anything up there?"

"Not a thing. Everything's fine."

"Good. I just got back from Battalion commander's conference."

"Oh? What did they have to say?"

"Not too much. The road to Wonsan is still blocked. A company-sized patrol only got about three miles outside the city before they were turned back. Aerial observers say that there's a general drift of guerrillas converging around our position."

"Great," said Bayard. "That's all we need."

"The S-2 says there are strong indications that we'll be attacked tonight."

"That's a brilliant deduction. Anything else?"

"Just that tomorrow's the tenth of November—the Marine Corps birthday. All company commanders are to read the birthday message. They passed out mimeographed copies."

"Whose bright idea was that? Major Mansell's?"

"No, the birthday message business came straight from the Old Man himself. He's got the battalion mess section baking the cake tonight. We had to send a couple of our stretcher bearers back to help out."

"What are they using for field ranges?"

"The artillery battery has a couple. Those people travel first class. Do you know they've been feeding hot rations all the time we've been here?"

"That's all right with me if it gives them enough strength to poop out a few shells if I have to call for them."

"Well, that's about it, Captain. I hope you have a quiet night."

"I hope so too. But I'm afraid that if we do, some of our people will be disappointed. I'll see you in the morning. Good night."

Bayard rang off. He took a swallow of coffee. Baby-san handed him the opened can of cherries. Bayard ate a scrupulous half of the contents and passed the can back to his runner. Baby-san finished the cherries and then broke the plastic spoon between his fingers and put the pieces into the emptied can, bending the tin-plated lid back into place.

The night was now completely dark. Only a few stars were out, and the moon had not yet risen. "These new parkas feel good, don't they?" said Bayard.

"They're warm enough," said Baby-san, "but I'll be glad when they get rid of that mothball smell. It makes me feel like I'm inside a footlocker."

"But they're warm," said Bayard.

"Warm and heavy," said Baby-san. "They'll slow a man down when it comes to fighting. I wonder why they dropped them to us now?"

"It's getting cold."

"Yes, but not so cold we couldn't make out with our field jackets. Do you suppose that they're planning on us staying here all winter?"

"Well, that would be all right, wouldn't it?"

"Well, I don't know," said Baby-san dubiously.

"If you look at a map of Korea," said Bayard, "you can see that this would make a pretty good winter line. This is the narrowest neck of the peninsula. It's only about a hundred miles wide here. We hold Pyongyang on one coast and Wonsan on the other. They give us two good anchors for our flanks. This might be a very good place for us to spend the winter."

"Then why's the Eighth Army heading for the Yalu?"

"I think that's mostly political. We don't have enough men to cover the whole Manchurian border. The line of the Yalu is almost six hundred miles long. I think that before the really cold weather sets in, the Eighth Army will be coming back. Then we'll have enough men for a solid line from Wonsan to Pyongyang."

"Would you call that tactics or strategy?" asked Baby-san. "I can never keep the two straight."

"That would be strategy. Strategy is *where* you fight the enemy. Tactics is *how* you fight the enemy."

There was a minute of silence. "I bet Jones feels like the cheese in a mousetrap," said Baby-san suddenly.

"How's that?"

"Well, he's got a pretty good position up there, but he knows damn well that he couldn't get himself or his people out of there if he had to."

"He isn't coming back. He's staying there."

"I know, but what if somebody is wounded bad? We'd never get him out of there."

"He could be carried straight back along the trail. We left that route open."

"The gooks wouldn't be likely to let us get away with that," said Baby-san gloomily. "The trail'd be the first thing they'd cut off."

"All right. In that case we would have to wait until morning to get him out. That's the chance we have to take."

"Is this strategy or tactics we're talking about now?"

"Tactics."

"I think I like strategy better. You want to get some sleep, Captain? I'll mind the phones."

"I'm not sleepy," said Bayard.

"I'm not either," said Baby-san.

Every fifteen or twenty minutes Jones would call back on the CE-11 to report everything secure on the Nose, but the tension was building up. "Somebody's out there," said Jones. "I can feel it."

"Maybe it's just a patrol," said Bayard. "Maybe they'll pull back then they'll run into our wire."

"Maybe," said Jones, "but I don't think so. I think we're in for it."

Bayard could do nothing but wait. Wait and listen with the CE-11 pressed close to his ear. He could hear Jones's breathing. He could hear the rustling fall of loose earth as Jones turned in his hole.

It was almost with relief that shortly after midnight he saw the green fireball of an enemy flare arc across the sky. It was followed by the short staccato blast of a bugle.

"They're coming!" Bayard heard a high-pitched excited voice, not Jones's, over the CE-11.

"Knock it off." Jones's voice was reassuring, hoarsely insistent. "Don't none of you people start shooting until they get into our wire." Then, directly into the mouthpiece so that his voice came through more strongly, he asked, "Did you see the flare, Captain?"

"We saw it," said Bayard. "Do you want your barrage fires now?"

"Not yet," said Jones. "I want to wait for them to get into our wire."

A trip flare popped somewhere out in front of the Nose. The trees in front of Bayard changed into black, dodging shadows against the backdrop of the flare's white magnesium light. Kusnetzov's machine gun started firing. Bayard recognized its regular pulsating rhythm. Kusnetzov was working his gun beautifully, getting off about eight to ten rounds in each burst. Bayard could visualize Kusnetzov methodically traversing his sector of fire.

The BARs and rifles joined the machine gun. Then the mines started going. The concussion was heavier than that of a grenade. Even at this distance Bayard could feel the jar of the explosions in his hole. "Okay," he shouted to his artillery observer, "let's have the barrage fire!"

A rain of shells came down on the Nose, gathering momentum. Soon the entire crest was being pounded on all sides. The 105s, the 81s, the 60s, the incoming mortar shells, the exploding mines, the small-arms fire, all combined into an indistinguishable din. Bayard clung to his telephone, talking first to Jones, then to the artillery observer, then to Mansell.

Mansell told him that there were probing attacks all around the battalion perimeter. Easy and Fox Companies were both being hit. In front of Bayard the action reached a sustained crescendo and then began to thin out.

Bayard experimentally halted the barrage fires. Jones reported that the incoming mortar shells had stopped. The trip flares around the Nose popped with lessening frequency. The small-arms fire died more slowly, subsiding and then breaking out again in brief angry exchanges.

Bayard felt that the fight for the Nose was over. "How does it look?" he asked Jones.

"Everything's fine up here," said Jones.

Bayard hesitated before asking the next question. "Anybody hurt up there?"

"Let me check," said Jones. Then, after a pause, he responded, "Nobody. All that shooting and stuff, and nobody hurt."

"That's good," said Bayard with relief.

"Now what do we do?" asked Jones.

"We wait and see if they come back for another dose of the same."

"They won't be back," said Jones. "We tromped them good."

"Pass the word to go on 50 percent alert," said Bayard. "I think I'm ready for some sleep myself."

Securing the phone, he pulled his sleeping bag over his boots and up to his waist, and then, hunching down inside of his parka, he wedged himself as comfortably as possible in the narrow hole. He dozed off almost immediately.

chapter twenty-one...

When Bayard awakened, he found the OP suffused with the gray light of night giving way to morning. There was a covering mist—not so heavy a fog as the preceding day's but dense enough to obscure the rising sun. His body was stiff and aching from the cramped position in which he had slept. He worked his way out of his sleeping bag and stretched. His throat was coated with phlegm. He hawked it up and spit it out.

"I'll have some coffee in a minute," said Baby-san. He was sitting on the edge of the hole, pumping the plunger of the gasoline stove.

"You should've awakened me," said Bayard, "so you could have gotten some sleep yourself."

"I got some sleep," said Baby-san. "The first sergeant spelled me on the telephones. We figured you needed the sleep more than we did."

By midmorning Thompson had gone forward with a fresh detail to relieve Jones's squad.

"Get the place cleaned up," ordered Bayard. "Replace the mines and flares that have been expended—but be goddamn careful in doing it."

Bayard left the OP and went down to Dog Company's command post. He told Gibson he wanted to be left alone for a while. Going into his hut, he pulled off his parka, field jacket, and boots, and threw himself down on the lower bunk. He was very tired. His earlier feeling of elation had oozed away.

Gibson came into the hut at about noon to rouse him. "How do you want to work the birthday celebration, Captain?"

"The what? Oh, the cake—I had forgotten about it."

"Turner from the mess section is outside."

"I'll see him," said Bayard. He pulled on his boots and field jacket and went out into the open.

Turner, who was assigned to Dog Company as a stretcher bearer except for those rare intervals when there was a battalion mess, was standing in front of the hut with two of the other mess cooks. Each was holding two baking tins of cake. "We figured six pans would be enough, sir," said Turner. "Of course, the pieces won't be very big."

"They'll be big enough," said Bayard. "Now, where are we going to set this thing up?"

"I thought we could seat our people over there on the slope," said Gibson. "We got a table knocked together to hold the cake and a sort of lectern for you to use when you read the message. I figured we could bring back half the company at a time. That means you'll have to read the message twice—if that's all right with you."

"It's all right with me," said Bayard. "When do we get started? Let's get it over with."

"It shouldn't take long," said Gibson. "We could have the first half of the company here at 1330 and the second half at 1500. That'll give them plenty of time to get down and back from position."

"Good enough," said Bayard. "Pass the word." He walked with the three mess cooks to the selected area.

"It's a lot different than last year at Camp Lejeune," said Turner at his elbow. "I worked all night last year getting the holiday meal ready. I don't think you were with us then, Captain, but we really put out a chow—shrimp, turkey, ham, six or seven kinds of vegetables, a couple of different salads, and about a two-hundred-pound cake. Colonel Quillan cut the cake with his sword. I never worked so hard in my life, but it was worth it. This is a pretty sorry cake we got this year, Captain. We did the best we could, but we didn't have nothing to work with."

"It'll be all right," said Bayard. "Don't worry about it."

By half past one, the first group of marines had come filing down from the MLR and were seated on the ground in a semicircle around the table holding the six pans of white-frosted cake.

"I think we're ready," said Gibson.

Bayard stepped behind the lectern, which was a wooden box turned upside down and nailed to four shaky legs. He took the mimeographed sheet of paper from his pocket and smoothed it out. He had not bothered to read it over in advance. There were about eighty men seated in front of him. They had taken off their helmets and were sitting there, most of them, with their helmets and individual weapons cradled in their laps. Bayard looked into the taut, weathered faces of his Dog Company marines.

"As you know," said Bayard. "It is a Marine Corps custom to read the Birthday Message each year before the cake-cutting ceremony. This message was first published by the thirteenth commandant—that was Major General John A. Lejeune—in 1921. General Lejeune had commanded the Marines in France and Germany during World War One. The old-timers say he was the greatest leatherneck of them all. He wanted this message published to all marines around the world as a reminder of the honorable service of the Corps. And we have been doing so on the 10th of November ever since. This year it is a little different because we are in the field. Now, if you will give me your attention, we'll get on with it."

Bayard cleared his throat, held the mimeographed sheet flat against the rough surface of the lectern, and read:

"On November 10, 1775, a Corps of Marines was created by a resolution of the Continental Congress. Since that date many thousand men have borne the name marine. In memory of them it is fitting that we who are marines should commemorate the birthday of our corps by calling to mind the glories of its long and illustrious history.

"The record of our corps is one which will bear comparison with that of the most famous military organizations in the world's history. During ninety of the 146 years of its existence the Marine Corps has been in action against the nation's foes. From the Battle of Trenton to the Argonne, marines have won foremost honors in war, and in the long areas of tranquility at home generation after generation of marines have grown gray in war in both hemispheres, and in every corner of the seven seas that our country and its citizens might enjoy peace and security.

"In every battle and skirmish since the birth of our Corps, marines have acquitted themselves with the greatest distinction, winning new honors on each occasion until the term 'marine' has come to signify all that is highest in military efficiency and soldierly virtue.

"This high name of distinction and soldierly repute we who are marines today have received from those who preceded us in the Corps. With it we also received from the eternal spirit which has animated our Corps from generation to generation and has been the distinguishing mark of the Marines in every age. So long as that spirit continues to flourish marines will be found equal to every emergency in the future as they have been in the past, and the men of our nation will regard us as worthy successors to the long line of illustrious men who have served as 'Soldiers of the Sea' since the founding of the Corps."

Bayard stopped reading and looked up. The Dog Company marines were sitting there quietly, whether sullen, somber, resigned, or contemplative, Bayard could not tell.

"Now, we will serve the cake," said Bayard. "I think the cooks did very well to get any sort of cake baked for us this year under the circumstances. If we can have a single line go past the table, you will each get your piece. There's also hot coffee."

"We couldn't get you a sword," said Turner in a low voice. "But we cleaned up this here Ka-Bar knife."

"You want me to cut the cake?" asked Bayard, taking the knife by its leather grip.

"Yes, sir," said Turner. "You're the company commander."

The cake had been scored into three-inch squares. Bayard pried loose a square with the point of the knife and held it balanced on the blade.

"Don't forget about the oldest and the youngest," came a soft prompt from Gibson.

"That's right," said Bayard. "Who's the oldest? I guess that's you, First Sergeant."

"I'm afraid so," rumbled Havac, taking his piece of cake from the blade of Bayard's knife. "You read that real well, Captain. I've had the Birthday Message read at me a lot of times, but today was the first time I really heard the words."

"Now," said Bayard, "who's our youngest marine?"

"I guess I am, sir," said PFC Howard. "That's what the company clerk says anyway."

"How old are you?" asked Bayard.

"Eighteen," answered Howard. "I reached eighteen on board ship coming over."

Bayard put the piece of cake into the machine gunner's outstretched hand.

"Happy birthday, sir," said the boy.

"Happy birthday," said Bayard. "Good job up there on the Nose last night."

The rest of the audience had queued up, and Bayard served each man his piece of cake.

"That leaves us three pans for the rest of the company," said Turner. "How about a piece for yourself, Captain? It isn't too bad, I don't think."

"After you," said Bayard. He held out a piece of cake to each of the three mess cooks. He then took a piece himself.

"Happy birthday," he said.

chapter twenty-two...

Happy birthday! thought Bayard, sitting there in the garden outside the Hotel Otsu. He closed his eyes experimentally. The whisky seemed to be wearing off. The world no longer spun about. He was quite sober now, but restless and disturbed. He didn't want to go to bed. He was certain he wouldn't be able to sleep. He decided to go back into the bar. Perhaps the three women from the hospital were still here. He could talk to them, strike up some sort of conversation. Maybe it would lead to something.

He entered the hotel lobby. The same clerk was at the desk. The bell captain was dozing on his bench. The American girl was still at the writing table.

"That must be quite a letter," said Bayard, stopping in front of her. She looked up.

"Why?" she asked unsmilingly.

Bayard waved emptily at the air with his hands. "You've been at it a long time. You were here when I finished dinner, and you're still here."

"It really isn't any of your business, is it?"

"No," said Bayard. "It isn't. I'm sorry. I didn't mean to intrude."

"You're back from Korea. The forward area?" asked the girl, relenting a little.

"Yes. How could you tell?"

"It isn't hard. The replacements—the ones who are going in the other direction—have a different look."

Bayard looked at the wedding band on her left hand. "Your husband— is he in Korea?"

"Yes—or he was. He was killed in April."

"I'm sorry."

The girl lifted her shoulders in a tired little shrug. "You had no way of knowing. There's no reason for you to apologize."

"I'm not apologizing," said Bayard. "I was just trying to say that I was sorry that your husband had been killed. And I am sorry."

"Thank you," she said.

"Have you got that letter just about finished?"

"Just about."

"Then why don't we have a drink together?"

"If you will wait till I finish this last page."

"Fine," said Bayard, and he went over and looked once more at the cheaply done damascene cigarette cases and compacts in the gift-shop showcase. Tomorrow he would have to see about getting those pearls for Donna. Then the girl was at his elbow.

"I'm ready," she said smiling. She was much more attractive when she smiled. It erased the tired, set expression from her face. Together they went into the bar.

Bayard paused just inside the door.

"Looking for someone?" she asked.

"No," said Bayard, "just getting my bearings." The three women from the hospital were gone. They must have left while he was in the garden. "Just looking for a table. How about the booth in the corner? Is that all right with you?"

"Any place is fine with me."

They went to the booth and sat down. "Now let's get acquainted. My name is Bayard—George Bayard."

"I'm Alice Gardner."

One of the Japanese boys came from behind the bar over to the table. "What'll it be?" Bayard asked her.

"I think another bottle of beer. Make it Japanese beer."

"Wouldn't you rather have a highball? I've been drinking Scotch."

She hesitated slightly. "All right," she said. "Make mine Scotch too. Scotch and water."

The waiter went off to get their drinks.

"You'll be going home soon?" asked Bayard.

"Yes, very soon," she said looking at his left hand. "Are you married?"

"No," said Bayard, fingering the empty space between the second and third joint of his ring finger, "I'm not married. Do I look as though I should be?"

"Well," she said, "I had assumed—most men your age are, you know."

"Not married," reaffirmed Bayard, "not even close to it."

Donna would not be flattered by the drift of this conversation, thought Bayard.

The waiter set their drinks down on the table, and Bayard paid him from his damp, wadded ball of military scrip. The girl was studying him closely. "I'll try again," she said. "You're not regular Marine Corps, are you?"

Bayard smiled and twisted his glass in his hand. "How could you tell? I thought I had become a pretty good facsimile of a marine."

"There's something," she said, "I mean, the regulars of all the services have a kind of a stamp. My husband was regular Army. You're different from him."

"So far you've scored one wrong and one right," said Bayard. "What else would you guess about me?"

"Is this a game we're playing?" she asked smiling again.

Bayard decided that she was quite pretty when she smiled. "We can make it a game," he said. "What sort of stakes should we play for?"

Alice held up her glass. "We used to play a game something like this at school. I think it was called Prince of Wales. A drink for a wrong guess. How's that?"

"And what about right guesses?"

"Then you take a drink," she said. "If I guess wrong, I take a drink."

"It sounds like a very fine game," said Bayard. "The score is now one to one. That's a drink apiece."

They touched glasses.

"Cheers," she said.

"Cheers," said Bayard. He drank about a quarter of his highball.

"Proceed with the game," he said. "It's still your serve."

"You're from the East?"

"Not exactly—unless you count Ohio as East. I've always thought of it as being in the Midwest. But I went to school at Princeton and I've lived in Baltimore."

"Are you on rest and rehabilitation?"

"In a way. But I'm not going back to Korea. I was released from the navy hospital in Yokusuka yesterday. We have an administrative center here in Otsu. Once I get my papers straightened out, I'll be going home."

"I'm glad you're out of it," she said. "The whole rotten mess."

"What about you?" asked Bayard. "When will you be leaving for home?"

"Soon. My husband was a captain in the 1st Cavalry Division. When the division went to Korea, we stayed on in Japan, my daughter and I. My husband was a tank officer. His name was Joseph Gardner. Maybe you met him one time or another?"

"I'm afraid not," said Bayard. "I didn't know any army tankers by name. But we worked with them sometimes."

Maybe we passed on the road north of Seoul, thought Bayard, a captain in dark green fatigues and a yellow scarf.

"I didn't really expect that you would have known him," said Alice. "It's just a question I've gotten into the habit of asking."

Bayard realized that the palm of his hands were wet. He wiped them dry with a paper napkin.

"What's the matter?" asked Alice. "Aren't you feeling well?"

"I'm all right," said Bayard.

"You look ill," said Alice. "Are you sure you feel all right?"

"I'm all right. I feel fine."

"Your wound—was it a bad one?"

"Not so bad."

"That gold star on your Purple Heart—that means that you have been wounded twice, doesn't it?"

"That's right."

"Were both of your wounds in Korea?"

"Yes, that's why I'm going home. It's in regulations. Two wounds, and you go home."

"Am I asking too many questions?"

"I don't mind."

"Was the first wound a bad one?"

"It was very slight." Bayard thought again of the *Mercy* and of Anna the nurse and wondered if she were still with the ship.

"When was it?"

"Last December."

"You were with those marines who were trapped up by that reservoir, weren't you?"

"We didn't consider it to be a trap."

"It must have been horrible."

"It wasn't as bad as it sounded in the papers."

But it had been bad, thought Bayard. Worse than Seoul. Much worse than Madong-ni.

chapter twenty-three...

The battalion had stayed on at Madong-ni until just before Thanksgiving. Then an army division newly arrived from the States had taken over the Wonsan sector, and the 1st Marine Division was freed to consolidate to the north in the vicinity of Hungnam. An army infantry battalion, its peacetime skeleton filled out to strength with Korean conscripts, had relieved the marines at Madong-ni after a two-day march from Wonsan. Bayard had walked out his line with a captain recently transferred from schools troops at Fort Benning. The captain had been a machine-gun instructor and had some criticisms to make concerning Bayard's positioning of his automatic weapons. Bayard stood it for a while, but his patience soon wore thin.

"Captain," he said wearily, "once I pull Dog Company off this hill, you can do any goddamn thing you want to with your own machine guns. But don't tell me how to use mine."

The guerrillas in the surrounding hills were now quiescent. The battalion made its motorized march back to Wonsan without incident. They were billeted a day or so in a half-destroyed Catholic school, and then they went north by railroad in open freight cars to Hungnam.

They received the rest of their winter gear in Hungnam—the shoe-pacs with the felt innersoles, the mittens with the wool liners, the winter trousers. They had gotten some enlisted replacements too, and Dog Company was brought back almost to full strength. But there had been no officer replacements, so Dog Company had to go into the winter campaign two lieutenants short.

They moved into the high ground north and west of Hungnam. To their right front, elements of X Corps had gone north almost as far as the Yalu, but there was nothing on their left flank but high and inhospitable mountains. At first, there was no enemy except the weather, which had turned bitterly cold. Then their patrols began to make contact with a new enemy. Naheghian's Forty Thieves were the first to bring in any prisoners—half-a-dozen of them in new padded-cotton uniforms of an unfamiliar type.

Jim Kim questioned the prisoners briefly before they were delivered to the battalion S-2. "They Chinese," announced Dog Company's interpreter.

"Chinese? Are you sure?" asked Bayard.

"I sure. They say four weeks ago they leave Shanghai. They say many Chinese cross the Yalu."

But the intelligence summaries that came down to the 2d Battalion continued to deny the presence of a Chinese army. First it was claimed that the Chinese were simply Chinese nationals living in Korea who had been conscripted into separate formations of the North Korean army. Then it was postulated that they were a token force sent south by Peiping to screen the withdrawal of the remnants of the North Korean army into Manchuria.

The 1st Marine Division advanced against this shadow army on a broad front, its regiments and battalions widely separated. The temperature now fell to below zero every night. The men learned that the new shoe-pacs were treacherous. Marching soaked the felt innersoles with sweat. If these liners weren't changed regularly, a man's feet soon became frostbitten. Dog Company lost six or seven men that way before they learned to carry their extra felt innersoles and heavy woolen socks inside the waistbands of their trousers, where they were dried by body heat.

The resistance in front of them thickened and toughened. Gradually the forward momentum of the division slowed, then halted. The 2d Battalion found itself defending a perimeter thrown around a hydroelectric plant—one no longer functioning but not yet destroyed—that fed itself from a reservoir marked on some of their maps as Changjin and on some Chosin.

Fresh identifications of new Chinese units now came almost daily. The red rectangles and numbers on the S-2's situation map multiplied ominously. Each night brought sharp attacks against the 2d Battalion's perimeter. Each morning marine patrols sallied forth to probe the enemy. Each day the patrols were engaged a little closer to the perimeter, driven in a little sooner.

Then there came the morning when the 2d Platoon was only a half-hour out and the sound of rifle fire came back to Dog Company.

"I'm stopped," radioed Thompson.

"Where are you?" asked Bayard.

Thompson gave him the map coordinates of his position in code. Bayard unshackled the code and plotted the position on his folded map. "You're only a half mile out," said Bayard.

"I know it, but I'm stopped," said Thompson.

"Push him and see what happens."

Minutes later, there was a fresh outbreak of angry rifle and machine-gun fire. It continued intermittently for twenty minutes or so and then subsided.

"He's there to stay," reported Thompson. "I can't move him. I've got three casualties. What do you want me to do?"

"How big a force?" asked Bayard.

"At least a company. I can't find his flanks."

"Come on back in," said Bayard. "Do you need some covering fire?"

"Yes," said Thompson. "I'll let go a red smoke grenade, and then I'll pull out. Put the mortars just beyond that."

Bayard alerted the 81mm mortars. A few minutes later a swirling plume of red smoke rose above the snow-covered hills to their front. The mortars began firing.

It took an hour for the 2d Platoon to extricate itself and get back into the perimeter. They had four wounded and one dead. Thompson's face was gray with fatigue and strain. Bayard looked at him with concern. "I'll go with you to Battalion," offered Bayard. "While you make your patrol report."

"Thanks," said Thompson with an uncharacteristic smile. "I need the company." Then he collapsed in the snow.

"Corpsman!" called Bayard. Pilnick scurried over. "What's wrong with him?" Bayard asked.

"I think he stopped one on the way back," said a member of the 2d Platoon. "I saw him fall down like he was hit, but he got right up again."

"He's got a bullet in the shoulder and has lost a lot of blood," said Pilnick. "I got to get him in a tent where it's warm enough to give him plasma."

Thompson was evacuated. It was a critical loss. Thompson's strong, if irritating, leadership of the 2d Platoon would be missed. He hadn't the common touch that endeared Naheghian to the 3d Platoon, nor did he have the iron nerve of Martinez. But in his own way he had been the steadiest and most professional of the platoon leaders.

Bayard transferred Reynolds to the 2d Platoon and gave the machine-gun platoon, with some misgivings, to Gunnery Sergeant Agnelli—a technically competent gunny, but not a Havac or a Martinez.

Dog Company's strength was wearing away. Night attacks against the perimeter became routine. Company administration was reduced to a notebook carried in the pocket of the first sergeant's field jacket. Each morning Havac totaled the night's losses and recalculated the company's strength.

On the last day of November, Bayard was summoned to battalion headquarters. The little group of tents was wedged into a ravine and thus protected somewhat from shellfire. The Chinese were using more and more mortars, and a troublesome battery of 76mm field guns sporadically took the battalion perimeter under fire.

Bayard ducked through the canvas tunnel that acted as a windbreak for the operations tent and pushed under the doubled blanket that served as an inner door. Although it was broad daylight outside, no light penetrated the windowless walls of the tent. A gasoline lantern hissed and filled the tent with its greenish white glare. Except for a wet circle immediately above the heat of the stove, the inside of the tent's canvas was gray with frost. The stove, an oil-burning space heater the size and shape of a quarter-barrel beer keg, sat in the middle of this sixteen-foot-square space that was the nerve center of the battalion. The smoke pipe followed the pole up through the peaked top of the pyramidal tent. Someone had nailed short sections of board crosstrees-fashion to the tent pole above the stove, and these were hung with heavy boot socks. The tent smelled greasily of damp wool, fuel oil, and gasoline. A half-dozen opened cans of C rations bubbled on top of the sheet-metal stove.

The battalion commander was sitting on an ammunition box close to the stove. Red Snapper had wrapped himself in a blanket and hardly looked up when Bayard entered, barely acknowledging Bayard's salute and greeting. He looked old, very tired, and only half alive.

Major Mansell was at the map board. There were two maps pinned to it under the acetate. One was large-scale, showing the situation in all of North Korea. The other was the battalion 1:50,000 battle map. Bayard, starved for news of what was happening outside the narrow circle of the battalion perimeter, stared hungrily at the grease-pencil markings on the large-scale map. A grouping of blue symbols represented the Eighth Army, strung out along the west coast. A smaller blue grouping showed the X Corps scattered along the east coast from as far north as the Yalu down to south of Wonsan. In between the Eighth Army and the X Corps and south of them were the thickly massed red symbols representing the Chinese divisions.

Major Mansell tapped the other half of the map board with his pencil, calling Bayard's attention to the smaller-scaled map, which showed in detail the 1st Marine Division's zone of action. The grease-pencil symbols automatically translated themselves in Bayard's mind into a summary of the local tactical situation.

Stabbing at the 2d Battalion's perimeter were three red arrows. Small, numbered rectangles at the base of their shafts identified them as the 701st, 702d, and 703d CCF regiments. The "CCF" stood for "Chinese Communist Forces."

Bayard let out a low tuneless whistle through frost-stiffened lips. "So that's what hit us last night?"

"Elements of three regiments," said Mansell.

"That means we're surrounded by a division."

"At least," said Mansell calmly, almost with a note of satisfaction.

Bayard looked closely at the major. The faintest of smiles lifted the edges of the thin tight line of Mansell's mouth. The bastard's enjoying this, thought Bayard. He shot a look at the colonel, sitting there swathed in his blanket, eyes dull, cheeks sunken. More and more it was getting to be Mansell's battalion. Now that Major Crenshaw had been evacuated, Mansell was both operations and executive officer. Mansell's usually well-groomed mustache had grown a little ragged these last few days.

"How's your company?" The colonel's voice was only a husky shadow of its old rasping self.

"All right, sir," said Bayard. "I have one hundred and forty effectives."

"Dog Company is the strongest company we have," said Mansell. "That's why it is a job for them."

"I asked Bayard," said the colonel testily. Mansell said nothing more but smiled his thin tight smile.

Bayard stood there self-consciously, waiting uncertainly. This little flare-up by the Red Snapper was embarrassing.

"You look like you could use something hot to eat," said the colonel. "Why don't you grab some of these hot rations? Can of beans or something. I think we got some coffee too."

"Thank you, sir," said Bayard. He was hungry. He had eaten very little these last few days: the effort in thawing out the food was too great. He pulled off his cloth-and-horsehide gauntlets and let them dangle by their strings of parachute cord. Bayard had a dim memory of his mother a long, long time in the past pinning his mittens to his winter coat before sending him out to play. Now a man tied his gloves to his parka so he wouldn't forget them or lose them in the snow, because his hands left unprotected would freeze in an hour.

Bayard's own hands felt strange. The heat of the stove set them to tingling. His fingers were swollen, stiff, and mottled red and blue. He fished awkwardly in an inside pocket for a plastic spoon and picked up a bubbling can of spaghetti from the stove. He knew that the bent-over lid by which he was holding the can must be hot, but his fingers didn't feel the warmth.

He was aware that Major Mansell was waiting impatiently to proceed. "Well, Major," said Bayard. "What is it for Dog Company?"

"If you will come closer to the map board," said Mansell, "I'll show you."

Bayard moved once more to the battalion's battle map.

"You're familiar with the general situation," said Mansell. "You know that the Eighth Army has been hit very hard and that there is no physical contact between X Corps and Eighth Army. The 1st Marine Division has now been given the mission of facing to the left and attacking across the peninsula so as to hit the Chinese flank and thus relieve some of the pressure against the Eighth Army. The division will be pulling together its regiments and concentrating here, where we are presently."

Mansell paused in his briefing and tapped the battle map a few inches west of the blue ring that marked the 2d Battalion's perimeter. "As you know, this is the one good transverse route across the mountains. I believe your company has already patrolled this road as far as Toksu-nyong—the first major pass. This is about four miles west of our battalion perimeter. As far as we know, the enemy hasn't fortified the pass, but at the first indication that the division is concentrating here, he undoubtedly will. Therefore, we can save considerable time and effort if we secure the pass prior to the arrival of the main body of the division.

"That's the job we're giving Dog Company. Tomorrow morning you will leave the perimeter ostensibly to patrol westward in company strength. We're gambling on the enemy letting you through as far as the pass in the expectation of ambushing you on your way back. This would be consistent with the tactics they've been using against our patrols. However, you aren't going to return. You're going to organize the high ground in the vicinity of the pass and hold it."

"For how long?" asked Bayard. A weak, empty feeling began growing deep in his stomach.

"Not more than three days," said Mansell. "Perhaps not even that long. As soon as the rest of the regiment closes on our position here, we should be able to move up and take over the pass with the entire battalion."

chapter twenty-four...

The night following Bayard's receipt of the order to take Dog Company to Toksu-nyong Pass was fairly quiet. The 2d Battalion's perimeter received only occasional probing attacks and a light mortar shelling. Dog Company suffered no casualties.

At first light, a provisional platoon made up of Headquarters and Service Company people was scheduled to relieve Dog Company of the responsibility for its present sector of the battalion perimeter. Bayard passed the word for Dog Company to be ready to move out when the platoon arrived. While he waited, he breakfasted on a cup of soluble coffee and a chocolate bar. The night had been a cold one to spend in the foxhole. How cold was it? No one had a thermometer, and there was considerable speculation on the subject.

"One thing's for sure," said Baby-san, urinating in the snow and watching it congeal into yellow ice. "It's cold enough to freeze the piss out of you."

The platoon from Headquarters and Service Company arrived. The lieutenant in charge was Three-Able, Mansell's assistant operations officer.

"It's all yours," greeted Bayard. "We're ready to move."

Three-Able eyed the length of the line of foxholes being vacated by Dog Company. "Shit," he said in disgust. "How am I supposed to hold this goddamn line with forty men?"

"That's not my problem," said Bayard. "You'll have to take it up with your boss." Bayard then turned to Havac, "First Sergeant, start moving the company down to the road."

The company filed down from the hill and formed up on the road in a double column facing west. It had been weeks since Bayard had seen his company so assembled, and as he walked from the rear of the column to its head, he was struck by how worn and shabby his marines had become.

The only remaining mark of uniformity were the shapeless parkas and the clumsy shoe-pacs. Less than half his men still had their steel helmets. Of the helmets that remained, many had lost their cloth camouflage covers, and several were burned black from being used as cooking pots.

Some marines wore the pile-lined hoods of their parkas pulled up over their peaked cloth caps for extra protection against the cold. Others, about a third of the company, had army winter caps. These had earflaps, the wearing of which permitted a certain individuality of expression. Some men wore the flaps tied up Cossack-style. Some wore them hanging down like the ears of a hound dog. Some wore one flap up, the other down— presumably to favor a frostbitten ear. Several enterprising members of the company had gotten themselves Korean caps made of dog fur. Sergeant Martinez had a shaggy black-and-white fur headpiece, the earflaps of which stood straight out from the sides of his head. Kusnetzov, Bayard noted, was still wearing his knitted blue watch cap.

Some of Dog Company were prepared to march with their sleeping bags rolled into a short, tight roll and fastened to the bottom of their haversacks. Others had abandoned their packs altogether and rolled their sleeping bags, and perhaps a poncho or shelter-half, into a long horseshoe roll, which they looped over a shoulder.

Gibson and the property sergeant were waiting for Dog Company on the road close to the west roadblock. Each man, as he passed the sergeant, was handed an extra bandolier of rifle ammunition and two 60mm mortar shells to add to his personal load. A Russian-made truck, which Bayard recognized as part of the battalion's booty from the fighting in Seoul, and a one-ton trailer were parked by the side of the road.

"That's all the transport they'll give us," said Gibson. "The truck's about shot. It's only got a two-wheel drive, you know. These hills with that trailer have just about pulled the guts out of it. I guess Battalion figures it's expendable."

"What kind of a load do you have on it?"

Gibson consulted his pocket notebook. "Three units of fire for the small arms and machine guns, two units for the 60s, three pyramidal tents, three space heaters, seventy-five gallons of fuel oil, seventy-five gallons of water, three days' C rations, thirty reels of barbed wire and some iron pickets, a dozen bales of sandbags, eighty antipersonnel mines, two hundred fifty hand grenades, a couple hundred pounds of TNT and composition C, and some primacord."

"Too much," said Bayard. "It's overloaded."

Gibson nodded his head in agreement. "I know it, but there's nothing on board we could safely leave behind."

"Will it get as far as the pass?" asked Bayard.

"I think it will—if we baby it along."

Bayard looked at his watch. "I hope you're right. Anyway, it's time for us to be moving."

He took his place at the head of the column, raised his arm above his head, and brought it down. Dog Company started westward along the road. In front of them, the west roadblock was marked by an M-26 tank that had lost a track to an antitank mine, then had been pushed into its present position so that its 90mm gun and its machine guns could be brought to bear along the road. A little knot of Weapons Company people manning the roadblock had gathered at the road's edge to watch Dog Company pass through.

Bayard saw also a jeep that he recognized as the battalion commander's. As he got nearer, he saw the shrunken figure of the Red Snapper standing by the jeep. A curious impulse stirred in Bayard. "Let's make it look good for the Old Man," he said in a low voice to Gibson. Bayard turned around and, marching backward, faced his company. "Comp'ny," he bawled. "Atten*shun!* Quick time. March! Pick up the step! *Wun . . . Tup . . . Thrip . . . Four!*"

There was a shuffling of feet, a wavelike motion down the length of the column, as a surprised Dog Company shifted from route step to quick time and began to march to a cadence that was now being chanted by the equally surprised platoon sergeants.

Bayard faced around to the front again. Baby-san was at his left elbow. The gold-and-scarlet company guidon had miraculously appeared on its pikestaff. The slapping thud of the shoe-pacs striking the frozen roadbed had a solid, reassuring quality. Bayard felt better, more confident, than he had in days. He was now almost abreast of the Red Snapper. The Old Man had drawn himself up to stiff attention. Behind him stood Major Mansell and the battalion S-2.

Bayard jerked his eyes to the right and brought his hand up in salute. Out of the corner of his eye he saw the guidon sweep downward. The Red Snapper, eyes straight to the front, face impassive, came to a rigid salute and held it. Bayard marched on, cut away his own salute, saw Baby-san bring the guidon staff back to the carry. Bayard faced around again and looked down the length of his marching company. It was a sadly shorter column than the big company that had marched into Seoul. He moved to left side of the Red Snapper at the edge of the road and joined him in saluting each platoon as it passed.

The durable Martinez marched at the head of the 1st Platoon. It didn't seem to matter how Bayard deployed his company, the 1st Platoon, whether it was on the right flank or the left, in the assault or in support, always seemed to get hit the hardest. The members of the platoon took a curious and perverse pride in their casualty rate. They called themselves the Bloody First. Someone in the platoon had cut a square of red silk from a cargo chute and wore it as a neckerchief. The rest of the platoon then followed suit, and the red scarf became the badge of the Bloody First.

The staunch 2d Platoon with its new platoon leader, Mr. Reynolds, followed the Bloody First. The 2d Platoon had been with Thompson for so long, how well would they do under a new officer?

The machine guns and the mortars marched next, Dog Company's indispensable crew-served weapons. The machine gunners regarded themselves as the elite of the elite. The mortarmen exhibited their own pride by wearing in their caps, as a sort of unofficial badge, the safety pin from a mortar shell fuze.

Naheghian's Forty Thieves brought up the rear of the company. Even now, when all of the company was so shabby and threadbare, they managed to look a little more disreputable, a little dirtier, a little more lacking in uniformity than Dog Company's other platoons.

Bayard saw the Red Snapper hold his salute until the last man in the company had cleared the roadblock and the ramshackle Russian truck at the tail of the column had rumbled past. Then he and his company headquarters dogtrotted to a position in the column just behind the 1st Platoon. To his front Bayard could see the first intervening ridge and beyond that, blue in the morning air, the higher ridge. A vee-shaped notch showed against the skyline. That was Toksu-nyong Pass.

At Bayard's signal, Dog Company deployed into an approach march formation. Ahead as advance guard and point went Martinez and the 1st Platoon. Reynolds moved to the right flank with the 2d Platoon. Naheghian echeloned to the left with the 3d Platoon. In the center moved the company headquarters, the mortars, and the road-bound truck and trailer.

A minimum of engineering, dating back to the Japanese occupation, had gone into the construction of the road. It zigged and zagged its way up the slope of the first ridge, finding the easiest natural gradient. As a consequence, the elements of the company marching along the road traveled twice the distance of the flankers climbing the rougher yet more direct route.

Initially, no opposition hindered their movement except that offered by the rugged nature of the terrain. As Major Mansell had anticipated, the Chinese made no effort to thwart the departure of the company from the protection of its battalion perimeter. The first ridgeline attained, Dog Company could look down into the minor valley that still separated them from the heights of Toksu-nyong. The lower ground in front of them was desolate, white with thin drifted snow except for the gaunt black skeletons of a burned-out cluster of houses, relics of a village destroyed by an air strike brought down by an earlier patrol.

Dog Company slid down into the valley and then began the steeper climb upward to the pass, which now could be clearly seen. The road made its precarious way along a series of narrow shelves hacked into the side of the mountain. The truck shuddered in protest, threatening to slide off the outer shoulder of the road into the precipitous depths. The clutch was slipping badly, and the transmission had developed an ominous whine. Dog Company got behind the truck, heaved and pushed, and the driver drove with one foot out of the cab, ready to jump.

The climb continued, though, without incident. By noon Bayard was standing in the notch where the road passed over the dorsal edge. His map indicated that the elevation was 1,639 meters—he was about a mile above sea level. The ridgeline at this point ran from southwest to northeast, where the ridge climbed to a height of 1,967 meters. To the southwest the differential in elevation was even more marked, the peaks rising sharply to over 2,100 meters.

Bayard remembered a Marine Corps Schools definition that a saddle was the high point between two low points that was also the low point between two high points. It was a ridiculous definition until one thought about it. Here he stood precisely at such a point. There was a valley to his rear, a valley to his front, higher ground to his left and right. Here, and here alone, the road found its way across the mountains. He thought of other mountain passes: Thermopylae, Brenner, Khyber, Manassas Gap, Kassarine.

A sharp cold wind blowing from the north and funneling upward through the notch threatened to tear the map from Bayard's hands. He turned his back to the wind and tried to refold the map. It was a 1:50,000 Japanese Imperial Land Survey map copied in black by the 64th Engineer Base Topographical Battalion and surprinted in red with anglicized place-names and a thousand-meter military grid. It was a good map if you could translate in your mind the neatly drafted contour lines into the realities of razor-edge ridges and plunging chasms.

"That wind's going to make this place as cold as a witch's tit," said Baby-san. "Where're we going to set up the CP, Captain?" Bayard looked around. There was no shelter, no defilade, in this wild windswept place. In the saddle itself the ridgeline was somewhat flattened. As the ridge-line rose on each side of the pass, the crest grew sharper-edged, jagged with outcroppings of granite.

"Here, just off the road," said Bayard. "That truck is going to stick up like a sore thumb, but there's no place to hide it."

Baby-san had pulled the company guidon down from the truck. He tried to jam the pikestaff into the ground, but the earth was frozen hard as iron. He kicked together a little pile of rocks around the base of the staff. "That'll have to do until I get a chance to dig it in." Bayard summoned his platoon leaders. "While your people are catching their breath, let's look over the ground."

Dog Company's perimeter, as they eventually decided it, was to be peanut-shaped, bulging out at each end toward the higher ground that formed the shoulders of the saddle. Bayard divided the perimeter into three sectors. The north sector he assigned to Reynolds and the 2d Platoon. The south sector he gave to Naheghian and the 3d Platoon. He held Martinez and the 1st Platoon in the center with himself and the mortars. This was the position most exposed to enemy fire but least accessible to direct assault. From here he could shift a squad or so from Martinez's platoon to any threatened segment of his line.

Dog Company had five hours of remaining daylight in which to organize its position. The men were tired from the march and the climb, the cold was enervating, and they had to be pushed into making the effort to get themselves a decently protected hole.

The truck and the trailer were off-loaded. The three pyramidal tents with their space heaters were set up as warming tents, one for each defensive sector. Like the truck and trailer, these tents could not be satisfactorily concealed, but some place had to be provided for the men to thaw out the bone-deep cold.

The cans of fuel and water had to be taken into the tents. Even mixed with gasoline, at these temperatures the fuel oil thickened like molasses so that it wouldn't pass through the carburetors of the tent stoves until it was warmed. There was no way to keep the water from freezing except to cluster the five-gallon cans close to the stoves, and this in turn absorbed most of the heat that was being thrown out by the burners.

At dusk, in company with Gibson, Havac, Agnelli, and Baby-san, Bayard walked the circuit of his mountain fortress. Dog Company had done as well as could be expected in getting itself ready. Some of the holes were dangerously shallow and would have to be deepened in the morning. It was virtually impossible to dig a satisfactory foxhole in this frozen earth, underlain as it was with rock. They had used up a portion of their TNT and composition C blasting holes in the more stubborn locations. The outcroppings of rock themselves offered a species of protection, but Bayard knew that granite struck by high explosive shells could splinter into fragments as deadly as shrapnel.

Not all of the wire had been strung, but there were comforting thickets of it at each end of the company position, where the ground rose toward the two foreboding crests that looked down upon their position. From these heights, Bayard knew, as did every man in Dog Company, the greatest threat would come.

The mines were set out, and so were the flares. The machine guns had their sectors of fire assigned. The mortars had fired in their primary concentrations—although not with the precision and nicety that Sergeant

Laski would have liked: mortar ammunition was too scarce for that.

As darkness settled over the position, Bayard put Dog Company on 50 percent alert, decreed that not more than six men should be in a warming tent at a time and then for not longer than twenty minutes. If they adhered to that schedule, each man in the company could anticipate a twenty-minute thawing-out every three hours, time enough for a cup of coffee or a heated can of C ration.

These arrangements completed, Bayard returned to the hole Baby-san had scraped for him just off the road. There he found the familiar collection of field phones connecting him with his platoon leaders. In a nearby hole was Brown with the SCR-300, which gave him his radio link with Battalion.

"I can hear them and they can hear me, but that's about all," said Brown. "We got the height here and reception should be good, but these Jap batteries don't stand up in the cold. They look good, but they don't last."

The artillery sergeant was equally pessimistic about his backpacked radio equipment: "I wish they had let me bring the jeep so we could have more positive communications. This gear is apt to go out when we need it the most."

Bayard boiled some coffee over his little stove and made his supper of that drink and a bar of chocolate he had kept thawed in his shirt pocket. Chocolate was about all he had the energy to eat these days. You heated a heavy unit from a C ration, and as soon as you took it away from the flame, the frost crystals started to form around the inside of the can.

The leaden winter sky was growing darker. The air grew colder as the faint warmth of the sun subsided. Soon it would be totally dark. The wind, which had been blowing all day, now came through the notch in galelike strength, shrieking and moaning.

In his hole Bayard worked at getting his body below ground level to escape the chilling blast. The hole was shallow and crowded with his essential impedimenta: his telephones, his sleeping bag, his haversack, his map case, his binoculars, the gasoline stove, the box of C rations, his pistol belt with its holstered .45-caliber pistol, the magazine carrier with its two clips of cartridges, his compass, his first-aid pouch and packet, his canteen with its water frozen into a solid, useless chunk of ice. Even when he flattened himself against the bottom of the hole, he could barely get below the worst of the wind.

Bayard had no thought or hope of sleep. He lay there and waited. He felt very alone, yet he knew that in a similar hole five yards to his right, Havac was also lying there in the dark, waiting. And to his left was Brown with his radio. And next to Brown was Baby-san with his BAR. A little further away, over by the pile of supplies off-loaded from the truck, was Gibson with the other elements of the company headquarters—the company clerk, the property sergeant, the wireman, and Gibson's runner.

Pilnick had established the company sick bay in the 1st Platoon's warming tent. The silhouette of the tent was a sharp black triangle against the night sky.

A paralyzing chill crept into Bayard's body. Was this what is was like to freeze to death? His mind went outside his body, and he was able to view the process with a certain degree of detachment. An interesting problem of heat transfer, he thought, remembering his high school physics. He could almost see those textbook thermal units, those little square calories of heat, oozing out of the pores of his skin, filtering their way outward through the layers of underwear, woolen shirt, woolen sweater, alpaca vest, blanket muffler, field jacket, parka liner, parka shell—sucked upward from the hole by the cross-blast of the wind and then dissipated, lost.

"What are you trying to do? Heat the whole outdoors?" his father had said to him one winter day in Columbus as he had stood with the back door of the High Street shop wide open.

I am cold now, thought Bayard. I was never cold before. I thought I was cold when I was twelve and we visited my grandfather's place in Marysville and they put me in that unheated third-floor bedroom. I thought I was cold that Saturday afternoon sitting in the stadium watching that Michigan game being played in a snowstorm. I thought I was cold during that night problem at Quantico when we waded the Chopawamsic Creek. But that wasn't being cold. This is being cold. That was relative. This is absolute. You couldn't be any more cold than this. Those little bits of heat—they keep seeping away. When they are all gone, you will be dead.

Here he was with one hundred and forty marines and they were all freezing to death. In the morning the sun would rise on one hundred and forty hard-frozen corpses. How many people were there in the United States? One hundred fifty million? One hundred forty marines were less than a millionth, an infinitesimal part, of the American whole. Their loss wouldn't cause the slightest tremor in the upward climb of the population curve. They had a clock in the Census Bureau in Washington that tick-tocked the population growth. Maybe sometime during the night it might miss a tick or a tock, and that would take care of the loss of the one hundred forty members of Dog Company.

Something rapped against his helmet. Bayard jerked his head up and saw a dark shape leaning over his hole. He grabbed convulsively for his pistol, his awkward mittened fingers stubbornly opposed by the cold-stiffened leather of the holster flap.

"It's me, Skipper—Havac," said the dark shape. "It's your turn for the warming tent. You better get over there and get thawed out."

"I'm all right," said Bayard sullenly. "I'll stay here." To get to the warming tent, he would have to move out of his hole. It was too great an effort.

Havac shook him roughly by the shoulder.

"Watch what you're doing, Sergeant," said Bayard angrily. "I told you I was all right."

"I think you better go over to the tent," said Havac. "Get yourself a cup of coffee."

Havac waited. Bayard made no effort to move. "Skipper," said Havac. "If you don't get out of that hole, I'm going to pull you out."

"All right," said Bayard. "I'm getting out. I told you I was all right." He slid his legs stiffly out of the sleeping bag and pushed himself to his feet. When he stood up, the hole came only to his knees. "I'll be back in a couple of minutes," he said to Havac.

"Take your full time," said Havac. "Twenty minutes."

Bayard bent forward against the weight of the wind and stumbled the short distance across the rough frozen ground to the black triangular shape of the tent. He ducked in under the door flap and saw inside a half-dozen marines in the faint illumination of a grease light. You improvised a grease light when you had no candles. You poured the lard from the C ration sausage patties into an empty can. A twisted piece of undershirt made a wick or, better, the asbestos packing used to seal the water jackets of the heavy machine guns.

The circle of six marines opened to make room for Bayard by the stove. "We got a can of joe going, Captain," said one of the marines, whom Bayard recognized as a rifleman in Martinez's second squad. "Want some, sir?"

"Thanks," said Bayard. "I could use it."

The tall marine sloshed a couple of inches of black liquid into a canteen cup and handed it to Bayard. "That's a real blizzard blowing out there," said the marine. "I don't think I've ever been so cold. Not so bad in here, though."

Bayard sat down on a fuel-oil can. The wind blowing across the top of the smoke pipe created a terrific draft, and the stove metal was glowing cherry red. The low sidewalls of the tent were lined with stacked cases of rations. These offered some slight additional insulation and a species of protection from enemy fire. Not as good as sandbags, but filling sandbags with this frozen earth was slow work. It would have to wait until tomorrow or the next day.

"Do you think we'll get it tonight? An attack, I mean, sir," asked one of the six marines.

Bayard shrugged. "Your guess is as good as mine. Our job is to be ready for them if they do come."

"They won't attack tonight," said the first rifleman firmly. "Those fuckers are human. They can't stand this cold any better'n we can."

"I hope you're right," said Bayard.

"He hasn't been right yet," said the marine who had asked about the possibility of an attack. "He's the one who was so sure the war'd be over as soon as we took Seoul."

"Him and MacArthur," said one of the marines to no one in particular.

"I know one thing for sure," said the tall rifleman. "If I was company commander, this here is where I'd be spending the night. Right here in this tent. I wouldn't be freezing my ass in a foxhole." He gestured toward the sidewall of the tent. "I'd break out one of Pill's stretchers and flake out on it here where it's warm. How about it, Captain?"

Bayard looked up sharply. In the dim light he could not see the expression on the tall rifleman's face. Bayard had been studying the stretchers stacked along the wall and the pile of blankets. It had occurred to him that they might as well be used. He was the company commander. No one could challenge his right to stay in the tent.

"Our time is up," said a corporal. "Let's get back to our holes and give the other guys a chance."

The corporal got to his feet. Two other marines, one of them the tall rifleman, also reached for their weapons and stood up. They moved slowly, reluctant to leave the warmth of the stove.

"Come on, you guys," said the corporal impatiently. "Let's go."

The corporal ducked under the door flap. The tall rifleman was the last to follow. He looked back at Bayard before letting the flap fall. "Go ahead,

Captain. Grab yourself one of those stretchers. Nothing's going to happen tonight anyway."

Bayard looked again at the stretchers and the pile of blankets. The provident Pilnick had those ready for the casualties they would receive when they were attacked. But there were no casualties as yet. It wouldn't be as though he were depriving a wounded man of the space and warmth. And there was plenty of room. The tent could hold twenty people. The rule of six at a time was just so there wouldn't be too many people in the tent in the event it was taken under fire or hit by a mortar shell.

Here in the tent his earlier thoughts of freezing to death seemed ridiculous. The canvas walls couldn't stop bullets or shell fragments, but somehow the warm glow of the stove and the faint light of the burning grease were reassuring, giving him a feeling of safety and security.

Three more marines, replacing those who had left, came in from the outer cold, stamping their feet and swinging their arms.

"Christ, it's cold," said one. "Oh, it's the captain. How are you, Captain?"

Bayard got to his feet. "Here," he said, "I was just leaving. Take my place by the stove." He moved to the doorway. "I'll be seeing you in the morning, men." He dodged under the frost-thickened canvas flap and went back out into the night, retracing his steps to his foxhole.

Baby-san was there minding the phones, sitting half erect, a blanket wrapped around his shoulders and his BAR gripped between his knees. "Your turn," said Bayard. "Go get yourself warmed up."

When Baby-san had gone, Bayard got back into his hole. He slid his sleeping bag over his boots and trousers, bringing it up as far as his waist. It was 10:10. Three more hours, and he would take another turn in the tent.

The revitalizing effect of the warming was short-lived. His legs were soon aching again, all the way from his knees down to his ankles. He thought of getting all the way into his sleeping bag, zipping it closed. That way he would be warmer. But Battalion had a rule against men on the line zipping themselves into their sleeping bags. It was a hard rule to enforce, a hard rule to discipline oneself to.

The bag was always a temptation. You pulled the thing over your legs to keep warm. This was permitted. Then you found yourself inching down further and further into the bag. You pulled the zipper shut, you were warmer, and then you fell asleep. If your position were overrun, you could die that way, caught in your sleeping bag, asleep or helplessly awake, a creature without useable arms or legs. Bayard flexed his legs and his arms experimentally. He thought again of the unused stretchers and blankets in the warming tent.

Someone whistled over the sound-powered phone. Bayard picked it up, sliding the receiver under the flap of his winter cap. Reynolds was on the line. "Someone's out there, Skipper. We can hear them in the wire. Out in front of my center squad. Can we have some illumination?"

"Are you sure?" said Bayard. "I don't like putting up flares unless you're pretty sure they're really out there."

"We're sure," insisted Reynolds. "I can hear them myself. It must be a wire-cutting party."

"Very well," said Bayard, "I'll tell Laski to put up a sixty."

The mortar section had one of its tubes laid in over the north sector. The gunner pulled the pin from the nose of an illuminating shell and dropped the round into the smooth-bored barrel. The little mortar *ka-chunngged*, a tongue of flame leaped out of the tube, and the shell was on its way. The canister popped open, the magnesium flare lit, and the light came swinging down on its parachute from the sky in front of Reynolds's position.

"See anything?" queried Bayard.

"They're out there—" Reynolds's words were cut off short. There was the rippling burst of an enemy submachine gun, a high-pitched scream.

"Are you all right?" asked Bayard.

"I'm all right," said Reynolds. "But there are a lot of them out there."

Bayard heard the heavier sound of a Browning light machine gun. That would be Kusnetzov, he thought. He has the gun in the center of Reynolds's position. "Get some high explosive out there!" Bayard yelled to Sergeant Laski.

Pop—pop—pop went the 60s, throwing out their shells. Brave little weapons, thought Bayard, but the shells are too light to do much good. "See if we can get some 105s or 155s," he called to the artillery observer.

There was another voice on the telephone. This time it was Naheghian. "They're out in front of me, Captain. A whole goddamn army of them."

Bayard heard Naheghian's machine guns firing, joined in by his BARs and rifles. He told Laski to keep two tubes shooting in support of Reynolds, to switch one tube to the support of Naheghian. He told his platoon commanders he was working on getting some artillery help. He told them to hold on.

"I can hold," said Naheghian.

"If Naheghian can hold, so can I," said Reynolds grimly.

Then, as the Chinese got deeply enmeshed in the wire, the mines started going. They exploded upward in a sort of fountain of flame, going up a hundred yards in each direction from Bayard. The concussion shook him in his hole. He had kicked himself free of the sleeping bag and was now on his stomach, head raised above the level of the parapet. Silhouetted against the bright white magnesium light were a myriad black dodging shadows. In the dancing light of the flares, it was not always possible to distinguish the black outline of a rock or a scrubby tree from that of a man.

A sudden drenching rain of shellfire came down on the center of Dog Company. Bayard flattened himself in his hole, burying his head in his arms. He smelled the choking odor of white phosphorus. He groped frantically for the telephone to the artillery observer. "Get them off us! Get them to lift their fire!"

"That not ours," said the artillery sergeant in a strangled voice. "That's incoming. We're not shooting Willie Peter."

A shell hit the warming tent. The fuel oil mixed with gasoline exploded with a whooshing roar. A marine burst out of the tent and ran crazily around the command post area, a flaming torch, clothes saturated with burning fuel oil. A dark pursuing figure threw a blanket over him and wrestled him to the ground, his screams stifled in the blanket.

Bayard hugged the bottom of his hole, a telephone gripped tightly in each mittened hand. "How about some help?" he snarled over the line to the artillery observer. "Can't you get those goddamn guns shooting?"

"It's on the way. They're shooting now," said the sergeant. "But only one battery. The whole regiment is being attacked and that's all they can spare us."

"They've gotten into my center squad," reported Reynolds. "I'm going to push them out."

Bayard saw Reynolds's tent go up in flames, saw in this new illumination numberless black scurrying figures, saw that the Chinese had penetrated the 2d Platoon position and were coming down the slope into the notch of the pass. "Martinez," he yelled, "they've gotten through the 2d Platoon! They're coming our way!"

"I see them," Martinez's voice called back from the darkness. "We're ready for them."

Baby-san had shoved his BAR over the edge of his foxhole. "I can't see to shoot from here," he said impatiently. "I got to get me a field of fire." He seized his weapon and wriggled away through the darkness in the direction of Martinez's blocking position.

The dark shapes reached Martinez's line. There was an angry exchange of rifle fire, the glassy explosions of grenades. The dark shapes dwindled in number; then there were none.

"We stop them!" Martinez shouted exultantly.

Bayard got to his knees, but his legs and arms were reluctant to obey. He had pulled his pistol free of its encumbering holster. He had to use both hands to release the safety. Now he was on his feet.

"Martinez," he yelled in a voice he wouldn't have recognized as his own, "get two squads ready to counterattack! We're going back up the hill. Gibson, you take the remaining squad and face around to support Naheghian in case he needs help. Havac, you come with me!"

He found Martinez thirty yards or so away. "Let's go," he said. "Guide on the burning tent. One squad to the right. The other to the left. Let's go." Bayard started up the slope. He stumbled. His legs didn't want to go up the ridgeline. If he had let them, they would have turned him about and sent him flying back to the protection of the hole he had just left. He cursed his body as a weak thing and forced it to go forward.

Then Bayard's pistol went off in his hand. He was not conscious of pulling the trigger. The noise and the solid punch of the recoil were reassuring. He straightened out his arm and leveled the pistol at a dodging shadow. He pressed the trigger. "Squeeze it gently, like your dolly's titty," the gunnery sergeant had said on the Quantico pistol range an eon ago.

They reached the burning remnant of the 2d Platoon's warming tent. Bayard tripped over a prostrate form in a padded white uniform. The body came alive and enveloped him in its arms and rolled over on him. Bayard caught the sharp stink of garlic. He pushed the muzzle of his pistol into the padded uniform and pulled the trigger. The Chinese grunted and went suddenly lax. Bayard got to his feet.

He saw Martinez in front of him, face ruddy in the reflected glare of the flames. "All right, Captain?" asked Martinez coming toward Bayard. "You all right?"

"I'm all right," said Bayard shakily.

Martinez stopped. A surprised look spread itself across his Indian face.

"I'm all right," repeated Bayard.

Martinez dropped the butt of his rifle to the ground. He leaned wearily against the rifle for support. He tried to speak. He fell to his knees. His hands slipped reluctantly down the barrel of his rifle. He fell forward into the soiled and trampled snow.

Bayard got to Martinez, bent over him, saw that nothing could be done. He picked up Martinez's rifle. Ahead Bayard could hear the reassuring sound of a Browning light machine gun. He could see the orange-red fingers stabbing their way up the slope. One gun at least was still being served.

Bayard looked around, saw dimly the hesitant figures on his right and left. "Come on, marines," he said. "Let's get this thing finished." They went on.

They reached the machine gun and found Kusnetzov and Howard still behind it. They found Baby-san sharing a hole to the left of the gun with a dead rifleman, protecting the flank of the machine gun with his BAR. Bayard looked at the dead rifleman's face, saw that it was the tall marine who thought that Bayard as company commander should stay in the warming tent.

They found Reynolds in a foxhole, his face mangled by a .45-caliber slug from a Chinese Thompson submachine gun. But Reynolds was still alive. The Chinese submachine gunner was dead.

The back of the attack was broken. Rifle fire still crackled spitefully from the higher ground leading up and away from the pass, but the Chinese were withdrawing. Bayard thought suddenly of Naheghian, looked around and saw, across the notch, that his firefight, too, was subsiding.

Bayard had no way of knowing, could not yet tell, what his casualties for the night had been. He saw Turner and his messmen stumbling down the rocky incline with their burdened stretchers, but it would be morning before the first sergeant could be expected to get an accurate count of who was left. Bayard grabbed Baby-san by the arm. "Go get Mr. Gibson," he said. "Tell him to get up here and take over the north sector. He's to consolidate what's left of the 2d Platoon and these two squads of the 1st Platoon."

The blackness of the night was beginning to gray. It was almost morning, realized Bayard. Sometime during the night, he could not remember when, the wind had died down. It seemed less cold now.

Baby-san returned with Gibson, who reported that Naheghian's platoon was intact and in good shape, with very few losses. Bayard gave him orders to reorganize the sector. Gibson listened soberly and then set about the business of reforming the squads and reassigning his remaining NCOs.

Bayard was suddenly very tired. He wandered around the shattered position aimlessly, looking at the dead and debris, looking without emotion at each huddled body in padded white but feeling a soul-deep wrench of dismay, a mounting sense of failure and inadequacy, at the sight of each green-clad body. There were a lot of them—far more than he wanted to count.

He stopped at Kusnetzov's machine gun position. Kusnetzov and Howard were sitting on the edge of their emplacement sharing the biscuits from a C ration. Their position was knee-deep in expended cartridge cases. "Looks like you did a lot of shooting," said Bayard.

"Ten boxes, Captain," said Kusnetzov with pride. "This little gun she work like a charm."

It was then that Bayard heard the sound; at first he thought it was the moaning of the wind. "What's that noise out front?" he asked.

Kusnetzov looked scornfully out toward the mist-enshrouded underbrush. "You mean our communist friend? He has been crying like that all night."

"Can you see him?"

"We've been looking. Not yet. Maybe now that the light is getting better."

The three men, Bayard, Kusnetzov, and Howard, concentrated on the ground to their front. "I think I see him," said Howard after they had spent several minutes in silent searching.

"Where?" asked Bayard.

"There by that squatty tree with the double trunk," said Howard, pointing.

"I see him now," said Kusnetzov. "See him, Captain?"

Bayard squinted along the line indicated by Howard's gloved forefinger. He saw the prostrate figure of a man in a dirty white uniform, saw the man raise himself to his elbows and pull himself along for a foot or so and then fall forward on his face once again.

"A mine must have blown off his feet," said Kusnetzov.

"It's a wonder he hasn't bled to death," said Howard.

"I fix him," said Kusnetzov. Still in a sitting position, he reached for a rifle and raised it to his shoulder.

Bayard kicked out with his foot and knocked down the barrel of the rifle. "The man's wounded. You can't just shoot him."

Kusnetzov shrugged. "Why not? Are we to leave him out there all day to listen to?"

"No," said Bayard slowly, "we've got to do something—"

"What we do, Captain?" jeered Kusnetzov. "Go out there and get him?"

"We've got to do something," repeated Bayard.

"You mean go out there and get him," said Kusnetzov.

"When the light gets better, so we can be sure of the mines," said Bayard.

"The light is all right now," said Kusnetzov. "You want him so much. I go get him." The big machine gunner jumped to his feet and started out through the barbed wire entanglement.

Bayard followed him to the first strand of wire. "Get back here," he ordered.

Kusnetzov turned and grinned, his teeth showing whitely through his tangled black beard. "In a minute, Captain. I be back in a minute." He moved slowly, raising his big feet high as he stepped carefully over the wire.

"I said get back here," said Bayard sternly. He took a step forward. The wire caught at his trousers. Bayard went no further.

Kusnetzov continued his painstaking way through the entanglement, reached the wounded Chinese, and knelt over the prostrate body. He looked back toward Bayard, wagging his head in mock sorrow. "Too late, Captain," he called. "Our little friend is already dead."

"Get back here," said Bayard once again. "And for Christ's sake, be careful."

Kusnetzov started back through the wire, moving toward Bayard with a repetition of those same high, deliberate steps. Then the mine blew up underneath him. Bayard flung himself to the ground, covered his head until the debris was through falling, and then looked up.

Kusnetzov was still on his feet, standing there about a hundred feet in front of Bayard. Or rather, the remnant of the man was standing there. The blast had sheared away Kusnetzov's face. The eyes were gone. The lower half of the jaw was gone. The white teeth of his upper jaw showed through the mask of blood in a macabre caricature of a grin. A gobbling noise came out of the shattered face.

He raised his arms in a sort of supplication. The hands were blown off. The bones of his arms stood out like sticks through the mangled flesh.

Then he started forward again, toward Bayard, moving with those same high, deliberate steps. The barbed wire caught at the green winter trousers, but the legs, moving as implacably as pistons, tore free of the wire, and Kusnetzov continued his grotesque, high-stepping march.

The occupants of the north sector could do nothing but watch in horrified silence. Kusnetzov's tottering body stumbled across the last strand of wire and fell forward across the parapet of his emplacement. A flailing arm struck the barrel of his machine gun, canting it off to the side. One more convulsive movement racked the shattered body, and then it lay still.

"Is he dead?" asked Howard.

"I don't know," said Bayard. He turned the body over gingerly and saw that his mittened hands were slimy with blood and pulpy flesh. "His chest is blown in," said Bayard. "He must be dead."

A faint frozen exhalation came up from the mangled face. "He's breathing," said Howard. "He's still alive. I can see his breath."

"He's dead," said Bayard harshly. "That's just a sort of steam from his body hitting the cold air."

"I wonder if he feels anything?" asked Howard.

"He can't feel anything," said Bayard angrily. "He's dead. I told you he was dead. Now cover him up with a poncho or something."

"I don't guess he can feel anything," said Howard dubiously. "I might as well use his own shelter-half to cover him." He reached for the neat pack that had been pegged to the wall of the machine gun emplacement, undid the blanket-roll straps, and pulled loose the camouflaged shelter-half. "Which side out?" he asked with a foolish giggle. "Green or brown? I never know which side goes out."

"Shut up and get him covered," said Bayard. Together, they draped the multicolored cloth over the body.

"I'm getting sick," warned Howard.

"Go ahead and throw up," said Bayard. "You'll feel better."

chapter twenty-five...

The Chinese did not bother them during the daylight hours that followed
that first night attack. Dog Company was given time to reorganize, to
shorten the circumference of its perimeter to a length more manageable
with its reduced strength. The previous night's narrow-margined victory
acted as a bitter-tasting tonic. Holes were dug deeper, the barbed-wire
entanglements thickened, exploded mines replaced, on-position reserves
of ammunition replenished. But no amount of reorganization could make
up for the losses in men and material. A sizable share of the company's
rations, fuel oil, and, most damaging of all, the spare batteries for the radio
sets had been in the two tents that had burned.

By noon, Brown and the artillery sergeant were reporting that they
no longer could raise Battalion on either the tactical or the artillery nets.
"Goddamn it!" exploded Bayard. "What were you thinking of when you
put all the batteries in one tent?"

Brown attempted to stammer an explanation, the batteries would have frozen—

"All right," said Bayard contritely. "What's done is done. Now what do we do about it?" There was no point in blaming Brown, but the loss of radio communication was critical, Dog Company's isolation made all the more complete, more impenetrable, by the speechlessness and deafness.

"We might try to warm the batteries that are in the sets," said Brown tentatively. "Sometimes they recuperate."

"Where do we warm them?" Bayard's frozen lips stretched painfully in a humorless grin. "Where do you suggest?"

The one remaining tent, which was in Naheghian's area, was riddled with holes and scarcely usable. Bayard had offered it to Pilnick to use as his company aid station, but the corpsman had shaken his head. "Too exposed," he said. "With the captain's permission, I'd like to dig in under the belly of the truck. That would give us at least some protection." Bayard had given his consent, and the frozen ground under the otherwise useless truck had been hacked away until Pilnick had a saucer-shaped hole for his sick bay.

"We could put the batteries in the sick bay," suggested Brown, seeing Pilnick's new refuge.

"Try it," said Bayard. He laughed again, mirthlessly. "We've got nothing to lose." So the batteries from the radios were placed in the sleeping bags of the wounded. Perhaps the warmth would revive the cells enough so that the marines could send out at least one emergency signal.

When night came, the Chinese attacked again, this time more boldly and without subterfuge. They announced their coming with flares and bugles. Anchored in its deeper holes, Dog Company responded with machine guns, rifles, and mortars. But it was doubtful that this would be enough to throw back the attack.

This was the time to try the radio once again. Brown and the artillery sergeant, with Bayard watching, reassembled the SCR-300, stringing together the inert batteries in parallel in an effort to boost up a flicker of current.

Nothing. They were dead. There wasn't even enough current to activate the transmitter. Bayard felt his last hope of surviving the night fade and die. He had no way of calling for artillery support. Without artillery support . . .

Then, quite miraculously, at the height of the Chinese assault, a barrage from a full battalion of friendly 105s began. The Chinese were stopped by a wall of high-explosive fire. Bayard had no explanation for the miracle except that perhaps the gun flashes from his fight had been seen two valleys away.

When morning came, Dog Company was still in possession of the pass, and Bayard, half-frozen and bone-weary, felt almost buoyant. Part of this, he told himself severely, was light-headedness from lack of sleep. He doubted if he had slept four hours out of the last forty-eight. But this was the beginning of the third day, and Major Mansell had said that they would not have to hold the pass alone for more than three days, that by then they would be joined by the rest of the battalion.

They waited out the morning, eager for some sign of the approach of the relieving force. While they waited, there were new aggravations with which to deal. The Chinese had posted snipers on the adjacent high ground so that a marine had to be extremely circumspect in his movements. A carrying party that was moving rations from the notch to the north sector had two members hit by rifle fire. Gibson asked permission to take out a patrol to clear the snipers from the hills, but Bayard did not dare risk this further dissipation of force.

By early afternoon their hopes of the battalion's reaching them that day had begun to wane. It was still early enough, they argued, for the battalion to get to them before nightfall. But their arguments lacked conviction as they measured with haggard eyes the downward course of the sun in the western sky.

Then, late in the afternoon a Marine Corps transport plane came over their position, orbited, and signaled that it was going to make a drop. Dog Company looked upward in expectation. The Douglas R4D Skytrain came down low to tumble out its load. The hurtling dark bundles blossomed each in turn into a red, green, or orange flower as the opening parachutes caught the air and checked the rate of descent. But the razor-edged mountain ridge was an elusive drop zone and the blasting wind carried most of the drop far down the ice-covered slope. There the bright splotches of color of the chutes beckoned to the Dog Company marines.

There were rations, ammunition, maybe even batteries down there—the very substances that would keep Dog Company alive. Bayard deliberated, weighing the consequences, but there was only one decision he could make. He ordered Naheghian to take out a fifteen-man patrol and bring back into the perimeter what he could and to destroy the rest. He told Naheghian to look particularly for batteries.

Naheghian was completely shapeless in his filthy parka. The earflaps of his fur cap hung down loosely. The moisture from his nose had run down the ragged ends of his mustache and had frozen there, like the tusks of a walrus. He carried three firearms now. He still had the sniper's rifle. That was his daylight weapon. In a shoulder holster he had his .357 Magnum revolver. And for nighttime use he had a Thompson submachine gun he had taken from a dead Chinaman.

He handed the Tommy gun to Bayard. "How about keeping this for me, Skipper, until I get back. I'll be needing it tonight."

Bayard took the submachine gun in his left hand and held out his mittened right hand. "Good luck," he said, "and hurry back."

Naheghian gripped his hand tightly. "Don't worry, Skipper. This is the sort of thing the Forty Thieves are good at."

The Chinese let the patrol get to the first cluster of parachutes. Then they opened on them with a converging fire. Watching through his field glasses, Bayard saw a marine stumble and go down. He saw Naheghian bend over him. Then he saw Naheghian himself slump forward.

"Extricate. Extricate," gritted Bayard through his teeth.

As though his orders were transmitted telepathically, the patrol began a fighting withdrawal from the baited trap. If they lost their nerve, if they broke and ran, they wouldn't have a chance. Bayard had Laski put down a covering fire with his 60s. He had his machine guns seal off the flanks of the patrol. This was all he dared do.

"How about going out to help?" asked Gibson. Bayard ground his teeth together and shook his head. The patrol would have to make its own way back.

Like dirty green chessmen being moved across a rough ice-covered board, the patrol slowly climbed back up to the notch. Then, suddenly, a rush, a zigzagged run to a new firing position. An angry exchange of shots. Another rush to the rear. A tableau being played out against a background of mortar fire, with the wings of the stage outlined by machine-gun fire.

The patrol made it into the perimeter with Naheghian's body, two wounded marines, and very little else. They had retrieved some of the ammunition and several colored parachutes, but they had found no radio batteries.

Bayard looked despairingly at Naheghian's dead body, the half-closed eyes, the parted lips. He couldn't be dead. That small, dark, frozen spot on the front of his parka couldn't be the mark of a lethal wound. Gunnery

Sergeant Agnelli had come up alongside of Bayard. Bayard told him to take over what was left of the Forty Thieves. There now remained just two officers in Dog Company: Gibson and Bayard himself.

Bruised by the loss of the airdrop, Dog Company's spirits sank lower as darkness closed on them without any sign of the relieving battalion. That night they were attacked again. Bayard retained no very clear memory of what happened that third night, only a confused recollection of vivid white-gold mortar bursts and red-orange streaks of tracer and the incessant, hammering din of explosions. It was as though his brain had been excised from his skull and was laid on a butcher's block and was being beaten by a mallet.

Bayard fought through the night with his telephones clenched in mittened fists. As long as those slender wires linked him to Gibson, to Agnelli, to Laski, the Dog Company continued to exist as an entity. Then came the shattering moment when he could no longer raise Gibson on the sound-powered phone.

"He isn't here," answered a frightened voice.

"What do you mean, he isn't there?" snarled Bayard into the mouthpiece.

"I don't know," answered the voice. "There was some trouble over on the left flank. He didn't come back. There's nobody here but me."

Bayard dropped the telephone and called across the parapet of his hole to Havac: "Mr. Gibson is missing. It sounds like they're pretty shaky up there in the north sector. You better get up there and take over."

Havac made no complaint, no protest. "Aye, aye, Skipper," he grunted. Bayard heard him vault heavily out of his hole, saw a glimpse of his broad back as he moved up the ridge to Gibson's position.

They found Gibson's body in the morning, a short distance from in front of his position. He had a grenade in one hand and his carbine in the other. The carbine was set on full automatic, and the magazine was empty. Turner and the messmen, who had fought all night themselves as riflemen, carried his body back to the notch on a stretcher.

Bayard looked silently at the white face. He touched the cheek. It was frozen hard as marble. He nodded, and Pilnick zipped the sleeping bag closed over the dead lieutenant's face. The litter bearers picked up the body and carried it over to the line of other stiffly frozen shapes shrouded in olive drab. Bayard counted the sleeping bags. There were twenty-three.

"How many wounded we got?" Bayard's face was crisscrossed with cuts where frostbite had split the skin. His face was stiff with matted beard and the ice that formed from the moisture of his breath. It was painful to talk.

"Nineteen who are in bad shape. Two froze to death last night. I don't know how long the rest will last," said Pilnick.

Bayard looked at the weary little corpsman. "Not much like Baltimore, is it, Pills?"

"Not much," said Pilnick. "I used to think that corner by the Pratt Library was cold and windy. It would seem like Miami compared to this place. The wind never stops blowing. I've used the last of my gasoline, Captain. What am I going to use to heat my sick bay?"

Bayard thought of his apartment near Mt. Vernon Place. It was a high-ceilinged pair of old rooms with drafty full-length windows overlooking Charles Street. There was a boarded-over fireplace with an ornate marble mantle. Bayard had installed a gas log. He had liked sitting there on winter evenings facing the gas flame with the high back of his chair toward the windows.

Now he doubted if he would ever again be warm. His hands and feet ached continually with the cold. He knew that his toes and fingers were frostbitten. Only by the sheerest willpower could he force himself to struggle with the clumsy shoe-pacs every three or four hours and replace the sweat-frozen ski socks with the second pair that had been warming under his shirt.

"What about fuel for the space heater?" Pilnick asked again.

"Christ, I don't know!" exploded Bayard. Then, regaining control, he said: "Pull the carburetor out of the stove and burn whatever you can find in the thing. Scrounge around. Maybe there're some ration boxes or ammo boxes that haven't been burned yet. Break up the benches in the truck if you want to."

Bayard swung himself around in a slow, staggering about-face, taking in as he did so all of Dog Company's shrunken, minute world. Altogether the circumference of his line must be about five hundred yards. He had about eighty men left. His chilled brain struggled numbly with the division. Eighty men to cover five hundred yards. That was more than six yards of front to a man. And now there were no other officers, just himself.

That morning a flight of four Marine Corsairs came overhead. Dog Company had its recognition panels out, and after a cautious first look, the flight leader came down low. He roared over the position, rocking his wings in greeting, and then led his flight away while Bayard watched impotently, unable to talk to the plane.

"Going off to get a hot breakfast," sneered Baby-san.

"At least they know we're still here," said Bayard. Wearily, he summoned Havac, and the three of them trudged the circuit of the perimeter.

The landscape was white and gray and black. The snow covered the ground only thinly, and in unsheltered places the wind had bared the frozen earth and barren rock. In this desolate region, trees and shrubs grew sparsely, and their winter-blackened trunks and limbs thrust up grotesquely, like beckoning arms, through the snow. In front of Dog Company's foxholes were the tumbled shapes of the enemy dead in their quilted cotton uniforms, some mustard-colored, some dirty white. Their faces and hands were puffed and frozen bluish black. And there were stark reddish trails where the wounded and some of the dead had been dragged off.

Bayard had made a careful count of the enemy dead. There were 126 bodies in front of Dog Company, singly or lying in discernible lines where they had been caught in the final protective fires of Dog Company's machine guns. Exercising his numb brain, Bayard applied certain rules of thumb, a sort of score-keeping: for every dead Chinese out there, their comrades had probably dragged away at least one other dead body. That would be about two hundred fifty dead. And for every enemy killed, there should be four or five wounded. That was the usual ratio. Enemy casualties, then: twelve hundred and fifty to fifteen hundred. Dog Company had exacted a price, but was it a fair exchange? What satisfaction was there in trading the life of a man you knew for that of ten of these nameless faceless enemy?

Four wounded Chinese prisoners were in Dog Company's sick bay under the truck. They lay stolidly on their pallets, smoking the cigarettes Dog Company had given them from their own meager stores and answering the questions put to them by Jim Kim.

They were from the Chinese People's Volunteer 56th Division. Six weeks earlier, in October, they had been in garrison in Shanghai. They were issued winter uniforms and moved by train to the Yalu. They crossed into Korea three weeks before the attack against the Marines.

Some of Dog Company stared stonily at the prisoners and muttered "Kill the bastards," but this was just talk. Perhaps if Kusnetzov were still alive and had the opportunity, he would have done it, either with his bayonet or his big powerful hands. But Kusnetzov was dead.

Those dead Chinese lying out there, bodies frozen into grotesquely improbable attitudes, padded uniforms powdered lightly with snow. . . . Bayard looked at them and felt nothing, neither anger nor hate nor compassion nor pity nor contempt. Nothing. It was as though these inert, improbable shapes were less than human, simply the debris carried up on a beach by a breaking wave and left there by the receding tide. Later the tide would sweep in again. . . .

Bayard's mind was too tired, too bitterly numb, to conjure up any further images. The Chinese would come back tonight, and if Dog Company lasted, they would be back the next night and the next. Their plan never changed. Sometime after ten o'clock the green flare would go up, arcing across the black winter sky. The bugles would sound, and the dark shapes would converge on Dog Company, coming down from the higher reaches of the ridgeline.

It wasn't fear that Bayard felt. With fear, there would have been an excitement, a surge of adrenaline, a stimulation. What had seeped into his body along with the cold was a dull, bitter acceptance. He saw the same apathy in the eyes of his men and in the empty grins they gave back in response to his forced pleasantries as he made his plodding way around Dog Company's line. "They don't look good, Skipper," muttered Havac. "This outfit's about fought out."

"How do you think we'll do tonight?" asked Bayard.

"I don't know," said Havac. "Chow we can do without. But ammunition is something else again. We got plenty of small-arms and enough machine-gun, but the mortar's about all gone, and so are the grenades."

"How about searching the Chinese dead for grenades?"

"We've done that, and we've gotten some. They're lousy grenades, but they're better than nothing. We can use them."

Bayard stopped in his tracks and looked at the first sergeant. "Let's face it, Top. If they want to take us tonight, they can do it. We don't have enough poop left to stop them."

"Yeah," said Havac, "but we'll take a lot of the bastards with us."

Then they heard the pulsating beat of a low-powered aircraft engine somewhere to the east. They searched the sky and finally discerned the shape of a small helicopter struggling toward them. "I didn't think a chopper could get up here," said Havac wonderingly.

Bayard pulled his binoculars out from under his parka and focused them on the helicopter. In the distance it looked like a bulbous, blue dragonfly. The cold morning sun caught on the plexiglas nose. Bayard could see two figures seated side by side in the cockpit. Underneath, by the landing skids, were hung the coffin-shaped pods that could carry out two of Dog Company's most severely wounded.

The whirling blades beat at the cold, thin mountain air. The attention of all Dog Company was now on the aircraft. It nearly attained the altitude it needed to clear the pass, then trembled and fell off down into the valley. The pilot brought it around, and once again it struggled for the height it required to reach Dog Company's perimeter.

The helicopter, buffeted by the winds funneling through the notch in the mountains, fought its way into a hovering position over Dog Company's heads and then began setting itself down on the small open landing zone that Bayard had marked with red recognition panels formed into a cross. A down blast of air from the rotor blades struck Bayard's upturned face. A small whirlwind of debris kicked itself up and danced across the abbreviated landing zone as the helicopter settled itself delicately onto the red cross. The skids of the craft touched the earth. The rotor blades began to droop as the pilot cut back on the throttle. Bayard thought it had safely landed. Then a gust of wind came roaring through the funnel of the pass, caught the craft broadside, and sent it skittering sideways. A rotor blade dug into the ground, and the helicopter flipped over on its side. The flailing blades smashed themselves to bits against the frozen ground. The engine, relieved of its load, raced briefly and then was still. The fuselage came to rest with its landing skids—and the pods that could have lifted off two of Dog Company's wounded—jutting straight up in the air.

"Get them out! See if they're hurt!" Bayard heard himself yelling. He was the first one to reach the helicopter. Wrenching open the door, he saw that the pilot and the passenger were tumbled into a heap in the plexiglas nose. He got his gloved hands under the pilot's armpits and hauled him free of the wrecked aircraft.

"I'm all right," said the pilot, pulling away from Bayard. "Get the colonel out. See how he is."

Bayard and Havac each got a grip on the passenger and lifted him free of the helicopter, seeing as they did so that it was the Red Snapper. Once on his feet, the battalion commander impatiently pushed away the helping hands. No sooner had he done so than he sat down abruptly on the ground.

"Christ, my ankle," he said. "I think the fucker's broken."

"Corpsman!" yelled Havac unnecessarily, because Pilnick was already there.

The corpsman bent solicitously over the battalion commander. The Red Snapper brushed him aside. "Leave me alone for a minute, son," he said. "Well, Bayard, it looks like we've got ourselves in a fine fucking mess."

Bayard looked at his battalion commander sprawled on the ground and felt the last of the brief ray of hope that had been tanned up by the helicopter's appearance go out. He now felt nothing but cold, abysmal dismay.

"What's your company strength?" The Old Man seemed more wizened, more ineffectual than ever, sitting there on the ground in his oversized parka.

"About eighty," said Bayard. "I'm the only officer."

A slight grimace of pain flicked across the Red Snapper's face. Pilnick had crept back and was gingerly removing the Old Man's shoe-pac. "Goddamn it, lad, watch what you're doing," protested the battalion commander. "Are you trying to pull my fucking foot off?" He turned his attention to Bayard. "And you. We haven't heard from you for days. What're we supposed to do—guess what's going on up here?"

"We had no way of communicating," said Bayard. "Our batteries are dead. We didn't get any from the airdrop. We had no way of talking to you." Did he have to justify himself to this querulous relic of a half-forgotten past?

The Old Man jerked his head around toward the pilot. "You think you can make the radio in your contraption work?"

"I don't know," said the pilot dubiously. "I can try."

"If you want to ever see your home, loved ones, and flight pay again, you goddamn well better make sure it works," said the Red Snapper.

"I'm afraid your ankle might be broken, sir," said Pilnick. "At least, it's badly sprained."

"Put a bandage on it and let me get up before my ass freezes to the deck."

"If I put a bandage on it," warned Pilnick, "it will stop the circulation, and your foot will freeze."

"Thank you for your expert opinion, Florence Nightingale," said the Red Snapper. "Now put on the goddamn bandage like I told you."

The pilot was back from his exploration of the helicopter's cockpit. "I can send a little. I can raise the battalion forward air controller. But I haven't much power. Just enough for a couple of minutes transmission."

"All right then," said the Red Snapper. "Do this: Tell them we're here and okay. Tell them I'll be calling back in an hour to let them know what we're going to do."

"Is the battalion on its way?" asked Bayard.

The Red Snapper looked at him pityingly. "Son," he said, "the whole fucking front has collapsed. The Eighth Army is hauling ass for Pusan. The X Corps is scattered in pieces from Wonsan to the Yalu. The division is turned around and heading for Hungnam. I never thought I'd see the fucking day that a buncha goddamn Chinamen could run off an American army. Now get me on my feet, and we'll take a look at this here Dog Company of yours."

Bayard and the first sergeant helped the battalion commander to his feet. The Red Snapper took a tentative step, grimacing as his weight came down on the damaged ankle but pushing aside the would-be helping hands.

"If you try to walk on that foot, sir," warned Pilnick, "you're apt to do irreparable damage to your ankle."

"I can walk all right," said the Red Snapper. "Let's look at your position."

The cold alone had caused a bone-deep pain in Bayard's own ankles and feet. Whatever the Old Man felt, it did not show on the wizened face. Was the soul inside as withdrawn and shriveled as the exterior the man presented to the world? The Red Snapper lurched along with a puppet-like stride, swinging his injured leg stiffly. Bayard, following at his elbow, watched and wondered.

The Red Snapper stopped behind a rifleman lying in a shallow foxhole. The rifleman's weapon lay in a shallow cradle scooped out of a parapet built of bits of earth and rock cemented together with hard-packed snow. The rifleman turned over on his back and looked up dully, incuriously, at his visitors.

"What's the zero of your piece, son?" asked the Red Snapper.

"Eight clicks elevation, three left windage," answered the marine mechanically.

"Let me see your weapon," ordered the Red Snapper. The marine rolled over on his side and pushed his rifle up toward the battalion commander. The Red Snapper took the rifle in his left hand, pulled off the outer shell of the mitten on his right hand with his teeth, and unlocked the rear sight. He twisted the knob and ran the rear aperture all the way down. The faint clicks sounded as loud as drum taps in the frozen air. Then he ran the sight back up, counting off nine clicks, and locked it again.

God, thought Bayard, he thinks he's back on the rifle range at Camp Lejeune.

"See that dark speck about five hundred yards up there near that crevice in the rock?" said the Red Snapper. The marine rifleman nodded dumbly. Bayard looked and saw nothing.

The Red Snapper lifted the rifle slowly to his shoulder, took a breath, held it, and squeezed the trigger. He rocked back under the recoil of the piece. The bright brass cartridge case spun out of the receiver. "I think I got me a Chinaman," he said. "Offhand, at five hundred yards." He passed the rifle back to the rifleman and put the mitten shell back on his right hand.

They walked on. Bayard looked back and saw the rifleman talking to his fire team leader and pointing up the ridge toward the crevice in the rock.

The Red Snapper asked the name of every marine. He squatted down behind each machine gun and automatic rifle and checked its sector of fire. He asked the mortar-section leader to point out his primary target areas.

Hunky Havac had trailed behind Quillan and Bayard as they had made the circuit of the perimeter. When they were back at the command post, Havac suddenly rasped: "It's good to have you with us, sir." Bayard looked at Havac sharply. Wasn't even the granite first sergeant immune to the Legend?

The Red Snapper looked at Havac appraisingly. "It's good to be here, Hunky," he said in his thin, improbable remnant of a voice.

Christ, thought Bayard, am I to spend my last hours on earth with a pair of posturing idiots?

The three of them took shelter under the scant protection of a cargo parachute. "What a fucking farce," said the Red Snapper. "Smedley Butler must be spinning in his grave. In '27 he could've marched the old brigade from Tientsin to Shanghai and back, and the whole four hundred million of the slant-eyed bastards couldn't have stopped us."

Bayard, crouching under the orange nylon canopy, said nothing.

"The Chinese don't have a ring around you," said the Red Snapper. "When I flew in here in that goddamn chopper, I didn't see a goddamn Chinaman on the road from here back to Battalion. He's perched up on the high ground, where he can watch you during the daytime and come down on you at night. He thinks we can't move at night. He thinks an American can't take a piss after dark, that he can't find his prick without a flashlight, and he's goddamn near right."

"What do you want me to do?" flared up Bayard. "Walk out of here?"

"Exactly," said the Red Snapper. "We're going to get up on our hind legs and walk out. Now, where's that chopper pilot?"

The helicopter pilot was found in the shelter of the aid station. He and the battalion commander went over to the wrecked helicopter. The Old Man took the radio handset and talked at length to Battalion until the power supply ran out. "This thing all through now?" he asked the pilot. The lieutenant nodded. "Then get rid of that silly-ass flight jacket and get yourself a parka and a rifle. From here on in you're a platoon leader."

The Red Snapper turned to Bayard. "Give this guy a job. At eleven o'clock tonight, there's going to be the goddamnedest artillery barrage that ever hit a point target coming down on this position. I've asked Regiment to get us a time-on-target shoot with every goddamn gun in the division that'll bear on this pass. I figure by just about that time this goddamn position ought to be crawling with Japs."

Japs? thought Bayard uneasily. Just what war does this shriveled old man think we're fighting? Is he completely out of touch with reality?

"But by that time," the Old Man went on, "we'll be halfway back to Battalion."

"How," asked Bayard, not believing what his ears told him, "are we going to do that?"

"I told you before," rasped the Red Snapper testily. "We're going to get up on our hind legs like men and walk out of here."

"As easy as that?" said Bayard.

The Red Snapper looked at him steadily and the dead-gray eyes had turned as hard as flints. "No, not easy, Captain. Rough. Real rough. But I don't believe that Christ in his infinite mercy means for us to die on this goddamn hill. He will see us safely through the valley."

"How do we evacuate the wounded?"

"We carry them out," said the Red Snapper. "Have your corpsmen check the number of litter cases. If a man can walk, he walks. If he can't, we carry him. Put your people to work making extra stretchers. Use blankets, ponchos, whatever you've got."

"What about the dead?" asked Bayard, afraid of the answer.

"They must be left," said the Old Man. "We'll have barely enough able-bodied men to carry the wounded."

Bayard looked out from under the canopy of the parachute toward the row of bodies encased in sleeping bags. "Just leave them?" he said shakily, "to be torn to bits by our own shells? Not even to be decently buried?"

"Son," said the Red Snapper gently, "we're going to need every ounce of energy we can muster to get ourselves and our wounded out of this place. We can't waste our men's strength in hacking out graves in this frozen rock."

"Some of the foxholes are deep enough," said Bayard. "We could bury them in their fighting holes."

"With their weapons beside them," said the Red Snapper in an odd, faraway voice. "A fitting grave for a fighting man. Visigoth, Viking, Sioux Indian—my marines come to join you in your warrior's Valhalla, their weapons in their hands. . . . But make goddamn sure that the weapons we leave behind won't work. Smash them up good." The Red Snapper waved an impatient hand at Bayard. "Well, get on with it," he said.

Bayard went over to the sick bay Pilnick had burrowed under the body of the truck. It was a blatant target, made more so by the flamboyant red, yellow, and green cargo chutes that Pills had stretched out in place of tentage to extend the space available for his patients. Inside, under the parachutes, it was warm, and the space heater glowed a cherry red. "I got the gasoline out of the helicopter," explained Pilnick. "I hope it don't blow up."

"We're leaving here tonight," said Bayard. He then relayed to his chief corpsman the Red Snapper's plan.

"It'll be quite a job," said Pilnick, dubiously looking around at the crowded huddle of patients. The aid station was roughly circular in shape, with the space heater in the center and the patients on their pallets arranged around it like the spokes of a wheel.

"We'll manage somehow," said Bayard. "How's Mr. Reynolds coming along?"

Pilnick dropped his voice to a whisper. "I don't know whether he's asleep or not, sir. I don't think there's much chance for his eyes. The left one's gone for sure—the bullet went through the cheekbone and angled upward. I don't know about the right eye. Maybe definitive surgery could save it."

"Which one is he?" whispered Bayard. After the glare of the sunlight on the snow, he found it difficult to see in the gloom of the aid station.

"That one there," said Pilnick pointing.

Bayard leaned over the pallet of his last remaining platoon commander. The wounded man's breath was passing noisily through the hole in the bandages that covered his face. Bayard couldn't tell if Reynolds were conscious or not. "Don't worry, old horse," said Bayard softly. "We're going to be out of this pretty soon." Reynolds's hand came out from under the sleeping bag and groped feebly in the direction of Bayard's voice. Bayard gripped the hand in both of his own. "How are you fixed for morphine?" he asked Pilnick.

"I can't give him any morphine," said the corpsman. "Not with a head injury."

"I don't mean just for him. I mean for the others."

"I got enough."

"I want you to dope these people as much as they can stand before we leave here. I want you to make the trip as easy for them as possible."

"I will," said Pilnick. "It's going to be a rough night." He paused. "What about the four Chinese? Do we take them with us or do we leave them here?"

Bayard hesitated.

"We could leave them," suggested Pilnick. "They'd be pretty well protected by the body of the truck until their own people got here and took over."

Bayard thought of the planned artillery time-on-target. The wounded prisoners' chances of survival would be small. "No," he decided. "We'll take them with us."

The night, when it closed around Dog Company, was fortunately very black. Bayard could scarcely make out the shapes of his marines forming in column—four men to each stretcher. Almost none of his marines were not so encumbered. All carried out their rifles, their ammunition, and hand grenades. Everything else had to be jettisoned. Steel helmets were left behind, as much because of their telltale silhouette as their extra weight. The crew-served-weapons marines had smashed their mortars, machine guns, and rocket launchers. This came hard to the prideful gunners, severing those hard-forged invisible chains that bound them to their weapons.

Shoe-pacs crunched in the thin snow underfoot. The canvas of the stretchers creaked under the weight of their silent, benumbed burdens. Bayard looked at his watch. It was almost nine o'clock. If the enemy were on schedule tonight, its probing patrols would soon be feeling out Dog Company's defenses. In the distance to the east was the dull red glare of a bombardment; the sound carried to them faintly. Battalion must be getting it or giving it out.

The Red Snapper moved to the head of the column. Swinging his injured leg stiffly, he walked with a crude crutch that someone had improvised for him from a section of aluminum tubing from the helicopter fuselage. He raised his free hand over his head and swung it down. "Let's move out," he said.

A strange macabre ritual, thought Bayard, we are our own pallbearers delivering ourselves to our graves. He stepped into the column behind the Red Snapper. After him came the first sergeant and then Jim Kim and the wounded prisoners, each of these begrudgingly borne by four marines.

The column threaded its way out of the old perimeter, through a gap cut in the thin belt of barbed wire, and along a path gauged to be free of mines. Bayard looked back and sensed rather than saw the dark shapes closing the gap in the wire and arming the personnel mines behind them. To their slender supply of mines, Dog Company had added an improvisation: all of the ammunition they could not carry—the mortar shells, the belted machine-gun ammunition, the TNT blocks, and the plastic explosives—had been carefully brought together into a half a dozen piles. Each pile was trip-wired and booby-trapped. And in the center of the perimeter, where the Dog Company guidon had stood, Pinky the company clerk had left a sign made out of a ration box and translated into Chinese for him by Jim Kim: "We, the U.S. Marines, will be back."

They marched in silence except for the squeak of rubber soles on frozen earth or ice, the sound of an occasional stumble and a muted accompanying curse. Bayard counted his steps, translating them into a rough estimate of time and distance. Ten minutes. A quarter of a mile. Slippery progress sliding down the slope from the saddle. Floundering now and again in pockets of snow. Stomach clutched up into a knot, waiting for the inquiring stutter of a Chinese burp gun. Waiting for the crunch of a mortar shell. Nothing. Just keep moving. Watch the shoulders of the man in front of you. Watch the unreal, bobbing figure of the

Red Snapper lurching along. Impervious. Untouchable. Unbelievable.

The Red Snapper raised his arm and signaled a halt. The men of Dog Company shuffled to a stop. A green flare, familiar from many night attacks, arced across the sky to the west. The sound of a bugle carried to them thinly. They saw a cluster of white phosphorus mortar shells fall on Dog Company's old position. The shells burst brightly, fountains of flame feathered with white plumes of smoke. Dog Company could hear the rattle of small-arms fire. The Chinese were closing on the empty perimeter—empty except for the company's dead, buried in their foxholes, a ghostly garrison.

Bayard looked at his watch. It was almost eleven. The Chinese had attacked on schedule. The distance and darkness were too great, but he thought he could see black figures moving in silhouette against the still bursting white phosphorus.

Someone pushed his arm and turned him around so that he faced east. The dull red glow that marked the battalion and regimental positions flickered brighter. An orange-red flame stabbed upward from the horizon, a wide flame coming from many places. Dog Company first felt the sound, rather than heard it. A murmur, then a sighing, and then the sky overhead was filled with the freight-train rush of many unseen projectiles rifling swiftly to their target.

The shells came down on Toksu-nyong in a solid, deadly rain. The cacophony of bursting shells shook the ground under Dog Company's feet. The yellow-red glare reflected itself against the men's exultant faces. Four battalions of artillery were emptying their tubes on the target as fast as their gunners could pull their lanyards and reload and pull their lanyards again.

Bayard felt a great wild delight as the barrage tore the night to shreds. "Kill the bastards. Kill the bastards," he heard himself chanting, and he did a little capering dance.

Then abruptly it was over. How long had it lasted? Thirty seconds? One minute? Three? Five?

"Show's over," said the Red Snapper. "Let's go." Dog Company picked up its burdens. The stretchers felt lighter now. The cold wind was less biting. The trek seemed less impossible. They marched on, led by the incredible little man with the lurching stride and the aluminum crutch.

The axis of their march paralleled the road. The footing was not bad.

There were no stars, no moon, or else the marines would have stood out starkly against the snow. As it was, now that they had progressed well down from the crest of the ridge, Bayard could not distinguish at twenty-five yards between a man's shape and the scrubby pines that sparsely covered the slope.

It couldn't last. He knew that their luck couldn't hold. The exhilaration he had felt during the bombardment was beginning to fade. The paralyzing cold was creeping back in.

Then from a short distance off to the left front of the column came the sharp quick sound of a voice, unintelligible but unmistakably a challenge. The Red Snapper halted, raising his arm in silent signal for the column to halt, a signal to be relayed by the men behind him. Bayard, in turn, raised his arm and froze in his tracks, bracing himself for the shock of the submachine-gun bullets he felt were sure to come.

Silence from the unseen Chinese. How many of them were there? Was it just a frightened outpost? Or a patrol? Or had Dog Company stumbled into the enemy's reserve assembly area? Should the marines stand there waiting, exposed to the unseen? Or should they take their chances and try to punch their way through?

Red Snapper brought his hand down, and the column moved on. Bayard took his place behind the battalion commander, still half-expecting the shock of a string of machine-gun bullets or the burst of a grenade. There was nothing. The column continued to make its way through the black night, and there was nothing.

They reached the floor of the valley. Ahead was the lower intermediate ridgeline. They started to climb. The stretcher bearers were tiring now, and the rate of march slowed. They worked their way upward, groping for handholds and foot purchases in the icy slope.

Ahead of them was the Red Snapper. It was inconceivable that he could climb that slope with a broken ankle, but he did. Somewhere in front of them in this high ground should be the battalion's outposts.

How long had they been going? Bayard pushed down the canvas cuff of his mittens and looked at his watch. The luminous dial was blurred, but the time appeared to be close to one o'clock.

Then, unexpectedly, orange-red fingers of tracer bullets came stabbing out of the darkness, and there was the unmistakable, deliberate pounding of a Browning heavy machine gun. Bayard fell to the ground, his mittened fingers digging at the icy crust. To get so far . . . to die like this in the crossfire of your own machine guns.

"Knock it off!" Havoc's bull roar came out of the night. "This is Dog Company, you shitbirds!" The firing thinned out. "This is Dog Company!" Havac roared again.

"Christ, it's the Hunky," said a wondering voice from somewhere out in front of them. "Okay, you guys, come on into the perimeter."

chapter twenty-six...

Bayard was hit the morning following their march down the pass from the Chosin Reservoir. They had thought it was all behind them. They had fought their way through the last roadblock. The ships were waiting in the harbor at Hungnam, ready to take them off. Trucks were supposed to be waiting to shuttle them the rest of the way to the port. Havac had given him a head count that morning of fifty-seven effectives.

Dog Company—bearded, tired, frostbitten, but still on its feet—was walking through a bedraggled village called Sudong-ni toward the point where the trucks were scheduled to meet them, when a sniper fired down from the surrounding hills. The bullet snapped into the frozen slush of the road a half-dozen feet or so in front of Bayard. Immediately Dog Company swung the muzzles of its rifles up toward the sound of the shot. "Don't fire up there!" someone shouted. "The Army's up there. The Puerto Rican regiment."

"If that's so," said Baby-san morosely, "somebody better get the word to 'em that we ain't gooks."

The crack of another rifle shot echoed down from the hill. Something plucked impatiently at Bayard's sleeve. He looked at his arm and saw a little triangular tear in the sleeve of his parka. He felt something warm course down the flesh of his arm and into his glove. He pulled off his mitten shell and the knitted inner liner. A little rivulet of blood ran out from his cuff and splattered onto the dirty snow. Bayard flexed his bare fingers curiously.

Then Pilnick took him by his uninjured arm and led him off the road to the cover of the bordering ditch. Pilnick gingerly helped him off with his parka and field jacket. The corpsman cut through the remaining layers of clothing—Bayard's sweater, flannel shirt, and undershirt—with his scissors so that he could examine the wound. "Clean through the biceps," declared Pilnick. "Missed the bone completely. This one won't even get you back to Japan, Skipper."

Pilnick put on a battle dressing. "How does it feel, Captain? Do you want me to give you a shot of morphine?"

"I don't think so," said Bayard. "It just aches a little, and my fingers feel sort of numb."

"If it starts giving you a bad time, let me know."

"Thanks," said Bayard. "We better get going."

Pilnick helped him with the field jacket and parka, improvising a sling for the wounded arm by pinning Bayard's sleeve to the front of his parka. Corpsman and company commander got back on the road and caught up with Dog Company in the line of march. They found the trucks waiting for them at the designated spot. Dog Company boarded the trucks and bounced over the broken roads the last twenty miles, through Hamhung and on to a place called Chig-yong-ni.

There, they found a bivouac with long rows of pyramidal tents set up and waiting for them. "It ain't tactical," criticized Dog Company's younger members as they scrambled down from the trucks.

"It don't have to be," said the veterans. "We're so far back from the fuckin' front it don't have to be tactical. This is strictly rear area."

"That may be, but I'd feel better if we had a perimeter. Where do you reckon we go from here?"

"We got to go around to the other coast and rescue the friggin' Eighth Army."

"Balls on that," said a machine gunner, handing down his weapon to his assistant gunner waiting on the ground. "I wish t'Christ we'd go to Indochina to help the friggin' Frogs. At least it'd be warm. I thought the Marines did their fightin' in the friggin' tropics."

"That was the last war," said a sergeant whose service dated back to the hazy days of 1942.

The company formed up in the street and was assigned to its tents. Ten tents for Dog Company were ample. Once the men were settled, Bayard—with a reminder from Pilnick—went to see Dr. Goldberg about his arm. The battalion surgeon replaced the compresses and gave him a shot of penicillin to keep down the infection. "I ought to turn you in with that arm," said Goldberg.

"I'm the last officer in Dog Company," said Bayard. "I better stick around."

"They could get along without you," said the surgeon.

"I know that," said Bayard, "but I don't want them to find that out. As long as this doesn't bother me any more than it has been, I'll stay with the company."

They spent two days at Chig-yong-ni, and then the tents were struck and the battalion entrucked for the embarkation area in Hungnam. Gray-painted ships filled most of the harbor. Not since Okinawa had Bayard seen such a concentration.

"Maybe we *are* going to Indochina," said a rifleman.

"Christ, if you're going to make any predictions, make it a good one," said the corporal who was his squad leader. "I hear we'll be in Tokyo for Christmas and San Francisco for New Year's."

"In a pig's asshole," said Pinky. "I got it straight from the communicators. We're going to Pusan so the fucking Eighth Army has some place to retreat to."

"Here at Hungnam we got twenty thousand marines, fifty thousand doggies, Christ knows how many ROKs, and not a goddamn Chinaman within twenty miles—still we're running away," said the machine-gun platoon sergeant, a scholarly type who read field manuals and military history. "With what we got here, we could hold this port all winter and then attack to the north again in the spring. This war don't make sense."

LCTs ferried them out to the ships. The whole regiment boarded one transport. While they were considerably fewer in number than a regiment should be, there still numbered twice as many troops to be embarked as the civilian-crewed transport—the same class of ship as they had taken from San Diego—was designed to carry.

It was almost midnight. A ship's officer met Bayard at the top of the gangway and asked him if he would like to clean up before having a midnight chow. The officer led him to his own stateroom and gave him a thick white towel and a change of underwear. Bayard took a shower, favoring his wounded arm, which was swollen and sore to the touch.

After he had washed and shaved, he redressed in the clean underwear and dirty outer clothes and went to the officer's wardroom, where the midnight meal was being served. The mess steward insisted on piling his plate high. "Don't you worry, Cap'n. They's plenty more in the galley. You help yourself."

Having eaten, Bayard went out onto the still-crowded deck. From far out to sea, the big ships of the fleet were hurling their shells into the hills behind Hungnam. The muzzle flashes of the great guns flickered along the horizon like a strange sort of northern lights.

"They say the Mighty Mo is out there," said a marine standing in front of Bayard.

"I don't know what they think they're shooting at," said the marine next to him. "I don't think there's a fucking Chinaman within fifty miles of this place. Got a cigarette?"

"Sure."

The flame of the match illuminated the two faces. "Thanks," said the first marine. "What outfit you in?"

"Dog Company, Second Bat."

"Dog Company? You were the guys that nearly got wiped out."

"Wiped out? Shit, we could've held that fucking pass all winter."

"The shit you could."

"The shit we couldn't."

It was only a two-day run to Pusan. Two marines were assigned to every bunk, and this led to ribald comment. The mess lines never ended, but the food was good. The transport's crew treated the marines with a strange and unfamiliar courtesy, and the men of Dog Company learned that they were heroes. And although they couldn't pronounce the word, they learned from the radio that the 1st Marine Division was Xenophon's ten thousand in a new *Anabasis*.

During this time, something went wrong with Bayard's arm. The battalion surgeon felt under Bayard's armpit and located the swollen lymph glands. He probed them gently. "Hurt, George?"

"Enough," gritted Bayard through his teeth.

"When we get in at Pusan, we'll see if we can't get you admitted aboard the hospital ship. I could open it up here in the sick bay, but—" The surgeon raised his hands in an age-old Jewish gesture, "You might as well get some rest and decent chow while you're about it."

So when the transport discharged the regiment onto the docks at Pusan, Bayard found himself with a smaller detail of sick and wounded, waiting for a small craft to take them out to the *Mercy*, while the rest of the regiment entrained for the division assembly area at Masan.

The *Mercy* was all stainless steel and white enamel, and the smell of soap and disinfectant was stronger than the smell of sweat, paint, and fuel oil, which was to Bayard the smell of all navy ships. The surgeon who operated on his arm gave him a local anesthetic, opened the wound, probed impersonally into the depths of Bayard's bicep, and fished out a bit of uniform cloth.

"Here's your focus of infection," he said laconically, and then he threaded a drain through Bayard's arm. "This'll give it a chance to heal from the inside out."

Bayard was to be a patient on the ship for about a week. The doctor said that his system was run down and that he should remain quiet until the infection subsided. Except for an occasional twinge from his arm, Bayard didn't feel bad, and it made him restless to be confined.

A nurse came through the ward twice a day, looking at temperature charts, checking dressings, and issuing instructions to the corpsmen. She had a pleasant face, capable hands, a full bust, a broad behind, and round solid legs. Bayard learned that her name was Anna something. The last name was Polish, and he wasn't certain of it. She was a navy lieutenant, his contemporary in rank and, he supposed, in age. She would come through the ward, squeezing past the narrowly separated beds, so close that Bayard could smell the starch of her uniform, her cologne, the faintly antiseptic smell of her hands, and, underneath all this, the slightly acid woman odor.

On the fourth day after his arrival she was not wearing a brassiere, and when she bent over him, he could see past the vee of her uniform collar down into the deep cleft between her ample breasts. He caught a glimpse of jutting nipples surrounded by brown areolae. Later that day, as she paused to straighten his sheets, it seemed to him that she let her fingers trail over the length of his sheet-covered leg.

By the end of the week he was spending most of his time building erotic fantasies in which he stripped Anna bare of her nurse's uniform. He imagined the flicker of her tongue in a kiss, the feel of her breasts in his hands, and the surging response of her thighs.

In combat, things like this hadn't bothered him. He went for weeks without so much as a wet dream. He supposed that the nervous tension of combat soaked up the vital juices, turned them inward. Or perhaps combat was the quintessence of destruction and sterility in all its forms— the opposite extreme of fertility and procreation. He had noticed that even the obscenities of the men's language tended to become sexless. The words remained the same, but they lost their lewd connotation. It was only when you got to the rear that the old urges came back, magnified perhaps by the very fact of their repression. Maybe it was all just another facet of the old life cycle—man's subconscious drive to plant his seed before he himself is destroyed.

On Thursday, Bayard was lying on his bunk, trying to interest himself in a Mickey Spillane novel, when Anna made her rounds. She examined his bandage professionally and then made a note on her clipboard. "Not much wrong with you, soldier," she said.

"Marine, please, lady. Not soldier," he said. "When am I going to get off your lovely boat?"

"Ship, please, marine. Not boat," she said. "I should think day after tomorrow. Saturday. Right after the captain's inspection. We need these beds for people who really need them."

"Do you ever get ashore?" asked Bayard tentatively. "Do you ever get off this sea-going bedpan?"

"Once in a while," she said. "We get ashore now and then."

"Then what do you do?

"Oh, I don't know. Shop at the PX. Go to one of the officers' clubs. Why?"

"I thought maybe we could get together."

Anna said nothing, half smiled, turned to leave Bayard's bunk. "No, I mean it," said Bayard. "I ought to be able to squeeze a day or so out of my orders before getting back to my battalion. Couldn't we sort of look around the city together?"

Anna looked at him appraisingly. "Would you really like to?"

"It would mean a great deal to me."

"We'll see," she added. "We'll see how things work out."

Bayard was discharged from the *Mercy* as scheduled on Saturday. Once ashore he found that some of the techniques learned in the rear areas of the Pacific in World War II were still current and workable. Twenty dollars to the steward of an army officers' club got him two fifths of whiskey. One fifth went to a motor pool sergeant and got him the use of a jeep. Twenty more dollars to the corporal behind the desk of the Victorian monstrosity of a hotel next to the railroad station got him the private use of a room.

These preliminaries completed, Bayard still had half a day to kill before Anna could be expected to arrive at the fleet landing. Pusan was the first sizable Korean city Bayard had seen that hadn't been bombed or shelled. But in a way, he found it a more revolting reminder of the war than the shattered ruins of Seoul. Situated at the lower tip of the Korean peninsula, Pusan was like a giant grease trap catching the sediment and scum of the war, swollen three times its prewar size with the refugees, the opportunists, and much of the displaced South Korean government. To all of this was added the vast and involved logistical phantasmagoria needed to support the United Nations forces.

Crudely painted signs offered entertainment that was no doubt as dubious as the spelling: "Stark Club, 50 Butiful Girls Dance With Lonley GI, Beer, Wisky, Gin, All Kins Ammerican Drink," "BlacK Cat, Lovely Hostisses, Continus Showings, U.S. Drinks," "Miami Club, Hot Womans, Cold Beers."

Two Negro quartermaster sergeants, a giggling Korean girl on the arm of each, elbowed past Bayard. The girls wore fur coats and slacks. Their black hair was permanent-waved, their ochre faces plastered white with powder, their lips heavy with greasy lipstick.

A trio of British soldiers stalked by in fuzzy, olive drab battle dress, their brown berets jaunty, their hobnailed shoes bright with black polish.

A giant U.S. Army sergeant—his parka grease-stained and fire-singed, the flaps of his fur cap awry, the lower half of his face a tangle of yellow beard—strode angry-eyed through the crowd, a gaggle of shoeshine boys at his heels. Like a bull baited by dogs, he turned on them. "Me Russki," he roared thumping his ample chest.

It was a senseless gesture, but it had its momentary effect. The shoeshine boys fled to a safe distance and then, recovering their aplomb, closed once more around the sergeant, importuning him for cigarettes and candy. "Ah, hell," said the sergeant. Ripping apart a package of cigarettes, he tossed its contents high in the air. The shoeshine boys scrambled for the cigarettes as they fell into the mud of the street. The sergeant saw Bayard, laughed, and said, "Goddamn little fuckers're like leeches."

A string of stall-like shops lined the street. Flagrantly displayed were many of the items that had been in short supply at the front. Bayard saw row after row of Coleman lanterns marked "20 U.S. dollars" and dozens of navy flashlights being offered at five dollars each. Up north, Dog Company had made out with candles, when and if it could get them. Half the teeming, pushing, Korean civilians seemed to be wearing GI fatigues and field jackets. A large number of young Koreans—neither refugees nor ROK recruits, but sleek members of that species a black market invariably breeds—were wearing jackets made from the pile liners stripped from somebody's supply of winter parkas.

At three o'clock Bayard took his borrowed jeep to the fleet landing. A raw winter wind was blowing across the water. Here in the south, there was a wet cold, not the subzero temperatures they had experienced in the north. He parked the jeep where he could sit and watch the liberty boats unloading, lit a cigarette, and waited.

An hour passed. He fished in the crumpled pack for a fifth or sixth cigarette. It was empty. He got out of the jeep, favoring his arm, which was still tender. He walked over to a chief petty officer wearing a shore-patrol brassard. The chief was bulky in a navy parka; his pistol belt was loose and drooped untidily around his hips.

"What's the story on the liberty party from the *Mercy*, Chief?"

"Whaddya mean, liberty party?" he replied with an air of hostility.

"Well," said Bayard, "wasn't there supposed to be a party of nurses coming ashore at 1500?"

A sly, knowing smile slid across the chief's face. "You got a date with one of them, Captain?"

"Sort of," said Bayard.

"Then you've been had, Captain," said the chief. "Because there ain't no nurses coming ashore from the *Mercy* today."

Bayard stood looking at him for an irresolute, embarrassed moment. "Thanks, Chief," he said. And turning on his heel, he went back to his jeep. He still had the bottle, and there was still the hotel room. He had a strong hunch that the smart U.S. Army corporal at the desk might be able to provide a Korean girl for the night. He found a parking place near the hotel to park the jeep. He parked the jeep, remembering to padlock the gearshift. He took the rotor from the distributor as an extra precaution.

But once inside the hotel, he did not stop at the desk. He went straight up the staircase to his room. He threw his few personal things—there was nothing except his toilet articles and the bottle—into his haversack and got ready to leave. He knew that it wasn't a Korean girl that he wanted.

Downstairs again, he tossed the room key to the corporal and said that he was checking out. The key bounced across the chipped marble of the desk counter. The corporal caught it and hung it back on the key rack. "Better luck next time," the corporal said.

"Yeah, sure," said Bayard.

He took the borrowed jeep back to the motor pool and found the sergeant dispatcher. "Got anything going to Masan tonight?" Bayard asked.

"Masan? Tonight?" said the sergeant. "Gee, Captain, I thought you were all fixed up for tonight."

"I changed my mind," said Bayard shortly. "Have you got anything or not?"

"I got a truck convoy pulling out at eight, but what do you want to leave now for? You'll get there in the middle of the night. Why don't you wait until morning?"

"I want to get out of here," said Bayard. "The sooner the better. This town has a real bad smell. In fact, it stinks."

Anna sent him a note later. He received it at Masan. She wrote that it wasn't her fault that she hadn't gotten ashore. A batch of wounded had come in from the north. Maybe this was so. Bayard never answered her letter, nor during the time the division remained at Masan, did he ever go again to Pusan.

chapter twenty-six...

By the time Bayard had been discharged from the *Mercy* and got to Masan, the replacements had arrived. Dog Company had six new lieutenants, all reserves who had just finished a refresher course at Quantico before being flown out from the States. Two-thirds of the enlisted strength at Masan was new. Bayard was doubtful that the company could absorb such an influx of replacements and ever regain its old effectiveness. But it did.

A month of low-intensity combat was fought in late January and early February against guerrillas west of Pohang, and this was the best sort of training for the new men and officers. When they went back into the attack north of Wonju in late February, Dog Company was as good as ever. Well, almost as good. You had to give the credit to the remaining old dependables, such as Havac and Agnelli, and to youngsters like Jones, who had moved up to be the acting platoon sergeant of the 2d Platoon.

Mansell had taken over the command of the battalion after the Red

Snapper was evacuated, and he had held on to the command all that spring even though he was still a major. A story circulated that the Red Snapper had told the division commander that Mansell should keep the battalion.

The newspapers called it the "UN counteroffensive." The Eighth Army called it Operation Killer. Dog Company was content simply to say "the Division is back in the attack." It was a vicious, wearing offensive that took the 2d Battalion away from the roads, away from its supporting armor, away from the friendly sea and up into the hills of central Korea.

They were just below the 38th Parallel when the division came out of the lines at the end of March. The marines of Dog Company had it figured out that when they went back into the attack, it would be Battalion's turn to be in Regimental reserve and Dog Company's turn to be in Battalion reserve. So the situation had looked then—wrongly as it had turned out—as though it would be a good long time before Dog Company was again committed. Perhaps as much as two weeks.

That would have given them time for a little rest, some B rations cooked up by the battalion mess—not all of Dog Company thought this better than individual C rations—and a little training for the replacements. More new men were in. Baby-san and Pinky went down to the battalion CP to get them. Twenty-four, the sergeant major had said over the phone. Almost enough to bring Dog Company back up to strength. It was funny about replacements: they always arrived at night. Even here, twenty miles behind the lines, there seemed to be an administrative conspiracy that new personnel must be received and processed in the dark.

Not so dark tonight, though. Battalion had relaxed the blackout discipline because, while there was a possibility of enemy aircraft, the danger was certainly remote. Consequently, the better part of Dog Company could be seen sitting around the warm, bright light of a dozen campfires. In the hills above the company bivouac, the serpentine line of a brushfire burned with the orange-red glow of a gigantic neon sign.

The night was not quiet. Trucks bearing the rear echelons of the army division that had relieved the Marines in this zone of action roared northward along the main supply route a hundred yards from where Bayard was sitting. (Dog Company, before settling down to its campfires, had thoughtfully erected a roadside sign: "If you dogfaces want to retreat, use the stream bed, as us marines will be counterattacking up the MSR.") Tracked vehicles clattered by, churning up dust, the dry smell of it competing with Bayard's pipe. From further north in the valley came the echoing sound of the 155s and the eight-inch howitzers beginning their pre-preparation fires for the army's continuation of the attack in the morning.

Bayard was sitting on a water can in front of his headquarters tent, listening to the 2d Platoon sing. Gunnery Sergeant Agnelli had cooked a spaghetti dinner for company headquarters—the components had been given him by Havac's friend, the battalion mess sergeant. Bayard felt warm, well-fed, and content with the world. "When Johnny comes marching home again, hurrah, hurrah. . . ."

The great-great-grandfathers of some of them might have sung that along the line of the Potomac or outside Vicksburg, thought Bayard. Second Platoon looked something like a Civil War scene, the men sitting there with their short-billed cloth caps and the firelight shining in red and gold on their faces. "And pretty Red Wing, as she lay sleeping . . ."

The ballad of Red Wing's love life in all its biological detail was shouted out into the Korean night. A string of marines came marching into Dog Company's area. From the silhouette of the field transport packs on their backs and the seabags on their shoulders or clutched in their arms, one knew these were the replacements. "Fresh meat," said someone.

"Gee, Mom, I want to go, right back to Quantico," sang the 2d Platoon.

"Knock it off," growled Havac to the singers. "Bring 'em over here," he called to Baby-san.

Baby-san halted the replacements with a flourish in front of company headquarters. Tonight the scarlet-and-gold guidon stood in front of a pair of shelter-halves shared by Bayard and the first sergeant. The replacements dropped their seabags and grounded their equipment at Baby-san's command. A slung rifle slid off a shoulder and banged noisily into a helmet.

"Detail, 'ten*shun!*" roared Havac in his drill-field voice. Then, turning to Bayard, he said in his lower, first sergeant-to-company commander tone, "Do you want me to take care of the assignments, Skipper?"

"I'll do it," said Bayard. "Pinky, you got a roster?" Pinky handed him the transfer order. Bayard flicked on his flashlight and looked at the list: one sergeant, two corporals, and twenty-one privates and PFCs. The personnel officer had seen fit to send Dog Company twenty-four men all with names beginning with *H*—"Hall" through "Hyland." The last time they had gotten replacements there had been seventeen *Mac*s and *Mc*s.

Bayard stepped out in front of the detail. The men's backs were toward the campfires, so he couldn't see their faces. But he was sure he knew how they felt. The 2d Platoon had quieted down, waiting for the captain's speech. The captain always gave the new men a speech. "At ease," said Bayard to the new arrivals.

The words came easily enough; he had said them often enough before. "You have just joined Company D of the 2d Battalion. I am Captain Bayard. This is First Sergeant Havac. It's a good company and a good battalion. We landed at Inchon on 15 September. We fought from there into Seoul. Then we went on board ship again and landed at Wonsan. We had a fight at a place called Madong-ni, and then we went north to the Chosin Reservoir, where the Chinese came into the war. We fought our way back to Hungnam and sailed for Pusan. Since February we've been fighting in central Korea. Altogether this company has had over 100 percent casualties since landing in September. But we have also had sixty-eight men recommended for awards, not counting Purple Hearts. The men you are replacing were pretty good men."

Yes, they had been good men: Almquist, Lewis, Kusnetzov, the two Smiths, Martinez, and the rest. Some he had known well. Then there were others, just shadows, who had arrived in the dark of one night and were gone before he had gotten to know their faces.

"How many of you men are reserves?" Most of the men raised their hands. "Any of you veterans of the last war?" Only one hand went up. Bayard flicked his flashlight over in that direction. It was the one sergeant who had his hand up. He was a Negro. "What outfit were you with, Sergeant?"

"I was in antiaircraft artillery, sir—51st Defense Battalion."

"Well, you're all marines," said Bayard. "There's no difference out here between regulars and reserves. And it takes only one day of combat to make you a veteran. But that first day is important. Between now and then, learn as much as you can from the old timers. You've all got too much gear. In the morning sort out the things you think you really need and then cut that amount in half. Tag your seabags, and we'll see to it that they get to the rear. From here on, everything goes on your back. You can only carry so much over these hills and still do your job."

Bayard, Havac, and Pinky then conferred, and the new men were tolled off to their platoons. In benediction, Bayard told them, "You'll be lonely at first. Things are always strange for a replacement. But you'll get to know your way around. We'll get to know each other better. That's all. Good night."

Yes, he would get to know them better—some of them.

At Havac's order they shouldered their gear, and Baby-san marched them off in the direction of their platoons. "Aw right, you guys," said Baby-san, "keep low goin' by them mortars." The twenty-one privates and PFCs obediently hunched down and crept cautiously by the three menacing muzzles, to Baby-san's delight. "Hey, guys," he yelled to the 2d Platoon, "these boots don't know a piss pipe from a sixty-millimeter mortar."

"Time for our people to hit the sack," Bayard said to Havac.

Havac nodded and roared down the street of shelter-halves: "Lights out. Douse them fires. Turn in, you buncha heroes."

Second Platoon sang one more song, "The Battle Hymn of the Republic." That had been Gibson's favorite. The campfires winked out one by one, and soon all was dark and quiet in Dog Company area except for the occasional challenges of the sentries as they walked their solitary posts.

They were still in reserve when General Sung Lee, the local South Korean commander, who was eager to do things in the American manner, sent over his brass band to give the marines a concert. Neither Bayard nor Dog Company was much interested in a Korean band concert, but Major Mansell decreed that each company would turn out at least a third of its personnel.

It rained the morning of the performance—a slow, soaking spring rain that returned the improvised parade ground to its original bean-patch state: the entire area in front of the Headquarters and Service area was ankle-deep in odoriferous mud. At 1400, on command of the battalion adjutant—a shrill, yelping, little terrier of a man—the spectators formed a square around the improvised bandstand. They stood there waiting, rain pinging softly on their helmet liners and running in rivulets down their ponchos. For the officers and staff NCOs, benches had been improvised from boards balanced on water cans. Major Mansell arrived, his runner carrying a folding camp chair. The runner placed the chair in front of the officers' benches, and Major Mansell sat down. He half turned around in his seat and nodded coldly to the company commanders.

"Checking to see who is here," said Bayard in a low voice to Beale.

"Piss on him," said Beale.

The band arrived in its Japanese truck a little behind schedule. The bandsmen were dressed in U.S. Army olive drab uniforms, already growing soggy from the rain, and lacquered helmet liners. Except for their Korean faces, they looked like stubby, two-third-sized American GIs. They arranged themselves on the bandstand. Their leader—a ROK lieutenant, according to his insignia—walked to the front of the stand and raised a yard-long baton.

As the baton came down, the band, their brown faces impassive, crashed into a welter of sound. At first the music failed to register with Bayard. Then the tune began to emerge. Someone must have worked out the score for the band by ear. The melody was distorted, the rhythm was all wrong, but the song was "When Irish Eyes Are Smiling."

The jangling, bouncing music was like that of a merry-go-round organ. When he was a very small boy, the adventure of the summer for Bayard had always been the picnic at Buckeye Lake. He closed his eyes. The wooden horses flew round and round. The lights flashed back from the mirrors set in the carousel. Apples on a stick. Cotton candy. The smell of popcorn and hot dogs heavy in the summer heat. All these things came back to him as the triangle tinkled, the bass drum boomed, and the melody romped mechanically along.

His childhood in Columbus, growing up—it was another world. He tried to remember what it had been like just before the war. Columbus had been a citadel of isolation; he remembered that. He had been only vaguely aware of the war in Europe, and the chances of the United States getting into it had seemed remote. As an underclassman at Ohio State he had not been interested in ROTC—the U.S. Army's Reserve Officers Training Corps. It was a dull sort of thing—close order drill in poorly fitted olive drab uniforms with blue lapel facings and a smattering of horse-drawn field artillery with red facings. He had not applied for the advanced courses that would have given him a reserve commission.

Then suddenly there was Pearl Harbor, and the alternatives seemed to be the draft or one of the officer procurement programs. He had enlisted in the Marine Corps's officer training program after an interview with a first lieutenant wearing a magnificent blue uniform and a gleaming Sam Browne belt. There had been a medical examination, a confusing set of forms to complete, and finally, he found himself in the company of four other boys from Ohio State and one from Capitol University, raising his right hand and being sworn into the Marine Corps Reserve. The lieutenant had given him a warrant as a private first class and an identification card and told him he would be called to active duty for officer's training as soon as he graduated.

When he announced his enlistment to his mother, she had gone promptly to bed with a case of the nerves. His father, in an unprecedented burst of independence, invited him out for a drink. There was never any liquor permitted in the house, for it was one of the family tribulations that his father "drank." The two of them, father and son, had made the rounds of the High Street bars, his father proud and animated in a way George had never seen him before. He had told him tales of France and World War I—although they both knew that George's father had been in a military police battalion that had gotten no closer to the front than Brest—and for a little while George could see in his father the young soldier in the photograph on the mantel.

Bayard had accelerated his graduation date by going to school during summer quarter. He graduated in December 1942 and in January went to Quantico and into the strange new world of the Marine Corps. While he was still in Candidates Class, his father closed the shop on North High Street—after all those years—and went to work at the new Curtiss-Wright plant on the east side of the city. He knew his trade, and they made him a foreman of a department. After twenty-six years of bleak fidelity to his wife, he began an open affair with a machine operator in his department. She was in her middle forties, a hearty, outspoken woman with hair bleached the color of polished brass. The two of them had left for California, where he went to work for Consolidated. Now each year at Christmas, Bayard received a card from San Diego signed "Dad and Marge."

His mother had left Columbus and had gone back to Marysville to live with her aging father and her two sisters. The old doctor had slipped into senility and finally had died in 1947, leaving the three sisters the gloomy old house and fifty run-down acres, all heavily mortgaged, and very little else. Bayard's mother died the following year, and he came home to bury her in the family plot, saddened because he could feel so little sense of loss.

That was the only time he had been back to Columbus since the war. He drove down from Marysville after his mother's funeral and stayed at the Fort Hayes Hotel. He walked up High Street toward Union Station past the old shop. It had changed. A ceramic tile front had been added. The neon sign jutting out over the sidewalk said "Restaurant Interiors." The words were repeated on the single show window, and underneath them, it read "Restaurants—Bars—Grills—Institutions." In the lower right-hand corner of the window were the words "I. Babashanian, Proprietor." Behind the glass were a sheaf of plastic upholstery materials—their bright colors a little sun-faded—and a display of chromium fixtures, their brightness a little dimmed by a speckling of soot.

Bayard had stood so long studying the window and the shop that a man had come outside. "Can I help you," asked the man. He was perhaps forty, stocky, very dark, and with a thick shock of black hair. "Are you—" Bayard looked again at the name on the window, "Mr. Babashanian?"

"Yes, I am. Can I be of service?"

"I used to live in this neighborhood," said Bayard. "Didn't this used to be a sheet-metal shop?"

Mr. Babashanian, seeing that Bayard was not a prospective customer, grew much less cordial. "I don't know," he said impatiently. "I've only had this place since the war. I think I've heard there was a tinsmith here once. I think he went out of business during the war. Couldn't get materials or something."

"There used to be a dry-cleaning shop next door," said Bayard, "called the Paris Tailors. It was run by a man named Rocco Giachetti, and he had a daughter, Rose. Did you ever run across them?"

Mr. Babashanian looked at Bayard suspiciously. "What are you, with the FBI or something? You want to find out about these people, why don't you go to the post office or police station?"

"I'm not with the FBI," said Bayard. "I've no ulterior motives. How are things with you? How's business?"

"Fine," answered Mr. Babashanian, still faintly suspicious. "Why shouldn't it be fine?"

"I'm glad to hear that," said Bayard. He wondered if Mr. Babashanian lived with his family in the narrow rooms over the shop. "Thank you very much, Mr. Babashanian. You've been a big help." Bayard walked away, half-melancholy, half-amused, feeling Mr. Babashanian's suspicious eyes boring into his back.

Bayard made one more try. He visited Central High School. Mr. Cavendish was still there, thinner, grayer, older. Mr. Cavendish had an elaborate story to tell of having served with the OSS and having been with the Maquis in France. Bayard told him that he had just returned from a year in Paris. Unabashed, Mr. Cavendish quickly rewove his account so as to eliminate some of the more glaring discrepancies.

chapter twenty-eight...

Then, finally, there was that morning in April. All the previous day Dog Company had watched the war-blighted valley of Soto-ri from its triumphant position on Hill 416. The men had seen it lying there deep between the sharply rising hills that had been terraced into gigantic staircases by a hungry and industrious people.

Bayard, studying the ground before him with a careful company commander's eye, was conscious, as he had been for the last several days, that the eternal miracle of spring was beginning to touch Korea with its magic. The earth in the valley had thawed and was coming to life. In the terraced squares, hard-won from the begrudging hills, thin ribbons of bright new green showed in the dark brown furrows. But the floor of the valley was pocked with shell holes and torn by the ripping treads of the tanks. Even the healing touch of spring could not close all the wounds of war.

On both sides of the valley the hills grew into mountains that were colored brassy yellow and bronze with the dead leaves of the poplars and oaks, blue-green with twisted and stunted pines, and black in charred ugly patches. The lower hills bled from the clay red gashes of entrenchments. Higher up, the mountains turned gray with rock, and in the distance, remote and higher still, they were blue with ice and white with unmelted snow.

That morning, very early, as Dog Company started down from Hill 416 along the mountain trail leading into the contested valley, they had passed a very small shrine, set jewel-like in a grove of gnarled and twisted pines. It perched high on a rocky crag overlooking the turquoise and deep green of the river and the whitish gold of the sandy river flats. A gravel path led to the temple gate. On the path lay a saffron-colored hand, neatly severed at the wrist. Someone had placed a lighted cigarette between the fingers of the hand. A thin curl of smoke made its insouciant way up into the warming morning air.

Here and there down in the valley, white phosphorus shells—the Willie Peters—still burst and sent up their cottony plumes. As the long gray-green column of marines threaded its way slowly down from the heights, the ghost of the white phosphorus remained—that Fourth of July smell.

They could now see plainly what was left of the village of Soto-ri. On a hillside close by were the grass-covered grave mounds marking the passing of a dozen generations, a reminder that the valley had been untouched by time for perhaps the past five hundred years. Now, however, Soto-ri was changed, freshly colored with the reds and blacks of a primitive painting—red with the burnt mud of the crumbled walls and black with the charcoal of seared rafters and thatch. Over the ruins, a pall of yellowish smoke still hung in mourning.

Dog Company was carrying down its own burden of dead from Hill 416. The wounded had been sent out the night before. There hadn't been enough stretchers, even for them. The dead were forced to be content with a poncho for a winding sheet and to be tied with signal wire to a carrying pole hacked from the half-grown pines. Four marines bore each pole, two at each end, with the stiffening corpse suspended in the middle.

A foot slipped, a marine stumbled and went down on one knee, a poncho-shrouded body swaying precariously. Bayard heard a boy's voice say, "Don't let his head hit the ground."

They were bringing down seventeen bodies, and half of Dog Company was needed to bear the burden. The wounded who had gone out the night before would get well, most of them. But the dead—death has a finality about which nothing can be done.

The gradient lessened; the trail grew broader and the way easier. Dog Company reached the road that paralleled the river. Here the trucks met them. Here they could leave the dead, and here waiting for them was an issue of rations and ammunition. Bayard lit a cigarette and broke out his map to study the next leg of the day's march. "Skipper," interrupted Havac, "the rations are five-in-ones instead of Cs. How do you want me to handle them?"

"Five-in-ones?" questioned Bayard irritably. "They're no good in a moving situation." Five-in-ones were fine for the artillery or service units, but what a rifle company needed were individually packaged C rations.

"I know they're no good," said Havac in patient agreement. "But that's what we got. Do you want to pass them out or not?"

"Break up the rations and divide them the best you can," said Bayard, and then with sudden suspicion he asked, "What about the shoes?"

"No shoes, Skipper," said the first sergeant, "just the rations and the ammunition."

Bayard's irritation flamed into anger. He still had men wearing shoe-pacs, and in this warmer weather they were ruining their feet. He had been promised shoes when they came off the hill.

"Where's Mr. Gibson—I mean, Mr. Burke?" For a split second, Bayard had forgotten that Gibson was dead—dead for four months now. If Gibson were still the company executive officer, he told himself grimly, the shoes would have been there and so would the C rations.

"Mr. Burke is at the truck with the gunny and the platoon guides, waiting to see how you want the five-in-ones handled," said Havac in a carefully neutral voice.

Bayard turned to his runner, Baby-san. "Go tell the Gunny to divide up the five-in-ones the best he can. And tell Mr. Burke to report to me." Bayard stood staring in stony silence down the road, to where it made a right-angled turn across the river and into the village, waiting until Burke, the new executive officer—he was the second since Gibson—approached.

"Good morning, sir," said Burke tentatively, eyeing Bayard with some apprehension.

"Good morning," said Bayard acidly. He took Burke by the arm and led him a few steps away from Havac and Baby-san. "Did you have a good night's sleep?"

"Yes, sir, I did," said Burke slowly. "I stayed with the S-4. He had a tent."

"I'm glad," said Bayard with saccharine sweetness, "but that isn't why I sent you to the rear last night, is it?"

"No, sir."

"Why did I send you to the rear?"

"To arrange for the rations and ammunition."

"And what else?"

"And the shoes, sir."

"Where are the shoes?"

"The S-4 said we'd have to wait until the battalion went into reserve."

"What about the rations? Why did you bring back five-in-ones instead of C rations?"

"The S-4 thought they'd be a change for the men. Besides, that was all he had in the battalion dump."

"Those aren't very good answers, lieutenant."

"I'm sorry, sir," said Burke in desperation. "But if Battalion didn't have the stuff, how was I supposed to get it?"

"If it had been a routine issue," said Bayard with ominous patience, "the company property sergeant could have taken care of it. I wouldn't have sent you."

"I'm sorry, sir."

"You're going back with the trucks," said Bayard. "If Battalion doesn't have the shoes, you're going to Regiment. If Regiment doesn't have them, you're going to Division. In fact, Lieutenant, I don't give a damn if you have to go all the way back to Pusan, you're going to get the shoes and you're going to get them issued to the men before we move out tomorrow morning. Understood?"

"Aye, aye, sir," said Burke, looking thoroughly miserable.

"Then get with it."

"Battalion, sir," said Bayard's radio operator coming up to him and passing him a hand-set.

The message was brief. "Dog Company Six? This is Firebrand Three-Able. Resume the march. Do you roger? Out."

Bayard nodded to Havac. Havac shouted a command. The marines of Dog Company fell in on the road. They moved out in a double column of files, the old familiar march formation, a staggered row of marines on each side of the road. The concrete bridge that crossed the river had been partially destroyed, then repaired with wooden timbers, and now it was destroyed again. Dog Company left the road and tramped sullenly down to the ford. They entered the river with obvious and audible distaste. The cold water worked its way through leggings into shoe tops, soaked trousers legs to the knee, and then got hip deep.

Someone passed the word that the stream bed was mined. In mute corroboration, an old Sherman tank was lying there half submerged on its side in the middle of the river. Bayard felt a crawling uneasiness in his testicles that could not be accounted for by the coldness of water alone. He had seen the wounds that mines could cause: they blew off a man's feet and legs, they gutted him, they ripped off his genitals. Today, however, Bayard's fears were groundless. The column emerged wet but unscathed from the river and marched into the village of Soto-ri.

Along the street, there was a stirring of life and a few filthy beings, scarcely identifiable as human, emerged from the rubble to stand watching with folded hands and blank eyes as the marine battalion trudged past. Although two other rifle companies had gone through Soto-ri before them, Dog Company marched with caution, trigger fingers ready to snick back the safeties.

It had taken a week's fight to get Soto-ri. The other two battalions of the regiment had tried for five days to take the heights that controlled the village, clawing their way up in a frontal attack. Then two nights before, the 2d Battalion, until then waiting with apprehensive impatience in reserve, had been committed. Yesterday morning, after a long climbing march, the battalion had come in on the enemy's position from the higher ground on the flank. A vicious day-long fight had ensued. Then had come the inevitable night counterattack. The 2d Battalion held on to the rocky ridgeline. Now the enemy was withdrawing to the north, and the battalion had come down into the valley.

Bayard did not entirely trust the village. He had been feeling a nervousness, catlike jumpiness these last few days that he regarded as a premonition. The battalion radio crackled an order to halt the column. Bayard raised his arm and shouted, and Dog Company shuffled to a stop. He wondered why they were halting, but it was not his business to interrogate Battalion. He was grateful for the break. His company headquarters and the 1st Platoon had reached the far edge of the village. The rest of Dog Company was strung out behind him along the ruined street. From where he stood, he could see his whole company.

He looked back the length of the column and saw that all of the platoons except the 2d had posted march security. The leader of the 2d Platoon was new, but that was no excuse. "Get Mr. Hunter up here," Bayard ordered Baby-san. His runner raised his automatic rifle to high port and dogtrotted down the road to the 2d Platoon. He returned shortly with its commander.

Bayard chose to ignore the lieutenant's half-diffident salute. "Hunter," he demanded, "how long have you been with this company?"

"Three weeks, sir." Hunter was one of a draft of second lieutenants who had been flown out from Quantico as soon as they graduated from Basic School.

"That should be long enough to learn how we do things in Dog Company."

"Yes, sir."

"Then, goddamn it, why didn't you put out security when we halted?"

"Well, sir, I figured in this case—well, the whole battalion has gone through the village. I figured it was secured."

"I don't give a good goddamn if the whole division has gone through the village. It's SOP in this company that every time we halt we put out security. Is that understood?"

"Yes, sir."

"Then get back to your platoon and do it." The lieutenant started back for his platoon at a dead run. Watching him go, Bayard felt his anger fade. Here the day was only half over, and already he had reamed out two of his lieutenants. Given time, Hunter would make a good platoon leader. He had done well up on the hill.

Bayard was physically very tired. He felt old and worn out. Just now his legs were trembling with fatigue from the morning's march. He found a grassy spot along the edge of the road and sat down. He slipped his arms free of his pack straps and flexed his shoulders to work out the cramp that had set in. He was perspiring. If the weather stayed warm, he would be able to get rid of the woolen undershirt he was wearing. It was soaked through with sweat, but he was too tired just now to go to the trouble of taking it off.

His legs were still wet to the thighs from wading the river. He knew he should at least change to dry socks. If there was much more hiking to be done, the wet wool would blister his feet. He fished around in his haversack and found a pair of dry, if not-so-clean, socks. He worried loose the stubborn wet knots in his bootlaces and pulled off his boots and socks. The grass and sun felt good on his bare feet.

It took a great effort to fight down the languor that threatened to engulf him. Any minute now, Battalion would be passing the word to move out, and he would be caught sitting there with his boots and socks still off. He pulled on the stiff dry socks he had found in his pack and relaced his wet boots.

Bayard looked around at the scattered members of his company headquarters. Because he was tired and his earlier anger was spent, he now felt relaxed and in a philosophical mood. It pleased him to fancy that each of the members of his official family revealed something of themselves in the manner in which they used this brief respite.

First Sergeant Havac was standing ramrod straight in the middle of the road, not willing to sit down, not willing to admit that he was tired.

Pilnick was sitting primly on an abandoned reel of communications wire. He didn't need the stenciled petty officer's insignia on his sleeve to distinguish him from the marines.

Jim Kim was eating, stolidly jabbing at a tin of jam with a hard C ration biscuit.

Baby-san, with his youthful energy and insatiable curiosity, was prowling around the ruins of a nearby house.

Perkins, the radio operator who replaced Brown when he had been wounded there weeks before, had pulled out the long antenna for his SCR-300 and was diligently switching channels back and forth, trying to monitor both the regimental and battalion tactical nets.

Gunny Agnelli was engaged in earnest professional conversation with the machine-gun platoon sergeant, something about worn-out barrels and overhead fire.

They're all acting in character, thought Bayard, and so am I, sprawled out here on the grass, a worn-out company commander.

"Hey, Captain, come here." It was Baby-san, beckoning from the doorway of the house. "You, too, First Sergeant." It was an ordinary mudwalled, thatch-roofed house, now bullet-riddled, with one corner that had been knocked away by a shell burst. Bayard got to his feet reluctantly. Baby-san was always unearthing some inconsequential treasure. Bayard walked across the road as his runner ducked once again into the house.

"That goddamn kid better have something worth showing us," growled Havac, following a few feet behind Bayard.

Campaigning didn't wear the first sergeant down, thought Bayard. He just got tougher, more leatherlike.

"I think this place must have been a gook regimental headquarters or something," said Baby-san, meeting them at the door. "Look, they got a Russian switchboard in here, and a couple of radios, and a big leather box full of papers."

Bayard ducked his head and went through the low doorway. At the opposite end of the room he could see the switchboard and the leather trunk. Baby-san bent over the opened trunk and lifted out a handful of papers. "I bet some gook sergeant major is getting his ass fried about now for leaving these behind," he said.

But Bayard never had a chance to examine the papers. As he crossed the floor toward Baby-san, something dropped past him from the open rafters overhead. A black Chinese stick grenade bounced onto the wooden planks. Bayard saw it very clearly. He could even distinguish the white Chinese characters stenciled on it. Then it exploded.

It was as though someone had kicked him in the stomach hard. He doubled up and fell forward. He sensed rather than saw Baby-san spin about and fire his BAR from a crouch. Dimly he heard Havac's bull-like bellow of rage. A body fell from the rafters, landing on top of Bayard. Lying there under the weight, he felt a hot stickiness running down the back of his neck and around and onto his face. As the world faded away, he was not conscious of any pain, only a sensation of relief, of escape.

chapter twenty-nine...

"We were married for almost five years," said Alice Gardner. "We met in Germany. I had gone there to teach in a school for dependents. He was in an armored division. Then he was transferred to Japan. All our married life we lived overseas. I have a little girl. She's almost three. We're waiting for transportation to the States. I don't know what I'll do when we get back home. Teach school again, I suppose."

"We face the same prospect," said Bayard. "I'm a school teacher too."

"I wouldn't have known it. You don't seem like the school-teacher type."

"A little while ago you said that you didn't think I was a regular," smiled Bayard. "Now you say that I'm not the school-teacher type. What am I, then?"

"Oh, I don't know. I think you're a very nice person, whatever you are. Where did you teach?"

"At a boy's preparatory school in Baltimore."

"A private school. That's not quite the same as teaching in a public-school system. Are you going back to it? The prep school, that is."

"I don't know. I haven't quite made up my mind. Before this Korean thing came along, I was thinking about going into the Foreign Service."

"You'd look good in striped pants. Do they really wear striped pants?"

"I don't really know. I don't think so. Would you like to dance?"

"I'd love to."

They walked across the floor to the jukebox. No coins were necessary. The box was wired to play without cost, courtesy of Army Special Services. Alice ran her finger down the list of selections, hesitated, and then punched the button next to "Good Night, Irene."

"I know it's corny, but I like this one," she said. She held up her arms. Bayard felt a pulse banging in his ears. It was the first time in a year that he had embraced a woman. He wondered if she could feel the trembling in his arms. "I haven't danced with anyone since Joe was killed," she said. "You're the first."

Korea is never very far away, said Bayard to himself. You forget it for an instant, but it's always there, like a cork pushed under the water, always ready to bob back to the surface. You remember they served Dog Company hot cakes and syrup that night when you came into the battalion perimeter after coming down from the pass at Toksu-nyong. You remember the anxious, solicitous, yet triumphant look on the face of the battalion mess sergeant as he supervised the chow line.

"Goddamn it, Hunky," the mess sergeant had said to Havac. "They tried to tell me you'd never get back. But I said you would and that when you did I'd have a hot breakfast waiting for you. I only got ten men left in my mess section, but I told them that I was getting hot cakes and hot joe ready for Dog Company and nobody else was going to get anything to eat until you guys got in."

You remember the look on Dr. Goldberg's face when he cut away the shoe-pac and the bandages and saw the Red Snapper's leg. The Old Man eventually lost his foot. The surgeon who performed the operation in Tokyo wrote to Goldberg that fortunately he had been able to save the knee joint and that with a proper prosthesis Lieutenant Colonel Quillan would have good residual articulation.

Bayard had heard that Thompson had been released from the hospital and was now instructing at Basic School in Quantico. Thompson had not written, and Bayard didn't find this too surprising.

There was a letter, however, from Reynolds. "The surgeons here at Bethesda have rebuilt the eye socket and have given me an artificial eye," wrote the machine-gun lieutenant. "They've still got some plastic surgery to do, but I keep telling them that I was no beauty to begin with. I was lucky not to lose the other eye. Of course I'm finished so far as a Marine Corps career is concerned. As soon as they're through with me here, I go before the retirement board. I'm enrolling at George Washington and am going to try to get my degree in education. Maybe I'll wind up a professor like you. I don't know whether you knew it or not, but that's what the men used to call you—the Professor."

Thompson and Reynolds—they were the only two left. Gibson, Naheghian, Burdock, Miller—all dead. There were others. What were their names? It was strange. The originals you remember, but the replacements came and went so fast that it was difficult to keep them straight. Burke, Robinson, Fagan, Conrad, Bliss, and Barron. Those were some of the names. They had turned out to be pretty good men. At the time he was wounded in April, Burke and Robinson were still with the company. Perhaps they still are.

The music ended, and it seemed to Bayard that Alice clung to him for just an instant before they parted. They walked back to the record machine hand in hand and punched another series of selections.

"You're a good dancer," she said. Bayard smiled to himself. He wasn't a particularly good dancer, and he knew it. He also knew that convention demanded that a woman pay this compliment to a man the first time she danced with him. But they did move smoothly together. The music that came out of the machine was a syrupy blend of sound with a strong, unmistakably accented beat. He felt very good, utterly relaxed for the first time all evening. The girl in his arms lost her identity and became any girl—a pleasant-to-hold, pliant form.

Then the music ended again, and Alice was leading him back to their table. The room was now empty except for themselves and the Japanese bartender in the cowboy shirt. The bartender was busy taking the liquor down from the back bar and putting it away for the night. What remained of their highballs was thin and flat. "Hey," Bayard called to the bartender, "let's have another round of drinks over here."

The bartender came to their table smiling obsequiously and holding a towel in his hands. His cowboy shirt was magenta with yellow embroidery. "Sawree, sir. Bar is closed. Is late. Is after hour." He had short, bristly black hair. He talked and smiled at the same time. His teeth were large and ugly and capped with gold.

"I said we wanted another drink," said Bayard belligerently.

"Sawree," said the bartender. "Bar is closed. Better to go home now."

Alice laid her hand on Bayard's arm. "We better go now," she said.

"All right," said Bayard. "Let's go." He laid an uncounted crumpled pile of military scrip on the table for the bartender. They left the bar, walked across the miniature lobby, past the basilisk stare of the night clerk, past the sleeping bell captain, and started up the faded red carpeting of the staircase.

"I'm on the second floor," said Alice. "Room 209."

As they walked down the corridor together, her thigh kept brushing his. He caught her hand and linked her arm through his. They reached her door. "You got your key?" he asked.

"It isn't locked," she said. "The hotel sent up a mama-san to baby-sit for me." She turned around and faced him, with her back against the door. "It was nice meeting you," she said. "Talking to you helped me."

"Well—" said Bayard.

"I'd ask you in," said Alice, "but we might wake my little girl."

"We could go to my room."

"I don't think so."

Bayard stepped close to her, put one arm around her waist, and with his free hand caught her under the chin and tilted her face upward. He kissed her. She didn't resist. "Let's go to my room and have a drink," he said.

"Just one," she said. "Just a drink and nothing else."

"All right," he said, "just a drink. Nothing else."

They relinked arms and retraced their steps down the corridor. Bayard opened the door to his room and flipped on the light. Alice walked past him to the open balcony doors. Outside the moonlight was still bright and white—whiter than the yellowish glare of the electric light.

Bayard went to the dresser, turned up two tumblers, and poured an inch of Scotch from the bottle of Ballentine's into each. He added a like amount of water from the carafe. As he picked up the glasses, his arm brushed Baby-san's letter and sent it coasting down to the floor. Briefly, like a knife-stab, Bayard thought of Dog Company and wondered what bit of hill top was its current universe. "I'm afraid it's warm," he said, passing one of the glasses to Alice.

She sipped her drink. "It's a beautiful night," she said, turning back to the opened balcony doors.

"It certainly is," said Bayard. He finished his drink in a single swallow, put down his glass, and stepped behind her, reaching his arms around her waist. She settled back against him so that the roundness of her buttocks fit smoothly against his thighs. Growing bolder, he moved his hands upward and cupped her breasts. She let them remain there for a moment and then gently carried them down to her waist again. He grew more insistent. This time, she did not move his hands. Her breasts were small and firm.

He dropped one hand down to her waist again and moved it downward across her belly. She turned to him abruptly, pushed up against him, pressing hard. They kissed open-mouthed, his tongue finding hers.

They had backed gradually toward the bed. Bayard felt the edge of the mattress against the back of his knees. He sat down, pulling her with him. "You better get the lights," she said in a husky whisper. Bayard rolled out of the other side of the bed and flicked off the light switch by the door.

A square of white moonlight shone in through the balcony doors. She stood up again and began taking off her dress. Watching her, Bayard swung his legs over the edge of the bed and fumbled with his bootlaces. Getting them undone, he took off his boots and stretched out across the bed. As her dress fell to her feet, he groped for her hand and pulled her down beside him. His hands moved over the wonderful, almost forgotten, satiny feel of her slip. He then unbuckled his belt and kicked off his trousers.

They were matching each other, piece for piece. At last their under-clothing came off, and they were lying together nude. As she fit herself against him, they kissed hard and exploringly. He moved his hand up the inside of her leg. "Not yet," she said. "Make it last."

They lay together for what seemed a long time. Bayard gently explored again between her legs with his hand. She did not stop him, and he felt a wetness on his fingers. Finally he raised himself slightly and looked down on her. She lay there with her mouth slightly parted and her eyelids half closed. With the moonlight falling across her face and bared breasts, she was quite beautiful.

"Now?" he asked.

"Oh, yes," she said, eyes closed. "Love me hard, Joe, hard, hard."

"Joe?" repeated Bayard mechanically. Then he remembered. "I'm not your husband," he said in a harsh, tight voice.

Her pliant body turned tense and rigid. She turned abruptly away from him. "I think I better have a cigarette," she said. The passion had gone out of her voice.

Bayard tried to turn her toward him once again. She resisted him. "Please," she said, "a cigarette." He took one from the pack on the night table next to the bed, lit it, and passed it to her. He lit one for himself and, lying on his back, looked up at the blackness of the ceiling.

"I'm sorry," she said. "This isn't very fair to you. For a moment I thought—"

"It's all right," said Bayard coldly. The ghostly specter of a dead husband had drained all of the desire out of him. He could hear the quiet sounds of her dressing. He did not try to restrain her, nor did he turn his head to watch.

She was dressed now, and she walked around to his side of the bed. "Will I see you tomorrow?" she asked.

"I suppose so," said Bayard.

She bent over the bed and kissed his cheek. "Good night," she said.

"Good night," said Bayard. She went to the door. Bayard did not get up. He heard the door close and the latch click into place. Left behind was the faint scent of her body and her perfume.

Bayard felt guilty and unclean. Not because of Donna—because, after all, he was under no obligation to remain celibate, so far as Donna was concerned. The last time he had seen Donna was when she said good-bye to him at Washington's Union Station and he had taken the train to Camp Lejeune. That was a year ago. His continence since then had been forced by circumstances, but Donna had been under no such constraint. She had not been a virgin when he met her. He had not been the first, and he had no deep, abiding reason to believe he was the last.

Nor did he feel particularly bad about Alice. She was an adult, and he was certainly not her keeper. No, what bothered Bayard was her dead husband. It was as though Alice's husband had entered the room and caught them in the act.

Her husband had been a tank officer. Bayard thought of that last April day before Dog Company had gone down into the valley of Soto-ri. His marines had won the heights. They were waiting there, he and his company headquarters, watching the blighted village below them for some sign of life, when they saw the two tanks—M26 Pershings—crawl slowly, tentatively, into the valley. Somewhere behind them, the tanks had left, or lost, their infantry support.

They were army tanks, their olive drab paint not quite so dark as the forest green of the Marine Corps. Swinging their great 90mm snouts around, they seemed to be searching the ridge tops with their myopic eyes. Then a turret hatch clanged open, the sound carrying thinly to Bayard's hilltop position. The tank commander's helmeted head and shoulders emerged from the bowels of the squat green monster. The commander scanned the valley floor and the ridgelines with his field glasses, his map spread out in front of him. As remote and detached as a spectator in a theater, Bayard watched the scene through his own six-power binoculars.

The turret of the second tank opened, and its commander also appeared. The two seemed to talk. The first pointed a gloved hand toward the left fork of the valley. The commander of the second tank nodded and waved and then disappeared into his tank, the turret hatch banging shut. The giant motor roared, the sound filling the valley and carrying loudly to Bayard and his headquarters group.

"If they try going up that left fork," muttered Havac, "they're going to run into nothing but trouble." The Pershing lurched from the road, its broad treads and forty-six tons of steel grinding through the first dike. The paddy mud splashed and churned, and the tank wallowed forward, leaving behind two parallel black scars in the paddy.

Then an immense column of brown mud and smoke pillared up, and the marines watching from the hill heard the dull, booming explosion of a land mine. The tank teetered ponderously, then hung motionless, its gun pointing skyward and its left tread dangling helplessly from its road wheel. The turret swung around in a slow search. The hatch again opened.

With both hands, the tank commander pushed himself out of the turret. He crawled forward onto the front plates and looked down at the crater that had formed under the bow of his M26. The other tank, which had been waiting at the road's edge, now lumbered forward, following in the broad, black tracks left by the crippled tank. It wheeled around, great gobs of soft brown mud spinning out from behind its treads. Gently it poked its rear toward its injured mate.

A second crewman climbed out of the stricken tank. The two tankers dropped down into the mud and made their way over to the stern of the rescuer. Uncoiling the heavy steel towing cable from the rear of the uninjured tank, they dragged its weight back to their own vehicle and bent its stiff length around the towing hooks. The pair of tankers then stood back. The rescuing tank inched forward. The towing cable tightened. The second tank sloughed along sidewise in the mud and came to a stop. The engine of the first tank thundered, the treads spun, and the tank bucked forward under the double weight.

The long stuttering cough of a heavy machine gun came from the far side of the valley. The two men standing by the cable fell face forward into the mud. The commander of the uninjured tank pulled at the operating handle of his .50-caliber machine gun, crouched down, and fired a long burst at the sound of the enemy gun. His incendiary bullets burst in lemon-yellow splashes on the hillside and a necklace of little fires started up in the dry grass.

Then the enemy appeared. They came out of the culverts, from behind the ditches and dikes, from the holes dug into the hills where they had been hiding. They waddled forward, grotesque in the padded winter uniforms they still were wearing. Their rifles banged; their submachine guns began their high-pitched chatter. The tank commander was hit and slumped down over his gun.

"Christ, can't we do something?" said Baby-san. "Can't we help them?"

"I don't know how," said Bayard. "We're too far away to get there in time. Where's the artillery FO?"

The first knot of Chinese to reach the tanks hurled a barrage of stick grenades. The crew of the second tank was slow in pulling the body of their commander back into the tank. Before they could close the turret cover, a couple of the grenades found their way through the open hatch. The 90mm gun of the second M26 boomed futilely into the empty sky. The tank's .30-caliber machine gun rattled frantically. Some of the Chinese were throwing bottles of gasoline and these burst into oily splashes of flame on the tank hulls. Then the enemy began to crawl over the tanks, their olive drab hulls half-obscured by the greenish yellow bodies.

"Can't you help them out?" Bayard yelled to his artillery observer. "I can't reach them with anything I got!"

"I'm trying," said the artillery lieutenant. "I got a fire mission on the way. I've asked for VT fuze."

There was the familiar freight-train rumble from behind them, the tearing sound of 105s passing overhead, then the brownish black puffs of the airbursts breaking over the heads of the Chinese. Then full battalion fire came crashing down, the shells filling the valley with a bouquet of great black flowers. The exploding shells peeled the Chinese off the tanks like a sharp knife cutting the rind from a cheese. The crashing fire multiplied, and soon the only greenish yellow figures remaining in the paddy were the dead and the dying.

Fires had started deep in the hulls of the two tanks and the oily black smoke from both joined into a tall black column rising up from the valley floor. "Not a fucking thing we could do," said Baby-san. "How do you suppose those army apes could be so stupid as to go out into that valley without their infantry?"

In his room in the Hotel Otsu, Bayard finished his morning cigarette and ground it out in the ashtray on the nightstand. The moonlight had paled. The sky was graying. It was almost dawn. There was no point in trying to sleep. He decided to take a bath and redress. He swung out of bed. On the floor he saw the white square of Baby-san's letter. He picked it up and, snapping on the light, read it again.

> *Dear Captain,*
>
> *I got some bad news for you. First Sergeant Havac was killed the day before yesterday. I don't know whats been in the news but we've been fighting pretty hard at a place we call the Punch Bowl. We were running one of those razorback ridge lines when the company got clobbered with mortars and the 1st Sgt got it.*
>
> *Major Mansell has been promoted to Lt. Col. and also got the Navy Cross.*
>
> *Pills and the Gunny are okay. Theres still a couple of the old guys left around.*
>
> *We got a replacement first Lt. for a company commander now. I guess he'll be alright.*
>
> *Your Friend,*
> *Wade Hampton Caldwell*
> *(Baby-san)*

Bayard refolded the letter and put it back on his bureau. It was hard to believe that Havac, the indestructible Havac, was dead. He wondered how good the new company commander would be. With Havac gone, he'd have to be good. Dog Company. It had changed, but it was still Dog Company.

Bayard had struggled with his thoughts all night long, ever since Alice left the room. He now finally resolved what he must do.

The administrative section of the transient center would be open at eight o'clock. It was now five. Maybe if he got his orders endorsed first thing, he could get out of here today. The business of the two Purple Hearts was just a technicality. If he was willing to waive it, they would be glad to change his orders.

Bayard started the water in his bathtub. One more bath, and he would be ready to go back to Dog Company.

about the author...

Born at Billingsport, New Jersey, almost on the site of an American Revolution battlefield, Edwin Howard Simmons claims to have done his first bit of writing about war at age fourteen. He now lives near Mount Vernon, Virginia, on a half-acre of what was once George Washington's River Farm. He came into the Marine Corps in June 1942 from Army ROTC at Lehigh University. Having served in World War II, Korea, and Vietnam, as well as North China and the Dominican Republic, General Simmons has commanded in combat, or been acting commander, of every size unit from platoon through division. This service has been rewarded with numerous personal decorations including the Distinguished Service Medal, the Silver Star, three Legions of Merit, two Bronze Stars, a Meritorious Service Medal, and what he calls an "unavoidable" Purple Heart. Retiring from the active service in the grade of brigadier general in 1972, he continued for nearly a quarter of a century as the Director of Marine Corps History and Museums and is now, since 1996, the Director Emeritus. *Dog Company Six* is his first novel, although he has been a prolific writer of short stories and nonfiction. His most recent books are the third edition and revision of *The United States Marines: A History* (1998) and the large format, award-winning *The Marines* (1998).